KT-526-425

WINSTON GRAHAM

Warleggan

A Novel of Cornwall 1792–1793

PAN BOOKS

First published 1953 by Werner Laurie Ltd
First issued in Fontana Paperbacks 1969

This edition published 1996 by Pan Books
an imprint of Pan Macmillan Ltd
Pan Macmillan, 20 New Wharf Road, London N1 9RR
Basingstoke and Oxford
Associated companies throughout the world
www.panmacmillan.com

ISBN 0 330 34496 X

3 5 7 9 8 6 4

A CIP catalogue record for this book is available from
the British Library

Typeset by CentraCet Limited, Cambridge
Printed and bound in Great Britain

For Peter Latham

BOOK ONE

Chapter One

In that coastal triangle of Cornwall lying bëtween Truro, St Ann's, and St Michael, social life did not extend far in the 1790s. There were six big houses – or six inhabited by gentlefolk – but circumstances did not encourage inter-course between them.

Into one of these, Mingoose House, the oldest and most easterly, Ruth Treneglos, *née* Teague, had done her utmost to bring a new social zest; but childbearing had cramped her style of late; her rough-booted husband John was interested only in hunting, and her father-in-law was too deaf and scholarly to care who came and went in his front rooms. In Werry House, the largest and most disreputable, Sir Hugh Bodrugan sprawled and belched like a lecherous volcano while Constance Lady Bodrugan, his stepmother, who was young enough to be his daughter, bred dogs and fed dogs and talked dogs most of her waking hours.

On the other and western side of the triangle Place House, an unbecoming Palladian residence put up in the early years of the century, was occupied by Sir John Trevaunance, a widowed and childless baronet; and Kille-warren, which was not much more than a glorified farm-house, by Mr Ray Penvenen, who was richer and even more cautious than his neighbour.

To the two houses in between, one actually on the coast, the other near it, it would have come natural to look for more enterprise, not only because they were where they were but because each was occupied by a young married couple of whom social occasions might have been expected. Unfortunately, neither household had any money.

Between Sawle and St Ann's, on high ground but protected by trees, Trenwith House, Elizabethan and mellow and beautiful, was occupied by Francis Poldark and his wife Elizabeth and their son, who was nearly eight years old, and Francis's great-aunt, Agatha, who was so old that everyone had forgotten to count. Three miles to the east was the sixth and smallest of the houses, Nampara, Georgian and utilitarian and never properly completed but not without a certain individuality and charm, which was characteristic too perhaps of its owners. Ross Poldark lived here and his wife Demelza; and their son Jeremy had just passed his first birthday.

So of the six houses, the first two were preoccupied with dogs and babies; the second two had the means to entertain but not the will; the last two the will only. Therefore some surprise and speculation were caused when, in May 1792, five of the households received an invitation from the owner of the sixth to a supper party on the twenty-fourth of the month. Sir John Trevaunance wrote that he was taking the opportunity while his sister was staying with him and while his brother Unwin, a Member of Parliament for Bodmin, also was down.

This seemed such a poor reason for breaking with the habit of years that everyone cast about for a stronger motive. Demelza Poldark at least had no difficulty in finding one.

When the letter was delivered, Ross was up at the mine,

the new mine where he spent nearly all his time nowadays, and Demelza waited impatiently for his return.

As`she laid things for the light meal they would have – supper was not until eight – Demelza wondered what the outcome would be of this latest and probably last gamble. Wheal Leisure, the mine on the cliff, which Ross had started in company with six other venturers in '87, continued to prosper; but last year he had sold half his holding in it and had sunk the money in this much more speculative enterprise.

The result so far had been failure. The fine new pumping engine, designed by two young engineers from Redruth, had been set up and all the claims made out for it had been confirmed. But the thirty-fathom level, which was as deep as the old men had gone, offered nothing but worked-out gunnies; and the new forty- and fifty-fathom levels they were driving to strike the lodes again had been most unproductive, yielding poor stuff where there was any yield at all. The engine might work with the greatest possible efficiency; it still used coal; and while things stayed as they were, every day brought nearer the day when silence would fall on the valley and the engine begin to rust.

As she glanced up through the window, she saw Ross coming across the garden in company with his cousin and partner Francis. They were talking attentively, but Demelza could see that it was over no sudden discovery. Often she watched Ross's face as he came in.

She picked up Jeremy, who in his efforts to walk was threatening to pull the cloth off the table, and with him in her arms went to the front door to meet them. The wind billowed the skirt of her green-striped dimity frock.

When they were near enough, Francis said:

'Demelza, you never grow up; you look seventeen. I hadn't intended to come today, but damn it, I feel revived for the air; I think tea with you might complete the cure.'

She said: 'Is this your first time out of doors? I hope you haven't been down the mine.'

'My second. And I have not. Ross has been exploring on his own again, with the usual measure of success. Jeremy boasts another tooth, I believe. I fancy there were only three last time I looked.'

'Seven!' said Ross. 'You're on dangerous ground.'

They laughed and went indoors. The early part of tea Jeremy made sure was devoted to him; but presently Mrs Gimlett came in to bear him away, and the adults were allowed some peace. Demelza, a little breathless and with a curl rakishly over one eye, poured herself a second cup of tea.

'And are you truly better, Francis? The fever is quite gone?'

'It was just the influenza,' said Francis. 'We all had it, but I the worst. Choake bled me and gave me Peruvian bark, but I recovered nevertheless.'

Ross stretched himself, easing his long legs. 'Why do you not have Dwight Enys? He's keen and up-to-date and has a knowledge of the latest physical ideas.'

Francis grunted. 'Tom Choake has always looked after us. Personally I think these medical jockeys are much the same. Anyway, our friend Enys is in a little trouble himself over old John Ellery, I understand.'

'What's the matter with him?'

'It seems he had a toothache and Enys took out three teeth but dug for the roots, as is his fashion. Choake

6

contents himself with twisting off the crowns, as you know. But this time something has gone wrong with Dwight's methods and Ellery has not been out of pain since.'

Demelza said: 'I thought Dwight looked a small matter worried when he called yesterday.'

'He takes his failures too much to heart,' said Ross. 'I should think it a great disadvantage in his profession,'

'It is a great disadvantage in any profession,' said Demelza, carefully not looking at him.

Francis raised an ironical eyebrow. In the brief silence that followed, and to cover it, Demelza took down her envelope from the mantelshelf.

'We have an invitation, Ross! Just think of it in these bad times. Have you had one, Francis? I suppose it will be quite a big affair. I wonder if we should dress. What does Elizabeth say of it?'

'From the Trevaunances?' said Francis while Ross read it. 'Yes, we had a note today. The old man has grown extravagant with his grey hairs. I feel there's some motive in his madness, though, knowing Sir John.'

'Ah,' said Demelza, ''twas much the same thought came to me.'

'What motive?' asked Ross, looking up from the letter.

Francis glanced at Demelza, but she was waiting for him. He laughed. 'We're uncharitable, Ross, your wife and I. Ray Penvenen's niece, Caroline, is an heiress in her own right. Unwin Trevaunance has been stalking her for two years. This may well be to announce the kill.'

'I did not know the girl was back again.'

'She returned from Oxfordshire, I believe, last week.'

'But then,' said Demelza, 'should it not be – if it were to announce an engagement – should it not be Mr Penvenen who give the party? I thought that was the way. Ross, you promised once to buy me a book on etiquette, but you never did so.'

'You behave better without it. I like a wife who is natural and not stiffened up with all manner of artificial observances.'

Francis said: 'Anyway, Ray Penvenen would never give a party even to celebrate his own engagement, so that need not discourage us from the speculation.'

'You will go of course?' asked Demelza.

'I think Elizabeth had her visiting look on when I left her this afternoon.'

Ross said: 'I hope if they intend to join up, those two, they'll be sharp about it. If Caroline Penvenen is to be in the neighbourhood for long, it is likely to unsettle Dwight. I'd be glad to see her safely tied to Unwin.'

'I heard there was something between her and Enys last time she was down, but I should think he's wise enough not to get himself entangled there.'

Demelza said: 'It seems to me no man is wise enough if the woman is not wise enough.'

Ross glanced up good-humouredly. 'That's an acute remark. D'you speak it from personal experience?'

She met his eyes. 'Yes, Ross, from personal experience. Think how foolish Sir Hugh Bodrugan would be over me if I let him.'

Not until he spoke had he seen the latency of what he said, which might even refer to their own marriage; and he was glad that – she had taken it in the right way. He did not reflect that two years ago he would never have any doubts on the point.

*

At about the time Francis and Ross walked down from the mine to tea, George Warleggan was dismounting from his horse outside Trenwith House.

To look at him one would not have thought him the grandson of a blacksmith, the first generation of his family to be genteelly educated – unless the clothes he wore told the tale they were intended to disguise. No country squire would have dressed so well for an afternoon call, even had he wanted to impress the lady of the house, as George did.

When Mrs Tabb showed him in and, rather in a flurry, went to look for Mrs Poldark, George strolled about the hall tapping his boot with his crop and staring up at the ancestral pictures. This was a different poverty from the poverty he might have seen at Nampara House three miles away. Francis and Elizabeth might be no better off than their cousins; but you do not reduce a mellow Elizabethan house to dilapidation in a few years. George was staring at the magnificent window with its hundreds of small panes of glass when he heard footsteps and turned to see Elizabeth skimming down the stairs.

She slowed as soon as she saw him and came down the last steps hesitantly.

'Why, George . . . when Mrs Tabb said – I couldn't quite believe . . .'

'That I had really ventured to come.' He bowed over her hand politely. 'I was passing near, so brought my godson a birthday present. I thought perhaps I might be permitted that much.'

Still uncertain, she took something that he handed her. 'But it isn't Geoffrey Charles's birthday for months.'

'Last year. I'm late, not early.'

'Does Francis . . .'

'Know I'm here? No. But if he does? Surely this rather childish enmity has gone on too long. Really, Elizabeth, it gives me such pleasure to see you again. Such pleasure . . .'

She smiled at him, not flushing as she would have done a few years ago, but warming all the same to his admiration. She did not know how much of George was genuine, but she knew this was. She thought he had grown more stocky since they had last met, so that one saw in his greater bulk the shadow of the middle-aged man he would become. But however he had behaved to Ross – and that she certainly resented – he had never been anything but scrupulously fair with Francis and unfailingly charming to her.

In the winter parlour she unwrapped the small parcel he had brought, and found it was a gold watch. She tried to return it to him, troubled and feeling him overgenerous, but he would have nothing to do with that.

'Drop it in a drawer for a while if you feel he's too young. The quarrel surely doesn't include him. By the time he's old enough to carry it, perhaps we shall all be friends again.'

She said: 'The quarrel was not of *my* seeking. We are very quiet here nowadays, and I should be glad of all my friends. But you know Francis as well as I do. He is wholehearted in his feelings, and if he were to come in now the – our friendship might come to worse hurt than ever before.'

'In other words he would try to kick me out,' George said pleasantly. 'Well, no doubt you'll think me overdeliberate in all things, but I have posted my manservant on the rising ground near Sawle Church. If he sees Francis coming, he can give me good warning, so you needn't fear a brawl.' He hunched his shoulders. 'I should have hesitated to do so if I believed there was risk of your thinking me a coward.'

Elizabeth sat down on the window seat and looked out over the herb garden. George watched her carefully, like a business deal to be negotiated.

Elizabeth said: 'Before anything else I want to thank you for your kindness to my mother and father. My mother is still so unwell, and to ask them to your home . . .'

'I told them especially not to tell you.'

'I know; Father said so. But he wrote of it all the same, and of all your kindness while they were there.'

'It's of no moment. I have always admired your mother, and think her so brave in her eye trouble. I wonder they don't sell their house and live with you here.'

'I have – thought of it myself sometimes. But Francis does not believe it would be a good arrangement—' She checked herself.

George sat down and put the silver end of his riding crop against his teeth. 'Elizabeth, I don't expect you to be in any way disloyal to Francis's views of me and this quarrel, but don't you *personally* think it time it was forgot? What good is it doing any of us? Francis is cutting off his own hand. You know as well as I do that, were there any malice on my side, I could bankrupt him tomorrow. To you it's not a pleasant thing to say, but can you doubt it?'

'I don't doubt it,' Elizabeth said, flushing now.

'I only wish it were different. I should like to help to make it different. But while this feud continues . . . I should like you to help me heal it.'

She unloosed the catch of the window and opened it a few inches to let in a gentle breeze. Her profile was clear-cut like a cameo against the brown of the curtain.

'You say you'll not ask me to be disloyal and then press me to take sides—'

'No. Not at all. To mediate.'

'Do you think my mediation would have so much effect? George, you know Francis's mind just as well as I do. He believes you to have been behind the prosecution of Ross, to have—'

'Oh, *Ross*...'

As soon as he spoke, he saw he had said the wrong thing; but he went on, keeping the resentment out of his voice.

'I know you have a vast affection for Ross, Elizabeth. I wish I could enjoy the favour in your eyes that he does. But let me put this clearly to you. Ross and I have never seen eye to eye since we were at school. It is – something fundamental. We do not like each other overwell. But on my side it is no more than that. On his it is a disease. He plunges headlong from one misfortune to another and blames me for them all as they come upon him!'

Elizabeth had got up. 'I wish you wouldn't say this. It isn't fair to ask me to listen.'

She might have walked away across the room, but he didn't move aside and she found herself at close quarters with him and not quite able to get out of the window bay.

'Don't you hear Ross's side? Why is it unfair to hear mine? Let me tell you of his position and what he has done to extricate himself.'

She said nothing more. Aware that he had overcome the first hurdle, George went on: 'Ross is impulsive, over stiff-necked, rash. You can't blame me for that. It is the fault of being born with money, coming from generations of people who have always had money. But no one need behave as he has behaved. Four years ago he began this ill-conceived plan for smelting copper in Cornwall. He blames me for its failure, but it was doomed to failure from the start. Then, when he was hard set as a result, he was too proud to go to his friends for assistance; and so, added to his other debts, he signed a bill for a thousand pounds at a usurer's rate of interest – it has but now come into my uncle's hands, that is how I know – and Ross has been paying this interest on it ever since. Nor is he satisfied with this, but he last year sold the half of his interest in a profitable mine and induced Francis to go into partnership with him in this white elephant, Wheal Grace, which his father exhausted twenty years ago! When he ultimately beggars himself and you as well, no doubt he'll blame me for having stolen the copper out of his ground overnight!'

At last she escaped and walked across the room. He was overstating his case, but the truth might lie somewhere midway between his argument and Francis's. Her feeling for Ross had never quite been definable to herself, and there was some grain of perverseness which took pleasure in seeing the other side.

George did not follow her. After a minute he said: 'You know, don't you, that you're one of the loveliest women in England.'

The clock on the mantelshelf began to strike five. When it had finished, she said: 'If what you say were even half true, it would be – kind of you; but I think, with Francis not here, a liberty. As I know—'

'If the truth's a liberty, then I've taken it,' George brushed a hand down his embroidered waistcoat, not perfectly at ease but not at all in retreat, 'because the truth it is. I move in society a great deal and I assure you I am neither flattering you nor presuming. Turn round. Look at yourself in the glass. Or perhaps you know yourself too well to realize. Men realize. Other men besides myself. And there would be many such, of both sexes, if you moved about more freely and were to be seen. Even now I hear people say, "D'you remember Elizabeth Poldark – Chynoweth that was? Now *there* was a beauty for you. I wonder what's come of her."'

'Do you suppose—'

'If,' said George, 'if Francis would let me, I could help him. Let him play with his mine if he wants to, but that need only be a side issue. Once before when I came here I mentioned sinecure positions. Today I could get him nominated for two. There is no disgrace in them. Ask your parson how he gained his church or your major his battalion – by having a friend speak for him at the right time. This – this existence is no existence at all for you. Your poverty is not only undeserved – it's unnecessary!'

Elizabeth was silent. Whatever she thought of George's compliments, it was a sore spot he touched. She was twenty-eight now, and her lease of beauty was not indefinite. She could count on the fingers of one hand the number of her outings since her twenty-fifth birthday.

'Oh, George, you're very kind. Don't think I don't know that. The more so because I realize you have nothing to gain. I—'

'On the contrary,' said George, 'I have everything to gain.'

'I scarcely know quite what to say. You heap favours upon my mother and father, upon my son, and would on Francis if he would allow you. I wish I could see some end to this quarrel, I truly wish I could. But – in suggesting that it's a trivial thing, don't you deceive yourself? None of it's as simple as you make it sound. I wish it were. I should be happy enough to see our friendship restored.'

He came over to the fireplace. 'And will do your part to restore it?'

'If you will do yours.'

'How?'

'Help to convince Ross that you are not his enemy.'

'I am not interested in Ross.'

'No, but Francis is Ross's partner now. You'll not reassure one without the other.'

George stared down at his riding crop. Perhaps the look in his eyes was not for her.

'You credit me with supernatural powers. What do you want me to do?'

'If you'll do what you can,' said Elizabeth, 'I'll do what I can.'

'I hope I may hold you to that bargain.'

'You may.'

He bent over her hand and this time kissed it, with a rather dated formality which yet conveyed what he meant it to convey.

He said: 'Please don't bother to show me out. My horse is at the door.'

He left the room, shutting the door after him, and crossed the great empty hall. The wind was rattling a loose window. As he reached the front door, Aunt Agatha came out of the small drawing-room and began tottering across in his direction. He tried to avoid being seen, but – although she was nearly stone-deaf – her eyesight was sharp enough.

'Why, if it isn't George Warleggan, or I'm a dunce! Don't mumble now! People will mumble. 'Tis years since you put foot inside our place, I'll swear. Getting too grand for us, are you?'

15

George smiled and bowed over the withered hand. 'I salute you, old hag. The worms must be tired of waiting. It's not seemly when people rot while they're still above ground.'

'Getting too grand for us, I b'lieve,' said Agatha, one trembling claw going to join the other on her stick. 'Look at that waistcoat. I remember you when you was a boy, George, not hardly bigger'n Geoffrey Charles. Quite over-awed you was, coming here that first time. Different now.'

George smiled and nodded. 'There should be a law to poison off old women, ma'am. Or a pillow pressed over the face would not take long. If you were the last of the Poldarks, I'd do it myself. But never fret, your great-nephews are digging their own graves. It won't be long.'

A slow bead of water escaped from Aunt Agatha's eye and slid diagonally down one of the furrows on her cheek. This was no sign of emotion, it just happened from time to time.

'You was always Francis's friend, I remember, never Ross's. What's that you say? Nervous you was, that first time, and hardly fledged, an' Charles saying, what's the boy brought home from school with him now? Well, times has changed. I mind the years when you couldn't have rid over from Truro in all that falallery without being turned heel over tip by some footpad or needy tinner. Have you seen Francis?'

'I've seen Elizabeth,' said George, bowing again. 'You remind me of forgotten things, old woman. Die soon, won't you, and be forgotten yourself.'

'Goodbye,' said Aunt Agatha. 'Come again and stop to supper. We're uncommon short of company these days.'

Chapter Two

Francis reached home just before six. He found Elizabeth sitting by the window, embroidering a stool cover, and Aunt Agatha crouching over the tiny fire.

'Whoo, it's hot in here.' He went across to one of the windows and opened it. 'Really, old lady, you'd be better in bed than cramping your old bones there.' But he did not say it unkindly.

Aunt Agatha screwed up her eyes at him. 'You've missed our visitor, Francis. Missed him by a skin, I should say. 'Tisn't often we've a visitor these days. You should have asked him to supper, Elizabeth.'

Francis looked at his wife and she flushed, furious that the old lady had forestalled her and furious that she cared.

'George Warleggan came.'

'George?' The way Francis said the word was enough. 'You saw him?'

'Yes. He didn't stay long.'

'So I should think not. What did he want?'

Elizabeth raised her grey eyes, which at times like this could look especially candid and virginal. 'I don't think he wanted anything. He said he thought it unnecessary to go on with this quarrel.'

'This quarrel . . .'

'And very cordial he was too,' said Aunt Agatha. 'For-

17

tune's improved his manners, or I'm a dunce. Quite like old times, 'tis, having a man make a knee to you.'

Francis said: 'I wonder if he knew my back was turned.'

Elizabeth went on with her embroidery. 'He said he and you had been friends since childhood, he did not wish the estrangement to continue as it was. He had, he said, no desire at all to intrude on your private affairs or Ross's, his only wish being to help us to a fuller enjoyment of our lives . . .'

'You speak as if you have learned the lesson well.'

Elizabeth's fingers flickered uncertainly over her work basket, selecting a new colour. 'That was what he said. You may take it or leave it as you please, Francis.'

Aunt Agatha said: 'I mind it was the year of that Du Barry scandal, or was it the year after, that you first brought him here. Stuggy lithe boy, he was, and the clothes they sent him in! Velvets and silks, you could see his mother'd no taste; and he staring about like a bull calf that had strayed from its stall.'

'He has an easy, oily tongue,' said Francis, 'and a persuasive damned way of putting things. I know it to my cost. Does he suppose we shall live a fuller life because of the boon of his friendship? I don't think his flatteries can convince you of that.'

'I can form my own judgments,' Elizabeth said. 'Though I couldn't but be aware that if it wasn't for his forbearance in the matter of mortgages we should not be living a life at all.'

Francis bit his thumb thoughtfully. 'I confess I don't understand his forbearance. It's out of character. Now that I'm in partnership with Ross . . . That's why the adventure at Wheal Grace is in Geoffrey Charles's name. But George makes no move.'

'Except towards friendship,' said Elizabeth.

18

Francis went to the open window and let the cool air waft on his face. 'I can't help but feel that I owe my immunity to you.'

'To me? That's silly. Really, Francis—'

'Silly? Far from it. George has been making sheep's eyes at you for years. I'd never supposed him to be sufficiently human to let any warmer feeling interfere with his business aims, but lacking a better explanation . . .'

Elizabeth got up. 'I hope you'll find a better. I must go and read to Geoffrey Charles.'

As she passed Francis, he caught her arm. The relationship between them had been kinder these last two years, though it was never warm. He said: 'We may disagree, but I think his coming today has a plain enough reason. Whatever you may think he feels for me or I may think he feels for you, we can't doubt what he thinks of Ross. If by befriending us he can put a new division between us and Ross, he will certainly have gained his object. Do you want him to do that?'

Elizabeth was silent for a moment. Then she said: 'No.'

'Nor I.' He released her arm and she went slowly out.

Aunt Agatha said: 'You should have asked him for supper. We've plenty as it happens. But 'tisn't like it was when Charles was alive. I sadly miss your father, boy. He was the last one that knew how to entertain in a proper genteel way.'

On his way home, at Bargus Cross where the gibbet stood, George met Dwight Enys, who was coming from the direction of Goon Prince. Dwight would have saluted and ridden on, but George halted and the two horses closed together.

'Well, Dr Enys, you ride far on your medical duties. Never to Truro, I suppose?'

'Seldom to Truro.'

'And when in Truro you do not venture as far as the Warleggans.'

Dwight made some show of quieting his horse while he thought out his reply. He decided to be frank. 'I've had nothing but friendship from your family, Mr Warleggan, and feel nothing but friendship in return; but the Poldarks of Nampara are my chief friends; I live on the edge of their land, work among their mining folk, sup at their table, and share their confidence. In that event it seems better that I should not attempt to get the best of both worlds.'

George did not move his neck but allowed his eyes to explore Dwight's shabby velvet coat with its gilt buttons.

'Are the two worlds so divided that an independent man cannot pass from one to the other of his own free will?'

'I have taken it so,' Dwight said.

George's face darkened.

'Men's tongues in some things outrun women's. Your own affairs prosper?'

'Well enough, thank you.'

'I was at the Penvenens' place last week, and gather that you are the regular physician there now.'

'Mr Penvenen keeps in very good health. I don't see much of him.'

'They tell me that his niece is back.'

'Indeed.'

'I understand you did some clever operation on her throat and saved her life.'

'I think men's tongues have outrun the women's in that also.'

George did not greatly appreciate having his own words

turned back on him. He began to feel a growing dislike for young Enys, who spoke so bluntly and hardly bothered to hide his sympathies. George did not spend his time in company which cared nothing for his approval or disapproval.

'For my part,' he said, 'I have no faith in physicians or apothecaries, I think they kill as many as they cure. My family is fortunate in not yet being effete, as so many of the older families are.'

He rode on, followed by his servant. Dwight stared after him, then tugged on his horse's rein and went his way. That he had offended an influential man he knew. In his profession he would have preferred it otherwise, but he had long since chosen his friends. What did concern him was something else. 'They tell me that his niece is back,' George had said. If Caroline Penvenen was really home, it meant the destruction of his peace of mind.

Dwight's business was in Sawle; and as he was leading his horse down the steep slippery lane to the fish sheds at the bottom, he heard a clatter behind him and saw that Rosina Hoblyn had fallen, on the stones. She had been carrying a bucket of water, and he looped the reins of his horse over a post and went to help her to her feet. But he could not get her up. Any tentative approaches he had made to the subject of why the nineteen-year-old Rosina walked with a bad limp had been headed off by her family, who seemed to be afraid of the subject. Now her pretty thin face was white with pain, and he had to lift her to her feet.

''Tis my knee, sur. 'Twill be all right in a moment. Sometime he go like this and I can't move him at all. Thank you.'

Her younger sister Parthesia came skipping out of the house and retrieved the bucket and curtsied at the doctor and put an arm out to help Rosina.

'No, not yet,' she said, and to Dwight: 'if I wait, 'twill ease off.'

After a few minutes they got her inside. Dwight was glad that Jacka the father was not there, as his moods could go all ways.

With his 'no nonsense' face, Dwight waved away Rosina's and Mrs Hoblyn's protests that it was really all nothing at all, that if she sat on the table and swung her leg it would pass off, and bent to examine the knee, half fearing to find heaven knew what scrofulous condition. He did not find it. Swollen certainly and a little red, but the skin was not shiny or hot to the touch.

'You say this trouble began eight years ago?'

'Yes, sur, 'bout that.'

'Does it hurt all the time?'

'No, sur, only when it d'go stiff like this.'

'And have you had the same trouble with your hip?'

'No, sur, there's nothing amiss wi' that.'

'Do you ever have a discharge from the knee?'

'No, sur. 'Tis just as if someone turn a key and lock it,' said Rosina, pulling down her skirt.

'Has any other physician seen it?'

He had the feeling that they were exchanging glances behind his back. Rosina said: 'Yes, sur – when it first went wrong in '84. But 'twas Mr Nye, and he's gone dead since then.'

'What did he say?'

'Didn't say nothing 'bout it,' Mrs Hoblyn put in hastily. 'Didn't know what 'twas at all.'

The feeling of the house was so obviously discouraging that Dwight told the girl to use a cold compress and said he would see her again next week when the pain had gone. When he came out, dusk was almost falling and he had his most unpleasant call still to make.

At the bottom of the hill was a flat green triangle of grass and weed above the shingle, and on one side of it were fish sheds with cottages and shacks built over them. You crossed a narrow humped bridge to reach them. Dwight stood for a moment staring out to sea. The wind was rising and the farther cliffs were hardly visible in the gathering dusk. It was still possible to see the grim jaws of the narrow inlet. An old man fumbled with a net over one of the boats. Seagulls fought for a fish head behind the inn. A candle glimmered in a window.

Above the rush of the waves Dwight fancied he could hear the whispered voices of the villages. ''Ere, heard about John James Ellery, 'ave ee? Had toothache, that was all – went to the surgeon over to Mingoose: surgeon took three teeth away. John James has been in mortal pain ever since, and like to die! I'd fight shy of 'e, if I was sick!'

Dwight turned to go, and as he did so a man came quietly from behind the inn and seemed to want to avoid him. But Dwight stopped and the man stopped. It was Charlie Kempthorne, whom Dwight had cured of miner's consumption, and who was laying suit to Rosina Hoblyn, though he was a widower of forty-odd with two children and she only nineteen.

'You're out an' about late, sur, aren't ee? 'Tis no eve to be anywhere but home by the fireside – that's for them as is lucky t'ave a fire to sit by.'

'What I was about to say to you.'

Kempthorne grinned and coughed. 'There's business best done in the half-light, y'understand. When the Customs men don't see ee.'

'If I were a Customs man, I should be at my busiest in the half-light.'

'Ah, but they d'like their firesides, like other sensible folk.' There was a trace of uneasiness in Charlie's expression as he slid past.

Phoebe Ellery opened the door for Dwight and led him upstairs. You climbed to John James Ellery's room by a wooden ladder from the room below where sacks of potatoes and nets and oars and cork floats were stacked. It was impossible to stand upright in the bedroom, and this evening the 'chill' had just been lit to fend off the encroaching night. Most of the glass had gone from the window, and the wind beat through, plucking at the sacking and bringing in a spatter of rain. A great black-and-white cat stalked about the room, scarcely ever still for a moment and making ominous purple shadows of his own. The sick man had his face wrapped in an old cloth and kept muttering: 'Lord, 'ave mercy on me, Lord, 'ave mercy on me.'

Phoebe stood in the doorway watching Dwight with relentless, reproachful eyes. ''E'll be better in a while,' she said. 'The pain last for an hour, maybe, and then d'go off for a space, see.'

There was little Dwight could do, but he stayed half an hour and administered laudanum and listened to the noisy waves, and by the time he left the spasm was passing.

It was a wild night and Dwight spent it restlessly, lost in a sense of his own failure and in the futilities of his profession.

Chapter Three

Ross and Demelza were among the last to arrive at the Trevaunances on the evening of the twenty-fourth of May, having been forced to borrow a horse from Francis, who still had three in his stables; and a company of about twenty people were already talking and laughing in the big drawing-room as they went upstairs. It took Demelza half an hour to change, and Ross, who had little to do for himself, read the latest copy of the *Sherborne Mercury* which had been obligingly left in the bedroom.

France was at war with Austria. Only three weeks ago the revolutionary pot had at last boiled over. The paper said M. Robespierre had opposed the move and had resigned his post as Public Prosecutor, but the others were mad keen for war and already a great army had invaded Belgium. A clash with the Austrian troops might be expected at any time. What of our own position? It was well for Mr Pitt to forecast fifteen years' peace, as he had done in March; prophecies cost nothing; but when they were accompanied by further cuts in our tiny army and skeleton navy, the danger to our safety and survival was plain.

Ross was so far gone that he did not hear Demelza's first words, and she had to repeat them before he looked up.

As he rose he was conscious that his wife's charm and attraction had not been lessened by three years of trial and near poverty. At times it got itself hidden under the everyday mask of work and the routine of living, but this made its emergence all the more startling. At such moments he recognized with instant attention the quality in her that made her attractive to so many men.

As he went to the door to open it for her, he said: 'D'you ever now have any fears about going into society – as you did in the old days? I never know now whether you're nervous or not.'

'For the first ten minutes my knees knock,' she said. 'But luckily 'tis the part of me best covered.'

He laughed. 'I know what will cure it.'

'What?'

'Port.'

'Yes, quite often, yes. But other things too.'

'Such as?'

She lifted her bare shoulders in a slight movement of doubt. 'Knowing other people have a confidence in me.'

'The other people including me?'

'Chiefly you.'

He bent slowly and kissed her neck in the soft part where neck and shoulder join. 'Might I prefer you that confidence now?'

'Thank you, Ross.'

He kissed her again, and she put up a hand to smooth back his hair by the ear.

'You still have some feeling for me?'

He looked at her in astonishment, staring deeply into her eyes. 'Good God, you should know that!'

'Yes, Ross, but there is feeling and feeling. It is the one and not the other that I am asking about.'

'Would you want to involve me in a philosophical argument with all your beaux waiting to flirt with you downstairs?'

'They are not my beaux. And I do not think it would be a – what you said argument.' She put her hand on the door.

He said: 'Demelza.'

'Yes.'

'If there are two feelings, then I don't think you can put them in separate compartments ever, because one is a part of the other and inseparable. You should know that I love you. What other reassurance do you ask?'

She smiled obliquely but with a new warmth. 'Only that I should be told it.'

'So now you've been told it. Does that make such a difference?'

'Yes, that makes such a difference.'

'I'll keep a note of it for Wednesdays and Saturdays in future.'

'Sundays is a better day. The thing will sound right on a Sunday.'

So they went down in a cheerful enough mood and found all their neighbours there, the younger Trenegloses, the Bodrugans, Dr and Mrs Choake, and of course the Penvenens.

And George Warleggan.

It was a blunder of the first magnitude on the Trevaunances' part to have invited him and Ross to the same party; but now it had happened, it had to be gone through with. Rumour had magnified the fight between them last year into vast and murderous proportions; and their presence here together tonight added a spice to the meal for those who had no particular concern for the outcome.

But George offered no provocation and for a time avoided all contact with the Poldarks. Whatever else being thrown over the stairs did, it gave one a physical respect for one's enemy.

At dinner Ross found himself near the top of the table with Constance Lady Bodrugan on his right hand, Elizabeth on his left, and Caroline Penvenen directly opposite.

He had heard so much of Caroline that it would have been strange if she had tallied with his expectations. He thought her not so beautiful as Elizabeth nor so charming as Demelza; but her clear-eyed, quick-thoughted vitality instantly took a man's attention. The emeralds about her milky-coloured throat precisely suited her; they changed suddenly like their wearer in different lights, were now cool and unfathomed, now sharp and glinting. He had no difficulty in understanding Unwin Trevaunance's feelings, always supposing him to be susceptible to other influences than gold. One wondered at their relationship, because it seemed strained tonight. Caroline treated him with bare courtesy, and one imagined that after marriage things would be different. A man did not have that leonine head and jutting bottom lip for nothing.

They were hardly seated when Sir John said: 'You have met Miss Penvenen, Ross? Caroline, this is Captain Poldark,' and Ross studied her wide-awake grey-green eyes.

Miss Penvenen inclined her head in acknowledgment. 'We met for the first time this evening, John; though in truth I have seen Captain Poldark before – in somewhat different case.'

'When was that?' asked Ross.

'Oh, you could not be expected to notice me. It was at your trial at Bodmin when you were charged, you will remember, with plundering two ships. I was one of the audience.'

'I remember well enough,' said Ross. 'But audience

suggests entertainment, and I can't suppose the entertainment was very good.'

'I have known worse. You see, in a play one knows virtue is going to be triumphant; but in real life one trembles on the brink of iniquity and fears for the outcome.'

'I think you must have been at the wrong trial, Miss Penvenen. There was precious little virtue in my case and no triumph in my acquittals unless it was a triumph for the wrongheadedness of the jury. Your sympathy should have been with the judge.'

Caroline's eyes flashed. 'Oh, it was, I assure you. I noticed how sad he looked when he could not punish you at all.'

During the first part of the dinner Ross talked to Elizabeth. Her pleasure was no less than his and was plain to Demelza who, near the foot of the table, found herself between Sir Hugh Bodrugan, who always had such a marked and possessive partiality for her company, and Captain McNeil of the Scots Greys. McNeil was that officer who had been in the district once before, some years ago, stationed here with a company of dragoons to watch over the unrest in the mining districts and to put down the smuggling.

Whatever anyone else might feel about the disposition of the table, Malcolm McNeil had no complaints. He only wished Sir Hugh wouldn't be so monopolistic. Again and again he tried to gain Mrs Poldark's attention, and again and again the hairy baronet grabbed it back. His first real opportunity came when Sir Hugh had to carve another piece off the joint for Mrs Frensham, Sir John's sister, and McNeil at once asked Demelza if he might presently do the same for her.

'Thank you, no,' said Demelza. ''Tis quite surprising

seeing you here, Captain McNeil. I thought you was gone back to Scotland and the clans.'

'Oh, I have been back in the meantime,' he assured her, screwing in his great moustache at her admiringly. 'And overseas. And in London and Windsor. But I grew an affection for this piece of country – and some of the people – and when the occasion came to revisit it and them . . .'

'With your dragoons?'

'No dragoons this time.'

'Not one?'

'Only myself, Mrs Poldark. I'm sorry to disappoint ye. I was ill with a fever, and afterwards, meeting Sir John in London, was invited to take my sick leave here.'

Demelza glanced at him amiably. 'You don't look a sick man, Captain McNeil.'

'Nor am I now, ma'am. Let me fill your glass. Is it canary ye have been drinking?'

'I know only three flavours, and it is none of those three.'

'Then canary it must be. And I have found a great amount of pleasure as well as health in admiring your beautiful coast line—'

'Not looking for smugglers?'

'No, no, Mrs Poldark; not this time. Why, are there some still? I thought my last visit had quite put them down.'

'And so it did. We was all downcast after you had gone.'

The Scotsman glanced at her with a twinkle. 'That is a remark capable of two interpretations.'

Demelza looked up the table and saw Ross smiling at Elizabeth. 'I didn't think, Captain McNeil, that you could have supposed me a smuggler.'

McNeil's chuckle, restrained as it was by his standards,

was enough to silence the rest of the table for a second or two.

Mrs Frensham said, smiling: 'If that pleasantry will bear repetition, I think you should not keep it to yourselves.'

Demelza said: 'Oh, it was not a jest on my side, ma'am. Captain McNeil was assuring me that he had not come down this time to catch smugglers, and I told him I did not know what else he could expect to catch in these parts.'

Sir Hugh Bodrugan rumbled: 'Damme, I differ as to the jest.'

Mrs Frensham said: 'Captain McNeil has been convalescent. His purposes here, he assures me, are wholly innocent; otherwise we should have put a guard over him and locked him in his room.'

'I truly believe, ma'am, you should do so at once,' said Demelza, at which Sir Hugh and the Captain laughed again.

At the other end of the table Sir John Trevaunance, with a not unobvious purpose in mind, had made a derogatory remark about young Dwight Enys. Ellery had died that morning, and Sir John was of the opinion that the scandal should receive public attention. Ellery, a hale and hearty man of sixty . . . Enys had so probed into the jaw that the wound had never healed. His old friend Dr Choake would bear him out . . . Ignorance and neglect. But Sir John found the move a mistaken one, because not only did Caroline speak quickly in Dr Enys's defence but she found an ally in Ross Poldark, and the baronet, to his annoyance, and still more to Unwin's, found himself between two fires. Ross had thought Caroline pert on their first introduction; but now for the moment they were in accord, and it was noticeable at the end of the argument that Caroline's eyes travelled over him approvingly.

Elizabeth said in an undertone to Ross: 'She's lovely, isn't she?'

'Very striking. Beauty's a maker of taste.'

'Is it true, do you think, that what the eye doesn't admire the heart doesn't desire?'

'Oh, without doubt. Do you know anything to disprove it? Well, it has been so with me. As you should know.'

'I know very little of you, Ross. How often have we met in five years? A dozen times?'

Ross was silent. 'I was not thinking of the last five years. But perhaps you're right. I am inclined to agree, I know very little of you either. And you've changed so much – inwardly I mean . . .'

'Have I? Tell me in what way the deterioration is most noticeable.'

'That's asking a reassurance, isn't it? You may have it. It's a different Elizabeth, that's all. The opposite of deterioration. But startling at times. I understand now how young you were when you promised to marry me.'

Elizabeth put her hand out to her wine glass but only fingered the stem. 'I should have been old enough to know my own mind.'

Something in the way she spoke surprised him. The sudden feeling in her voice was like self-contempt. It swung their talk right away from the polite, slightly flirtatious conversation that had been passing between them.

He looked at her, trying to weigh this up, said cautiously to provide her with the normal escape: 'Well, let us agree you were young . . . And then you thought I was dead.'

Elizabeth glanced down the table to where Francis was talking to Ruth Treneglos. The emotion had perhaps caught her unawares too. Or perhaps she decided she had escaped too often. In a perfectly cool, young voice she said:

'I never really believed you were dead. I thought I loved Francis better.'

'You *thought* you loved him . . .'

She nodded her head. 'And then I discovered my mistake.'

'When?'

'Quite soon.'

His rational mind still refused to accept this sudden conversation at its full value, but somewhere inside him his heart was beating, as if the intelligence reached him through another channel. Twenty-odd people at this table, his own wife talking to the cavalry officer with the big moustache, Sir Hugh at her other hand waiting to break in; George Warleggan, for the most part silent and intent but his gaze every now and then flickering up from his food or from his partners to rest upon Elizabeth's hair or mouth or hands. Incredible that Elizabeth should choose this moment to make such a confession, after nine years. Incredible that it should be true . . .

'These damned mongrels that roam about,' said Lady Bodrugan feelingly, 'breeding and interbreeding; they make it uncommon hard to keep one's stock pure. You're that much luckier, John, dealing only in cattle. What did you say your dog was, miss?'

'A pug,' said Caroline. 'With beautiful black curly hair and a gold-brown face no bigger than the centre of this plate. Unwin regards him with the *utmost* respect and affection, don't you, dear.'

'Respect, yes,' said Unwin, 'for his teeth are devilish sharp.'

Ross said to Elizabeth: 'This is some pleasant joke you are trying on me?'

Elizabeth smiled with a sudden brittle brilliance. 'Oh,

it's a joke indeed. But it is against myself, Ross. Didn't you know? I wonder you never guessed.'

'*Guessed . . .*'

'Well, if you did not guess, it might have been more gallant of you to have met this barefaced confession halfway. Is it such an astonishment that a woman who changed her mind once could change it twice? . . . Well, yes, perhaps it is, for it has always been an astonishment and a humiliation to me . . .'

After what seemed a long time Ross said: 'That first Easter I came to you after you married – you told me then plain enough that you loved only Francis and had no thoughts for anyone else.'

'Was that when I should have told you? Only a few months after my marriage, and with Geoffrey Charles already alive in me?'

Something was taken away from Ross and another dish put in its place. Whatever the object of the party, Sir John was not sparing his cellar, and talk at the table was louder than it had been. Yet Ross had to struggle with himself not to push his chair back and get away. That Elizabeth should have chosen this moment . . . Unless it was that only the presence of other people had given her the courage to tell him point-blank what she had long wanted him to know . . . And where a few minutes ago he had made no sense of what she said, now he saw it as sensible enough. Every second that passed fitted it more inescapably into the pattern of the last nine years.

'And Francis?' he said. 'Does he know?'

'I've said already too much, Ross. My tongue. A sudden impulse – it had best be forgotten. Or if not forgotten, disregarded. What were we talking of before this?'

Three places down the table, Francis's slightly raffish

face, in which the vivid lines of youth were losing themselves in a too early deterioration ... As if conscious just then of something toward, he glanced up at Ross, wrinkled one eyebrow and winked.

Francis had known. Ross saw that now. Francis had known so long that his early outbreaks of disillusion and disappointment were far behind him. His own jealousy long spent, and perhaps his love with it, he felt no discomfort at seeing Ross and Elizabeth together. His quarrels in earlier years, the enigmas of his behaviour, were all explained. And now so far as he was concerned it was all past – part of an era best forgotten, in this new time of tolerance and good will.

Perhaps, Ross thought, that was why Elizabeth had now ventured to tell him; because *her* feeling was spent and she believed Ross's to be; she'd offered it as an explanation, an apology of things past, something due to him now that danger no longer existed for any of them in the confession.

Elizabeth had turned to answer some question put by the man on the other side of her, and it was a moment or two before Ross was able to see her face again. Even then she didn't meet his eyes, but he knew instantly by something in her expression – if he had not in fact known all along – that for her the question was not in the very least a dead one and she did not suppose it to be so for him.

After the ladies had left, there was half an hour with the port, and then the sexes were reshuffled for tea and coffee.

Ross had one other meeting with Caroline Penvenen. He was passing a small withdrawing-room when he heard angry words and recognized the voice as Unwin Trevaunance's. He had only gone a few more paces when he heard the door bang sharply and quick footsteps caught him up at the door of the main drawing-room. He stepped back to let Caroline go in before him. She smiled at him rather breathlessly, her eyes still glinting with a disappearing emotion.

As he seemed about to move away, she said: 'Might I have your company for a moment or two?'

'For as long as you wish it.'

She stood beside him, scanning the people with narrowed eyes. He was aware now how tall she was and how graceful.

'I'm gratified you are loyal to your friends, Captain Poldark.'

'Loyal? I hope so. But do you mean . . .'

'I mean to Dr Enys. Because I must tell you that when I met him first he was most loyal to you.'

'When was that?'

'Before your trial, of course. He was quite hot-blooded in your defence.'

In the general run of life people shied away from mentioning his trial to Ross. His was not a face that encouraged liberties. But this girl seem to suffer no hesitation. She spoke either from a complete lack of perception and sensitiveness or else out of her own particular conception of honesty which admitted no taboos. Since she seemed to wish to be friendly, he took the charitable view.

'Must I suppose from that that you gave him reason for defence?'

'Oh, yes, of course. For if you wish to discover a man's true feelings, it is always best to provoke him.'

'Are those the tactics you're applying now, Miss Penvenen?'

She smiled pleasantly. 'It would be presumptuous of me to imagine that I could.'

'Shall you stay with your uncle for the summer?'

'It depends. In October I shall be twenty-one – and then I shall be my own mistress. It's a provoking long time coming.'

'Perhaps before then you will be married.'

'Would that not only be exchanging one keeper for another?'

'Always supposing you look on a husband in that light.'

'Never having had one, I cannot tell. But having seen so many of them about, I should not have thought it an unflattering description.'

'At least it's unflattering to your uncle.'

Caroline laughed. 'But why? He has kept me. Isn't that being a keeper? There have been no bars across the windows – at least only invisible bars of conventionalism and disapproval. But I fancy I should like my freedom for a while.'

As they were talking Unwin went past them with a thunderous face, and Caroline kept Ross in conversation while the other man was in the room. Good-humouredly aware that he was being used, Ross reflected that his hope of seeing them quickly married did not seem likely to come off.

It deteriorated further when Unwin disappeared and was seen no more that evening. Cards were played until midnight, but the fact that there had been a tiff between the young couple was underlined by Ray Penvenen's sour face; and all this put a blight on the last part of the evening.

Just when the party was going to break up, George Warleggan found himself temporarily isolated with Francis and immediately took the opportunity of speaking to him.

'Good evening to you. May I say I'm glad to see you again after all this time.'

Francis stared at him. 'I'm sorry I cannot say the same, George.'

'If it's true, then *I'm* sorry. It need not be.'

'That's where we differ. I made my choice long ago. I prefer to keep my hands clean.'

George's face darkened. 'This empty spite ... In your cousin I have come to expect no reason—'

'Well, then, if that's reason, expect none in me.'

If George had had serious hope of a *rapprochement*, it did not survive this. He turned away and found himself face to face with Ross.

There was a moment's silence. One or two now watching hopefully expected an immediate battle. They edged nearer to catch the words which would provide the spark.

Ross stared down at the other man. 'Good evening to you, George.'

George's formidable face twitched slightly. 'Well, Ross, imagine our meeting here!'

'We must have supper together sometime.'

'I shall look forward to it ... I hope your mine prospers.'

'It will.'

'I wish I had your confidence.'

Ross said: 'Must you be envious even of that?'

George flushed and opened his mouth to say something as Ross moved away. But a word now would undo the restraint of years. Now for the first time he had Ross where he wanted him. Restraint was a virtue. He had only to endure in silence to triumph.

As Ross and Demelza rode home, accompanied for the first part of the way by Francis and Elizabeth, a half-spent

moon rose and tinselled the landscape for them, lighting
the dew on the fields and the spider webs in the hedgerows.
There was not much talk among any of the four. Elizabeth
was keyed up with what she had said and nervous as to the
result, because you could never predict what Ross would
do. Francis was sleepy. And Ross, lost in his thoughts of the
past and his speculations for the future, was curiously
detached from the scene though inescapably aware of the
figure of Elizabeth, cause of it all, riding on ahead of him.

Demelza, with her instinctive, animal perceptions, knew
that something quite fresh had cropped up in Ross's life.
She felt that Elizabeth must be at the bottom of it, but
could not imagine what new thing had suddenly grown out
of the old allegiance. 'I hope to be able to wait on you,
ma'am,' Captain McNeil had said, a very nice admiration
in his look. Of all the men she had ever met, Malcolm
McNeil was the only one who could begin to hold a candle
to Ross. 'One of these days *I'll* give a party, my dear,' Sir
Hugh Bodrugan had said, fingering her arm.

Just before it came time for them to separate, Francis
said:

'Is it true the tub-runners have had another successful
run?'

'Yes,' said Ross. 'I heard so.'

'Vercoe and his gaugers will be in an ill-humour.'

'I've no doubt.'

'There was a whisper about – I've forgot where I heard
it – but there was a whisper about that you were concerning
yourself in the Trade.'

Silence fell. Demelza pulled a little more tightly at her
horse's reins, and the horse shook his head with a jingle of
distaste.

Ross said: 'Where did you hear that?'

'Does it matter so much? It was some time ago and I think concerned that run in March.'

'There has never been a time when some foolish rumour has not been flying round regarding one of us, Francis.'

Another pause. 'Well, I'm glad there's no truth in it anyway.'

'Glad? I did not know you had any special feeling for the Customs men.'

'Nor have I, Ross. But I have some feeling for you nowadays. And I do not like this informer, this sneak, this telltale who is about. Everyone knows of his existence; no one knows who he is. If he was identified, he would soon come to a bad end. But while he is about there is a double danger. Of course if I were Mr Trencrom, with big stakes in the business, connections, and a sizable cutter to maintain, I should I suppose go on and trust in the Lord. I'd have to. But if I were an ordinary threadbare country gentleman, looking to turn an extra penny, or a miner or a blacksmith, thinking of smuggling as a side line, this is the last time of day I should want to have any hand in the work.'

It was a long speech for Francis, and as he spoke they had come to the fork in the track. The four riders halted.

Ross said: 'I suppose you'll do your best to quash this story if you should run against it again.'

'I will. Oh, I will. Well, good night to you both.'

Ross said: 'So far as the Trade goes, there are of course degrees of help one may render. Not all kinds entail running the boats ashore or bearing off the goods.'

'All kinds can be dangerous if there is an informer about.'

'If I were a threadbare country gentleman looking to

turn an extra penny, I might agree with you. But in some circumstances risk must be weighed against reward.'

'I think I should prefer not to know any more. My wish was to convey a friendly warning, not to pry into your secrets.'

'It seems you already know the secret. It will be a good thing if you have the details too. Some time ago Mr Trencrom came to see me, he being in some straits because the informer had made it impossible for him to run in a cargo at any of the usual places. He asked if he might use Nampara Cove. At the time the Warleggans were making themselves obnoxious by getting a foothold in my other mine, Wheal Leisure. I agreed to Trencrom's proposition, and he uses my cove and land – but twice only a year and for each landing he pays me £200.'

Francis whistled. 'It's a tidy sum. Enough to tempt any man. If there were not this danger, I should have jumped at it myself.'

'If there were not this danger, I should not have been offered it.'

'No . . . No, I see. But this money – is it to keep Wheal Grace in operation for longer than we'd planned? If so—'

'I have debts,' said Ross briefly. 'One of them carries an excessive rate of interest. With this money from Trencrom I am able to survive. Without it our mine would never have been started.'

'You should have told me.'

'What?'

'Of these debts. The money we've invested in Wheal Grace might have been better employed.'

'If Wheal Grace fails, it might have been better employed in some other venture. It has never been enough in itself to pay what I owe.'

Francis stared at his cousin's face, which was half lit by the climbing moon. He would have liked to clear up this point between them, but there were too many pitfalls. Their present friendship, their present partnership, meant too much to him to be jeopardized by an ill-considered question now.

As Ross and Demelza rode on alone, Demelza said: 'I wonder who told him.'

'About the Trade? It was bound to get abroad. When twenty or thirty men know . . .' As if reading her thoughts, he added: 'Oh, I know that's what you've always said. But it's a risk to be fairly taken. So long as no one learns the date of a run, all's well. Gaugers will not spend every night out.'

'I would rather go barefoot.'

'There is no risk of that.'

'There are worse risks.'

'I differ.'

'Don't jest, Ross. It's no jesting matter. You have been in too much trouble these last years.'

By now they were riding down into their own valley. On the other side the new engine of Wheal Grace slithered and sighed as it pumped the water up from the depths of the earth.

To divert her Ross said: 'And did you enjoy the evening? Did it come up to your expectation?'

'Yes, it was all very agreeable. Only we were separated, as you might say, at the very beginning and were almost strangers by the end of it.'

'It is the fashion of modern society. But I noticed Captain McNeil looked after you very well.'

'Yes, he did indeed. He's a very polite, genteel sort of man, Ross, and is going to call on us one day next week.'

'Hm. It is not an uncommon pattern. You only have to crook your little finger and they all come.'

'You have an awful wicked tongue for exaggeration, Ross. I wonder sometimes it does not drop off. And Caroline Penvenen?'

'Caroline?'

'Yes, you saw very much of her. What do you think of her? She kept you in a corner, did she not, and wouldn't let you come forth.'

Ross pondered a minute. 'She kept me in no corner that I did not wish to be kept in,' he said, 'but I certainly think she is the wrong wife for Dwight. She would wipe her feet on him.'

Chapter Four

Ellery's death made a big difference to Dwight. Surgical and physical skill could be exercised in a poor and primitive community only on a foundation of confidence and trust. Without that foundation you were lucky if you exercised anything at all. In two weeks more than half Dwight's patients disappeared from his doorstep or made excuses when he called.

His visits to St Ann's were at no time frequent, but he had one or two faithful patients there and among them, a paying one too, was Mrs Vercoe, the wife of the Customs Officer, whose youngest child he had pulled through an illness during the winter. On the day following the party, to which he'd not been invited, he paid them a visit and was just in time to see Vercoe himself separating at the front door of his white-washed cottage from a tall fair-haired man with a fine cavalry moustache. Although plainly a gentleman, the stranger had not come by horse, because he strode away across the fields towards the cliff path.

Inside the cottage Clara Vercoe greeted Dwight. Hubert was not so well, she said, had vomited after his latest bottle of physic and she'd given him no more. Hubert, looking papery and wasted, was brought forward into the sunlight falling through the open doorway, and Dwight cast a professional eye over him while pretending to admire his story book. It was a new kind, cheaply printed in Plymouth on sheets of stiff paper with line pictures illustrating *The History of Primrose Prettyface* and bound between covers of thin horn with a wooden handle. The first picture was of an angel, and Hubert had coloured the wings red.

Dwight wondered if this was another echo of the Ellery affair and if his draught was being blamed for some digestive upset. He said he would change the stuff, and poured some of it into a cup to examine and taste.

While he was there Jim Vercoe came back into the cottage for a telescope, and Dwight followed the direction in which it was pointed, towards a sail on the horizon.

You could not but admire a man who persisted in his task in the face of bribes offered, occasional threats, and the social ostracism that came his way. Something of the unpleasantness Vercoe often had to meet showed in his bearded face. Dwight would have admired him the more if there had not been also a trace of that grim satisfaction about him which some men find in getting disliked in the course of their duty.

'The sky's very clear this morning,' Dwight remarked as the Customs Officer lowered his glass.

'Sharp's a knife, surgeon. There'll be more rain afore nightfall.'

'We been watching for the revenue ship all week,' said Mrs Vercoe with a nod. 'Jim's been asking for 'er for long enough.'

''Twill be all over the village soon,' Vercoe said irritably. 'Women's tongues is too slipper in what don't concern 'em.'

'Eh, Dr Enys wouldn't say anything, would you, sir?'

'No more than I should if I saw a man with a cask of brandy.'

Vercoe stared at him resentfully for a moment. A man

with the standing of a physician had no right to be that impartial.

''Tis hard to do a proper job when all the gentry are against ee, surgeon, and when there's scarcely a place for an honest boat to find safe harbourage anywhere along this coast. They just won't venture in when the weather's heavy. Even Padstow's no safe refuge if a gale blow up. But ye can't keep a watch from Mount's Bay!'

'I should have thought the disadvantage works both ways. The seas that keep away your revenue cutter will stop men from landing a cargo.'

'Ah, 'tis not so simple as that. The runners will take more risks, and they d'know every rock and eddy like the back of their hands. What I need 'bove all is more men ashore. 'Tis fighting uphill all the way. And the worst thing of all mebbe is knowing that after all if you catch your men, as like as not they'll be brought before the local magistrates and acquitted and set free.'

Dwight said: 'I know it is hard, but I should not say that *all* the gentry are against you. Or even all the people. I understand you have your informers, and they should be worth their weight in – well, gold.'

Vercoe's face coloured with a dark, angry flush. 'That's what you come down to, surgeon, when you're hard set. You're not helped by the honest men, so then you've to use the rats.'

A few minutes later Dwight rode into the main street of the village and dismounted at the little shop where his medicines were made up. He stooped in and waited among the multicoloured bottles and the bundles of coloured straw for making bonnets and the green canisters of mixed tea until Irby, the druggist, squeezed himself out of the dungeon where he mixed his prescriptions. Irby was a little fat man with a stub of a nose and steel spectacles with lenses no bigger than the acquisitive eyes behind them.

Dwight began by asking pleasantly to see the order he had made out and asking Mr Irby to taste the draught and to note the amount of sediment in the bottom of the bottle. Mr Irby was effusive, co-operative, but astonished; there would of course be sediment: the drugs Dwight had ordered would refuse to mix and a precipitate would form. Dwight with deference corrected him. If the drugs were pure, it was quite impossible, etc., etc. At this point the conversation, while still polite, began to carry a sediment of its own. Dwight said he wished he might examine the drugs from which the physic was made up. Mr Irby squinted round the sides of his spectacles and said that he had been practising in St Ann's for twenty years and no surgeon had ever cast a reflection on his competence before. Dwight said that in this respect he did not doubt his competence; it was a plain question of whether the drugs were adulterated. Mr Irby said he had never bought cheap drugs and he did not propose to be accused of that now. Dwight said he was sorry to have to insist, but he had a right by law as a physician to enter and examine the drugs in any druggist's establishment, and this he intended to exercise. Followed by Mr Irby, he went down the steps into the dungeon and peered about him in the uncertain light, at the Glauber's salts, the Dover's powders, the gamboge, the nux vomica, the paregorics, and the vermifuges.

The noise of Mr Irby's annoyance brought Mrs Irby from a deeper dungeon behind the first, but Dwight went carefully on with his examination. He found what he had suspected; that cheap substitutes had been bought and labelled for more expensive drugs, and in two cases the powders had been adulterated with something, ground bone or chalk. All these he tipped into a wooden pail. When it was full, he walked out through the shop with it, followed by the druggist angrily demanding recompense and justice. As he went he saw a tall woman standing in the shop, but it was so dark that he did not take much note of her. He carried the pail round the backs of the houses, found the nearest open cesspool, and tipped the contents in. When he came back he saw that the woman was Caroline Penvenen.

Five minutes later he left the shop, trying to dust the powder from his breeches and boots. Mr Irby followed him to the door calling down the wrath of God, but abruptly disappeared – being lugged in by his wife, who was a powerful woman as well as an astute one and did not wish their neighbours to know more than could be helped.

Dwight glanced at the splendid chestnut held by a mounted groom, but he didn't stop. As he got to his own horse, Caroline came out of the shop.

He took off his hat and the breeze fanned his face.

She said: 'Dr Enys, as I'm alive! How diverting. And with such an expression as if the Last Trump'd blown. I almost mistook you for a vision of Judgment.'

He had been expecting, half dreading this meeting. Now that it had come, it had all the anticipated sense of shock, it brought all the old feelings alive. In the middle of his anger he recognized them, every one. Her brilliant hair blowing in the breeze was a renewed offence; so was the curve of her strong feminine mouth, the laughter in her eyes.

Dwight said: 'There are times, ma'am, when we can't

wait for the Last Trump, but must pass a little judgment by the way.'

She swung up on her horse, and the animal side-stepped spiritedly on the cobbles. 'And who is next to receive a chastising? May I accompany you for the entertainments?'

'You may accompany me, but I've no entertainment to offer. I'm riding home now.'

She shook her head. 'You underrate yourself, Dr Enys. Your company is fair entertainment for me any day.'

He bowed. 'Thank you, but we differ as to that. Good day.'

He rode off fairly boiling. She thought him a fool, and no doubt she was right. His life seemed bounded with futilities, and her being on the spot served to point them. He had just left St Ann's when he heard the thump of hooves in the lane and Caroline drew abreast of him. Her groom was left behind.

She said angrily: 'We meet after fifteen months and you haven't even a civil word for me!'

That, he thought, was a trifle cool. 'I'm old-fashioned in these matters, Miss Penvenen. I thought civility should be shown on both sides.'

'I might have known better than to expect any from you.'

'Indeed you might.'

'The truth is that you do not like to be laughed at.'

'That is the truth.'

They were silent for a little way. She turned her whip over and over in her gloved hands and glanced at him. 'I'm sorry.'

He looked at her, startled, and she at once laughed.

'There, Dr Enys, you didn't expect me to say that and it has quite frightened you. You see how dangerous it is to prejudge a person. I should have thought your medical training would have warned you against it.'

'So it should. The symptoms were deceptive.'

'And now that you find yourself undeceived, don't you owe *me* an apology?'

'Yes . . . I'm sorry.'

She inclined her head. 'Do you think that if I show a properly sober frame of mind and promise never to laugh again, we might share this road as far as Trenwith?'

'You're staying with your uncle?'

'Yes.'

'Unwin Trevaunance is down, I hear.'

'He is.'

The groom was not overtaking them but was following just out of earshot.

'And how is the scurvy in Sawle?' she asked.

'Not so bad as last year. The potato crop didn't fail, and I sometimes wonder if even potatoes help to keep it at bay. On the whole—' He stopped and looked at her face; but if she was secretly deriding him, she gave no sign this time.

'Perhaps I'm wrong in calling you Miss Penvenen.'

'Why? Oh . . . No, I'm not married yet.'

'Is it to be soon?'

She wrinkled her nose. 'Not soon. At least, not to Unwin. He's jilted me.'

'What?'

'Well, I'm not sure which way round it was, but Uncle says it was the other way. Uncle was in the greatest of a passion when he learned of it – said I had been leading Unwin a dance. But really, Dr Enys, there's no harm in a man performing a dance once in a while, is there? Why should I sell myself to Unwin just to become Lady Trevaunance when Sir John dies? I was not meant to be an MP's wife. I should get no pleasure in spending all my money furthering Unwin's career. I'd better prefer to spend it furthering my own!'

Dwight hoped his feelings did not show in his face.

'And what brought you to this sudden decision?'

'Oh . . .' A glint came into her eyes. 'I think it was my first real meeting with Ross Poldark.'

'Ross Poldark happens to be married.'

'Yes . . . and incidentally last night had no eyes for anyone but his cousin-in-law – that lovely fair-haired woman with the grey eyes. I think that's their relationship, isn't it? But it looked closer.'

'You misunderstood it. Anyway—'

'Anyway, he had no eyes for me, you were going to say. Quite true. I shouldn't object to Poldark as a husband, I believe, but someone spoke him first. No . . . what I mean is that when one sees a ship of the line, one is that much less content with a third-rater. Do you understand me, dear Dr Enys?'

'I understand you,' said Dwight, wondering what his own category was in His Majesty's Navy.

'So you can appreciate it is a very sad story,' said Caroline, 'of a young woman left almost at the church door, and no redress. Can you wonder that at any moment she may fall ill and go into a decline?'

'I can understand,' Dwight said, 'that she will now have more time on her hands.'

There was a long pause. After it Caroline said steadily: 'You dislike me very much, don't you?'

He flushed. 'D'you really think that?'

'Have you ever given me cause to think otherwise?'

They had already passed Trenwith, passed her turning for Killewarren. He said suddenly: 'If what I feel for you is dislike – for coming between me and my work sometime *every* day in the last fifteen months – if that's dislike . . . If being unable to forget your voice, or the way you turn your neck, or the lights in your hair – if that's dislike . . . If wanting to hear that you're married and dreading to hear that you're married . . . If resenting the condescension that pretends you're not out of my reach . . .' He stopped, unable to finish his sentences. 'Perhaps you can identify these symptoms for me.'

They rode on in silence, and then Caroline reined in her horse.

'I must go back. I shall be late for dinner as it is. Tell me, do you ever ride for pleasure?'

'Seldom.'

'I shall be out on Thursday early. Would you like to meet me at the gates soon after seven?'

At least she was not laughing now. He could hardly believe that within ten minutes of their meeting all his good resolutions had been tipped overboard, with apparently no effort on her part and no resistance on his. He knew as plainly as if it had been issued by proclamation that, Unwin or no Unwin, Caroline was not for him. Her uncles would make very sure that she either married a title or more money. A penniless doctor with a good name but nothing to it would be better occupied putting straws in his hair.

The groom was coming up with them. She said: 'Or I could be ill if you preferred it. How long does it take to develop the scurvy?'

'It's an unpleasant disease,' Dwight said, taking off his hat, 'and so bad for the complexion. I shouldn't advise it.'

A week passed before Malcolm McNeil paid his visit to Nampara. He walked over one bright summerless after-noon, without prior notice since he wanted it that way, and on foot since he was keen to harden himself before returning to duty. As he came down the valley, he noticed the changes that three years had brought. On the opposite hill was a new mine with a pumping engine hissing and clanking, and a whole litter of sheds and piles of refuse, and leets and a smithy and a spalling house. Industry had advanced at the expense of farming. More fields lay fallow than a rotation of crops justified, and there were few cattle or sheep or pigs about. A dark-lashed baby was asleep in a cot near the front door. The servant who let him in left him in the parlour, which seemed to him to have become smaller and poorer since his last visit. A kitten came and mewed round his legs, and he picked it up and gave it his forefinger to bite.

Mrs Poldark was about five minutes, and she looked flushed when she came in.

'I'm sure this is an ill-chosen time, ma'am,' he said. 'I was passing and thought to avail myself of your kindness . . .'

'No, not at all. But Ross, I'm sorry to say, isn't here. He's over to the mine. I'll send Gimlett to fetch him.'

McNeil vigorously protested, and she allowed herself to be persuaded, knowing that Ross was likely to be deep in some work – probably fathoms deep – and would not want interruption. McNeil sat down and fastened his moustache more firmly in and let the kitten slide on to the shabby rug.

Being a Scotsman and a widely travelled one, he had not been much impressed by the women in these parts on his last visit. But there had been three good-lookers at the party the other evening, and this Mrs Poldark was the one with that little something more than looks which teased his curiosity. He fancied he knew potentialities when he saw them; and a spark was seldom long absent from this young woman's fine eyes. It was like the glint of a soldier's sabre at night.

He said: 'You have heard the latest war news, perhaps?'

'War news? I didn't know we were at war.'

He smiled. 'Nor are we, ma'am. I mean the French war with the Austrians. The information has just come through.'

'Is it good or bad?'

'Oh, good. Without question. The French broke into Belgium like a rabble, it's said, expecting no doubt to make men run at the sight of their unshaven faces; but when they met the Austrians, one disciplined charge was enough; the whole French army tairned and ran from the battlefield. And when their own officers – their own generals – tried to stop them, they murdered them, stabbing them with bayonets!'

'And what does that mean? That France is defeated already? Have they other armies?'

'None in the field . . . So much for your revolutionaries. It's strange how nairvous people have been at the thought of these cut-throats let loose. Folk forget that when a country throws away its discipline it throws away its strength. I trust this will be a lesson to the noisy windbags in Paris.' He paused and stretched a booted leg and twisted his moustache. 'Though for myself . . .'

Demelza waited. 'What for yourself, Captain McNeil?'

'Well, I confess I should not have been discontented to have a tilt at them some way or another. I should not be wishing Britain into war, ye understand, but for a soldier a small bout of fighting now and then restores his self-respect.'

'I shouldn't have thought 'twould be likely *you* would lose that.'

'No, ma'am. But in times of peace one is sent on – one is liable to be called upon for distasteful and rather shabby missions which . . .' McNeil stopped and withdrew his leg and looked at Demelza. Demelza looked at him without a flicker of a change of expression. He swallowed and said: 'I'm sorry. I thought I heard a baby crying.'

She got up and went quickly to the window, peered out. 'No. I can see him. He's still asleep.'

'Perhaps it's your little girl. Though by now I suppose she will be—'

'She died, Captain McNeil. More than two years ago.'

'Oh . . .' He got up. 'Forgive me, ma'am. I'm sorry.'

Demelza came back. 'It's nothing to forgive. You were not to know.' She stood by the table for a moment, fairly close to him. 'Pray sit down.'

'It must have been a grievous blow. You will feel a gap in your life . . .'

'It is hard to explain, for 'tis more than a gap. Or it has been with us. There is a change. Nothing hasn't been the same since. Those who are left are different people trying to live the same lives.'

McNeil stood looking at her. He cursed himself for

having got the conversation on the wrong leg. Yet in what she said he detected an alloy of something besides sadness. She did not look in the least a discontented woman, but all clearly was not well between her and life. It might be a circumstance worth exploring.

Ross was not, as Demelza not unreasonably supposed, fathoms deep; he was in conference with Francis and Captain Henshawe in the changing shed near the mine. The two young engineers, Bull and Trevithick, who had built the engine, had been over to correct a minor fault, and Ross had taken the opportunity of sounding them on the potentialities of their child. It seemed plain to him, and they confirmed it, that the engine was capable of a good deal more than was at present demanded; and he proposed that the main shaft should be sunk another twenty fathoms so that two new levels could be begun. This meant engaging more men; but as he pointed out to Henshawe and Francis, the prospect of profit was increased out of proportion to the expense. The great expense was the engine. While it worked, let it do the maximum.

Francis the gambler was all for it, Henshawe more cautious; but inevitably, as the chief partners, the cousins had their way. Henshawe's interest was nominal, and in any case he was not an obstructive man. He knew Ross's overriding need of quick results. Nor did he comment, as he might have done, that in his wide experience of mines in this district he had seldom known the copper lodes to improve with depth, as was often the case further west. Nothing was so unpredictable as a mine – one reason why they were always feminine – and he was not prepared to take the responsibility of standing in the way of Ross's instinct.

After the meeting Ross walked home alone, content that the effort was to be made but content with nothing else.

Elizabeth's confession at the party had had an unexpected effect on him. Behind the strong and sometimes lawless impulses that moved him from time to time was a bitterly clear-minded critic who saw his own acts, usually after he had performed them, with great detachment. Sometimes, though not very often, this critic turned on others. It did so now on Elizabeth. She wasn't at all less attractive to him – much the reverse. But he found himself *liking* her less. Her single mistake had distorted all their lives, pulling them out of their natural pattern. Then, having picked the wrong man, she had let him know it, and he, deprived of her love but not of his need for her, had run the conversational course downhill watched and blamed by Ross who thought he had all he could desire. Their lives had been the tragedy of one woman who couldn't make up her mind.

Far better now if *he* had never known. The knowledge served no purpose but to destroy what was left of his peace of mind. The result of all this, contrariwise, had been a new warmth in his feelings for Demelza. He wouldn't have been able to explain why, unless it was that he felt Demelza incapable of any such behaviour.

When he got to his own front door he heard a man's voice and surprised the coattails of Malcolm McNeil, who was just taking his leave.

Demelza smiled over her visitor's shoulder. 'Oh, Ross, I was afraid you was underground, or I should have sent for you. Captain McNeil has been entertaining me with stories of the American war. I wonder you never speak of it yourself.'

McNeil said: 'Captain Poldark is more modest, I've no doubt. The latest news suggests we shall not need him again just yet.'

'Oh, you've heard it?' said Ross in slight disappointment. 'My cousin has just told me. It may of course be exaggerated.'

'From what I gather, the road to Paris is open. The sooner the city is occupied the better.'

'No doubt you're right. I confess I still have a sneaking sympathy for the republicans – if only they would behave like reasonable men and not like apes. If I were a Parisian, I should not want to open the gates to Francis of Austria.'

McNeil said: 'By the way, did ye hear more of the man who killed his wife when I was last here, and escaped from your cove?'

'Mark Daniel? No. I expect he was drowned. The dinghy he stole from us was barely seaworthy.'

'Indeed, so?' McNeil looked at Ross with an unbelieving eye. 'Well, I'll be on my way. I'm returning to Salisbury in a few days' time, but I doubt I shall be down again before long. It is a fascinating part.'

This last remark he seemed to address to Demelza. She said: 'I hope you'll take back a good report of our behaviour this time.'

McNeil said: 'How could I do otherwise, ma'am?'

Ross watched the Scotsman's broad-shouldered figure walking briskly up the valley.

'He is a thought less impressive out of his soldier's clothes. I hope he did not come here because he suspects us of being concerned in the tub-carrying.'

'Oh, no, he invited himself to call when we met last

week. He is here only for his health this time. He has no interest in smuggling at all.'

'Did he tell you so?'

'Yes . . . Yes, he did.'

'H'm,' said Ross.

Demelza's indignation grew with her alarm. 'I don't see that there is any reason to suspect him at all!'

'Only that that was his business last time, and Cornwall is a long way to come just for a convalescence.'

'I'm certain sure you're wrong.'

'You were careful what you said, I suppose?'

'Of course! You should know I am more frightened of discovery than you are.'

Ross said musingly: 'I think I shall ride over and see Tremcrom tomorrow.'

'Why? He promised there was to be no more landing in our cove until September.'

'No, nor shall there be. I want to locate Mark Daniel.'

'I should not suppose it safe for him to come back.'

'No. But he was in Cherbourg last Christmas. You know why we opened Wheal Grace. It was part on account of the old maps, part on account of what Mark told us when he hid in the old workings before we helped him to escape. Well, we have spent months trying to find out what he found. Why should we not get him to help us? In a few more months it will be too late.'

'I'd rather Mark came than you went, Ross. Up till now you've taken no real part in the Trade.'

'Well, the first thing is to see if he can be found.'

'No, Ross, that isn't the first thing.'

'All right, I'll not go if it can be avoided.'

Mr Trencrom lived in an unpretentious six-roomed house tucked away as if not to be seen behind a sharp cleft in the hillside half a mile from the village of St Ann's. Although it was known that he was a very rich man, no evidences of wealth were allowed to appear in his house or in the clothes he wore, and there was plenty of speculation as to where he kept his money and what he did with it. Nothing suggested the miser in the size of his body or the warmth of his welcome when Ross called the next evening; and Ross came straight to the point, explaining the inquiries he would like put in hand.

'Mark Daniel,' said Mr Trencrom, squeezing his small voice out of his large chest. 'Let's see, that was the one that killed his wife, wasn't it? On account of her going with that Dr Enys. Remember well. Quite a fuss. 'Twould be dangerous still, I conceit, for him to come back. To England. Have you asked any of my men?'

'No. I came first to you.'

Mr Trencrom acknowledged the courtesy. 'Might deliver a letter. But Daniel can't read, eh? I'll ask Nanfan or Paynter to inquire. Nanfan's best because he's a relative. I'll do that, Captain Poldark. Nights are too light just at present. Can have too much of a full moon, eh?' He coughed, a weak consumptive paroxysm, as if someone had sat on a rusty spring in his sofa. 'There's trouble about. That man Vercoe. And that military fellow up at the Place. Shall be glad to see the back of him. There's more in it than meets the eye. And look at France. Chaos. I should not fancy to be Mark Daniel. Living there these days.'

Ross got up to leave. 'I'll call and speak to Nanfan. Does he always go?'

'No. Leave arranging to me. Oh, Captain Poldark, as a favour – just one for another, as you might say. I thought of calling to see you. But it's a long way, and after dark these summer days. Not in my first bloom.'

'Yes?'

'One drawback to your cove. Frequently thought of it. Must be done in a single night. You've always insisted, haven't you, everything must be carried away. Don't blame you. But 'tis awkward. If we could store some of the stuff – two, three days. As we used to do in Sawle and places. Ten men do in three nights what thirty do in one. Less chance for the informer. Get the stuff ashore and *hide* it. The main thing.' Mr Trencrom tried to push himself out of his chair. 'See what I mean?'

'You're suggesting we should hide it for you in our own house?'

'Didn't say house. Not necessarily. Though even there – if a cache were carefully dug—'

'I'm sorry. That's putting my neck in a noose. At present I always have the defence that the run is being made without my knowledge. But if one item of your goods is found in my cellar . . .'

Mr Trencrom clasped and unclasped his fat hands. 'You ask a favour of me, sir. What's the difference? Oh, in degree, I suppose, something. But the obligation, the benefit . . .'

Ross had known Mr Trencrom for some years; it was not the first time he had found him less easygoing than he looked. 'If you prefer it, I can go to Falmouth and take ship to Cherbourg myself.'

'Have reason to believe Mark Daniel has left Cherbourg.'

'Where is he, then?'

Mr Trencrom nearly asphyxiated himself with a cough. Coming up purple and panting, he said: 'Captain Poldark, now. Have no idea. But my men would have a better chance. Your mine is not paying yet, I understand?'

Ross stared at him grimly. 'D'you wish me to confirm that or to acknowledge the blackmail?'

'Oh, please. Between friends. We work together, do we not? Profit of both. Have no wish to offend. But we can't do without each other – just at present. I suggested this – thought you might not object. Would be willing to make some small extra payment for the convenience, small of course; my profits negligible, just as a good-will token. Twenty-five guineas, say . . .'

'For each cargo?'

'Well . . . yes, I suppose.'

Ross reflectively flapped his gloves. His struggle to remain solvent had distorted his views on money, but not to this extent. He was going to refuse again, but Mr Trencrom said:

'Don't decide now, sir. Take a little time. If you think more of it, leave me know. In the meanwhile I will see after your friend Daniel.'

'Thank you. Are you any further forward in tracing how the leakage in your arrangements arises?'

'Nothing substantial. So far we have been able to avoid serious trouble this year. But am not happy about it. As you'll understand. When it began I thought 'twas someone outside our circle. Hard, you know, bringing in goods, using forty or more men – not to let it get about. The *village* knows. The countryside. But last September, as you'll remember, we began to run a cargo in at Strand Cove. Most unusual to be able to. Usually the heavy swell. I issued instructions to our riders where to go only six hours before the run was due to begin. But we'd floated no more than a dozen ankers ashore when Vercoe and his men sprang out of ambush. Six of our best men arrested. Only thanks to his shortage of men the rest escaped. It can't happen again.

It mustn't, Captain Poldark. And the *One and All* has been gravely imperilled.'

'Well, only Vercoe knows who is at the bottom of it,' said Ross grimly. 'And Vercoe won't tell.'

Mr Trencrom asphyxiated himself again. 'Perhaps even Vercoe – does not know. I sometimes – wonder. Perhaps he gets messages – under the door. 'Tis a dangerous game for the informer. There is very bad feeling about.'

At the moment Mr Trencrom said this the informer was in the Hoblyns' cottage in Sawle.

Chapter Five

Dwight had had a busy week. As well as riding with Caroline, he had had a crop of sudden ailments to face; and it was from the last of these, a case of bilious fever in Sawle, that he was returning when he decided on the impulse of the moment to call in at the Hoblyns' cottage.

The evening was well on, and he found all the Hoblyns indoors and with them Charlie Kempthorne, who had got Rosina in a corner and was making up to her under the lowering gaze of Jacka her father. Not that Jacka particularly disapproved of Charlie, except for his age; it was rather that courting in any shape or form was one of the great number of things he didn't hold with. He couldn't complain that it was happening under his own nose, because he had refused Charlie permission to take Rosina for a walk.

Dwight apologized for the intrusion, said he had come to see Rosina; Rosina said hastily her knee was *quite* better thank you; Dwight ignored this and said would she and Mrs Hoblyn come into the next room. This left the two men alone, for Parthesia was in bed.

Charlie hadn't liked the interruption. He fancied he had been making some progress, and now it was all set back. But perhaps this could be turned to account. After a minute he scratched his short-cropped head and said: 'Reckon Rosina's coming round t'our way of thinking, Jacka. 'Twill soon be a question of naming the day, like.'

'It isn't to my way of thinking,' Jacka said. 'I'm thinkin' nothin' yet awhile.'

'But you're not saying me nay,' said Charlie. 'An' Rosina'll see that for herself. She's always been a good obeying kind of girl—'

'She better be,' said Jacka.

'An' 'tis plain to she that with 'er crooked pinbone she'll be lucky to get a good steady man who's maybe a bit olderer than she but all the better for that. *An'* got a tidy nest egg, what's more. And adding on every day. You should mind that, Jacka Hoblyn.'

'I'll mind what I've the wish to mind.'

'Let 'er go get forced put by some farmer's boy, an' what's the end to it? A 'ovel no betterer than a pigsty. I can give 'er a *home*, with cloam cups to drink out of like she was a lady. And I'll tell ee another thing. That field that's to rent from Surgeon Choake's house. Corner of it runs down nigh to the top of the lane, back o' my yard. Next year I thought to take it. 'Tis just what I d'need to—'

'I can't conceit where you get all your money,' said Jacka.

Charlie looked at him keenly for a moment. 'Ah, but that's just it. Money d'add to money all the while. Start with just a little and treat it right, an' it'll go on growing while you're asleep. Mind, it need a steady 'and. But that's what I got. And sail-making's different from bal work. There's more profit to it. Reckon my consumptives was a blessed dressed up, else I'd still have been down mine and no better off at forty than thirty!'

Jacka knitted his black brows. 'Wonder what surgeon's

about, coming this time of night. 'Tis no concern of his to
visit when he's not asked.'

'D'you pay 'im for every time?'

'Nay, give him his due, he's no great one for that.'

Kempthorne spat on the sanded floor. 'Well, I shouldn't
like it ef 'twas *my* house. It don't seem right, 'im coming
round any hour of the day, fingering a girl's knee. That's
'ow bad things d'start.'

Jacka stared at Charlie. 'I thought you was a friend of
his. I thought 'twas he cured you of the miner's cough.'

'So 'twas. I've nought against him. I'm only saying as it
'pears to me. When all's said, he's only a youngster – and
you know what happened with Daniel's wife.'

There was a moment's silence. Jacka's eyebrows were
like a scar. He stared at Charlie without pleasure and then
strode into the next room.

He found Rosina sitting on the end of the bed, and
Dwight was putting a bandage round her knee. Mrs Hoblyn
glanced up nervously.

Dwight was cheerful, having at last discovered the cause
of their reluctance to let him treat Rosina. 'Oh, Hoblyn,
glad you came in. Mrs Hoblyn has been explaining about
Mr Nye.'

'Ah?' said Jacka.

'Mr Nye said it might be better to amputate the leg. Of
course there's no fear of that. A ridiculous suggestion. I
want you to keep your knee bound for a week until I come
again.' He finished his work and stood up.

'Yes, sur,' said Rosina.

'I don't see as 'tis necessary for you to be calling,
surgeon,' said Jacka, not quite confident of himself. 'Rosina
d'get along well and fine as she is. She been like it too long
now for a cure. When she's sick, that's different like.'

'Rosina gets along,' said Dwight. 'But it isn't a happy or a healthy way to live. I can promise no improvement, but I intend to try.'

'Sometimes more 'arm than good comes of probing at things.'

Dwight flushed. 'Have no fear: she'll not die of it.'

'Well, I believe in leaving well alone.'

'But you have hardly the right to deny your daughter the chance of proper treatment.'

This was treading on Jacka's corns. 'Who's no right?' he shouted. 'I've a right to do what I will with my own. Don't forget that, surgeon.'

'Jacka, please!' said Mrs Hoblyn.

'Hold your clack, woman!'

'I'll *not*!' said Polly, standing up to him for once. 'Dr Enys is doing his best, and takin' pains, and that's more'n have ever been done for my girl before. You ought to be shamed, turning on him like this!'

Dwight caught sight of Charlie at the door, and some expression on his face made Dwight feel that the little sailmaker was enjoying the scene. For some reason he didn't want Rosina cured. Was it because his own suit would then be less hopeful?

Dwight was in time to step in front of Jacka as he made a movement towards his wife. It looked as if there might be a scuffle, but Jacka gave way. As usual his anger was shortlived, and suddenly it changed its direction, towards the man who had primed it.

'Get out of the room,' he bawled at Charlie. ''Twill be time enough to come in 'ere when you're wed to my daughter and not before!'

Nevertheless, as Dwight took his leave he knew that his next visit would be very much on sufferance, and he would have to produce some result soon or admit failure.

The next Tuesday was the first warm day of the delayed summer. The toe of England, eddying along through cold and cheerless days, had suddenly and at last reached warmer water. Even at seven, which was the hour he had agreed to meet Caroline, the air was gentle and mild.

She always kept him waiting, but this time less long than usual. They cantered away from the gates of Killewarren in the early sun, and she suggested they should turn south, among trees long held in bud but now a sudden full brilliant green. She seemed to know her way.

When they had gone about four miles, she turned up a lane which petered out into a clearing azure with bluebells and she said: 'Let's get down, shall we, Dwight. I want to talk, and it's not easy on a nag.'

He dismounted at once and tried to help her, but she slid off as nimbly as a boy and laughed at him.

'Let's sit over here. It's good to be idle sometimes. Or *I* think so. Perhaps you feel always you should be tending someone.'

'Not always. Not now.'

They sat on a green mound punctured with rabbit holes, and Caroline picked a bluebell and swung it idly to make the bells quiver.

'I'm returning to Oxfordshire, Dwight.'

Something lurched inside him. 'When?'

'On Friday's coach. I shall be in Uncle William's bosom by Monday.'

'What has made you decide to go?'

'Oh, I didn't decide. Uncle Ray is very angry with me

about my treatment of Unwin, and he thinks I shall be better banished from this place altogether.'

Dwight looked at her. Her wide eyes were contemplative, narrowed with the sunshine; the bright light brought extra colours to them, greys and flecks of hazel and deeper greens.

'I don't know what to say. I thought – I hoped you'd be staying.'

'I hoped I'd be staying too.'

Overhead a blackbird was chattering. 'When d'you expect to come again?'

'At Uncle Ray's invitation? Oh, that's very doubtful. He no longer approves of me or of my doings. And I suspect that someone has told him of my morning rides with his physician.'

'It's understandable then that he wants to send you away.'

'Why?' she asked provokingly.

'If you lower yourself by being seen about with Dr Enys, and not even a groom in attendance, it will be Mr Penvenen's first duty to come between you and your indiscretion.'

Caroline threw away her bluebells. 'So you agree with Uncle Ray. You think I should better be kept out of harm's way until I am safely married.'

'If I were your uncle . . .'

'But since you're not my uncle?'

Dwight got up. 'What do you expect me to say?'

She leaned back on her elbows. 'I should have expected you to say no.'

'And so should I like to. You know, Caroline, without the need of words to colour it or make it more explicit, that I – that I . . .'

After a minute Caroline said: 'Sit down, Dwight. We can't talk if you stride about.'

He stopped and sat again, his knees in his hands, a little away from her, frowning, ill at ease, deliberately not looking at her.

She said: 'Tell me, Dwight, I never know; there are two men in you: the strong, confident, impatient one, that so often goes with you in a sick-room; and the oh-so-much younger, nervous, susceptible one that often rides with me. Which of them is it, do you suppose, that cares for Caroline Penvenen and grieves she goes and thinks of her in her absence?'

A rabbit scampered across the greensward and ducked quickly into a hole. Dwight said: 'Questions are always directed at me. Perhaps I'll face yours if you face mine. How much are you concerned for the answer?'

'You ask a great deal.'

'No more than you ask of me.'

'Oh, yes, I think it is.'

Dwight watched her fingers stroking the fold of her skirt. 'Very well, then. I'll answer yours first. There are no two men in me but only one – and that one thinks of you continuously so that the image of you is never absent. But ... what you complain of is not to be wondered at. Money was never plentiful for me, and studying took all I had. There was no time for drawing-rooms or polite talk. I was not brought up to know the right addresses to pay beautiful women. I hardly ever met women – except as cases. As cases I know them well. So when I have dealings with people now, I differ with the dealings. If you come to me with a sore throat or a bad knee, you are a patient and I know you well. I know what to do and I do it. And you think, that man has confidence. But if I meet you in a drawing-room, you're not a patient but a woman, someone whose moods and manners I've never learned to understand. I don't know the right prescription for gallantry: I never had leisure to learn it. I don't know how to flatter you, and if you laugh at me – as you not seldom do – I grow more tongue-tied each minute; and when you sharpen your wits on me, I feel a dullard and a clod. There's the explanation of it all. What I feel for you as a person doesn't waver between strength and weakness, it only wavers between hope and despair!'

She had stopped looking at him and was staring across at the other edge of the glade. The curve of her throat gave him pleasure and pain. As he explained himself he had gained in confidence.

He said at last: 'And you?'

She smiled a little and shrugged. 'You want me to answer your question now?'

'Yes.'

'Perhaps this is our last meeting, so perhaps I can. Poor Dwight, have I laughed at you so often? Have I shown such perfect confidence and poise? You flatter me, you truly do. What elegance I must display! How graciously I've been taught . . .'

'I wasn't criticizing you.'

'I'm sure you would not dare. But let me explain *my*self. You say you spent all your time learning to be a physician, and so had no time for the formal courtesies. I'm sorry for you. Dear, dear, I am. But do you know what I have spent my time learning to be? Why, an heiress, of course.'

She leaned over on her elbow and looked at him. Her auburn hair, tied with a ribbon at the back, lay on her shoulder.

'An heiress must learn *all* the courtesies. She must learn

to draw and paint and play a musical instrument even if she's tone-deaf and only makes horrid noises. She must know French and perhaps a little Latin; she must understand how to carry herself and how to dress and how to ride and how to receive the compliments of her suitors. The one thing she never learns is anything about the successful marriage she is being prepared for. So you see, dear Dr Enys, it would not be surprising if she *also* gave the impression of being two persons and with some higher justification than you. You say you don't know how to pay compliments to women or how to behave in the best manner. But at heart you must know women very well. How different in my case. I don't know men at all. I'm expected to be in love at the touch of a hand or at a prettily turned compliment. But until I marry – if my dear uncles have their way – I shall know nothing of what a man is really like.' She paused and straightened up. 'From hearsay, I know what happens when people sleep together. It does not sound excessively genteel. One can take a risk in the gavotte and come to no harm. One should be a little more careful, I fancy, before choosing a bed partner for the rest of one's days.'

There was a long silence. The confession had moved Dwight in a new way. It was a new Caroline he suddenly saw – not supremely sure of herself and contemptuous of his efforts to please, but as unsure in her own way as he was, and hiding her unsureness behind a mask of laughter and ridicule. He was suddenly no longer infatuated but deeply in love.

'And Unwin?'

'Unwin was a suitor ready made. He came with all the possible recommendations. And there was no lack of confidence within him, Dwight. He seemed to think I should be flattered at the idea of marrying a seat in Parliament. Sometimes I caught him looking at me, and then I knew that he was interested in my money first, my body second, but myself, for myself, little at all.'

'And I?'

Caroline smiled at him queerly. 'It is not very easy to say this to your face, is it? When we first met in Bodmin and quarrelled, I thought, there is a man who ... And again when you came to examine my throat. It was not that I *liked* you, it was that I felt—' She sat up. 'No I can't tell you. Let's go.'

'Tell me.'

'I don't know what I feel for you – there that's the truth. Now go away.'

She got to her feet and moved a step towards her horse, but he jumped up and barred her way. 'You must tell me, Caroline.'

She flared at him, but he caught her wrist and held it. She said: 'Well, you should *know* without being told. I wondered what it would be like to be kissed by you, whether I should like it or hate it, whether it would feed or kill my interest in you. But I didn't know and I haven't known and I shan't ever know – and now it does not matter, because I'm going away. Oh, there have been other men who've attracted and *plenty* more who will! But I shall not marry the first of them nor the second. In October—'

But she said no more. He put his hands on her elbows and pulled her against him and kissed her on the cheek and then on the mouth. After a moment her hands gripped his shoulders tight, not pulling him closer but slightly pushing him away, as a woman will whose critical mind is aware that she has got only what she asked for. They stood there so long that a chaffinch fluttered down and stayed pecking at the grass until one of the horses shuffled and frightened it off.

At last a flight of rooks cawing and settling in the trees separated them. There was a curious strained silence when they broke. Dwight was out of breath and he thought Caroline was too.

He said: 'And now no doubt you hate me.'

'No doubt I hate you.'

'And will be glad to go, cured of your curiosity.'

'You'd best,' she said, 'you'd best help me on my horse – if we're to get back.'

He moved to bend to make a step for her foot, but at the first contact of her skirt he straightened and she was in his arms again. They reeled against the horse, which shied and whinnied; a tree came up against them, and she leaned her back against it as he kissed her again, more deliberately this time.

Already the sun was higher than it should have been. This time he really helped her to mount, and then he climbed up on to his own horse, and the soft morning breeze wafted on their faces.

Their horses were ready to move off, but neither of the riders made any sign.

'When will you be back?' said Dwight.

'When I choose.'

'You'll write?'

'If you wish me to.'

He made a gesture of hopelessness. Did she want reassurance of *that*? 'If you come back . . .' he began.

'It will be the same over again? But in October there will be one change.'

'What is it?'

'I shall be twenty-one. Uncle Ray can do nothing to

prevent me from returning to this district after October the twenty-sixth.'

They moved off slowly out of the glade, and nothing was left but some hoof prints and a few broken bluebells to mark the emotion which had flared there.

Chapter Six

The fine weather did not last, and June ended wet, to be followed by a wetter July and August. The rain beat upon the crops endlessly, flattened them, and turned them black. High winds swept the country, and the sun drifted pale and lost across the sky among the intermittent storms. In the cobbled streets of Paris new and strange terrors stalked. The eruption which had cracked the surface of the continental despotisms had suddenly festered and turned in upon itself. Hopelessly menaced from the east, tottering to its fall, it was pulling down upon itself the whole structure of civilized society. In this last phase of *felo-de-se* no infamy was too bad. News of the butchery of three hundred priests was followed by stories of children playing with heads and four days' continuous slaughter of the packed prisons. Men whispered of the Princess Lamballe torn limb from limb, her head stuck on a pike, judgment pronounced by the mob and those found guilty cut obscenely into pieces on the spot among the corpses already piled; the prisons no sooner empty than filled again.

Mr Trencrom, keeping up his illicit traffic in spite of politics and the weather, reported that Mark Daniel was no longer in Cherbourg but had moved farther along the coast; they hoped to get in touch with him on the next trip. At Wheal Grace the excess of outgoings over revenue was

enough to depress the most obstinate mind; and every inch
of rain that fell added to the cost of fuel.

In August, Caroline Penvenen wrote to Dwight Enys:

Dear Dwight,

I am not a prisoner in a tower guarded by a wolf,
but in order to write to you and see it posted before
Uncle William's sultry eye falls on it is no mean
Achievement. Your last letter I snatched away from
under his very hand and in the nick of time; so when
you reply to this pray direct it care of Mistress Nancy
Aintree at the Black Dog, Abingdon, where I can
redeem it at my tenure. Never have I known a
month so long as this; its first fifteen days have
seemed like thirty; my adolescence dies hard. How is
your Ross Poldark, does his mine prosper and his
cousin-in-law continue to eye him acquisitively? How
are all your patients and especially the pretty one
with the bad knee? Is her father still suspicious of
you? I don't wonder. Can you recommend me some
genteel, not unpleasant Malady which I may take
leisure to develop between now and October the
twenty-sixth?

Oxford has many miserable French refugees
about its closes: aristocrats with powdered wigs and
holes in their stockings. They paint a picture of
streets running with gore; I wonder if they
overcolour, the more to excite our pity. Uncle
William entertains them, but when they have gone
he grunts, 'A few more heads and it would have
been the easier for us!' You see now where I come
by my Sensibility. The Penvenen family has no equal
for it.

Dear Dwight, I wonder if you truly miss me, or if I am like a recurrent fever that enters your Veins, creating a hectic flush of excitement and leaving you wasted and rabid after I am gone? I know I should leave you alone, I really do, but I cannot suppose myself strong enough for such Resolution. My first small experience of you, I must confess though it's unmaidenly, was endurable, so that it's not too much to suppose a second would be the same. Between now and October I will try to get into some flirtation here, partly so that when my birthday comes Uncle William will the more readily see me gone, and partly so that when I come down I may have some surer grounds for comparison.

This I think you are unlikely to approve at first thought; yet I know you will not really wish to deprive me of what modest experience I may be able to gain which will help to make me a Woman of discrimination.

Believe me,
Your sincere friend,
Caroline Penvenen

In early September, a small new lode was found at Wheal Grace bearing better results than the old ones. But the discovery could only postpone the evil day, not prevent it. Ross and Francis still spent two days a week in the old upper levels. Lack of air became one of the worst obstacles, for most of the old air shafts had been filled in. In other places the roof had fallen, and one had to choose whether to abandon the search in that direction or to bring out workers to dig or blast a way through.

On the fifteenth of September, Ross and Francis had

arranged to meet Zacky Martin and Jope Ishbel and to make some final investigations. They spent the morning blasting and trying to drain the old work, which was out of range of the engine. At noon Zacky went, and an hour later the cousins came up and changed out of their streaming things and walked down to Nampara for dinner. Ross found a letter waiting for him. Usually the man who brought the weekly paper carried the letters, but this had been delivered by a journeyman draper who called to see Demelza in the hope of tempting her to buy. The letter was from his friend and banker, Harris Pascoe.

Dear Captain Poldark,

I have not had the pleasure of seeing you for some months; and I should be glad to receive a call from you to sign your account with us, when it is convenient to you.

This letter, however, is of another matter, of which I have some knowledge though personal to yourself. When the Carnmore Copper Co. failed in '89 and you found events pressing you to discharge certain debts, I believe you raised a loan of £1,000 from Mr Notary Pearce at an abnormal rate of interest. This loan, I have always understood from you, was in the form of a second mortgage on your house and land, of which this Banking House holds the first mortgage.

As you know, I rarely stir from my home; but much information comes to me unsought and I have heard recently that this loan was not in fact raised upon a second mortgage but was in the form of a Note of Hand or a Promissory Note. Pray tell me if this is so, because the Bill – if it is yours – is no longer,

I am told, in Mr Pearce's hands but has found its way into the possession of Mr Cary Warleggan.

Your relationship with the Warleggans is your own concern, and I should not wish to intrude on it; but if it is what I suppose it to be, then I should not be astonished at your receiving notice at any time that the Bill must be immediately repaid. I do not know how your venture is prospering or whether you have been able to set aside any considerable sum to meet such an emergency, but as your friend I thought it my duty to tell you what I had learned.

Call in when next you are in town: we should be glad to have you dine or sup with us.

Yours etc.,
Harris Pascoe

At dinner Ross had little to say. Demelza sensed that the bad news, whatever it was, involved the Warleggans – Ross had a special face for them – but her pride would not let her ask when Francis was there. When the meal was near its end Ross said: 'I'll not be able to go down with you this afternoon. This letter calls me to Truro.'

'But you were there yesterday,' Francis objected. 'Can't this wait awhile?'

'No. I'm sorry. No.'

'You'll be back tonight?' said Demelza.

His eyes met hers over Francis's head. 'I'll try. But late. Don't wait up.'

She watched him as he left the room to change. She stayed talking with Francis; but when Ross came down, she slid out of the room and stood with him at the front door waiting for Gimlett to bring the mare.

Ross put his hand on her shoulder. 'I don't want to explain now. The letter was from Harris Pascoe – certain things I had overlooked. I'm going to see him, that's all.'

She looked up into his face. 'Bad, Ross?'

'Not good. But I shall know more tonight.'

'You'll not be in trouble today?'

'Should I be likely to be, with Harris Pascoe?'

'Not if you stay closeted with him. But there are others you might chance to meet.'

He smiled grimly. 'The weather is cold enough for November. Go in now and talk to Francis. Have you noticed how fond of our house he is become since the mine opened? He's as much here as at his own home.'

'I've noticed.'

'Go in and give him another glass of port and take one yourself.'

'I dare not before supper or I should tope all day. About this letter—'

But Demelza was interrupted by the arrival of Gimlett leading Darkie. Ross kissed her on the cheek and mounted and rode off up the valley. It seemed to his wife that the clouds were so low he was overtaken by them and half shrouded in them before he was lost to view.

When she went in, Francis had risen from the table and was sitting by the fire she had lighted an hour ago.

'No, don't get up,' she said. 'Ross bade us finish the port, but I can't take it myself, not so early; I'd do no work for the rest of the day else.' She set the decanter with his glass on a table beside him and took a seat opposite, stretching out her scarlet slippers to the warmth. 'In a minute I must go see if Jeremy is happy. He never takes his dinner so kindly from Mrs Gimlett as from me. Did you have no good fortune this morning, Francis?'

'We've chosen the most barren piece of land in the Duchy, I believe.'

'And the lowest levels?'

'A venture of faith without good reason behind it. Perhaps they'll succeed, because reason certainly has failed . . . Strange, Ross having to go in to Truro again. Can it be something to do with the Warleggans?'

She looked at him in surprise. 'I don't know. But I wondered the same. Always when there is a hint of trouble one wonders if it is the Warleggans at the root of it.'

'Or Francis,' said Francis. 'There was a time when I was at the root of it along with George.'

'Oh, I do not think so,' she said quickly. 'That time has gone anyhow.'

'That time has gone. But I don't forget it. At least I do not forget one thing.'

'I think I will go and see for Jeremy.'

'No.' He hesitated, rubbing his hand on the chair. 'No, I have long wanted to tell you this. It must come sometime . . . Years ago—'

'This is best not started, Francis.'

'Years ago – it would be August of '89 – when the copper smelting company was fighting for its existence – George came to see me one evening. It was the night Verity had left. I blamed you bitterly for her marriage – for everything. In a sudden impulse of anger I gave off information to George which enabled him to put pressure on the share-holders of the company to withdraw their support. That is the one thing I cannot get over or forgive myself . . .'

Demelza got up. 'Why d'you insist on saying this to me – now?'

'Because for long enough I have been facing up to it. I cannot go on accepting your friendship, sitting like a stray dog at your fireside, with this not completely cleared up between us. The more our friendship has become of value, the less can it be left as it is. I suspect that Ross already knows the worst – but he won't let me tell him in so many words, he heads me off, and at the last I turn coward and let the matter drop. And so it rests.'

Somewhere at the back Garrick was barking; he had been shut out and resented it. Demelza did not speak. Francis got up, put his hand over hers for a minute, and turned towards the window.

Demelza said in great distress: 'It was such a thing to do to us. Had you no other way of hurting Ross?'

'An angry impulse – and then it's too late. But I don't begin to make excuse. You also knew?'

'Yes – partly. But – but to hear it spoken outright . . .'

Francis looked sick. 'You can't rebuild a friendship by ignoring what has destroyed it. I had to tell you. I'll go now.'

'No, wait. Ross is right, isn't he?'

'Not in this.'

'Yes, in this. For if we break now, we shall injure each other the more. And the copper smelting could never have prospered, Francis, we know that. Even the Warleggans when they took it over could not make it pay. Sir John Trevaunance is selling the machinery.'

'Do you excuse a murder because the victim was dying anyhow?'

'Not excuse it, no. But I'll not condemn to order neither. Does Elizabeth know?'

'Does she know what I did? No. It doesn't concern her at all. Except that she does not understand my worst antagonism for George Warleggan.'

After a long silence she said: 'You – haven't finished your port.'

'No? ... All I've finished is our friendship – which I prized, though you may doubt it.'

'I don't doubt it, Francis, but I doubt if you have finished with it. One bad thing does not outweigh many good. 'Tis the balance that counts.'

'It did not count with me that night.'

'So ever after you regretted it. Should you wish me to make the same error?'

'Yes.'

'Well, then, I shall not.'

'Not even to please me?' said Francis.

'Not even to please you.'

'I don't wonder,' Francis said, 'that Ross loves you. For I could do so myself.'

She glanced at him quickly, soberly, then bent and put another billet of wood on the fire. 'Do you suppose he still does?'

'Ross? Of course. Why, what did you think?'

'I believe he loves Elizabeth better.'

When she stood up, neither of them spoke for some moments.

He said: 'Well, if this is the day of confidences, may I tell you something about yourself, Demelza?'

'Of course.'

'You have one failing, and that is you don't think enough of yourself.'

'Oh, I think very well of myself, Francis. You would be surprised.'

'I'd be surprised at nothing you think or do except that. You came here as a miner's daughter, married into this ancient derelict family, took its standards as your own. So you mistake your own value, your own vitality, even your value to Ross. There are two qualities in blood, Demelza. There's the quality of family and the quality of freshness. Ross was a wise man when he chose you. If he's as sensible as I think he is, he'll realize it. If you're as sensible as you ought to be, you'll make him.'

Demelza's eyes were warm. 'You're very kind.'

'*Kind* . . . You see. There you go.'

'Well, are you not? I think so. But Francis, 'tisn't so easy as you think. I have to compare against your wife, who's so lovely – an' has breeding as well. And not only that. She was Ross's first love. How do you compete with perfection?'

'I don't believe Ross is so silly. I think . . .' He stopped. 'I believe that a greater regard for yourself, a greater personal independence on your part . . . Now I sound disloyal to Ross – but it's true. If you look on his feeling for Elizabeth as something unreal, and by exposing to it your own warm blood and your own good sense . . . How can she stand against those?'

'But Elizabeth is – far from lacking in warm blood herself.'

Francis again did not reply for a minute or two. 'It's not my wish to speak against Elizabeth now; but whatever she lacks or has, she lacks perfection. Every human being does. Indeed, knowing you even so little – and noticing the effect you have on other men – I should have thought you quite capable of holding Ross at your side when you want to, if you're so minded.'

She glinted a half smile at him. 'I may not say you're kind, so I'll say thank you.'

'I can't answer for another man – and yet I'm pretty sure ... Get rid of the notion that someone has done you a favour by taking you into our family.'

She stood quite still, thoughtful, young, made a wry mouth. 'I will think over it all, Francis. I believe it will make company for me for the rest of the afternoon.'

'Think over the first part too.'

'No. Not that.'

'Yes, that.' He bent and kissed her cheek. 'For we can none of us separate ourselves from the consequences of our behaviour. I have been trying to for long enough.'

It was beginning to rain again as Francis walked back to the mine. The reaction from clearing his unquiet mind to Demelza had left him more at peace with himself than for a long time. He had spoken on impulse, but the impulse had been part of a long-standing desire to tell her, to put himself straight not only with her but with his own conscience. Her reception of the news, its natural healthiness, had made him feel better about it all. Her attitude and Ross's, he felt, excused him nothing, but it made possible a continuance of their friendship with a new honesty on his side.

He went into the changing-shed of the mine and picked up a few of his belongings. He had come this far almost without thinking. His horse was in the Nampara stables, he had had no intention of going down the mine again. But the shed was empty; and when he got inside, the thought came to him that the last thing he wanted was to go home.

His own house depressed him; Elizabeth depressed him. He knew that this happier mood would go quick enough;

for the moment he could not bear to part with it. He began to slip on the old drill trousers and the woollen coat.

There were few people about in the rain. In the engine house one of the Curnow brothers was tending the great pump as it sucked and slithered. He touched his cap to Francis as he came in, and moved round to meet him, ducking under the great beam as it swung easily down.

'Going 'low by yourself, sur? Thur's Ned Bottrell outside could go along of ee.'

'No, I'm all right. I shall do no more blasting but shall pick over the stuff that has come down.'

A minute later Francis was climbing down the ladder of the main shaft. This shaft had originally been the lode from which the mine had begun; so it did not go straight down but at a sharp inclination as the lode had run and as it had been mined. At the third platform and the two-hundred-and-fortieth rung he stepped off into the thirty-fathom level. All this part of the mine was now deserted. The rest of the workers were below.

On his way to the piece of ground they had been blasting this morning, he squeezed through narrow clefts where there was barely room for his pick, scrambled across heaps of rubble with echoing caverns as high as cathedral transepts, skirted great pits falling away into the depths of the earth, climbed up and up where the old miners had followed a lode on its underlie; finally he reached the underground shaft or little wind as it was called – with the ruins of the old windlass still beside it – and slithered down the shaft, as if down the chimney of a house, to the big narrow slit of a gunnies where they had been this morning.

Francis saw that the water at the bottom had gone down a foot since they left, the result of their blasting, but it was evidently not yet finding its way to the sump of the mine.

The air was close and bad here, and his only light, from the hempen candle in his hat, flickered smokily over the scene. He worked for half an hour cleaning the rocks from the mouth of the tunnel, but no more water seemed to be entering it. Not only the air but the water was warm, and after a while he swung himself up into another excavation about six feet above water level. He found that, instead of being shallow as it appeared from below, it turned sharply and increased in height so that he was able to stand upright.

Interested, he followed it for about a hundred feet, scraping here and there at the slimy walls, moving on until he came to a place where the old men had found the lode again and had left an arch of it to support their tunnel. Here they had worked downwards, in what was known as a winze, and here also it seemed this morning's gunpowder had had some effects, for the rocks were dripping and he could hardly keep his feet as he picked his way round the edge to another tunnel opposite.

This tunnel meandered on for a matter of a hundred yards; but then the air began to get fouler, and he turned back. As he did so, a flicker of his candle found some answering glimmer in the rock. He bent and rubbed with his finger. Here was the coppery green of metal-bearing ground.

The old men had missed it or had passed on. It might well be that their reasons were adequate. There had been other such places. One could not be sure of anything till one had picked away a few pieces, weighed them in the hand, examined in a better light the quality of the ore.

He needed his pick, which he had left in the big gunnies.

A quarter of an hour's work here ... If it looked like ore-bearing rock of any promise, he would carry a half-dozen specimen lumps up to grass.

Luck if after all this time ... While Ross was away and he down here alone! Silly to speculate, to imagine; it had happened before, the expectation and the disappointment.

He stumbled back as far as the winze and stopped to gain a breath or two of better air and to wipe the sweat off his face. Very hot. If this could be, it would give him not only a fresh entitlement to Ross's friendship but to his own self-respect.

He moved cautiously round the edge of the winze; and as he did so, his boots suddenly slipped on the slimy surface. He twisted sharply to save himself, slithered down the slope, bumping his head and shoulders, trying to clutch, to distribute weight. Then in horror he fell, into water, plunging into it, coughing, choking, smothering in foul water; to breathe, to suffocate; he came up in pitch-darkness, treading water, floundering in search of some rock to save him.

He'd never been a swimmer; his best a dozen strokes. His clothes kept him up, spreading out like a tent; then the water seeped in; they began to clog, to drag. His flailing hands found the wall and he clutched at it.

Although he'd fallen clear, he'd thought to find the wall so sloping that he could crawl out. Not so. He kicked with his toes to get footholds that instantly slipped, clawed with fingernails, barked his knees, hit his face against the rock. He'd slid down the slope into another underground shaft. The fall had been short, but he'd no true idea how far the water was from the top of the shaft.

Cough foul water out. Heavy boots dragging down, drowning in futile darkness, deep in the earth away from the comfort and the voices of men. His fingers found a hold ... Slowly, with infinite effort, he pulled his body a few inches out of the water.

While his fingers held, he could think: might be a ladder still in the wall strong enough to bear him. For that, when he'd recovered, he must gather the courage to flounder round the shaft. It was bigger than the other one but could still only be small; enough for a ladder and a bucket they usually said.

What might have been triumph had suddenly become disaster. Two years ago in Bodmin he had put a pistol against his head and pulled the trigger. It had not gone off because the powder was damp. Then he had wanted to die. Death now would be the crowning irony.

He had been trying to kick his boots off; his fingers aching, change hands; one boot off. Lighter, lighter; this old woollen coat. He had stopped coughing; lungs free at least. To shout? As well shout in your coffin with the sexton planting the flowers.

A surprise for you, Ross. Feel this piece. Not just killas, is it? And here's some crushed under the hammer. I thought I'd do it while you were away. At least it's a justification at last of your faith in me. Henshawe can't believe his eyes ...

The other boot off. Struggle out of the coat. Hot down here. Like a rat in a bucket. He'd watched one once, but had had to go away before it died. Persistent things, clinging to life. More persistent than he.

This was the moment to try to swim round. Why had he never been confident in the water? As much as he could do to force himself to let go.

Round he went, kicking out ineffectually with his legs but keeping just afloat. Quite big, probably seven feet across; perhaps not a shaft but just a plot, used when ore was being mined quicker than it could be got to the surface.

No ladder, and no certainty he could find the fingerhold again. Panic gripped; a great shout that went echoing round and round in the confined space. Noise was comforting, as light would have been comforting.

He missed the fingerhold but instead found a nail. There had been a ladder, but it was gone. Try to find a foothold in some niche below; none . . . Nor anything to reach above. A rusty six-inch nail was a better fingerhold than the one lost. Could hold on quite a long time. And it might *be* a long time.

Trying to keep the fear in hand, to fight away the loneliness and the darkness, begin to work it out. Down about four. The mine worked three cores, the next changing at ten. If it was five now, that might mean nearly *five* more hours before anyone saw his clothes in the changing-shed or remarked on them or began to ask. Ross had gone to Truro, could not be back till late. Demelza – what reason would she have? His horse in the Nampara stables. Any time she might notice this herself or later Gimlett would say . . . But hours perhaps before they did anything.

His own home. Elizabeth anxious? Not until seven.

Any reckoning in hours. And even if there was an alarm, the search would take time. His mind travelled back along the twisting dark tunnels to the main shaft – all the way he had come, all the great mass of rock that lay between him and the daylight and the air. The atmosphere in this pit was choking and foul. Hours of patience, hours of strain lay ahead. His fingers would give way, he would *drown* long before help came.

Fear his greatest enemy. Darkness the other traitor. Light had left the world. Nothing shone, no shine, no sleek water, no metal or stone. He'd still little idea how far below the rim of the pit he was; but the grim thought came that if they had not blasted this morning and allowed some of the water to drain, this pit might have been full and left him no harder task than clawing a way back up the greasy winze.

He changed hands for the twentieth time and as he did so the nail moved. Fear grip your throat, begin to shout, at the top of your voice, over and over again. Help, help, help, I am lost in the very deeps of the earth. Not eight feet underground but two hundred; blind already but not deaf, shuddering in the warm water, fingers burning last grip loosening; one nail, one rusty nail.

He tried to make himself let go, to splash around again in the darkness; he might have missed something last time, some better handhold; but he no longer had the courage to try; he might never find this place again.

Time passed. Try to count. Sixty minutes make one hour. He reckoned three hours had passed. Must be after eight now. Someone must come soon. They would of course come straight to the place where they had been blasting this morning. A drip of water somewhere, and this his ears again and again magnified into rescuing footsteps. To keep his sanity he counted up to two hundred and then shouted and began again. But he was getting lightheaded. And the strain on his arms. Cramp seized him often, his legs were leaden, already swollen and dead. Sometimes he forgot numbers and talked with people who came close to him in the water. His father, gouty and eruptive and purple. 'Francis, Francis. Where are you, boy?' Aunt Agatha, not as she now was but younger and severe, dandling him on her knee. He was running across the sands of Hendrawna with Ross after him, their feet glinting in the sun.

He began to count again; and then suddenly heard a crash of splintering wood and looked up and saw Ross kneeling at the edge of the shaft reaching down a hand to help him out. Ross said sourly: 'My God, why can't you learn to swim!' and Francis reached up a despairing hand to grasp the help. Their fingers seemed to touch, and then a foul swirl of liquid closed over Francis's mouth and nose and he kicked and struggled to get to the surface again: he had lost grip of the nail, had nearly lost life in his dream of salvation, only death had wakened him; only death; in time the automatic responses of the body. So it would be every time, every time until the last.

Try to reassure yourself. This time tomorrow ... In a few weeks you will be able to laugh about this experience. Or be dead ... This time tomorrow between comfortable sheets, recovering. Or a swollen corpse covered with a sheet in the great hall of Trenwith waiting an early burial.

His breath was going. That was the worst. If he shouted now, he had to suck at the air for half a minute afterward to recover. By now it was well after ten. Somebody must come soon. He *could* not disappear without trace and cause no comment! Curnow had seen him come down. They would grow anxious. They would think. What were their brains *for*! Henshawe was often at the mine between five and six. Ofter he joined Ross and Francis to see how the work was going. *Not* today. Not of course today.

Francis let out a higher-pitched shout, much nearer a

scream. He stopped, gasping at the air. The nail turned in his painful clutch. Any further movement and it would come out.

'Help, help!' he shouted. 'Help, help!' a dozen times, and a dozen times more. It went on and on and on, until the volume decreased and the breath in was as noisy as the breath out. Tears were running down his cheeks.

There's *reason* for me to live now! Oh, *God*, I don't want to die . . .

At about this time Elizabeth closed the book in which she had been teaching Geoffrey Charles to read.

'It's time for your supper, my darling. Papa will be home soon, and you know he likes you to be in bed by seven.'

'Just this bit, Mummy.'

'No. You've had more than your share today.'

'Can I go out and play until Papa comes?'

'No, darling. You can play until your supper's ready. Don't be far away when I call you . . . And put on your cap!'

Geoffrey Charles galloped from the room, and Elizabeth looked up at the clock. It was nearly half past six.

Chapter Seven

Ross was back just before eight. He found Demelza upstairs repairing for the fifth time the curtains over the north windows of their bedroom. She hadn't heard him come.

'Why, Ross! You're earlier than I expected. Have you supped?'

'Sufficiently. What are you doing?'

'A little tear that Jeremy made this morning. He dearly likes something to cling to for support.'

'Soon you'll have made new curtains with your stitches.'

'Not quite so bad. What was in your letter?'

He sat in a chair and began to pull at his boots; then as she came over, he let her pull them off instead. It was a relic of their old days which for some reason she liked to preserve. While she was doing it, he told her what the letter said.

'And it was true, about the mortgage, I mean?'

He nodded. 'True enough. When I borrowed the money, my first concern was to get it; I didn't greatly care how. It was Pearce when I went to him who first spoke of a second mortgage. The next day he produced the money and I signed the paper for it . . . I accepted this as a form of mortgage, though in fact it was a promissory note. I suppose I knew, but I paid no heed to it at the time. Nor should I have needed to if Pearce had kept possession of it, as any friend and honest man would. I went to visit him. D'you think me a bully, Demelza?'

'Were you rough with Mr Pearce?'

'I didn't put a finger on him, but I suppose I was rough in manner; I thumped his table and broke the lid of his snuffbox. He quivered like a jelly, all fat and no backbone; but the damage is done. The bill has been passed on as Pascoe said, and Cary Warleggan now possesses it. So we have to face that.'

'You didn't go to see *him*?'

'I called at his house, but he was away. I think it was the truth, for the blinds were down.'

'And what now, Ross?'

'The Warleggans can do nothing until November. Then they can give me a month to redeem the note. In December I must find fourteen hundred pounds or default.'

She put his boots beside the chair but remained kneeling, her elbows on his knees, looking not at him but into space.

'Can we borrow no money elsewhere?'

'I don't know.'

'What shall you do?'

'There are seven weeks before the notice can be given. I have Pascoe to thank for that. And four more after that before it takes effect.'

She did not much like the look on his face, and she wriggled her knees round and got up.

She said: 'Are you sure Cary will do this, will demand repayment?'

'Would you not if you felt as they do for me?'

'Have I ever seen Cary?'

'At that party. A man of fifty-odd with small eyes and an uncomfortable way of using them. George, though I detest him, has certain principles – at least I think so. Cary has none. He's the moneylender of the family, the scavenger. George is accepted in most circles of society. Soon he will be in all. That will impose some standards on him. Nicholas, his father, of course, is reputable enough. Uncle Cary is the best hated of them all.'

She shivered. 'I wish I could earn money, Ross. I wish I could help you in some way. All I do is – is mend your curtains and bear your child and see after the farm and cook your meals and—'

'I should have thought that one person's work.'

'But there's no *money* in it! Not even a gold piece. One thousand four hundred pounds! I'd steal it if I could, turn highwayman or bank thief! Harris Pascoe would never miss it. Why does he not *lend* it you?'

Ross looked at her gravely, wryly. 'This is a new phase. Always before you've been pressing me to keep within the law—'

He stopped as there was a knock on the door. It was Gimlett to say that Tabb was below and wanted to know if Mr Francis was still here.

'Here? Of course not.' Ross looked at Demelza. 'What time did he leave?'

'About an hour after you. He walked up to the mine. At least—'

'His horse is still here, sur,' said Gimlett. 'I give him his feed, but didn't think to tell mistress as I reckoned she'd know about it.'

Ross pushed past him and went downstairs. Tabb was standing in the hall. Tabb explained that Mrs Poldark had been getting anxious, so she'd sent him over just to make sure Mr Poldark was come to no harm. Usually, now the nights was drawing in, the squire belonged to be home by seven. Ross went round to the stables. Francis's horse was there right enough and looked up expectantly at the sound of footsteps.

Demelza had followed. Ross said: 'Did he not say anything when he left? Perhaps he's walked over to Mingoose House.' To Tabb he said: 'Ride to Mingoose House, will you. In the meantime I'll go to the mine and see how long he stayed there and in what direction he left.'

A new moon was out and the misty rain had cleared. Demelza walked with Ross, hopping now and then to keep up, though her own stride was long. The engine house was lit and there were lights in two of the sheds.

Ross went into the changing-shed, where a lantern burned low. On a peg were Francis's ordinary clothes.

Outside, Demelza was thoughtful, waiting.

'I think he may be still here.'

'Here? But, Ross . . .'

They stared at each other for a moment; neither spoke.

Below ground eight hours was the usual core, but tending the engine twelve. This change was made at eight, and the elder Curnow was now in charge. His brother, he said, had told him nothing when he went off. As they were asking, Captain Henshawe came in and Ross explained the situation to him.

'Well, sur, he may be down there still, forgetful of the time; but I should not suppose so. Hold hard a minute, and I'll fetch a couple of men to go down with us.'

Demelza stood in the engine house. The curious slow, regular sucking motion of the great engine was like an animal gasping, a giant sea mammal newly landed, breathing out its life on the wet sand. A strange conviction of fatality had come on her. She had no reason for knowing, yet felt as if she knew.

Other men had come in now, and they watched Ross and Henshawe and Jack Carter and young Joe Nanfan climb into the bucket and lurch bumping out of sight. After they had gone, those that were left clustered in a self-conscious group; and she knew they would have been more at home if she had not been there. She, the miner's daughter become squire's wife, had more than the disadvantage of womanhood.

But she forced herself to go towards them and ask if none had seen Mr Francis this afternoon and if someone would go and knock up Daniel Curnow and find out what he knew.

Then came a long wait. Gimlett had stolen up from the house and stood beside her. 'The wind's cold, ma'am, shall I get ee a coat?' 'No ... thank you.' It was not the cold of the night that she felt but an inner cold that no coat would cure. Tabb came galloping back. They'd not seen Mr Francis at Mingoose. 'You'd best go tell Mistress Poldark,' said Demelza. 'Very good, ma'am.' 'No, wait. Wait a little while.'

Looking back, Demelza could see the lights in Nampara, the one in their bedroom that she had left. Beyond it and to the right the sea, with a dagger of moonlight in the black heart of the water. 'We can none of us separate ourselves from the consequences of our own behaviour,' Francis had said. 'I have been trying to for long enough.'

One of the men returned from Dan Curnow's cottage. Curnow had seen Mr Francis go down about four but had not seen him come up. He had not thought of mentioning it to his brother. Peter Curnow spat in disgust.

A few minutes later a miner came running up the ladder. It was Ellery, who was working on the sixty-fathom level. Some of them had been told and were helping with the search. Francis had not been found but his pick had, standing with the handle out of the water near where they had been blasting this morning.

Demelza looked at Tabb. 'I think you had best go fetch your mistress.'

It was Ross, carrying a lantern, who first swung himself up into the tunnel which Francis had followed. Like Francis he was surprised to see that the tunnel went on, and he beckoned Henshawe to follow him.

They were tired of shouting: their voices only beat back against them from the walls of rock or were thrown away in the echoing darkness. They reached the winze and tried to cross it, but Ross's foot slipped on the slimy rock and Henshawe had to catch his arm.

'Thanks. It's a place for—' Ross stopped and crouched on his heels and turned the light of the horn lantern down the winze. Just within sight was water, and floating on the water was a miner's hat. And there was something else there besides the hat.

'Have you your rope?'

'Yes . . .'

'Put it round my waist.'

He went down and found the body floating. Francis had been dead about an hour. In one of his hands, clutched so that they could barely unfasten it, was a rusty nail.

BOOK TWO

Chapter One

On a late afternoon in mid-November 1792 a private coach was making its way at a fair pace along the main highway from Truro to the far west. A fine misty rain was falling, as always in that terrible year, and the woods which ran intermittently beside the road were already dark and vaporous. The road was in bad condition, potholed and rutted deep in mud; but the driver, who had not been this way before, kept his whip constantly flicking across his horses because full darkness was not far away and he did not like the look of the country they were passing through. His mistress had told him that they were nearly home, but women were unreliable in their estimates, as today's journey had proved; and in this wild county they would be a fat and easy prize for any highwayman who happened to be lurking near.

They had just emerged from one lowering copse whose branches nearly met overhead when his courage bumped into his boots at the sight of a man standing by a dismounted horse at the roadside. Coming across those wild and boggy moors this morning he had cursed himself for ever having accepted employment under a strong-headed, wrong-headed slip of a woman, and this was the outcome. He rose in his seat and lashed at the horses; but as they lurched forward, the coach splashed into a deep hole and dipped wildly and almost toppled him into the road. By the time they had gained a proper speed again they were past the horseman, who was only sufficiently interested in them to raise his head.

They were past him by a few dozen yards when a loud rapping caused the coachman to lift the hatch, and he heard his mistress telling him to stop.

'It's right enough, ma'am. No 'arm or damage done. The 'orses—'

'Stop, I tell you. That gentleman. I want to speak to him.' Sulkily the driver brought the coach to a stop. Its back wheels cut and slithered in the mud; and the solitary rider, who had been attending to his own horse, again lifted his head. He was now too far behind to hear any of the conversation, but presently the coachman got down and came splashing gingerly back to him.

'Captain Poldark, sir?'

'Yes?'

'Mistress Penvenen, sir. Would like a word with ee.'

In the coach were two women, one a maid. Ross took off his hat and Caroline extended her green-gloved hand.

'You're late to be on this road, Captain Poldark. My coachman thought you were a highwayman.'

'If I were, I should choose a more opulent highway. One might wait here six nights in seven and not see a private carriage.'

'Oh, sir, I'm very poor,' said Caroline. 'But seriously, I thought you might be in trouble.'

'Thank you, it's nothing. My mare has cast a shoe.'

'Well, that can be a trifle more than nothing. What shall you do, walk home? It's a fatiguing long way.'

'I can get her shod in Chasewater. You're just returning to Cornwall, Miss Penvenen?'

'As you see. Too early to be Santa and too late to be

Guy. Why don't you share the coach to Killewarren and borrow one of my uncle's horses? We can have yours shod and send her over in the morning.'

Ross hesitated. He was tired and wet and depressed, and the suggestion was not a bad one. But he was a bit chary of this forward young woman.

'Thank you. Perhaps if I might come as far as you go on the Chasewater road . . .'

'We turn off soon. Baker, will you see that Captain Poldark's mare is securely tied to the coach. And proceed slowly, please; you need have no fear of highwaymen now that we have captured one of our own.'

That this was just raillery the maid, Eleanor, seemed slightly to doubt, for when the coach began to move again she stared open-mouthed at the big man opposite, bent uncomfortably on his occasional seat, with his muddied boots and his pale, lidded eyes and the scarred side of his face towards her.

Caroline, perhaps herself a little surprised at the size of him in a confined space and not as much at ease as she wanted to be, changed her tone.

'I was greatly sorry to hear of your cousin's death. Uncle Ray is not prolific with his letters, but he wrote about that. It was a very tragical occurrence. It seems no time at all since we all met at the Trevaunance table.'

'It is no time at all. We miss him very much.'

'I hope it has not brought your mining venture to a stop. I – understand you and he were partners.'

'It goes on. We've been able to continue it.'

'Profitably?'

Ross met her candid gaze. 'Not profitably.'

'As yet, I suppose you would add. Uncle William was saying that if this war spreads it will help the price of metals. Is Francis's widow intending to live on in that big house alone?'

'Eventually, I think, her mother and father will live with her. But she is not alone. There is her son and her aunt and two servants . . .'

'And how is Dr Enys?'

Well, at least she was not one to beat about the bush. 'As diligent as ever.'

'Only diligent?'

'It was not meant as a derogatory term.'

'Of course I should have known that,' said Caroline. 'The last time we met it was to form a common front on his behalf.'

'I do not think we shall need to be so ready in his defence now. Everyone then was accusing him of killing off old Ellery. Now they're loud in wonderment because he has cured a village girl of her lameness.'

Caroline lifted her face quickly. 'Rosina Hoblyn?'

'Oh, you know her?'

'By name. Dwight mentioned her. She is *cured?*'

'Cured. She walks as straight as you or I, and the villagers think he is a miracle worker just for a change.'

'How very diverting! And how did he come to perform it?'

'He has an explanation, but no one listens to it. Last Saturday he had fourteen lame people waiting outside his house.'

Caroline smiled and pushed away a strand of her hair. The roof lantern, which had been lighted when Ross got in, swayed with the lurches of the coach, and her expression seemed to change among the changing shadows.

After they had turned off the main road, he said: 'What time is your uncle expecting you?'

'He's not expecting me.'

'Oh . . . A sudden decision, I suppose—'

'Not a sudden decision on my part, Captain Poldark. One carefully prepared for. This coach, the coachman engaged, my luggage packed. But Uncle Ray has not invited me; and since we have come down probably faster than the post, I don't suspect he will have had any letter from Uncle William to warn him.' Seeing Ross's expression, she laughed. 'It's a way people have when they first become independent. You'll remember we discussed it at the Trevaunance party.'

So, thought Ross, she means to have Dwight if she can. Why did I get into this coach and accept a favour of her? To the devil with all women. And instantly, unbidden, his mind flashed away to that other woman, Elizabeth, frail in her grief and her black clothes, still out of his reach yet dangerously closer to him; his first love, and loving him – so she had said – depending on him now in all things; the contacts increased with the impediments half gone; she now half shareholder in the mine on Geoffrey Charles's, her son's, behalf; he the only near male relative, head of the Poldarks now and executor with Elizabeth of his cousin's will.

Francis's death had left an unexpectedly big gap in the life of the countryside. Duties and responsibilities had been expected of him which now devolved on Ross. Mr Odgers, the curate of Sawle-with-Grambler, came to Ross for everything, even seemed to expect Ross to share the family pew and the weekly victualling of the Odgers family. And another magistrate would have to be found. There had been a Poldark to do the job since the days of William and Mary. Could a man be invited to sit on the bench who before now had expressed his contempt of it? It was all very difficult.

In the coach silence had fallen. Today Ross felt he had touched rock bottom in his fortunes and in his spirits. Yesterday he had received a formal notice from Cary Warleggan that the accommodations of the bill were to be withdrawn in four weeks' time, and today he had been making a last effort to find the money. Credit was tight everywhere, but that was not the main difficulty. The greatest obstacle was Wheal Grace. Everyone who knew anything knew that she was failing. You might loan a thousand pounds to a needy squire and take the risk for the sake of the interest. But no one would lend money to a man whose mine was on the point of foundering. If you did, you visualised your capital going down the common drain. That, no doubt, was one of the reasons Nathaniel Pearce had unloaded the bill, glad to be rid of it when its chances of redemption were small.

Ross would not altogether have blamed him had the thing gone to anyone but the Warleggans. But of course no one but the Warleggans would possibly have taken it. They didn't want the money, they wanted the man.

A week or so after Francis's death a small bunch of good ore had been found in the tunnel he had been exploring at the time, but that had been almost the extent of new discovery since September. Mark Daniel perversely had chosen this time to disappear into the maelstrom of France, and no one so far had traced him. In parts of England the blackened corn still lay in the fields. Miraculously preserved by the sloth of their enemies, the French had found fresh heart and fresh armies and last week had captured Brussels. The shadow of famine and of war lay on all men's minds.

The coach at last turned in at the gates of Killewarren, and the coachman steered a cautious way up the shrubby drive towards a welcome light above the front door. He had to ring three times before it was opened by a servant girl who said: 'Why, Mistress Caroline, good life, an' we was cleanin' your room only this morning. Why, ma'am, do ee come in. Is the master expecting you?'

Ross followed Caroline into the hall: it was a very ordinary house for so warm a man, shabbily genteel but no more; three candles in glass globes thinly lit the black polished oak cupboards, the marble busts at the foot of the narrow stairs. 'With your consent I'll not intrude on your uncle this afternoon. I know you'll be tired from your journey, and his pleasure at seeing you again . . .'

Caroline smiled at him as she unfastened the strings of her hat.

'Will not be so great as you predict,' she said quietly. 'So it would not be an unkind act if you came up while your saddle's changed. Do not fear you'll be detained overlong, for a glass of wine is all you'll get from him, if that. While I am here, he improves; but I've been gone some months and I expect he will have slipped back into the old ways.'

Demelza sent for Dwight about seven and, being free, he came straight over and examined Jeremy.

'It is the usual thing: a sore throat and a touch of fever. He is prone to this overheating.'

'Too prone,' said Demelza, allowing Jeremy his rather tetchy freedom. 'Every time it happens, I think of Julia and get in a fever myself. Julia never was like this; at least – not till the last time. . . .'

'It's a way some children have and some have not. But I'd like you to call me always, just in case. Ross is out?'

'. . . He went to Truro – on business – and then was to have gone on to Redruth to see Trevithick. Something is not quite right with the engine, though I think 'twould be all the same now if no one bothered.' Demelza swooped quickly to catch Jeremy as he lurched drunkenly across towards her. She looked up sidelong, experimentally, at Dwight, a curl falling across her brow as she did so. 'Do you think I coddle him, Dwight?'

Dwight smiled. 'Yes. But it's natural – and right. In three or four years it will be different—'

'I don't want to be like Elizabeth and Geoffrey Charles.'

'Don't worry on that score. Look at him already – twice the child he was a few months ago—' Dwight stopped. 'Is that Ross now?'

'I think so. He's long overdue.' Demelza went to the window and peered out. 'Yes. But on a strange horse. I hope there's been no mishap.'

For the moment she could not leave Jeremy; and when at last she got him into bed and went down, Ross was already in the parlour and insisting that Dwight should stay to supper. Dwight made several excuses, all of which were ignored; so smilingly he gave it up, and Mrs Gimlett laid a third place.

Ross said: 'We need a visitor, Dwight. We've been pretty much down these last days, and it's as much your duty to see after our moral welfare as our physical. If there's anyone with broken bones tonight, they'll trace you here quick enough; so set your conscience at rest.'

'My conscience is all right. But I'm sorry to hear of your condition.'

'I'll tell you more later. I have been trying to raise money all day, and it's a subject that can only decently be spoken of on a full belly.'

'I hope you've not sold Darkie,' Demelza said, 'for that would spoil my supper before it began.'

'No ... She cast a shoe near Stickler's Wood, and I was offered a lift in a private coach to Killewarren and so came home on a loaned horse.'

There was a sudden silence. Demelza raised her eyebrows. 'Killewarren? It was Mr Penvenen's private coach?'

'Mr Penvenen doesn't own a private coach,' said Dwight.

'It was Caroline Penvenen,' said Ross. 'She'd driven down from London – or Oxford, is it? Her uncle wasn't expecting her. Were you, Dwight?'

'Yes ...'

To fill the succeeding pause Demelza said: 'I expect she wanted to surprise her uncle. When was she last here, was it May or June? It must be strange to have two homes.' When neither man spoke, she leaned forward and snuffed one of the candles. 'Will they send Darkie over tomorrow, Ross?'

Ross said: 'There's no need to discuss it if you choose not, Dwight. But we're old friends, and sometimes it's good to have things out. She asked me how you were and said she hoped to see you before long.'

'How did her uncle receive her?'

'Not graciously. I think she was glad of me as a foil. But she's hard to withstand when she lays herself out to please – as perhaps you know – and he looked to be coming round when I left.'

Dwight's long, slight hands fumbled with his doily napkin. 'You're not merely old friends but my oldest and best. If good would come of discussing this – this between myself and Caroline – I'd gladly discuss it. But I see none ... Perhaps I owe you some explanation, and in that case—'

'You owe us nothing,' said Ross. 'But I'd be sorry to see a situation grow half-realized. You know how it is sometimes.'

'You mean, I know how it was last time. The dangers are different here, though, aren't they? Well, I confess I'm in love with Caroline, and we've written; and now she's here again, and for better or for worse, we shall be seeing each other soon. I have no money and she has a great deal, so the attachment ... Do you dislike her very much?'

This was said to Demelza, and she was taken aback by it. 'No, Dwight. I don't know her except to exchange a few words, and you can't not like a person you don't know. I am not the best one to judge.'

'Nor I,' said Ross. 'But I believe she's altered my opinion of her today – and I'm at a loss to say why. Certainly not for the favour of a lift ...'

'There's a hardness to her,' said Dwight slowly. 'I'd be a fool to deny it. It's like a – a brittle shiny armour, and its use has been the same. There is so much else behind it ... In any case these things do not go by measure. The alchemy's too subtle to be weighed up.'

'Yes,' said Ross, thinking suddenly of Elizabeth, and, as if there were telepathy between them, Demelza looked at him and knew what he was thinking.

Dwight said: 'The attachment's bad, no doubt; but I can't shake or break myself of it. Perhaps she will be wiser.

It's a discreditable situation which could come only to a weak man; a strong one would break the dilemma somehow.'

'The longer I live,' Ross said, pulling his brows together painfully, 'the more I distrust these distinctions between strong men and weak. Events do what they like with us, and such – such temporary freedom as we have only fosters an illusion. Look at Francis. Was there ever a sorrier or more useless end or one less deserved or dictated by himself, or more unfitted to the minimum decencies and dignity of a human being? To drown like a dog in a well, and for nothing – to miss help by the space of an hour – to go out from this room and walk over to the mine and within a short while to slip on a greasy floor and be dead, and for *nothing.*' Ross pushed back his chair in sudden vehemence. 'It is what I have always resented most in life: the wantonness, the useless waste, the sudden ends that make fools of us, that make nonsense of all our striving and contriving . . . You've been with me in most of the worst of it, Dwight: Julia's death and much else. If you see a difference in result between any strength or weakness that's been shown, I confess you're cleverer than I am.'

Dwight did not speak, but after a minute Demelza said: 'Oh, yes, that's true, Ross. But is it all the truth? I feel that there are some things good which have come to us for our own striving. And though, for the whole, luck has been against us, sometimes it has moved for us and may yet do again. Wheal Grace is failing, but Wheal Leisure has prospered – and, if there was Julia, there is also Jeremy – and there was your acquittal from the trial; and – and much else besides.' She stared into the candle flame for a moment with a curiously blind stare, then blinked and was herself again. 'It may be that if on balance we have been unlucky, Dwight will not be so. There may *be* some happy way for him and Caroline, and a little patience will find it.'

In spite of a matter-of-fact tone, she spoke, Dwight thought, with a curious sense of fatality, as if she knew things had gone wrong for herself and could not now be righted. It was the first time he realized what Francis's death had meant to her, to them both, in terms of their own relationship.

Chapter Two

November is a bad month for secret assignments out of doors; but Caroline had hunted the country too often to be at a loss, and she sent a note to Dwight to meet her at the old mine at the edge of the wood near Bargus. When Dwight got there, his pulse quickened at the sight of a horse already tethered to a tree. He slid off his own horse, looped the reins over a stump, and went quickly into the old stone house. Caroline was crouching beside the open shaft; and as he entered, she threw a stone down and listened to its echoing fall.

She straightened up quite casually. 'No wonder there are so many illegitimate babies in Cornwall, it's so easy to be rid of them. I suspect that these old shafts are kept open for the purpose, Dwight.'

It was very shadowy in here and he could not see her expression, but he came over to her determined not to be put out of countenance, determined this time to play her at her own game.

'Not only babies but women, who spoil one's sleep, who interrupt one's work, who send unprincipled letters, who flirt and have no heart. It's a good and easy way of disposal, and who should be the wiser? Does anyone know where you've come?'

She stood balanced on the edge of the shaft as if challenging him.

'No one knows, Dwight; but I don't tremble with fear. Were my letters unprincipled? Did they spoil your sleep? Were they not a source of pleasure also? Be honest. Confess to me.'

Dwight put his hand on her elbow, drew her away from the edge, turned her towards him. They looked at each other, unfamiliars but friends. She lifted one eyebrow slightly and smiled. He bent forward and kissed her. Then they stood for a while in each other's arms while a gleam of sunshine fell through the ruined doorway and the only sound was the movement of their horses outside. It was a reunion from which obvious passion was absent.

'Your letters were pleasure and pain in equal halves, as no doubt they were meant to be. Do you like to torment those who love you?'

She looked at him closely, searchingly, renewing her own acquaintance. 'No . . . Perhaps I like to torment myself. I don't know. I can't say. All I know is that I'm back, that my uncles are furious, that I'm my own mistress, that I've made an appointment with you, and that you have come. Just now it's uncomplicated – clear in my mind. Don't expect too much of me, Dwight. Don't press me too hard.'

'I love you,' he said. 'That's uncomplicated too. Whether for you this is just a sample of life to be taken and then conveniently forgotten—'

'No, it is not; and you know it is not. And that was only in a half of my letters or a third, and the nice parts you've wilfully overlooked. Anyway, I'm not used to writing love letters any more than I am used to being made love to. It is—'

'I hope your experiments in Oxfordshire were satisfactory.'

'Yes, *yes*. Delectable. Quite enchanting. So much so that

116

I've hurried down here as soon as the lawyers agreed to release my money . . .'

They talked on, aware of their temporary isolation and making the most of it, yet both knowing that secret meetings could not be secret for long. Convinced now of all that he needed to be convinced of, Dwight would have liked to face up to their difficulties at this very first encounter; but he sensed that Caroline was still groping her way towards an understanding of her own feelings. Until then one could only live for the day.

As the weather was lifting, they went out of the old ruin and she perched on a stone wall while he stood beside her.

'I met your Captain Poldark again,' she said. 'But of course he told you. The more I see of him the more I like him. I must confess that, if you want me to be honest.'

'You'll not make me jealous of him. I only wish his circumstances were happier.'

'Circumstances? Is it his cousin's widow who is the circumstance, or has he some other trouble?'

'Financial,' said Dwight, and hesitated. He'd no wish to betray a confidence; but some desire to turn her off the scent, to steer her away from asking him about the Elizabeth-Ross relationship, made him say more than he intended.

'I thought he looked a shade down-in-the-mouth when we met. And so you were having supper with his wife when he returned. Perhaps that's cause for jealousy on my part. Tell me, what's the hold she has on men? She's pretty enough, I grant, but so are others who get far less attention. Do you know the secret?'

'It's not a question of knowing a secret. It's just a question of knowing Demelza.'

'Is she the sort of woman that all men desire except her

husband? It so often happens. What an advocacy for married life! Don't you think I should be very ill-advised to marry, Dwight?'

'No, I don't think you would be ill-advised to marry, if you marry the right man.'

'Ah, the right man, of course.' She picked up two stones from the crumbling wall, weighed them in her palm, like subjects for discussion. 'But tell me what you have been doing yourself. I hear you've performed a miracle upon your little fisher girl and that she can now dance the cotillion. Is it really so?'

Remembering her earlier derision, he glanced quickly at her; but her face was serious enough. Then she met his gaze and laughed. 'No, no, I mean it. Tell me. Why should I not be interested?'

'Well, it was all greatly talked up, and I suspect you of pretending a polite attachment for the subject.'

'Then you don't understand me yet, Dwight. When last I was here I had to defend you against some supposed failure. Why shouldn't I be told of your triumphs?'

Perhaps it was something in one of her letters that still left him reluctant. 'The matter was made overmuch of, as I say. The girl had been lame for eight years from some disease of the knee. At least, one assumed disease. After some futile attempts to do good with blisters and the like, I made an effort to study the structure of the knee – first the bone formation, and then in other ways.'

'What other ways?'

'Last month a dead sailor was washed up on Hendrawna Beach and buried in the sand by the miners. I went down in the night and took part of one leg away and so was able to study the ligaments as they are in a living person.'

'You did?' she said, watching him, interested in this new light on his character.

'Yes. Then one day—'

'Did you not find it unpleasant?'

'Well, it wasn't pleasure I was looking for.'

'You may think it unfeminine,' said Caroline, 'but do you know I believe I should be interested to watch such work.'

'Would you?'

'Yes, I would. I see it shocks you. Go on.'

'It does not shock me at all. Then one day at the beginning of this month I was able to put the girl's knee right with my hands. It was nothing more than a displacement. But the years have caused atrophy of the muscles and some local inflammation. At present she is about with a bandage on it, but I think she can discard that when she has the confidence.'

Caroline put her hand over his. 'So now you are a miracle worker and have people waiting outside your house every morning. Bravo. I will tell my uncle. It will irritate him.'

'It irritates me,' said Dwight, 'but I can make use of it.'

'And no doubt your little girl looks on you with the most adoring eyes.'

'No doubt she does,' said Dwight shortly.

'And so she should. There are not many physicians of your accomplishments using all their energies to help the poor. How do you live, Dwight? Tell me that.'

He glanced at her. As always she asked questions frankly, bluntly, with no apparent awareness that she might be on delicate ground. Yet surely she, if anyone, had the right to know.

'I've an income of a few pounds a month, and this is supplemented by about £40 a year from the two mines and by those of my other patients who can afford to pay. Often I get gifts in kind from those who have no money to spare. In the main I keep out of debt. That's all I care for – or it's all I have cared for.'

'Will the Hoblyns pay you?'

'In some way. And not all the gentry on my list are as healthy as your uncle. Old Mr Treneglos, who would never have a surgeon near him, regularly calls me in—'

'That's what I mean,' said Caroline. 'Have you not thought of setting up in a town, especially a fashionable town – such as Bath or Oxford – where you would be able to work among people of your own kind? It is nice to help the poor, but charity – some charity – begins at home; and I believe you would be well received anywhere, not just among fisherfolk. Although you may not believe it, your manner at the bedside is an impressive one; and you have qualifications, Captain Poldark says, rarely met with outside of London . . .'

Although she did not think he noticed, he had seen the glance she gave his clothes when they came out into the daylight. But much that she implied by what she didn't say was salved by its obvious purpose.

He said: 'When I came back to Cornwall, I'd no thought but to open a business in a town; it was Captain Poldark who invited me here. But to help poor people was part of my own purpose – still is. And in a town – even in Bath and Oxford – the poor are in greater need of attention than the well off. I don't want to become a society pet.'

She slipped off the wall and went over to her horse, made some pretence of fumbling with the saddle. The wind stirred her tawny hair, lifting it away from her ear and letting it fall. He was at once angry with himself for sounding pompous, for having irritated her. Yet what he said was the truth! Would she have disguised her own feelings for *his* benefit?

He went over to her: 'Caroline, you may think—'

She turned and smiled. 'What should I think, Dwight? That you're the most noble of men? Or does it even matter? The sun has gone in and I'm chilly. That's of the chiefest moment. Let us ride.'

Before he could help her, she had pulled herself into the saddle, and her horse stepped spiritedly across the soft turf. She checked it while he mounted and came up with her.

'It matters everything what you think, Caroline; but because it matters so much, I can't pretend to you to gain an easy favour—'

'I'll race you. As far as Jonas's Mill, eh? You know the way?'

She swung her horse round and headed it for the rough common beyond the ruined mine. To gallop across this stonestrewn ground was asking for a fall; but she set off at a pace which Dwight with his inferior mount couldn't hope to equal.

But if Caroline knew the neighbourhood well, Dwight knew it better. He cantered along the track beside the common until she was safely across and had taken the stone wall at the other side. Then he spurred his horse forward down the track. A minute or two later a hamlet of four cottages was surprised to see the black-coated figure of their surgeon, who normally rode at a discreet trot, flying through as if for his life. Behind him in the settling dust children gathered and stared.

Dwight took the track which came out at Bargus Crosslanes and plunged as recklessly as Caroline could have wished through the rough scrub on the other side. Then he jumped from his horse and slipped and slithered with it down the slope beyond. Jonas's Mill came in sight and at the same moment Caroline again. Dwight swung into the saddle. The only way of getting to the mill before her was to jump the stream that worked the mill. It was quite narrow, but his horse was not a hunter. As Caroline saw him, he set his horse at the stream. They rose together and the horse landed half in and half out of the water at the other side, floundering and almost falling. Dwight slithered off its back into a foot or so of water and hauled the horse up the sloping bank. By the time Caroline came up he was mounted again and waiting for her, while the miller and the miller's wife peered in astonishment out of windows and a small boy driving a yoke of oxen forgot to call to his team.

Caroline reined in her horse beside him, her eyes glinting. 'That was very – clever of you, Dr Enys. It's obvious that such – accomplishments would be quite – misplaced in city life.'

'I have others,' said Dwight, more out of breath than she was. 'I have others – that would not.'

'But you can't bear the thought of Bath, Dr Enys.'

'And you can't bear the thought of marriage, Miss Penvenen.'

'I see no connection.'

'I am used to dealing with connections which – can be worked up.'

'To a man of such talents anything is possible.'

'Nothing is possible without you, Caroline.'

She sobered a little, meeting his glance. Her face was flushed with the gallop. She no longer looked displeased.

John Jonas came out of the mill rubbing his hands on his apron.

'All right, sur, are ee? Did the young lady's horse run away with her, eh?'

'No,' said Dwight. 'No one has run away with her yet.'

Chapter Three

She was in the winter parlour when Ross called. Black suited her. He hadn't yet overcome the feeling that he had no business at Trenwith without Francis to welcome him. Ever since Francis's death there had been a new constraint between them, coming from her confession months before; a barrier to replace a barrier, because without it . . .

She'd stood the bereavement well, as, considering her fragile look, she stood all strain well – for whether she loved Francis in the ordinary sense or not, he was her husband, the father of Geoffrey Charles, and long-standing ties of affection and habit had been broken.

'I have brought you the last returns of Wheal Grace,' he said. 'I copied them from the cost book last night. They don't make invigorating reading, but I thought you should have them.'

'Why?'

'Why? Because you're a partner, of course. Virtually so, since Geoffrey Charles is too young to look after his own interests.' He put the papers on the table and opened them up.

'Can you not tell me all that matters? I need no proofs in writing.'

'Yet you should have them. It's the business way, and others may think it needful if you do not.' He waited a moment, but she did not come to the table.

'What others are there?'

Pearce or your father, or – well, here the figures are for you to look at. What matters is that we shall not be able to go on later than January. I think possibly it would be better to finish at the end of the year.'

Her skin looked cool, as if the clothes she wore did not belong to it, their blackness some part of a world she did not quite inhabit. 'Ross, you know all of my finances, but I don't know yours. I know the end of this venture will hit you hard, but not how hard. From something that Francis said . . .'

'Yes?'

'I had the impression that Wheal Grace had become as much a gambler's throw for you as for him. Are you gravely in debt?'

'Grave is the word. One foot in and the other shortly following. But that's a risk I took. I can't complain because it has gone wrong. What I do much regret is losing your money also.'

'Well, it was Francis's money. And he also knew the risk he was taking.'

'Then I regret it for Geoffrey Charles's sake.'

On this she was without argument, without subterfuge even to herself. 'More than anything I feel my poverty because of him, Ross. I can't bear the thought of his coming into his inheritance and finding it . . . When Francis came into this estate, there was money to live – and would have been for our children. This last has been a *wise* investment compared to much of the rest. At least it was a gamble in a mine and not on the turn of a card!'

It was on Ross's tongue to ask if she realized how much she had contributed to this state of affairs, but his tongue was tied.

'If your father and mother live with you, it will help you and them, I suppose. They may get a good price for Cusgarne from one of the rich merchants; the expenses of living can be pooled.'

'Yes . . .'

'Isn't that your intention?'

She breathed deeply, gave him a painful smile. 'It was, Ross. But just at the moment it's too soon. I want time to think about these things. Francis's death is – is too close to me.' She came at last to the table, looked down at the papers he had brought, flipping them over in her fingers but not reading them.

Ross said: 'You've seen George again?'

'I had to. He's my chief creditor as you know. So much so that he's almost my only important one. It was a little difficult without you, but he quite understood that you could not meet.'

'What are his views on the debts?'

'Very generous. They always have been.' She raised her eyes again. 'I can't rob him of that credit. He was always generous to Francis too.'

Ross nodded, his face showing neither approval nor disapproval. 'Had he any fresh proposals?'

'Yes. He offered to waive interest on the debts for a period of years. Of course I could not accept that.'

'Why not?'

'Well . . . There have been enough favours. I don't feel justified in accepting more.'

Ross studied the colour moving under the delicate flush of her skin. 'It depends why, does it not? If you refuse his favours out of loyalty to me, it's a mistaken loyalty. My quarrel with George is not your quarrel. Nor even need Francis's be, now. George has always – admired you – tried to win your approval. If he still wants to do so, I should let him. You may well retain your private opinion of him just the same.'

She did not speak.

'If on the other hand,' said Ross, 'you feel that acceptance of his favours means you must offer him favours in return – such as . . .'

'Such as?'

He frowned at the papers. 'You can imagine them better than I. At the least you might feel that becoming a friend of his would alienate people you like better. That you must decide for yourself – I can't advise you.'

'I already have,' said Elizabeth quietly folding the papers unread.

Ross accepted them back, and they talked for a time desultorily about day-to-day things. But although what they said was unimportant, the saying of it was not. They had never before met like this, each week, confidentially, as friends. Each week tied the invisible strings.

When he left, she walked slowly back to the winter parlour and from the window watched his dwindling figure as he rode down the drive. If she had been given to self-questioning, she would have admitted that she had not been entirely honest with him over the help she was receiving from George – but would have pleaded excuse on the grounds that it was a necessary outcome of her bereavement. She not only wanted to be thought well of by both men, she needed to be. George had proposed that, being Geoffrey Charles's godfather, he should hold himself responsible for the cost of the boy's education up to the time of his finishing at Oxford. She could not refuse this, and Ross would not have expected her to. But she did not want to tell him of it, nor of the several smaller favours. It compromised the position she wished to take up in his mind. Perhaps more than anything else at present she wanted Ross's approval for herself.

But from the moment of Francis's death all her emotions had needed new names. A pattern set and grown in years had dissolved overnight. She wished the circumstances would have permitted her to correct the mistakes of past years. At present she was only groping towards an understanding of them.

When horse and rider had disappeared round a bend in the drive, she rang for Mrs Tabb to fetch Geoffrey Charles from his great-great-aunt's bedroom, where he was playing. Aunt Agatha was in bed today with rheumatism, and her strength, Elizabeth thought, was failing. When the little boy came, his mother kissed him fondly and began to give him his history lesson. These hours she spent with her son were the best of her day; she found mother love uncomplex and wholly satisfying; in such a relationship there were no mental reservations, no attitudes to be sustained, and no conflict.

She had not so far found her widowhood objectionable in the conventional ways, she felt little loneliness as such, she had more time to devote to herself and more for Geoffrey Charles. But she grievously missed a man to take the responsibility of day-to-day living. The making of decisions was always something she had disliked, and in an estate of this character there was no avoiding them. Some in fact could only be dealt with satisfactorily by a man. Tabb did what he could, Tabb did everything he could, but sometimes he traded on his new position and she had to watch that too.

While Geoffrey Charles was reading aloud to her, she walked across and studied herself in the mirror, twisting a strand of hair in among the rest, staring closely at her eyes and skin. There were a few little lines about her eyes which had not been there five years ago. But they were not enough to make any difference yet. When she smiled they disappeared. She must remember not to smile much in private, for that would deepen the lines, but to smile much in public, for that would hide them.

What had George said: one of the most beautiful women in England? His usual exaggeration. But beautiful enough. It was not conceit to know that. Nor did she think it disloyal to Francis to be aware of a growing freedom. She had been in a cage too long, confined within the bars of this house. It remained to be seen whether she had forgotten how to fly.

Demelza never asked what took place on Ross's weekly visit to Elizabeth, and he seldom volunteered the information. But on one thing Demelza was quite resolved. Whatever her inner promptings might be, she would never allow herself to entertain any suspicions of Ross's behaviour or allow him to suppose that she had any. Although she seldom voiced them, she had strong views on what a wife's attitude ought to be in such circumstances.

Today when he returned she had other news for him.

'There's a message from Mr Trencrom. Jud brought it. He says they'll be over tonight. He wouldn't say what he meant.'

'It's a matter I've intended telling you of. Mr Trencrom wants me to have a cache dug on my land for storing his goods during a run, so that they can be taken away at leisure. Of course he's willing to pay for it.'

'But will that not greatly increase the risk to us?'

'It matters very little. In a month we shall crash anyhow.'

She did not speak but went on brushing out the stable, where he had found her. He could guess by her face something of what she felt.

'That doesn't make sense to me,' she said eventually.

'Well, if I go to prison for debt, this will mean more money coming in. And the quicker the debt is paid, the quicker I shall be out again.'

'That is supposing the goods are not found on our land. You will stay longer in prison if you are convicted for that.'

'I do not think I shall be.'

'Where is this – this thing to be?'

'In the old library. It can all be done in one night, and nothing to show tomorrow.'

She was silent again. She would say no more in criticism, he knew, either to him or to herself; but that did not make her forbearance any easier to accept.

He said casually: 'And how was Jud?'

'Grumbling as usual. John tells me he has joined the Methodies.'

'I should not be astonished: he has always had a fancy for hell fire. Demelza, I wish you would not do this work; it's not right you should take it on yourself.'

'Gimlett was busy and you were out. But I like it, Ross. It stops me from thinking. About this hole, this cache, how many will know of it?'

'Four to dig it. Six or eight perhaps who use it.'

'Jud Paynter?'

'Possibly.'

'Well, I—'

'Oh, I know he's leaky in his liquor. But he drinks less since his recovery – and I think we underrate him. Look at his behaviour at my trial. Trencrom trusts him, and Trencrom can't afford to make mistakes.'

'Neither can we.'

'As you say.' He stared at her for a moment, disliking himself for comparisons which sometimes now rose uninvited in his brain. 'Demelza, I am not making much of our situation yet; for there's still a few weeks to go, and I may still find the money. If I do not, I have made arrangements with Mr Trencrom so that a sum shall be paid to you monthly for the favours he receives. My remaining shares in Wheal Leisure will go to meet part of the debt, so there will be nothing from that. But Mr Trencrom's dole will keep you comfortably enough, and anything you can save from it can be put aside to wipe off the rest of the debt. In no time—'

'You do not need to fear for me. I was used once to living on nothing, and can do it again. And Jeremy I shall see for. Don't worry about us. What matters is paying off the money you owe.'

He took the broom from her, and after a brief resistance she gave it up. He carried on with the work.

'I had some expectation of Mr Trencrom. I'm a deal more use to him out of prison than in; and if there is a forced sale of this house and land, the new purchasers may not be friendly to his schemes.'

'I thought your Mr Pascoe had promised that the property should not be sold.'

'So he has. Indeed, the property already belongs to him under the mortgage deed; but Trencrom does not know of the promise.'

Demelza pushed back her hair with her wrist. 'You'll soil your best clothes. 'Tisn't sensible to do that now.'

'Well I'd as lief wear 'em out as save them for the moths.'

She said vehemently: 'Why do you not appeal to your friends, Ross – or let me appeal for you? Sir John Trevaunance would be sympathetic, I know. And Sir Hugh Bodrugan, though you may not like him, has good will towards me. And Mr Ray Penvenen, and old Mr Treneglos. They might well join with Mr Trencrom in putting up so much each so's to save you from the bankruptcy. It is not charity, for they know you are honourable and would pay them back. Why not let me try? Do let me try!'

He stopped and leaned on the broom handle, his eyes lidded in thought. After a few seconds he smiled and shook his head. 'No good, my dear. The sum is too great and so is my pride. And since you've so good an opinion of these friendships, keep it, for they would not stand the strain you suppose. One or two would help, I know, but others would not; and we can save ourselves the disappointment. Anyway, I've never asked favours and will not begin now. We'll get through it as we may, and presently start afresh. When that time comes, I shall keep to farming and leave all mining alone. Even brushing out stables will be a kindly thing to come back to!'

The four to dig it was six, with Jud leaning on his stick to superintend. An overblown moon climbed above the sand hills at nine-thirty, so there was need only of one small lantern within the library. At ten the cores changed at the mine, and by half past the last of the miners had dispersed. From then on, three of the six men were busy wheeling the excavated ground across the valley to the nearest dump. No one would notice that it had grown a little in the night.

The six men were Ned Bottrell, Paul Daniel, Ted Carkeek, Will Nanfan, Whitehead Scoble, and Pally Rogers. About eleven there was an alarm, but it was only Charlie Kempthorne with a message for Ned Bottrell that he was a father for the fifth time. This was good excuse for a tot of brandy and some rough-and-ready jokes.

At one Demelza went to bed; but Ross stayed until an hour before dawn, when the work was finished. The seven tired men – Jud, who had done no work, complaining he was the most tired of them all – tramped back up the valley in the light of a moon which had grown smaller and paler as the dark hours passed.

Chapter Four

Caroline and her uncle had never got on so well since her
break with Unwin Trevaunance, and her return to Killewarren and attitude since had done little to smooth things
out. She spent every fine day riding, often with a groom
but sometimes alone, and was silent through her meals or
edgy if questioned. She paid few social visits in the neighbourhood and seldom wished to be found at home if called
on. Rumours had not been slow to reach him, but he
understood her well enough to know that he must move
cautiously if they were to be checked or countered.

One night at supper she provoked a discussion by saying:
'Tell me, Uncle, what do you know of Ross Poldark?'

Blinking, cautious, watching her as if he suspected some
deeper meaning in the question than he was privy to, he
told her what he knew. Ross's father, the best-known
libertine in six parishes; Ross's service overseas during the
American war; his return after his father's death and his
bitter disappointment, so people said, that Francis was to
marry the Chynoweth girl; his foolish marriage a year or so
later to a girl he had taken from some miner's cottage in
Illuggan; his starting of Wheal Leisure and, later, his
leadership of the proposal to begin copper smelting in
Cornwall; the failure of the scheme; the death of his child;
the shipwrecks and the riots which followed; his trial and
his acquittal; his—

'Yes, Uncle, thank you, I know from there.' Caroline took a sip of wine, and her eyes looked darker for the reflection from the glass. 'His father, you say, was bad-behaved with the women of the neighbourhood. I should imagine the son has sowed his wild oats also. Or he looks as if he has. You do not mention that.'

Penvenen regarded the girl dryly. 'I was not attempting to spare his reputation – or your delicacy. I do not know if anything specially unsavoury has clung to him in that respect – although it has in many others. Of course this taking a half-starved beggar girl, or whatever she was ... I was in London at the time, but I believe it caused trouble among the miners and with her father.'

'But he married her,' said Caroline.

'Yes, he married her.'

She waited while her plate was taken away. Beside her in a basket on another chair was Horace, and she picked him up and set him on her lap.

'Did you lose much in your association with Ross Poldark in the copper company?'

'Enough. Everyone lost money. It was an ill-conceived enterprise at best.'

'I understand you escaped somewhat earlier and somewhat better than the others.'

The candles were between them, but she saw his sharply raised eyes. 'Who told you that?'

She laughed. 'Unwin. He said once that you and Sir John made a deal with the Warleggans and left the ship to sink. That was his phrase.'

'The ship – as you term it – was already on the rocks when we came to an arrangement with the Warleggans. We did so only to preserve capital investments we had made, he in his furnaces, I in the battery mill. No one lost a penny more because of our action. Unwin knew nothing of the situation at first hand.'

She held a piece of meat under the pug's nose, but he only sniffed at it and turned away. 'Is the horrid beef not to your liking, my pet? Very well, you shan't be pressed. Thomas, bring me the sweet biscuits – you know the ones Horace adores.'

'Yes, ma'am.'

'But you shall have to go back in your basket for those, my sweet, or you would crumble them all over my frock. There, is that to your liking? . . . I hear Ross Poldark is on the verge of insolvency now.'

'Indeed.' Her uncle had not appreciated her comments, and his reply was short.

'He has some debts outstanding from that time, and the Warleggans have got hold of them and are pressing him hard.'

'You are well informed.'

Thomas came back with the biscuits, and she thanked him with a smile. For a minute or two she devoted her whole attention to Horace. 'Not so very well informed, Uncle, for I cannot ask him to his face and I do not know the Warleggans well enough to ask them. But it seems a pity that so big a man should be squeezed out for so small a sum, don't you think? If he went out at all, he should go in the grand manner – to suit his looks and his style.'

Mr Penvenen said: 'I imagine Dr Enys could enlighten you on any further details you wished to know.'

Horace snuffled over his biscuit in the sudden silence. Caroline said: 'I believe I shall go into Truro tomorrow morning. It is a poor place to shop, but I need some shoes made. In Oxford shoe buckles are quite out of fashion and I myself prefer the string. And do you know there is quite a craze for feathers in the hair. I don't personally favour them, I feel too much like yesterday's fowl.'

'I think,' said Ray Penvenen, 'that although you are now your own mistress, Caroline, you should not allow a natural pleasure in your freedom to obscure the observances of good society in which it has been my privilege and your Uncle William's to enlighten you since your parents died. Although we may seem to be in a rough and isolated part of the country here, it would be a mistake to think that the conventions do not obtain. For instance, to ride far and unattended in the company of a young man of eligible years is to invite comment of an unsavoury nature, whether one is in Cornwall or in Oxfordshire. No doubt this is quite innocently intended, but it can have far-reaching consequences and is neither quite fair to me, who may seem to be countenancing it, nor to the young man, who may derive encouragement from it and ambitions beyond his proper sphere.'

Soft-footed, the manservant closed the door and went out. After a second or so a breath of air imperceptible to the skin reached the candles and their flames trembled like fronds in a still pool.

Caroline said: 'I'd always thought – I've always believed – that a mark of true quality and rank is to behave according to one's personal lights and to pay no attention beyond that to the mesh of artificial conventions with which would-be people of quality surround themselves.'

'That is true to a point But a person of quality only acts in such a way so far as his behaviour affects himself. When it affects other people, he is no longer a free agent.'

'It was what I was going to say. There are only two people concerned in this beside myself, and that is you and Dr Enys. Your concern is that you might be thought to be approving of my behaviour. Is that it? Well, if I am too much on your conscience, should I not be better advised to leave this house and live elsewhere?'

'Possibly,' he agreed quietly, 'if it were not for the affection that we hold for each other.'

She frowned a moment, looking angry and troubled. Then she covered her feelings by turning to Horace. 'Another biscuit, my love? Uncle Ray is becoming cross with me. There will, I fear, shortly be angry words on both sides. And possibly a scene. And things would be said which we should both later somewhat regret. That is a pity, don't you think? Do you not suppose we should better change the subject?'

Horace made a gruff noise in his throat and contrived to lick her fingers and his own nose at the same time. Ray stared across at his pretty niece in perplexity, partly disarmed but not at all less suspicious. There was a genuine bond between them, and he often blamed himself for weakness in his treatment of her. But he did not know how to continue the attack without provoking the scene she forecast. He did not suppose that what he had said would make any difference to her early-morning rides, but he knew that insistence at this stage might well lead to her carrying out her threat – to the grief and detriment of them both. And such a move would completely defeat his object by taking her right outside his influence. He wondered if he was approaching this problem from the wrong quarter and through the wrong person.

Supper ended in peace. Later, when he was in his study, he summoned his servant and asked if he could find out what arrangements Miss Caroline had made for visiting Truro in the morning. The man came back to say she had ordered her carriage for nine-thirty. Mr Penvenen bit the end of his quill for a few seconds and then wrote a short note.

> Dear Dr Enys,
>   If you are free, I should be obliged if you could call on me tomorrow morning between ten-thirty and eleven. It is some time since you made a routine medical call.
>   Yours etc.,
>   R. R. E. Penvenen

About five minutes to eleven Dwight turned his horse in at the gates of Killewarren, not without a quickening of anticipation at the prospect of seeing Caroline again without the necessity of contrivance. But no Caroline was about when he went in, and he was silently shown upstairs into the big untidy drawing-room with its antlers and its sporting pictures where he had first met Ray Penvenen.

Mr Penvenen was there to meet him again, or rather was standing with his back to him, staring out at the grey day. His coat as usual was sizes too big for him, and the warts were noticeable on his clasped hands. After a studied pause he turned.

'Ah, Dr Enys, you had my letter?'

'Yes,' said Dwight, knowing now and blaming himself for not having known before. 'I hope I've not kept you waiting.'

'There's time enough. My niece happens to be in Truro, and I thought this would be an opportunity to discuss matters with you.'

'Medical matters?'

'No. I must apologize if my note gave you that impression.'

'Well, yes, it did.'

Ray Penvenen picked up his spectacles from the desk but did not put them on. His lashless eyes were lowered. 'Perhaps you would care to sit down.'

'No, thank you.'

Somewhere near at hand Horace was yapping monotonously. 'I imagine you have some idea why I have sent for you.'

'I don't think it is for me to speculate, Mr Penvenen.'

'I could have wished you showed a similar delicacy in all your dealings, Dr Enys.'

'I'm sorry you should think I have not.'

'Yes ... well, yes ... I think you have not – though I should be happy to learn that you have been offending thoughtlessly and without a full appreciation of what is involved. I refer, of course, to your growing friendship with my niece.'

'I wonder in what way you consider that offensive?'

Penvenen glanced dryly at the young man.

'Come, Dr Enys. You can't be so unaware of the ways of the world. For more than a month, if not longer, you have been paying attentions to my niece. You must know that your first duty was to approach me and ask my permission. The fact that you have not done so shows that you suspect such permission would not be forthcoming. Isn't that so?'

Dwight bit his lip, angry with himself as well as with the man in front of him.

'All you say is true.'

'Ah ... Well, then, what explanation have you to offer?'

'None at all. Except that none of it has been so deliberate as you suppose. One's feelings grow unsolicited and unencouraged. There has been no one point when I have said to myself ... But I now have such feelings for your niece; I won't attempt to deny that.'

'You have not considered how her ill-advised meetings with you reflect on her reputation?'

'No, I have not: I don't suppose—'

'There's no need for us to quarrel, Dr Enys.' Penvenen folded his hands under his coattails and smiled. 'Caroline is a forceful young woman, a thoroughly delightful person but as mettlesome as an unbroken colt. She has never been sufficiently curbed – it would be an ungenerous task, but perhaps I and my brother are to blame for not attempting it. We try to humour her so far as we can. It is nothing uncommon for her to take violent likes and dislikes to people – often she drops them as quickly as she has taken them up. It may be so in your case; it probably will; but even then I should be opposed to these quasi-secret meetings. As for a serious attachment, to a young man in your position ... Apart from consideration of money and blood—'

'I don't think blood need enter into it.'

'But I do, my dear sir. There was a Penvenen at Prince Rupert's side at Marston Moor. And we have lived in this district for ninety years—'

'An Enys fitted out and manned a ship to fight the Armada. Ninety years ago one of my ancestors was High Sheriff of Cornwall.'

Mr Penvenen cleared his throat. His careful geniality was not quite proof against this reply. 'And as to money?'

'I admit the obstacle.'

'Caroline is an heiress, Dr Enys. She is my heir and my brother's heir, so she will be – to say the least – rich in her time. She is far too important a person to become entangled with a penniless country doctor. I'm glad you realize it.'

Dwight had controlled his quick temper so far, but everything Mr Penvenen said made things worse. The fact that he was using arguments Dwight had used against himself added to the insult.

'Ultimately, isn't it for Caroline to decide her own life?'

Ray Penvenen took one of his hands out and grasped the velvet lapel of his coat. 'That is where you are in error. Caroline must marry with our consent or she will not inherit any money from us.'

'That again must be for Caroline to choose.'

'And how do you think she will choose when I put the choice before her? She had been brought up in the greatest luxury. Nothing for her comfort has ever been spared. D'you suppose she'll sacrifice all that for what you have to offer? Are you justified in expecting it?'

Dwight stared angrily across the room. The desk was open, with a litter of papers on it. Above the desk was a small water colour of a red-haired child.

'It may be, of course,' said Penvenen, 'that you think my niece has a large private fortune of her own. Let me—'

'I neither know nor care what money she has.'

'Very creditable of you. But hardly practical. Caroline has about six thousand pounds of her own. That is all you could expect to get if you married her Dr Enys.'

Dwight said: 'Up to now, Mr Penvenen, I've suffered your comments with a due degree of civility. I owed it to you as Caroline's uncle and guardian. But there are limits to what a man may stand. God knows I've never given you reason to imagine me a fortune hunter, and I should have thought that such knowledge as you have of me might have inclined you to a less offensive view. If you suppose that no man who has not an eye on her money can fall in love with your niece, you greatly underrate her charm and insult her as much as you do me—'

'Now there is no need—'

'When I came here today, I was as distracted – I suppose – as any man ever has been, over this matter of Caroline's money. For months I've faced an insoluble problem. At least today you've given me a slender hope for the solution of it.'

The whiter Mr Penvenen's face became, the pinker grew the rims of his eyes. 'You are going a little far, Dr Enys. I suppose you realize that this will mean the end of our professional relationship—'

'You've shown me a way out,' said Dwight, pacing across the room, 'by telling me that Caroline's fortune isn't as great as I thought. One of substance, I admit, but not an insuperable bar. It would be possible for a penniless doctor to marry such a fortune without being eclipsed by it. It would be possible with such a fortune for a wife to maintain herself and yet not entirely dominate the purse strings. Thank you, sir, for that!'

'You will leave this house,' said Ray Penvenen, 'and not come here again. You will have no further communication with my niece. I forbid it and shall take steps to enforce it. Good day to you.'

Dwight stopped in his pacing opposite the little cold man. 'Caroline is of age, Mr Penvenen. Your control can only be exercised within the limits of your property. But perhaps you yourself have pointed the solution to our difficulties.'

'I have nothing further to say to you, Dr Enys!'

'I have this to say to you, sir, in all deference. Just now you asked me if I thought Caroline would give up all you had to offer for what little I have to offer. That's the crux, isn't it? Well, we must leave it to her to decide!'

'I see I have been gravely mistaken in your character, Dr Enys. I very much regret ever having invited you here.'

'Many times in the last months I have very much regretted having come. But at least we understand each other now.'

'We understand each other,' said Ray Penvenen, as Dwight went out.

Harris Pascoe was not busy when Miss Penvenen was announced; but he had the appearance of industry, being occupied at his favourite pastime of juggling with figures. He was not a man of strong passions, and things like credit and debit balances offered to him the cold white peaks of aesthetic pleasure. When Caroline was shown in, he reluctantly closed the last book and stood up.

'Miss Penvenen. I haven't had the p-pleasure. I know your father, of course.'

'My uncle. Yes, it's on account of his speaking of you that I've come to you today. Not of course that he knows I'm here . . .'

Harris Pascoe rubbed the soft part of his pen along the line of his cheek. Although he found his dearest pleasure in mathematics, he was not insensible to figures of another sort, and he acknowledged to himself that this young woman was worth looking at.

'And can I help you?'

Caroline took off her long green gauntlet gloves, flipping them against her knee. 'It's a peculiar mission I'm on, Mr Pascoe; at least you may think so, and I shouldn't quarrel with you for having that opinion. I want to know if you can help me to help a friend of mine who is in trouble. There, it sounds rather mysterious, doesn't it? And not quite respectable. Would you like me to explain?'

There was a suggestion of mischief in her eyes, so Harris Pascoe was at his most stolid. 'If you please.'

'I have money, Mr Pascoe, and am seeking an invest-ment. I understand that Captain Poldark has a bill out which will shortly come due for redemption. Do I use the right professional words? I understand that the present possessor of the bill is not willing to renew it. I should like to buy that bill. Could you arrange the purchase for me?'

The banker pulled his snuffbox towards him, opened it, and stayed for a moment with finger and thumb poised over the box. Then he closed it unused.

'You are looking for an *investment,* Miss Penvenen?'

She nodded brightly. 'From what I hear it should be a good one. The rate of interest is exceedingly high. Of course if you prefer to call the transaction by some other name, I shall not quibble.'

'Forgive me, you have c-control of your money?'

'Since I was twenty-one.'

'What does your uncle – but you say he does not know of this visit. Does Captain Poldark?'

Caroline smiled. 'Do you suppose he would let me interfere in his affairs?'

'No . . .' Pascoe got up and dusted some loose snuff from his waistcoat. 'You are putting me in rather a d-difficulty, Miss Penvenen. Captain Poldark is a client of mine and also a personal friend. It is not my custom to discuss a client's affairs with any third person; but I'll not disguise from you what I think you already well know – that a renewal of this bill would be a matter of the utmost importance t-to him. But also – but also your uncle is a valued client of mine, and I should be doing less than my duty to him if I allowed you to make this rash purchase – even supposing it can be made – without warning you that you could hardly make a more risky investment. Indeed, I don't feel I could proceed as you suggest without consulting your uncle in the matter first.'

Caroline looked down and gently stretched the fingers of her gloves. 'I am an independent person, Mr Pascoe. If you consult my uncle, you'll be disclosing a private conversation to a third party. I thought you never did that. And if you refuse to make this investment for me, I shall have to go elsewhere.'

Harris Pascoe perceived that his visitor was not to be trifled with.

'You're aware that it's not a good risk?'

'I'm aware that most people would not think it a good risk. But we all have our own opinions.'

Pascoe went to the window and stared down into the street. Absently he took note of the smart private coach waiting outside, the man in green livery on the box, the gaping urchins, the citizens too who had stopped to stare. If the girl had plenty of money, why should he exert himself to dissuade her? There'd be difficulties enough . . .

'There are difficulties in your suggestion which would be not at all of my making, Miss Penvenen. For one thing, I do not think the present owner of the bill would be willing to s-sell it.'

'Why not? He wants the money, doesn't he?'

'There is more than money involved.'

'Oh, yes, the Warleggans, of course; I have heard something of it. But is there not a way round that difficulty?'

'Not by offering to purchase the bill. At the very least

they would, I think, demand some extortionate premium on it which would put it quite out of your reach.'

'You don't know my reach, Mr Pascoe.'

'Possibly not. But allow me at least to advise you on the most economical way of going about the business.' He came back to the table and sat down, picked up his pen in some irritation, and made a few figures. 'Obviously, if you are quite set on doing this, the best thing is to lend Captain Poldark the fourteen hundred pounds personally to discharge the bill and have him sign a new bill for this amount.'

For the first time Caroline looked a little confused. 'I'm afraid that's impossible. That's what I haven't told you yet. He mustn't on any account know who has advanced the money.'

Pascoe considered her dryly. 'I see. But I'm afraid it is unavoidable. I don't think there is any other way. I don't think you have the *least* chance of persuading Mr Cary Warleggan to part with the bill, at any price. You have no doubt read *The Merchant of Venice*.'

There was silence for a few moments. Caroline said: 'I don't for a moment think Captain Poldark would accept the money from me.'

'Hm ... No, it's possible. You're a friend of his, of course? But a woman. I see your point.'

Caroline got up. She was as tall as the banker, and her slightness made her look taller. She folded her gloves carefully, not looking at him. But something in the shape of her face made him aware of what the look in her eyes was likely to be.

'Well, thank you for seeing me. I shall have to go elsewhere. I can expect you to tell no one of my call?'

'I shall tell no one. But don't be in t-too great a hurry. I think I have a suggestion to make which might help us to overcome this difficulty.'

'Yes?'

'Pray sit down again. Give me a moment or two to work this out.'

Caroline resumed her seat. Through narrow long-lashed eyes she watched Mr Pascoe open his snuffbox. She waited, patient now, for him to make his suggestion.

Chapter Five

Lobb the Sherborner had spent the night locally, so a letter was delivered to Ross just as he was leaving the house for the mine. He broke the seal and read what Harris Pascoe had to say, hardly certain that the slanting December sunlight was not in some manner distorting what he read. Having come through it twice with the same interpretation, he moved quickly round to the stables and began to throw a saddle over Darkie. Gimlett heard him and stopped his work and came into the stable.

'Can I help ee, sir?'

'No . . . I can do it. Oh, Gimlett, where is your mistress?'

'Gone looking for Garrick, who ran off after a stray cat.'

'Tell her I've been called to Truro on business, will you? I hope to be back in time for tea.'

'Yes, sur.'

Before eleven Ross was dismounting outside the banking premises of Messrs Pascoe, Tresize, Annery, and Spry. He dropped his reins over the post, lifted the latch of the bank door, and went purposefully in. Harris Pascoe was not engaged, nor indeed surprised to see his visitor, though the swift response was several hours earlier than he had expected. He looked up speculatively at Ross's expression as he was shown in.

Ross sat down and crossed his long legs and rubbed a finger carefully across his upper lip.

'Good day to you, Harris.'

'Good day. You're an early caller this morning.'

'Not earlier than I wish to be. This letter . . .' Ross took it from his pocket.

'Oh, yes. You received it s-safely. I imagine the contents would come as a surprise to you.'

'Surprise is not an overstatement.'

The banker smiled at his ledgers. 'Naturally I was happy to be the sender of such tidings.'

'No happier than I was to receive them. What is the explanation?'

'You already have the explanation in the letter.'

'Not one that satisfies me. After trying desperately to raise the wind for six weeks, I feel a little sceptical that it has suddenly decided to raise itself. Who is this anonymous person who has suddenly come forward as you say and placed this money at my disposal?'

'I'm not at liberty to give you the name.'

'Is it you?'

Pascoe looked up and met the unquiet eyes. 'No.'

'Is it a friend of mine – someone I know?'

'I can't tell you.'

'If I know no more than this, how can I accept it? On what conditions is it loaned me?'

'You have them in the letter. A new promissory n-note on the same conditions as the old, but at a lower rate of interest.'

'And whom do I promise to pay?'

'It will be left blank. The note won't leave my keeping anyway unless you d-default.'

Ross got up, put his finger tips on the enormous desk. 'It's monstrous, Harris. It really is. Have you been deluding some poor fool into thinking me a better risk than I really am?'

'No.'

'So it is a friend. Damn it, I still suspect you. I can't think—' He stopped and pushed a hand through his hair.

'I'd be glad to take the credit. But in my position as a banker I was not able to lend the money ... Had I been able to, I should have advanced it weeks ago and saved you the anxiety.'

'Well, I really can't accept this money blindfold. It's asking too much.'

'Of whom?' said Pascoe politely.

Ross subsided in his chair. It was the chair Caroline had occupied five days ago. He picked up his crop and turned it round in his bony fingers. His finances these last years reminded him often of a man deprived of air, choking, but again and again reprieved at the point of death. But never before had he come so close to the end of things as this December. Even now he felt very little sense of relief. He couldn't at all believe it. He stared at the man opposite. Pascoe was about to sneeze, but the sudden stare stopped it and he had to content himself with a sniff.

'It is none of the Warleggans? No swapping of horses without betterment, or accepting some favour from George at Cary's expense?'

'It is none of them.'

'Can they do anything to stop this; I mean can they retain the bill they have?'

'Not this way. With your permission I shall go over tomorrow and redeem the bill. The money is immediately available when you sign this new note.'

Ross stared at the piece of paper as if by doing so he

would penetrate the secrets that were being withheld from him. 'Is it Mr Trencrom?'

'I cannot tell you anything more.'

'You can't give me even a hint?'

'I'm afraid not.'

'But you, knowing the person, advise me to accept the offer?'

'I, knowing the person, advise you to accept. You'd be criminally foolish if you did not.'

That was enough. Ross dipped the quill in the pot and slowly signed his name. 'Are you in communication with this bashful gentleman?'

'I may be from time to time.'

'Well, would you convey my compliments to him and tell him I shall not lie easy till I know his name. I'm in his debt literally and figuratively for a greater amount than I have been to anyone else ever in my life. As to the monetary sum, I shall feel as much constrained to pay it as if it were a debt of honour; and for the personal obligation, perhaps the occasion may occur when I may pay that too.'

'I'll t-tell the gentleman,' said Pascoe, fixing his spectacles more firmly on his nose. 'I'm sure your acceptance will make pleasant hearing to him. It's plain that he has your welfare at heart.'

'I have his also,' said Ross.

Garrick chased the cat up a tree, so Demelza tied him securely at a distance and then tried to entice the cat down. This didn't work so she looped up her skirt and climbed the tree herself. It was from the vantage point of the topmost branches, swaying dangerously, that she saw Ross riding up the valley. She coo-ed but he didn't hear, and she retrieved the cat and climbed down in an apprehensive frame of mind. Sudden changes of plan on Ross's part always betokened bad news.

Gimlett's story of a letter confirmed her suspicions; and she spent the day in some foreboding, hiding her worst fears in a flurry of work. In the afternoon, with Jeremy plucking at her skirts and getting into all sorts of trouble, she made butter, putting the scalded cream she had saved into her stone bowl and beating it regularly round with her hand. But today it would not turn, and she began to have fears either that the cow was sick or that this was some sort of omen. Sir Hugh Bodrugan had been over last week, pressing her to see a cow of his that would not calve, convinced beyond all reason that she was capable of white witchery. She had refused. Two lucky coincidences had given her a name, and the only way to retain it was not to tempt fate any more.

Prudie Paynter had had some doggerel she used for making butter turn when she was a servant here, and Demelza tried it over now; but perhaps Ross's scepticism had infected her, for nothing happened. The afternoon was very cold, her hands were very cold, and she found it hard to keep up an even, unhurried motion.

The day had been still, no air moving and quiet except for the roar of the surf. Often the sea was a continual unperceived noise, but on days such as this it overcame the mind's defences and life moved to its beat. It was as if a great army of heavy vehicles was passing near the house, and now and then the air tremored on one's ears. A faint mist drifted inland from the breaking waves, greying the edges of the cliffs and sand dunes. In the garden the birds pecked at the hard ground, and seagulls circled the upper air.

The Carnbarrow Hunt was to meet at Werry House next week, and Sir Hugh had invited her over. Demelza wondered if her refusal had been right. She knew Ross's views, but she still felt Sir Hugh might be persuaded to help them – at a price. She had coaxed a concession out of him once before and come to no hurt. Surely she might do so again.

The cream began at last to turn, and after a few minutes she went out and drew a pitcher of ice-cold water from the pump to wash away the buttermilk. She had done this and was patting the butter into shape when Ross came.

She didn't stop to carry her board out to the stillroom, but slid through the house, nearly upsetting Jeremy, who lurched suddenly into her path.

Ross was already in, an unusual thing, having left his mare by the door. His expression was hard to read; almost always she knew, but this time it didn't conform to any of the recognized patterns.

'There's going to be a hard frost,' he said. 'Some of the shallower pools are freezing already.'

'Yes, I thought the same,' she said. 'There's all the signs. That sky . . . Jeremy, darling, *where* did you get the jam!'

The little boy had come tottering in carrying a large jar from the lip of which a dark crimson streak was already beginning to escape. On the very verge of dropping it he was able to present it to his father before it slipped from his hands. Then he sat down with a crump on the floor and said, 'Gar!'

'Thank you,' said Ross, 'a very friendly gesture . . .' He put the jar on the table. 'He's more forward than Julia was, isn't he? I can't remember at this age . . .'

'She was fatter and more content to stay in one place. We shall have to watch his legs . . . Ross, why did you go into Truro?'

'Some extra business to do with Pascoe. A matter of small importance.'

She knew then from some glint in his eye that the news was not bad.

'What is it? What's to do? Tell me if it is something better. I have been thinking all day . . .'

He sat down and warmed his hands at the fire. Gimlett had come out and was leading Darkie past the windows. 'Pascoe was agreed that there was likely to be a frost.'

'No, Ross.' She went over to him. 'Don't play now! This is too important. Tell me, please.'

He looked up at her eager face.

'Someone – some anonymous person – has chosen very foolishly to take over my debt, my promissory note which the Warleggans hold. It means that – for the time at least – the urgency to find the money is gone. Of course, it will still have to be found some day. But not *this* Christmas.'

Demelza stared at him. 'D'you mean – that you won't have to default – that there's still a chance? . . .'

'There's still a chance. Just that.'

'Oh, my dear.' She sat abruptly in a chair. After a moment Jeremy sprawled towards her and she picked him up and covered him with kisses of relief. 'Oh, Ross, I can't hardly believe that. After all this worry it's *beyond* belief . . .'

'You describe it exactly. It's beyond belief. All the way home I've been telling myself that things are just as black as they ever were before this threat blew up – that we are still poverty-stricken to the last edges of pauperdom – that in a month or so the mine must close – that we have practically nothing to live on. But just at the moment those things don't mean anything at all.'

'And it's *true*! It's true! Oh, thank God!' She suddenly set Jeremy down and ran across and kissed him on the cheek. 'I'm that *glad* for you, Ross! But glad isn't the word! There must be a better. I wish I knew a better! What is anonymous?'

He pulled her down till she was sitting on his knee. 'No name. We don't know our benefactor.'

'Some friend?'

'Some friend. To whom I owe one thousand four hundred pounds. The percentage of interest is also halved, so that after this year I shall only pay him two hundred and eighty pounds each Christmas.'

'God bless him, whoever he is!'

'Amen, I say to that.'

'Have you no idea?'

'Vague speculations on the way home. Each seems more unlikely than the last.'

There was silence for some minutes. He said: 'Where were you when I left?'

'After a stray cat Garrick was chasing. 'Twasn't fair, for the creature had a bad leg and I've told him oftentimes not to touch cats. Might it not mean now that the mine could go on a little longer?'

'Where is the cat now?'

'In the kitchen in a basket.'

'I thought so.' Ross stretched down to a bag at his feet. Demelza, a bit unused to this situation nowadays, made a move to rise but he would not let her. 'I've bought you a pound of Soachong tea. It is better than the stuff we get through Trencrom. I thought you'd like to try it.'

'Thank you, Ross. That's kind of you . . . *Now* perhaps in a short time we shall not need to do anything for Mr Trencrom. D'you think it possible? Then we should be *really* free, out in the open, able to breathe again!'

'And I brought you a new brush and comb. I thought it

a good thing to have one in reserve before you broke the present one.'

Demelza took the articles handed to her, turned them over in her hands. The comb had a twisted handle, like a plait of hair. 'Very – extravagant,' she said indistinctly.

'Very. I also got two pairs of worsted stockings each for the Gimletts. They were not dear: two shillings a pair. They've had little enough of late. And I have here a bonnet for Jeremy and a pair of knitted gloves. I thought he might be jealous if he was left out. I'm not sure as to the size. I suspect they will smother him.'

Demelza got up. The light was going, and over the hill the winter's day was infinitely remote. Everything was still except for the muffled roar behind the house, and this was less dominant for the time because the tide was out. Already the secret spell of frost had been cast over the valley.

'They look a good fit. That's clever to have guessed. And what did you buy yourself?'

Ross said: 'I was in doubt between a silk cloak and a jewelled sword, so I put it off till next time. This was my last purchase.'

He got up too and handed her a pair of women's garters. They were very fancy.

'For me?' said Demelza.

'I notice you've been wearing no stockings often this winter, and can only suppose you were in some straits to keep them up.'

Demelza burst into tears.

'Oh, come, come, I meant no offence. It was just a passing thought. If you'd prefer not to have them—'

'It isn't *that*,' she said. 'You know very *well* it is not that.' She put her hands to her face. 'It is the relief . . . And then buying all these things.'

'They were none of them extortionate.' He put his arm round her, but her breakdown was checked by a sudden howl from Jeremy, who, unused to seeing his mother in tears, was moved to copy her. Demelza knelt over him and comforted him, wiping his eyes as well as her own. After a few seconds she glanced up at Ross.

'I'm sorry. It was the relief. You see – I love you so much . . .'

Ross stared down at them both, moved himself and happy. The light from the window glinted on her hair, on the curve of her back, on Jeremy's clutching hands.

'I must put them on,' he said.

Demelza looked up. 'You mean Jeremy's bonnet and gloves?'

'What else,' rejoined Ross, smiling grimly.

With the usual sort of difficulty, Jeremy was invested with his new regalia. It all fitted pretty well, and should have done, since the shopkeeper had tried them on her own child first. Presently he went tottering off, the bonnet at a rakish angle, one glove not properly tied.

She had known that Ross hadn't meant that. She held the garters in her hand, and he took them from her, so she sat down uncertainly. She was wearing stockings tonight, old ones, but they were black and her skin above them glistened like ivory. He put the garters on with a good deal of care. It was months, almost years, since there had been this sort of thing between them, that odd fusion of desire and affection for which there is no substitute. Her eyes in the gathering darkness glowed at him. They stayed for a while hardly moving, he kneeling and she leaning back in the chair. His hands were cool on her legs. Remember this, she thought. In the times of jealousy and neglect, remember this.

He said: 'So you are not to be rid of me, my love.'

'I am not to be rid of you, my love.'

Over in the corner by the door Jeremy thumped down and began methodically to pull off his gloves.

Chapter Six

Verity, Francis's sister, had written inviting Ross and Demelza to stay with them over Christmas; but with ruin coming apace, there had been no alternative to a refusal. This sudden reprieve changed the situation, and Ross agreed they should go over on Christmas Eve and stay the night. He did not feel he could leave the mine longer than that. Verity, so closely tied always to Francis, had taken his death hard; and as Demelza pointed out, it was their duty to be with her on this first Christmas after. Elizabeth was going with Geoffrey Charles, so that the family could be all together in this way, yet in a house and a locality with no memories.

At the last moment, to everyone's surprise and to Demelza's private relief, Elizabeth changed her plans. Her mother had been ill again, and she decided she must spend it at Cusgarne, her old home outside Truro. She told Ross of this when he paid her his weekly visit four days before Christmas.

His call was later than usual and he found her at supper, eating by herself in the winter parlour. He sat at the table talking to her, noticing how scanty the food was, refusing some himself. This room, the most used, was the most shabby. She looked tired and ill tonight, her delicacy suddenly fragile. Aunt Agatha was no better and seemed likely to become bedridden. An added strain of carried meals and all the other sickroom attentions. Tabb worked eighteen hours a day in the fields, and Mrs Tabb looked after the few animals they had retained. Ross could estimate the amount Elizabeth would have to do.

Afterwards he went upstairs, treading the dark corridors to Aunt Agatha's room. By the light of two candles Aunt Agatha was interviewed, propped up in bed, her bright beady eyes winking in the candlelight, plying him with ceaseless questions whose answers she could not hear, running off into long strings of reminiscence out of a past dead and buried for everyone but herself. She told Ross she was ninety-seven and was determined to live to be a hundred. Whether the age was right or not, he didn't at all put it past her to have a good try. She might be sinking, as Elizabeth thought, but she still had a long way to sink.

So Christmas came, Christmas Day being on a Tuesday and very windy and cold. In the night there had been flakes of snow, but these cleared before the day came. A fateful season, with Pitt calling out the militia, and associations of yeomen and gentry and shopkeepers everywhere being formed. And the French in Antwerp now, glowering across the Scheldt estuary, held in check only by a British guarantee of the Netherlands.

Ross, eating his Christmas dinner with the Blameys – Andrew, Verity's husband, on leave from his ship, and the two children of his first marriage, James a midshipman, boisterous and warmhearted, and Esther as reserved as her brother was open – Ross stared across the grey wind-flecked water of Falmouth Harbour, pondered on the prospects of war and whether he should go to France himself to find Mark Daniel while there was still peace; and who his benefactor was; and how he might discharge his own ethical debt to Elizabeth and to Geoffrey Charles.

And fifteen miles away his benefactor was eating an even quieter meal of roast beef and plum pudding in company with her uncle, her crisp auburn hair subdued into a tight coil, as her nature had been subdued these last weeks. When she came back from Truro, Ray Penvenen had told her of his interview with Dwight. They had quarrelled, uncle and niece, as he had expected that they should; but, rather to his own surprise, she had suddenly capitulated and there had been a semi-affectionate reconciliation. No definite undertaking on her part – he did not expect it – but the outcome was as he desired. For a time he was a trifle suspicious of his victory, and he still kept a watch on her movements through one or another of the servants; but he had slowly come to the conclusion that he had stamped on the attachment just in time. He expected to go to London in early February, and he proposed that Caroline should accompany him. She showed no splendid enthusiasm for the idea, but at least she raised no objection; and Mr Penvenen was privately determined that she should not return. He had a sister in London, married to a rich merchant, with seven children of her own. It would do her no harm in the world to have an eighth for a while.

And Dwight Enys dined alone and later than the rest, having been out and making the most of his time while the daylight lasted. Lottie Kempthorne, Charlie's eldest girl, who was nine, had developed the smallpox and was very ill. An ominous occurrence. This year, except for a high mortality from an outbreak of measles in June, there had been no serious epidemics. A disagreeable way of entering the new year, with one of the worst plagues to combat. While Dwight was in the cottage, he noticed Lottie's younger sister May playing with a new kind of story book. It was called *The History of Primrose Prettyface* and was printed on good stiff paper and bound between covers of horn. As he ate his dinner, he tried to remember where he had seen another such book; but his mind soon turned to thoughts of Caroline.

Among presents which had come to him today was one from the Hoblyns: a finely woven scarf. On an old piece of ruled exercise paper was printed: '*From Rosina, with love.*' He wondered who had done this, for he knew none of them could write. Other gifts had come in kind today: eggs; a piece of bacon; two loaves of bread; a cake; six tallow candles; a woven mat – tokens of gratitude from people from whom each gift meant a real sacrifice.

... And Elizabeth. Elizabeth did not spend Christmas Day at Cusgarne after all.

She found her mother less ill than she had expected, but did not on that account feel any less obliged to stay with them as planned.

But at noon a message came from George Warleggan saying he had just heard of her being there and inviting them all to the new Warleggan country house, Cardew, where he was entertaining a few close friends over the week-end. Mrs Chynoweth, reluctant to venture out, pressed acceptance on Elizabeth with glowing descriptions of its magnificence. Elizabeth struggled with her sense of duty and turned the invitation down. At two George himself arrived, having come to fetch her. So, rather to her own surprise, on this gusty cheerless day with a half-gale blowing itself out, she found herself sharing his carriage, having left Geoffrey Charles in the care of her parents.

Cardew, begun to Nicholas Warleggan's requirements only ten years ago, she found all that it was reputed to be:

a house with an enormous Ionic portico, lavishly furnished public rooms with massive fireplaces and moulded ceilings, and thirty-five bedrooms, beside staff quarters, gun rooms, workshops, stillrooms, stables, greenhouses, and walled gardens. In the front of the house the grounds had been laid out to give an uninterrupted view of an artificial lake with a rolling parkland beyond.

The house made Trenwith look like a country cottage and Cusgarne more down-at-heel than ever. And after Cusgarne it was so warm and draughtless. George derived enormous pleasure from showing Elizabeth over it all, a fact not unremarked by the other members of the Warleggan clan. There were about two dozen guests in the house, people carefully chosen by Mr Nicholas Warleggan for their likely value to him in his business or social dealings; and he would have been better pleased if George had not gone off in the middle of the day, to return with this young woman and devote the whole of his attention to her.

Had there been anything 'in it' for George, he would have felt differently. It was high time George was married, and the *right* time. There were three or four young women in their late teens whom Mr Warleggan had picked over, all eligible for one or more reasons but chiefly for title or blood connections – since George could provide the money – and Nicholas would have been pleased to see his son making some recognizable movement towards one of them. This long-standing sentimental infatuation for a delicate uninfluential widow was all wrong – especially for a woman who, even by marriage, bore the name of Poldark.

In any case, even supposing that some sort of a match were made of it – and Nicholas, knowing Elizabeth, thought the chances remote – and supposing one swallowed the disappointment of such a poor match, Elizabeth, with only one child by her former marriage and he eight years old, was unlikely to be fecund; and above all things Nicholas wanted to see several stout grandchildren about the house. He wished that it had been Elizabeth who had fallen down the mine instead of Francis.

Thought of the Poldarks took his eye round to his brother Cary, talking in a corner to the younger Boscoigne. Cary was becoming a responsibility to the more respectable members of the family. Being closely concerned in much of the Warleggan financial structure, he could not be pushed into the background like Grandfather Warleggan, yet in his dress and in his manners he refused to advance with Nicholas and George. He could not be induced to wear a wig or to discard his skullcap or to keep his old coats free from snuff and ink stains. By his presence he brought one down to his level. Tony Boscoigne must be secretly laughing at him now, perhaps taking note of his peculiarities so that he could ape them afterwards to his friends. It was useless having a fine house and all the splendour that money could buy if one had to countenance such relatives.

And Cary's influence on George was constantly a bad one. Neither of them realized as he, Nicholas, did the tremendous importance of personal and commercial probity. Establish that name, that reputation, and within the limitations of ordinary finance you could accomplish anything. Cary's only concern was to gain his end and let the principles go hang.

Nicholas thought of their recent meeting when Harris Pascoe had called upon them with young Poldark's draft in settlement of the promissory note. As it happened they had all been in the building, and Cary had stormed in to him with a face so white he had supposed him ill. There and then, with Harris Pascoe waiting in an outer office, they had had a passionate scene. Cary had fairly ranted, and George, though he controlled himself better, had really felt little different. It had taken all his own personal influence to calm Cary down, to persuade them both that this was nothing more than a normal business setback and should be treated as such. Indeed, no money was lost at all; money was made, for Mr Pearce had parted with the bill at a discount; and it would be beneath their dignity as men of affairs to be put out of countenance over some loss of revenge on an impoverished and unimportant country squire. They had long been too big for that. It did not become them.

So far as George was concerned, Nicholas was satisfied he had won his point; but with Cary one could never be certain. One supposed he was conforming to an agreed line, and then suddenly he would do something quite heterodox which showed he had never had any intention of acquiescing at all.

Ross nursed his own special problem through Christmas and nearly into the New Year. Then he went to see Harris Pascoe. He wanted first of all, he said, to sell his remaining thirty shares in Wheal Leisure. He had made six hundred pounds out of the last and expected no less from these. Pascoe grunted and shook sand over a document. 'I suppose you have to do it? It's a pity now. War's almost certain. This bringing of the King to trial will inflame tempers on both sides. Copper will be rising in price all the time.'

'I am not compelled to do it, I want to do it. Perhaps you can get more than six hundred for the shares.'

'It's a tidy price. I s-suppose you will use the money in some way to keep your other mine alive?'

'No. I'm reconciled to the loss of that. I want the money for a special purpose. I want to leave it in your hands for the moment. Since you consented to act for an anonymous client once, you can hardly refuse to do so again.'

Pascoe stared at his lean visitor, who at times was coming to have a wolfish look.

'I don't follow you.'

'Francis's widow and his family are in dire poverty. More so now than we are. And she has no man. Two years ago Francis sank his last six hundred pounds in Wheal Grace. I feel a sting of responsibility for the result. I want Elizabeth Poldark to have that six hundred pounds back.'

'And will she accept it?'

Ross brooded for a moment. 'No. Or I think not. That's where I want your help. When my shares in Leisure are sold, I want you to make her an offer for her holding – or her son's holding – in Wheal Grace, on behalf of an anonymous client you represent. She's bound to accept that, and the money can then be transferred to her.'

Ross watched the sleet melting and trickling down the windows. The old year was true to its reputation to the last.

He added: 'It's not an original idea, being cribbed from your friend who used it on my behalf.'

Mr Pascoe blew the sand away and shook his document backwards and forwards to be sure it was dry. 'You mean you are offering £600 for a half share in a mine which is about to close?'

'We are not closed yet, of course. The miracle may always happen.'

'And do you suppose your cousin-in-law will b-believe some stranger is foolish enough to make such an offer?'

'Could I believe anyone was foolish enough to accept a renewal of my promissory note?'

Mr Pascoe coughed. 'No . . .'

There was another silence. Pascoe's eyes moved to the clock. 'You'll take dinner with us?'

'Thank you.'

They got up. Pascoe said: 'As your banker and your creditor, I must try to dissuade you from making this quixotic move. F-frankly I consider it ill-advised. You can't afford it. Indeed you can't. This is the *only* money you have.'

'I can't afford it,' said Ross. 'And – I have my own wife to keep and my own son to care for. But I'm here to look after them myself. Francis is not. If I do this, I shall order my life with a clearer conscience.'

'Would it not be as satisfactory if you made over your *income* from the Leisure shares, I mean temporarily, until things improve for Mrs Poldark. One never quite knows how circumstances change. It wouldn't be a lot for her, no big lump sum, but it would mean a regular payment every quarter.'

'No,' said Ross. 'It would not be as satisfactory.'

Harris Pascoe went over to a side cupboard beside the window and took a decanter and two glasses from it. 'I did not s-suppose that any advice I chose to give you would be heeded.'

Ross rubbed his chin. 'Your advice is always welcome, Harris. Like your friendship, I know its solid value. But in these matters where blood and sinew come into it and sometimes affection and dislike, we have to behave according to the chemicals in us. This act would give us satisfaction and that would not. So we do things, make moves which can't seem sensible to an onlooker such as yourself.

But always it's good to have someone by who points steadily to magnetic north. That's what you do. And we remember it with gratitude, even when we remember it too late.'

Harris Pascoe clinked his glass as he poured out the canary. 'I will, of course, do what I can to help you, Ross. I cannot withhold that, though I withhold my approval. It is a very honourable gesture you are making. I hope you'll not come to regret it.'

The Fox and Grapes was a small rather lonely posting inn midway between Killewarren and Redruth. In it, at about this time, two other people were also drinking canary and making plans.

Fifteen minutes before, Caroline Penvenen and her groom had ridden up; and Caroline had said she wanted some refreshment and some shelter from the weather and he must go on ahead of her and assure the Teagues that she would be with them very shortly. The lad looked uncomfortable, hot, and reluctant to go, part betraying his secret instructions from his master; so Caroline impatiently told him to wait outside for her; she would rejoin him when her thirst was quenched.

In the little dark parlour of the inn with its framed needlework pictures, its Indian fern, and its pewter mugs, she peeled off her gloves and stood a moment warming her hands by the fire, uncertain whether the arrangement had worked out as planned. She had seen no horse outside, but it would be a common precaution to tether it out of sight. As the innkeeper's wife came bustling in with the wine, she drew a breath to ask; and then she saw two glasses on the tray and Dwight standing on the threshold of the door.

Very soon they were in each other's arms. A cynic would have noted the sharp advance in their relationship since Mr Penvenen's move. Caroline perhaps would have taken the same course in any event, but without opposition she might have been months longer taking it. Instead at the moment she was making the running, and Dwight was giving her her head – willingly and happily as to destination but doubtfully as to course. Perhaps something of the convict in his mind showed in his expression, for abruptly she broke away and said:

'Do you not feel as I do? I should be sorry to go too fast and too far.'

'Neither, my darling, for that would be impossible. I – only wonder as to method. By nature I dislike secrecy – as I know you do – if it can be avoided. I should like to go to your uncle now and tell him what we intend . . .'

'You don't know Uncle Ray. He has a streak of obstinacy common to all the Penvenens. But is there perhaps some special reason for your disliking the idea of an elopement?'

'Why d'you ask?'

'Because I feel there is.'

He came behind her chair, put his hand on her forehead. 'It's such a poor reason that I'm ashamed of it. You've heard of Keren Daniel?'

'The girl who . . .'

'Yes, the girl I fell in love with, though she was a patient of mine – the girl whose husband, Mark Daniel, found her unfaithful . . . and killed her – when he should have come to kill me.'

'Do you know, I heard a different version – that she threw herself at your head, etc. I can always be sure of one thing, Dwight, that your charity, which covers so much, never extends to yourself.'

'One version or the other, the facts are not in dispute. A man of my profession who acts as I acted is entitled to consider himself very low.' Dwight was going to move away, but she caught his hand on her shoulder. 'People were kind – charitable as you call it. The version that you heard has become the accepted one. Sometimes I accept it myself. But there is a stigma still. Therefore one's future conduct becomes of the greatest moment . . .'

'And marrying me . . .'

'Marrying you openly would set a seal on my happiness – yes, and on my respectability too – that I don't deserve – but gladly take. Marrying you in secret, running away with you at night – though I willingly, gladly take that too – smacks a little of the fortune hunter, of the morally equivocal person which my affair with Keren suggests I really am. To leave also all my friends and patients without a word hints at desertion too, a desertion vastly different from the affair of Keren but not altogether different in effect . . .'

He broke off and covered her hand with his other one. It lay quiescent between his, but he did not delude himself that that signified quiescence on Caroline's part. He had said more than he intended.

She said quietly enough: 'Do you liken me to Keren?'

'Good God, no! You're as far apart—'

'Isn't this really, truly, something in yourself, Dwight? Haven't you to overcome it in any case? Nowhere I've been have I heard a word of blame for you in Keren's death. She threw herself at every man. Why should anyone think worse of you for marrying me?'

'Not marrying you, no—'

'Or of running away with me.' She withdrew her hand but not angrily. 'Dwight, you may feel I'm unreasonable in

171

not doing as you want – but I have such a strong instinct that the other way is right. If we come out into the open before we go – now, with a whole month to wait, there will be all manner of complications, new difficulties to face. It will mean leaving my uncle's house, breaking with him directly; and although I know I can do that, I don't want to. I don't at all want to if it can be avoided. Although I pretend to care nothing what he thinks, my ties are really quite strong. I owe him things which I should not if he were my father ... If we leave in secret, run away, he will be furious. He will denounce us both in the strongest possible language. But he will denounce us only to himself, for there will be no one else to say it to. Nothing will be said to us which it would be impossible for his dignity's sake to withdraw. Nor should I say anything definite, final, wounding, as I should if confronting him to his face. This way, with luck, there should be nothing to stop a reconciliation in six or twelve months. He will accept what cannot be undone. But the other way there would be a "if-you-leave-this-house-you-leave-it-for-ever" scene, and his pride would prevent him from retracting.'

Dwight was silent, and was silenced. There was nothing to advance against this. It was true what Caroline said, that his reluctance was something he must personally fight and overcome. In any case, it was manifestly unfair to burden her with the aftereffects of an old love affair – for it was nothing more than that. He liked her better not less well for her loyalty to the old man, which was something she had not betrayed until it came to the point of defying him. Like most of her feelings, she had kept it well hidden.

Dwight still woke up sometimes with a sense of incredulity that this brilliant, vital young woman had consented to marry him at all. She was giving up so much to do so. It would be a measure of his own smallness and ingratitude if he queried her way of doing it.

A week later Elizabeth sent a message that she wanted to see Ross. He rode to Trenwith in the teeth of a northwest-erly gale. When he got there, he thought he had never known the old house so empty. The wind howled down the big open chimney in the hall, loose panes in the great window rattled ceaselessly, a worn mat by the door floated and flapped in the air current. Human life and warmth had gone from the place.

Elizabeth was upstairs, and he watched her come down the broad staircase in that swift, lightfooted way she had made peculiarly her own. She was wearing a little white masculine jacket over her tight-waisted grey dress. She saw his eyes light up at the sight of her.

'Ross.' She offered him her hand. 'Please come in. I am sorry to have brought you from your work. But I want to know what I must do.'

He followed her into the winter parlour, and she took up two letters from beside the spinning wheel. She gave him the first. Although he knew very much what its contents were, he went through it carefully, interested to see just how Pascoe had worded the thing. When he'd finished, he looked up at her.

'Well, isn't it astonishing?' she said. 'That anyone should offer us – at this stage – as much for my share in Wheal Grace as Francis first put into it? Has there been some new discovery of ore?'

'None. I wish there had. It's strange, I agree. Indeed, it's hard to understand. Everyone knows we must finish soon. And Pascoe says he may not disclose who it is. You had this yesterday?'

'Yes.' She hesitated, lashes dark on her cheek. 'My first thought was George Warleggan. You know of his attempts to help me. Indeed I think he tries to make things better for me just as persistently as he tries to make them worse for you. And I thought that by buying these shares he was perhaps seeking both ends at the same time . . . So I wrote to Mr Pascoe – sent it in by Tabb yesterday. Tabb waited for an answer.'

She offered him the second letter. 'Dear Madam,' Ross read, 'I thank you for your communication delivered to me today. I am able to assure you that, should you and Captain Poldark decide to sell your son's holding in Wheal Grace, the interest will not pass to any member of the Warleggan family nor to anyone representing them. The prospective buyer is an independent gentleman with your son's and your own best interests at heart. There will be no attempt to interfere with the present control of the mine. I have the honour to be, madam, Your obedient servant, Harris Pascoe.'

Ross handed the letter back. She was watching him closely, and he had to say something. 'Extraordinary.'

'And what do you advise? I do not know if we should consider it.'

'Consider it? We should accept the offer.'

'That surprises me too. I thought you would fear interference from an outsider.'

'In other circumstances I should. But there is Pascoe's letter. And I have to tell you of a certain good fortune which has come to me recently.' He explained about the anonymous loan to himself. 'I can only suppose the same person is trying to help you. Some eccentric with the Poldark good at heart ... He could not have come at a more opportune time.'

'Have you any idea who it might be?'

'None at all. But I trust Pascoe. I know he would not betray us into any false position.'

The tightness of her waist emphasised the shape of her small breasts as she turned away from him. 'I – this money would of course make all the difference.'

'We should be out of our minds not to take it – for Geoffrey Charles's sake. There's little prospect for the mine unless this newcomer will invest fresh money. He may have some such idea. If so it can only be to my benefit. I shall hope to meet him.' Ross thought he was coming through the interview rather imaginatively. But not without a curious feeling as if he were cheating Elizabeth instead of helping her at great cost to himself. He had not told Demelza what he'd done, and he hoped it would be a long time before she found out.

Elizabeth said: 'You're sure you feel this is right, Ross – for yourself, I mean? Perhaps you are pretending to like this because you believe it is best for us. I should dislike to think I was being false to our friendship.'

'You're not being false to anything, Elizabeth. I mean what I say. You should sell. It will enormously ease your position. I'm only grateful to you for hesitating, for your loyalty and for your interest all through.'

She smiled across at him with a new brilliance. 'Loyalty's not all on one side, Ross, nor ever has been. Thank you for coming this morning.'

He rode home feeling already well paid for his sacrifice but with the old allegiance grievously reaffirmed.

Chapter Seven

Mr Coke, the Warleggans' nominee, bought the shares, at £22 10s a share.

After paying Pascoe £600 for Elizabeth, Ross had £75 over. This he could put to the reduction of one of his other debts or could set aside for future interest payments. Or he could buy another month's supply of coal and keep Grace going through February.

Henshaw said: 'I think 'twould be a pity to hang on longer than we'd planned. I'm so disappointed as you, except that my loss is a hundred and not six. But there's such a thing as a feel about a mine. She've been awkward from the start. I'd never have believed the poorness of the yield.'

'We shall get little enough for the engine. I shall feel tempted to dismantle it and keep it for the time.'

'There's never been a *sign* of the Trevorgie lode,' said Henshawe, his eyes frowning at the map. 'I do believe 'twas an old wives' tale from first to last. First we drove seeking it from Leisure, and then from Grace. If 'twas there at all, we should have found some sign of it.'

'And Mark Daniel,' said Ross broodingly. 'All our prophets have been false.'

'D'you think he was in his right mind that night you speak of?'

'He may have been deceived by one or two of the false

176

promises that raised our hopes. There was that fine deposit in the northeast end of the thirty level . . .'

'Copper £103 a ton last week.' Henshawe bit the nail of his little finger. 'When we started Leisure, 'twas only £80. 'Twas a crying pity you had to sell your Leisure shares just now. I reckon we shall make a little fortune out of her before we're done . . . If there was any *quality* in the stuff we'd raised from Grace . . .' He took his finger out of his mouth and stared at it.

'What were yesterday's assays from the seventy level?'

'Copper, tin, silver, lead; some of each; not enough of any. 'Tis as if the lodes have gotten mixed, contaminated like. The copper's *less* both in quality and quantity than it was ten fathoms nearer grass.'

Ross lifted a piece of the ore-bearing rock, turned it over and over in his hand. 'I fancy there's more tin than anything in this.'

'Copper lodes often do peter out that way.'

'What happens farther down still? The fault will not disappear, surely. Isn't there a chance of a renewal of copper at increased depth?'

Henshawe shook his head. 'Nobody knows how the earth was made. Some do say that the sea runs far inland and underground and makes the springs, forcing them along and up, like to the blood of a man's veins. So the copper runs too, like to a bone or a sinew, and then stops for reasons we know naught of . . . She've been a grievous disappointment; but if I was you, I should not throw good money after bad.'

Ross stared out of the half-shuttered window. The pale, grey January light fell on the scar half hidden by the hair growing down in front of his ear. All the old disquiet in his face today. The old rebellion against the pressure of inanimate things, the stubborn secret anger. You could never get away from it, Henshawe thought, something inborn.

'How would it be this last month,' Henshawe said, trying to remove the look, 'if we drove down again – not exactly starting an eighty level, but following these poor indications as if they was good and seeing what another ten fathoms have to show. I don't give much for the prospect; but 'twould perhaps settle a query in your mind, like.'

'How long *can* we go on, with no fresh capital?'

'If this next parcel of ore fetch what the last did, I'd say three weeks. Of course if we closed the deeper level, I'd say two or three weeks more than that.'

'Your money's in as well as mine. I can't decide for us both.'

'You've six times my stake, sur. I'll abide by what you say.'

'Yet you're the mining man.'

'There's little or no mining in this now. 'Tis instinct so much as anything, and your instinct's so good as mine.'

'Very well,' said Ross after a moment. 'We'll go down.'

When Henshawe had gone, Ross stayed in the old library for an hour or more, checking entries in the cost book. Presently, it being reckoning day, a file of miners formed outside and came in one by one, made their marks in the book against their names, and received the money due to them. Almost all of them had their own private marks, few being content with the conventional cross. All of them knew that in a matter of weeks they would come here for the last time. Ross had a word for each one, often a joke or a wry comment. They were not his chief friends, most of whom he had engaged at Wheal Leisure when opening it; but they had become his friends during the last year.

When the last had left he still stayed on, though it was well after two. Again and again he weighed up the samples of ore, comparing what had been raised this week with what had been mined last. Several times he took up a hammer and split pieces off. Once he nearly went through the floor in doing so. It was as well that he was not immediately above the cache, which had been made at the far end of the room under the last window. Where the trap door had been cut two big metal trunks stood, hiding the joins in the floor boards.

That reminded him, he must see Mr Trencrom, for Mr Trencrom was not playing fair. The storage place had been made on the strict understanding that goods should be put there for a limited time only – three or four days at the most until they could be carried away. There were things in there now, a roll of fancy lace and ten five-gallon casks of Geneva rum which had been left more than three weeks. That wasn't good enough.

At that moment Demelza called him from the front door, and he put his head out and answered her. The house being L-shaped, he let himself out of the end door, slipped its padlock on, and was about to walk across the garden when he saw Will Nanfan coming down the valley.

Will was an old friend. For the time he was comfortably off, with a small holding, five grown children, and a pretty second wife. He was a big fair man in his fifties, still handsome, and played the fiddle.

'Good day, sur, I'm glad to find ee in. I thought 'twould be a good time to call.'

'Come inside, Will. You have news for me?'

'Yes, but I'll not come in if 'tis all the same to you. I just dropped by to tell ee we've found Mark Daniel.'

Ross looked up sharply. 'Found him? At Cherbourg?'

'No, sir, not at Cherbourg. He's in Ireland.'

Ross stared across at the mine chimney on the hill. It was throwing out black smoke, which meant inefficient firing. He did not speak.

'That's why we couldn't seem to trace 'im. The people he'd been with said he'd left, but they'd no notion where. Nine months ago there was a deal o' trouble in Cherbourg. All this kick an' sprawl over the revolution. There was house burning and what not. Folk began to look askance at Mark, him being a foreigner; so he bested to go to Ireland, and slipped away in one of the Irish ketches that run goods over from time to time. He's living, they d'say, in Galway; or 'twas some such outlandish name.'

'How did you find this out?'

'Got talking with the skipper o' one of the ketches. He's a friend of Mark's, it 'pears. We do business wi' the Irish vessels, upon times. They run into the Scillies same as we do; they've depots to leave goods there same as we 'ave. They haven't the size, y'know, and often come back that far laden to the gunnels.'

Ross said: 'When will you be seeing this man again?'

'O'Higgins? Next week, like as not. The *One and All* will not be sailing till near the end of the month, but I'm takin' the cutter over to the Scillies on Monday if the weather d'lift.'

'Will you give him a message from me?'

'I've already said for him to tell Mark Daniel ye are wanting to see him.'

'Good. I'll send a note to Mark. Someone will read it to

him, even if it's the priest. Come in here.' Ross unlocked the door of the library again and went over to the desk.

Demelza, who had been occupying her waiting time giving Jeremy his food, got up and went to the window just as Nanfan left the library. When Ross came across, he looked preoccupied but not displeased. They ate the meal in silence for a time, the sole conversationalist being Jeremy, who was intelligible only to himself.

Ross told her the purpose of Will Nanfan's visit. Demelza said simply: 'I'm glad we shall know.'

'Yes. I'd been afraid perhaps he was dead. It's so long.'

'Shall you get him to come here?'

'I've asked him to meet me in the Scillies. There's less danger for him there, and I'm sure he'll come.'

'And how shall you get there?'

'I may pay a fishing boat to run me out from Penzance. Or I can go when Trencrom makes his next run.'

'You won't be quite so sure, that way, as bringing Mark to the mine. I'm sure he'd be willing to come.'

'He would. But a half-hour's conversation, with a plan of the workings, is all I need. I shall know then just what he was talking about and where it is likely to be found.'

Lottie Kempthorne was a great deal better. As Charlie put it: 'She have very good symptoms upon her now, and the smallpox are coming out kindly.' Dwight watched the other child but there was as yet no sign. Nor was there another case in the village. It seemed too good to be true. He called in one afternoon and was not at all pleased to find Rosina Hoblyn and her mother there.

Charlie was in high spirits, and after a few moments Dwight learned why. Rosina, with her father's glowering

permission, had at last promised to marry Charlie. At this
Dwight glanced a little in surprise at Rosina, and she
flushed. He had never thought her enamoured of her
middle-aged suitor, and he was not convinced now. She
was following the line of least resistance, edged by his
persuasions down the path he wanted her to follow, her
father softened for his part by what Charlie could offer
her.

It might well turn out a happy marriage. This cottage,
with the improvements Charlie had made, was lighter and
much more comfortable than the one she would leave.
And apparently she would no longer need to spend her
whole day over a needle. Even as she was now, with her
lovely face and unhalting walk, the chances were that any
other offer she might get would come from some callow
boy earning five or six shillings a week with only a tumble-
down shed to offer her for a home.

All the same, thought Dwight, there might have been
love and youth between them; and even if the glow lasted
only a short time, it was not, in this drab world, a thing to
be lightly sacrificed. He knew that.

'We reckon,' said Charlie, 't'build on another room
next year, so's Lottie an' May can sleep to theirselves. Then
Rosina and me, if mebbe we get a family increase, can have
things fitty and proper, like.'

Dwight glanced round the room. He was not an obser-
vant man in the ordinary way of things, and the slow
changes which had taken place inside this cottage during
the last eighteen months were suddenly apprehended by
him as if they were the work of recent weeks. The new
curtains, the good earthenware cups, the matting at the
door, the candles in suitable sticks, the glass in the window.
He looked at Kempthorne, and Charlie, who by some

instinct had been driven to look at him, quickly lowered his eyes.

'I hope you'll be very happy,' Dwight said.

'And we hope you'll come to our wedding,' said Charlie quickly. 'Don't us, Rosina? Why, all we have we owe to surgeon. Rosina's lipsy leg cured. And me with my consumptives. If it edn been for that, I should never be living a decent life and making money from my sail-making.'

'And now Lottie on the mend,' said Mrs Hoblyn.

'When do you expect to have your wedding?' Dwight asked.

'Next month, sur. Banns aren't called yet, and 'twill take a little time for to get things ready. Lottie'll be out an' about 'fore then.'

'Oh, yes, she'll be out and about before then.' If the miracle happened and no one else caught it. Charlie was still watching him. Charlie was a mystery: good-natured, friendly as a dog, always working, always smiling, always grateful for what you did. He never allowed anyone to forget, in Dwight's hearing, that he owed his good health to the surgeon. Yet Dwight, more especially of late months, was not quite comfortable in his presence. In a crisis he felt he would sooner trust the slow scowl of Jacka Hoblyn than the ready show of Charlie Kempthorne's yellow teeth.

On his arrival home he did not see Bone about; and his visitor's horse was tethered round the side of the house, so that he walked into the parlour unsuspecting.

She was standing by the window, tall and straight as a lance, and she turned at once smiling at him.

'Caroline . . . Is something the matter?'

'Everything is the matter. I have surprised your secret life! *"From Rosina, with love."* Is that how your patients address you?'

She handed him the scarf that Rosina had made for him, to which the printed note was still pinned. He accepted it but put it over the back of a chair, took her hands.

'You should have sent a message, my love. Have you been allowed out without your faithful groom?'

'No, I gave him the slip. I mustn't stay long.'

'It's *more* than good to see you. Let me look at you. Always when you are away from me . . .'

'There is a complication to report, and I came to report it. Uncle Ray has advanced our departure for London by one week. He now proposes to leave Killewarren on the third of February.'

He stared at her. 'We can put forward our own going by a couple of days, then. That's all. It will mean a slight arrangement, but we can leave on the first.'

'Have you heard again from Paul Hardwicke?'

'Yes. He thinks there will be a clear opening in the town when Dr Marquis retires. Until then it should not be difficult, he says, to find full occupation in temporary work. He counsels against my setting up on my own.'

'No doubt there is a certain cliquishness among the apothecaries. Dwight, I think it would be a good thing if we fixed our going for the second. If I am supposed to be leaving for London on the morning of the third, it will make my packing that much easier. Instead of escaping with a bundle through a top window in the approved fashion, I can get my trunks downstairs and safely stowed in the coach.'

'Do you still very much insist on going in – your own coach?'

'Of course. Why are you so much against it? Because it looks as if *I* am running away with *you*?'

He frowned uncomfortably. 'Not altogether. But I – well I have a feeling for providing the means of travel. It's going to be a moot point with us many times in the future, no doubt; I shall have to accustom myself to having a wife with a will and money of her own—'

'Especially a will.'

' – but in the first instance I should have better preferred us to travel by my arrangement and at my expense. I admit there is no logic to it.' He smiled. 'You have the coach – why shouldn't it be used? But—'

'Why not indeed? Once we have left Cornwall no one is to know it is not your coach. I shall certainly not say any different.'

Bone could be heard outside, raking the gravel path near the front door. The interview could not last much longer, and they talked on at an accelerated pace. This meeting might be their last before they met to be married, but he would not kiss her.

'I care nothing for poxes, small, large, or cow,' said Caroline. 'But I am bitterly jealous of your Rosina – still Hoblyn by name if no longer hobbling by nature. A nice scarf, if a thought coarse for a gentleman. I chanced to see her only last week when I happened to be in Sawle. Pretty enough, I grant you. I hope you will not jilt me, dear.'

'I think I am a little sensitive to such jokes,' said Dwight, taking the scarf from her again, 'and therefore hope you'll not make them. If there is any jilting, it will be on your side, and you know it. I shall not rest easy until you wear a ring on your finger and I have put it there.'

'So long as it is not a ring through my nose, you may put it there as soon as you can.'

She began to pull on her gloves. He had gone over to a side table, a trifle put out by what she had said although he tried not to be. She followed him with her eyes, which were a little doubting under their mockery.

'You do not regret making this move, Dwight?'

He turned at once. 'Heavens, no! How could I regret it?'

'Often since we decided to go I have noticed a discomfort in you, an unease, call it what you wish.' She threw back her hair to tie her own scarf. 'Is it still against your principles?'

'No, nor ever was. Believe me, please.' He stared at her and then half laughed himself. 'You're incorrigible, Caroline. For a moment I believed you were serious. You must rate me for having so literal a mind.'

'I think,' said Caroline acutely, 'that you would not have taken it seriously if it had not been a serious consideration in your thoughts.'

'Utter nonsense. I could shake you.' He took her by the elbows but only held her firm. 'Caroline, look at me. I love you. Does that mean anything to you? Does it mean *anything* at all?'

'Oh, yes, quite a certain amount, I assure you.'

'That's an admission anyhow. Then perhaps you'll not goad me with these strange doubts which you put into my mind ready-made. It's very mischievous of you – and a little unfair. We are utterly agreed as to the end – how could I have second thoughts as to that? – and as to the method, what doubts I had I voiced long since and have now forgotten.'

She put her gloved fingers up to his stock, patted it, then allowed her hand to travel affectionately down the line of his cheek.

'I'm sorry if I plague you so grievously. It is only that sometimes I wonder when the "end in view" has become a commonplace, sitting at your fireside and sharing your bed and never absent from your table, I wonder whether then you will not perhaps sigh for your Cornish patients and your lost integrity.'

'Can I say more than no? And why should the doubts be all on your side? What of you, throwing away thirty or forty thousand pounds for a down-at-heel physician? When the first excitement's failed and the novelty's over and it means living to an economy you've never been used to ... not able to keep up with the rich people of Bath, hunting to a restricted purse, dressing and entertaining at the same rate.'

'In the first place, as you know, I do not suppose I am throwing away thirty or forty thousand pounds, not if we arrange to quarrel at a distance and leave loopholes for reconciliation. My uncles bark worse than they bite, and they have no one else to leave their money to except a hatch of nephews and nieces who're already well provided for. But if they do remain estranged and will their money to the Astronomical Society, I shall certainly not complain and shall think the exchange a fair one. I intend to live my life in my own way and shall not be bribed by them into remaining their domestic tabby. It will do me *good*, Dwight, to stand on my own feet, and I want you to help me ...'

'I'll help you, my darling,' he said. 'I think perhaps we shall have to help each other.'

Chapter Eight

A half-hour's conversation might be all Ross needed with Mark Daniel; but the arrangements for such a conversation, and its venue on one of a group of wind-swept islands well out in the Atlantic in mid-winter, needed a margin on either side to allow for delays. Ross estimated he would be away a week.

A message had arrived from Mark that he was willing to come. Ross had suggested the twenty-ninth of January as an approximate date, because Trencrom had said the *One and All* would leave on the twenty-eighth and they could drop him off at St Mary's the following day and pick him up on their return. Mark had agreed to the twenty-ninth, but, with his own journey in an Irish ketch even more dependent on wind and weather than Ross's, he might well be days early or late.

With such news Ross decided to risk his last £75 on the purchase of coal. What had seemed a useless gesture now looked a fair business risk.

As the month neared its end political crisis again overshadowed the personal worries of men. The long-drawn trial of Louis the Sixteenth had ended in a sentence of death. There was still chance of a reprieve, but few really believed it would come about. The Convention could hardly retract now. Changes took place in England overnight. The noisy Jacobin clubs silently closed their doors.

Arguments which had gone on for years in taproom and in coffee shop came to an end. Men waited. Some went home and looked out old fowling pieces and rubbed up relics of earlier wars.

On the twenty-fourth it was known that the execution had been carried out. That settled it. Few people in England had much admiration for Louis beyond the manner of his dying; and it was less than one hundred and fifty years since they had cut off the head of their own king; but sentiment does not derive from logic. Theatres closed, crowds demonstrated outside the Palace. The French ambassador was given his papers. Now it was only a question of time.

It was in this atmosphere that Ross took leave of Demelza on Sunday the twenty-seventh and made his way by easy stages to St Ives, where the *One and All* had been undergoing repairs. Her crew, mainly St Ann's men, had found their own way down the coast in ones and twos; and soon after six on the following morning the seventy-ton cutter slipped out on the flood tide. A thin layer of powdered frost lay on her decks and did not melt until the sun rose. It seemed to Ross, standing in the bows with the small waves lipping at the yellow gunwales as she went about, that the sun came up directly above where Nampara would be. To feel a deck under his feet again after so long was unfamiliar and exciting.

To Demelza, rising early and knowing that if things went according to plan he would be at sea before dawn, the wintry day was charged with apprehension. No study of the battered old linen map, showing the Scilly Isles far out of reach of the French regicides, was a complete reassurance. As she went about her daily work, she blamed herself for getting into the habit of worrying. It was entirely outside her nature so far as her own safety went, but with Ross the tendency had grown on her. She must check it; she must correct it. One could only wish that he was a man less prone to attract trouble.

Determined to be practical, she hummed and sang at her work all morning, and in the afternoon for the first time for months opened her spinet and played a few airs. Once she had taken lessons from Mrs Kemp, but that was in the happy days of moderate prosperity when Julia was alive. She wished she could find time and interest to take it up again. Just playing a chord sometimes gave her exquisite pleasure, it struck down into her soul, not merely heard but felt, emotion of a new kind. In the middle of this exercise Dwight Enys arrived.

When she opened the door to him he said: 'Was that you playing? I'm sorry, I'd no wish to disturb you. Is Ross in?'

His cloak was flecked with hail, though she had not noticed the shower.

'No, Dwight. He's ... from home for a day or two. Won't you come in?'

He took off his cloak and hat on the threshold and shook them. Over the hills the sky was as brown as an old blanket with the passing storm.

'Did you walk?' she asked as he followed her into the parlour.

'Yes. I came about five because I thought Ross was usually back then. I should have come days ago but have been putting it off.'

'You'll take tea? It's that cold. I wish 'twould snow and then the cold might come down.'

'Do you know when Ross will be back?'

'By Saturday, I believe. Is it something urgent?'

'Oh ... no, not urgent. Not in the ordinary sense.' Hesitating, nonplussed, Dwight sat on the edge of a chair. 'Jeremy is well?'

'Yes. Can you hear him? He has Jinny Scoble's two little boys in to play, and Jinny is minding them for me.' She turned to watch the kettle, which was making some preliminary, intermittent noises. 'I'll go fetch the teapot. I forgot to bring it in.'

When she came back, he was staring out of the window. Dusk had come suddenly, as if the sides of the valley had closed in, and the firelight flickered and glowed across the room. She thought, I wonder if he's safely there now; I wonder what the Scillies look like. She pictured them as high barren rocks. Dwight helped her to light the candles.

As the light flickered on her skin, she said: 'I know Ross wouldn't mind you knowing. You have all our other secrets, almost, so another makes small difference. He has gone with Mr Trencrom and is dropping off at the Scilly Islands to meet Mark Daniel, who has been found at last. The *One and All* will pick Ross up again and bring him home about Friday or Saturday, when they will – anchor off our cove.'

Friday was the first of February. Too late for him. 'I hope Daniel has some good news for you.'

The candles had died down to tiny pearls of light, and these now began to melt the tallow and to burn lozenge-shape.

'It seems a century since that night,' said Dwight. 'When you stood between us, you only, and Mark would have killed me. I'd have welcomed death, then, because I'd betrayed all the things I valued most and the people who trusted me.'

'We were all overwrought that night. I'm glad nothing worse happened.'

In a distant part of the house there was a bump and after a pause a giggle of children's laughter. Demelza, who had expected tears, relaxed again.

Dwight said: 'The last thing I want is to remember that time. Because I came today to see Ross to tell him that I am leaving this district very shortly . . .'

She waited for him to go on. 'Is it to do with Caroline?'

'Yes. We're to be married. But because of her uncle's opposition it must take place in secret. So we're leaving together late on Saturday night.' He went on to explain why any other solution was impossible, why they could not live here, why he owed it to her to start afresh in a town where neither of them was known. Demelza listened in silence, and her silence to his overstrained perceptions was a criticism.

She said: 'Well, I'm glad to hear it for your sake, Dwight; sorry for our own. 'Twill not be only in Sawle and Grambler that you'll be missed. We shall feel – quite lost. And Jeremy.'

'Thank you . . .'

The kettle now seemed to be bursting with steam and water, and the fire was spitting its protests. She made tea.

'I've been in correspondence with a physician who studied with me in London. He's ill and needs a change, so has agreed to come for six months on trial, with the prospect of staying. It will be far better than leaving no one at all. Wright is a good man, older than I am, but with similar views. I'm sure you will like him.'

'Yes.'

'Of course I know it will not be the same for a time. Without conceit I know that. And it means also something for me – on which I depend. I shall miss people – and of course chiefly you.' He frowned out of the window to hide his feelings. 'I want you to tell Ross, will you, how much I feel I owe to him, to you both, for your friendship. The whole thing has been a great grief to me.'

After a few moments Demelza brought him a cup of tea. 'Marrying someone you love isn't a time for grief, Dwight. The last thing Ross or I should want – or I'm sure that any of your friends would want ... Worry about us and our ailments so much as you like until Saturday. But after Saturday you should forget all that and begin your new life as if Sawle and Grambler had never been. 'Twould not be unfeeling to do that. It would be good sense.'

When Dwight had gone, Demelza cleared away the tea things. Time Jeremy was thinking of bed. Dwight's visit had left her lonelier than ever. The discussion had curiously skirted the character of the girl in the case. Ross had once predicted Caroline would wipe her feet on Dwight, but perhaps he had revised his opinion since then. Demelza knew Bath by repute. That it would suit Caroline was fairly clear. Whether Dwight would settle into the conventional pattern remained to be seen.

Strolling round the small bleak island of St Mary's, Ross waited impatiently for some sign of the Irish ketch bearing Mark Daniel. So far in two days there had been none. The winds had been contrary, veering and backing between northwest and east. An active man, and with so much at stake in this meeting, he found the time unbearably slow. Three French crabbers put into the sheltered water between St Mary's and Tresco on Tuesday when the weather was bad, but their crews did not come ashore.

Hugh Town was little more than a straggle of thatched cottages and fish cellars clutching the shore of the island where it curved in a natural harbour. Every night the new revolving oil light on St Agnes Island, only installed three years, sent out its warning to wandering ships. Previously the light had come from an oak log fire. Although in the centre of the island and eighty feet above sea level, it had sometimes been put out by the sea. For more than a hundred years now no local man had been permitted to be in charge of it, after one wreck when the fire wasn't kindled until the ship was on the rocks.

Dressed in old clothes, Ross was still conspicuous about the island, and at the tiny inn where he stayed conversation stopped whenever he came into the room. On the Wednesday he was rowed over to St Martin's and spent a couple of hours up the Beacon Tower, watching the horizon for ships. From this vantage point the multiplicity of tiny islands looked like an anchored fleet.

On the Wednesday, Mr Ray Penvenen told his niece that in view of the prospect of war he thought it better to leave for London on the Friday instead of the Sunday. He had certain banking interests, and he would prefer to be in touch with them as soon as possible. But Caroline did not like this at all. Apparently she was not ready to go. Nothing would induce her to leave before Sunday morning. If he wanted to go before, he must leave without her. After argument, in which she seemed needlessly downright, he gave way. She had been so considerate to his views in other respects that he felt he must humour her in this. Nevertheless his mind was not quite easy, and several times that evening she looked up from her reading to find his eyes on her.

On the Thursday, Dwight had to go into Truro to draw some money and to obtain letters of credit for his journey. On coming out of the bank he almost bumped into a tall fair soldier in the uniform of the Scots Greys. Such figures might soon become a commonplace of countryside and town, but this man's great moustache was familiar. Then Dwight remembered where he had seen him before – leaving the cottage of Vercoe the Customs Officer at St Ann's. It was almost twelve months ago: sometime last spring.

On Thursday afternoon a small fishing vessel appeared in Crow Sound and presently nosed her way into the quieter waters of the Road. She was fore-and-aft rigged, but she carried a large square sail on her mainmast. After about half an hour a dinghy brought a man ashore.

Chapter Nine

They had their interview in Ross's private room upstairs. Only in the middle of this room was it possible for either of them to stand upright. A fire burned in the tiny grate, flickering on the yellow stone walls and lighting an old needle-work sampler with 'God Save Our Queen' worked in red wool. The rough floor boards were covered with a home-woven rug, and threadbare heavy curtains over door and window kept out some of the draught.

A disastrous change in Mark. Once these two men, of an age and a build, had been superficially alike. Not so now. Mark's hair was white and had worn up at the temples. He was thinner, and the enormous power had gone from his hands and shoulders. He had not been able to live with his memories.

They gripped hands and sat down and passed the ordinary talk of friends who have not met for a long time. Mark was working for a boatbuilder in Galway. He had made few friends, he said, and had not married again. I d'feel I still am married,' he said. 'Nought will change that.' Ross brought out a bottle of brandy, but Mark would not touch it. 'I keep guard on my tongue,' he said. 'Night an' day. Night an' day.'

Ross told him what he could of his family, accepted messages for them all. Although the next hour would decide so much, he found he could not rush his fences.

They spoke of France and Mark's reasons for leaving it, the crisis now. Mark was more interested in England and the scenes he had left. All this life he was living now was an uneasy dream, something from which he still hoped to wake. Ross realised that he was living only for the possibility of being able to return some day to his own home. It was not an ambition in which Ross felt he could honestly encourage him. Too many people remembered, would remember for another twenty years. If he returned, the magistrates would be forced to move against him.

At length silence fell. Ross looked at the other man, who was twisting his bony knuckles and frowning. 'You know why I wanted you to come here?'

'Yes. You said in your letter, sur. I got it read. Ever since, I been tryin' to think.'

'You don't remember?'

'Oh, I mind what I said well 'nough. And I mind what I saw. But 'tis hard to remember just where I saw it. I was fair crazed that day. I wandered . . .'

'Would a plan of the workings help?'

'Oh, *yes*. 'Twould, there's no doubt.'

Ross lifted the model schooner off the plush-covered table and unrolled the plan he had brought. It was one he had drawn just before he left, carefully omitting any work which had been done since the mine reopened. A plan of a mine, so essentially a three-dimensional thing, is hard to put on paper; but he had tried to make it easier by using three colours of ink for the three levels which the old men had worked.

He spread the map carefully and pinned it down; then because Mark puckered his eyes he carried the table impatiently to the salt-rimed window, and they bent over it together. Now. Now. This was the moment. The preparation and the waiting ... But Mark was still hesitant to begin, unable to get his bearings. Never a quick thinker, the years of exile had slowed him down in every way. He could have been in his sixties instead of his early thirties. Presently, having related the plan to all the familiar landmarks above ground, he began to retrace the steps he had taken on Tuesday the twelfth of August, 1789.

A hard task, fraught with all the obstacles of bitter remembrance, on which his mind for four years had been trying to close the door. And while he struggled, Ross watched, knowing all that it meant for himself and Demelza and Jeremy. Had he been a praying man, he would have prayed now, to some deity, to some patron saint, that what this man said – some magical words he would utter – would change the picture from failure to success, would make all his striving and contriving into a sensible pattern that showed adequate return for work done, a prospect of money to be earned for money spent – no more senseless searching after a hopeless mirage, no more groping and wandering in the dark.

'I went down ... so far as I could tell there was water; then I walked – 'twould be in the thirty level – I walked – thinkin' to myself ... An' then I stopped and sat down. There was hours to spend. I thought to end everything by casting myself ... And then I went on, bearing east so far as I recollect. There's a deep gunnies here ...'

'That's so,' said Ross.

'I climbed across'n – a plank, 'alf rotten ...' He stopped. 'Ye've put a stone, sur? There was enough cash for a stone?'

'Yes. We put a stone. With the words you said. "*Keren Daniel. Wife of Mark Daniel. Age 22.*"'

He rubbed a hand across his forehead. 'Twenty-two, that's all she was. I did ought to've known better. She was but a child ... That surgeon, Enys, is he still around? I reckon 'twas he I should've killed.'

'Try to remember, Mark. What did you do then?'

Mark turned his tortured eyes back to the map. 'Well 'twas just above the gunnies, bearing right. There was an old pick down there; and to keep myself from thinking I began to cast around, just as if I was looking for a pitch to take. Soon enough, picking at the rock ... A fine bit o' ground it looked to me.'

'Where was it?' said Ross, pointing. 'Just here?'

'Yes, I reckon. There on. It ran at a steep inclination ...'

'We found it,' said Ross. 'It was good ground while it lasted, but there was no breadth. It was a foot wide where you saw it, but three fathoms down it ran as thin as paper, and above, of course, it had been stoped. Henshawe thinks it was an offshoot from the champion lode.'

There was silence. The wood crackled on the fire, and Mark Daniel breathed through his nose. 'Then I went on again. Climbin' now all the while ... An old air shaft—'

'Here,' said Ross, pointing.

''Twas filled in. I reckoned I was barely fifteen fathoms from grass. From there ye can turn two ways. I turned east.'

'This way?'

''S, I reckon. Sixty or seventy paces on you double back 'pon yourself, and in the turn ... There's a cross-course. And about it, 'tis all keenly country; mostly silver lead it 'peared to me, and iron.'

A man came up the street outside carrying a bunch of glimmering fish on the end of a stick. They looked like some exotic fruit he had plucked from the sea bed. His footsteps struck musical echoes along the cobbled street.

'You'd an amazing good eye to see it there,' Ross said grimly.

'Why?' Mark frowned at him. 'Did you . . .'

'We struck it twenty fathoms below. We've stoped all that ground. It's been our best find. The cross-course had thrown the old men out, and we picked up their copper vein forty-odd feet to the south of that turning . . . But something had gone awry with the lode just the same, for the quality's indifferent. At least it is if you have an engine to run. Perhaps in the old days it might have paid its way . . .'

Mark stared out to sea. The ketch that had brought him had already left. A week might pass before it came again.

Ross said: 'There's no hurry. We're marooned here. Take your time.'

'Nay. I'll go on now. 'Tis little more I can tell ee, I fear. I sat down an' dozed for a while, then I woke an' thought t'was dark time already an' I hastened back. But goin' back, at the big gunnies, I took the east level instead of the west. I'd went no more'n two hundred paces when I knew 'twas wrong. But I found my way back by a branch level. See here; here 'tis.'

'Yes. Yes, I see.'

'In this there's two narrow gunnies, an' betwixt them is good ground I'll wager. Ye go down over broken steps where the lode's been worked. But only the bottom's been worked. All the backs is untouched. There's fine quartzy rock, and gossan. 'Twas too high for me to get to'n, but I'd lay there was a mint o' money in that one place alone!'

Ross did not speak for a minute. He stared at the map and then got up as if to stretch his cramped muscles. He took out a handkerchief and wiped the moisture off the palms of his hands.

'And then after that you came up?'

'I waited nigh the main shaft, waited for the dark and

for Paul's light to show. I thought the day would never end . . .'

'Yes,' said Ross. 'It was an anxious time.'

Mark watched him as he moved across the room, stooping to avoid the beams. 'This last place I've told you of. Is it no betterer? Have ye proven it useless like the others?'

'Let's go for a walk, shall we? The room is close and there's no space to breathe or straighten. Fresh air will help us both.'

Mark stood up somewhat reluctantly as Ross opened the door. 'Aye, whatever you d'say, sur. But I'd be obliged if ye'd answer . . .'

'What you tell me will bear investigation, Mark, I'm sure of that. There's no doubt a deal of its promise has escaped us. I think you've given me several valuable hints.'

They said more on the way downstairs and out, until Mark seemed partly satisfied. He did not know how much depended on his answers, but he knew what was entailed in the opening of a mine, and he would have been grievously upset to fail his friend. So Ross's first concern was to hide his own feelings, and that at the moment was very hard.

He did not in fact feel that Mark had failed him – only that he himself had failed those who gave him their affection and their trust. By building so much on the chance utterances of a man crazed with rage and grief, he had brought himself to this present pass. Now, as he walked along with Mark by the side of the sea, and while the cold breeze stung his face and chilled the sweat which had broken out on him during the interview, now it seemed to him that he had known for some time that this last throw would fail. The expectation was too much. At the beginning it could have been true; but experienced miners could hardly explore the old workings for months on end and not find whatever good ground was to be found. In his heart he had feared this; but it was the old story of the drowning man and the straw.

This last discovery Mark spoke of had been the first Ross's men had found. What Mark had seen was one of those complex mixtures which abound in mineral-bearing ground; quartz in this particular case, with schorl and oxide of iron and oxide of tin. Any good miner might have expected results from it.

But the ground had hardly paid for the working.

By Saturday, Dwight had given up hope of seeing Ross again before he left. Demelza had had no word, and no one seemed to know when or where the run was expected. That was as it should be, of course. And even Mr Trencrom was dependent on wind and weather.

What Dwight did not know was that Mr Trencrom had business dealings with the owner of a farm on the windy sand dunes of Gwithian. Farrell, the master of the *One and All*, brought his vessel in close enough to be seen before darkness fell. Then he stood hastily away from the land again, for Hell's Mouth was not far off; and the farmer's son mounted an excellent pony given him by Mr Trencrom for the purpose and rode the fifteen miles to see his benefactor.

So in the early dusk there was unaccustomed movement in a number of cottages and farmhouses of the district, a quiet preparing for a night of strenuous but stealthy work. An emptying of sacks and a saddling of mules, a coiling of ropes and a fetching out of black-tarred lanterns. Here and there, too, a pistol was primed or a flintlock taken down from the wall.

But this was not the whole of the preparations going on. At St Ann's, about a cottage separated a little from the rest and overlooking the bay, other men were quietly gathering; and inside, in the living-room, the three leaders were making final arrangements: Captain McNeil, Customs Officer Vercoe, and his assistant Bell. Vercoe was titular head of this expedition, but McNeil by virtue of his rank was deferred to on all decisions of importance. He also commanded the largest part of the men at their disposal, seven dragoons.

Vercoe said: 'Well, sir, 'twill be safer to be off soon, for it would never do to be seen moving about later on when the tub-carriers are round. 'Tis a long cold time, I know.'

'It was a long cold time last night,' said McNeil. 'The colder for being fruitless. Your informer is reliable, I suppose?'

'He has been times before. He said he'd no means of knowing whether the run would be last night, tonight, or tomorrow.'

'With this latest news from London, I see no prospect of keeping my men longer than the end of the week – or of staying myself. So this is really the last chance. It would aggrieve me if this run took place elsewhere while we were watching an empty cove.'

Vercoe grunted and rubbed his beard. ''Twould grieve me more. For upwards of thirty months I've been waiting for a chance such as this, to make a big haul. If all goes well tonight or tomorrow, the whole Trade in these parts may be stamped out for a generation. That's what I'd want more than aught else!'

McNeil looked at him interestedly, wondering what

inner compulsions drove the man to make a crusade of his daily task. Then he shrugged his shoulders and rose. 'So be it. Bell, ye've impressed on your men that they do not stir till they hear Mr Vercoe's whistle? We do not want the trap to go off half cock.'

'Aye, aye, sir.'

'I'll answer for my own men, of course. And I've impressed upon them there must be no unnecessary bloodshed. Don't forget these smugglers are our own countrymen, and very soon there will be plenty of blood to let in another cause. The same dispositions as last night.'

'Aye, aye, sir.'

'Very well. We had best be starting.'

As the time for his leaving drew near, Dwight grew more and more restless. For the twentieth time he looked at the clock. It was half past nine. He had arranged to be at Killewarren at eleven. Ninety minutes to spend. There would be no possible excuse for starting for another forty-five minutes yet.

He rang for Bone, and when the young man came asked him a half dozen unnecessary questions and then dismissed him, not knowing how often before he had done the same thing. Nerves. Elopement nerves. At this moment what was Caroline doing? Would she suffer in the same way? Not from the goads of a conscience never easy for four years, but perhaps from nerves of another kind. The strong control she had of herself did not delude him into supposing her anything but highly strung.

All today Dwight had been unable to get the face of Keren Daniel out of his head. The interview with Demelza, and knowing Ross was meeting Mark, had suddenly brought Keren to the forefront of his mind. This was only a change of position, he realised that now; she had never been far away.

Sixteen minutes to ten. For Caroline he would willingly give up anything. The trouble was he was giving up nothing material; instead he was bettering himself. Self-flagellation . . . Well, that was all right to a point, but beyond that point neurotic. In two hours he would be in a coach with her. Would any of his friends deny him the right to happiness? He fancied not one. In two hours he must draw a curtain across his past life.

Bone had come into the room again. Had he rung once more in his agitation?

'If you please, sur, there's Parthesia Hoblyn at the door. Says her sister's took queer. She asked for you to go see her, but I said you was busy tonight.'

Dwight glanced at the dock. Lottie Kempthorne quite recovered. No other cases had followed, and that little short of a miracle; even May had escaped. But Rosina. How long ago? Was it possible? He counted. It was still possible. He went through into the hall and found little Parthesia slumped in a chair getting her breath. Three miles from Sawle, and she had probably run all the way in the dark.

'What is wrong with your sister?'

Parthesia got up. 'Oh, sur, 'tis her knee! But an hour gone, sur, she was climbing the cobbles and it went just like it used to go afore ever you cured it, only worse she d'say! Fathur carre'd her indoors, sur, and she was that locked we could scarce bring her to a chair, sur. So Ma says, go ee to surgeon and see if he can right it.'

Four or five minutes to ten. Sixty-odd minutes yet. Sawle on the way, a mile or so out, but that nothing on a horse. Time enough to discharge a last duty – if he wanted to, and if he could. He would greatly have preferred not. In the last week he had made a round of farewell visits, though no one else knew them as such. This call if answered . . .

But this call if *not* answered? Peace of mind on his journey to Bath? The knee locked again. If his cure had been a temporary thing, it might mean . . . But his valise, packed and ready to go. He could not ride into Sawle with it.

'Wait here,' he said to Parthesia, who had been watching him, and called Bone aside.

Bone knew everything that was planned. You could trust your confidences to him.

'I'm going with the girl,' Dwight said. 'But I can't take my bag or it will rouse comment. I want it at the gates of Killewarren by eleven o'clock. Can you do that for me?'

'Aye, sur, I'll see for it.'

'It's some miles. Perhaps you can borrow a horse.'

'Hatchard will lend me a pony if I say 'tis for you. I'll go straight over now.'

'Have a care at Killewarren. Don't let yourself be seen before I come.'

When Bone had gone, Dwight put on his cloak, his hat, stared a moment round the room, taking a last familiar look. Then he went out to join Parthesia. In another way this call was not unwelcome. It would pass the last dragging hour. The waiting was over.

Parthesia rode before him. Her added weight was nothing. A little sprite of a girl, thin of body and small of bone. It was a clear cold night, moonless, with a freckle of stars misted by high herringbone cloud. He wondered if Ross was home yet. The run was expected. Going about his work late this afternoon he had noticed one or two signs which observed in innocence would have meant nothing, but, seen with an informed eye, meant business tonight. Near Sawle they passed two men on horses who drew well off the track to allow them to pass. Dwight wished them good night, but neither replied. Their faces were hidden in thick mufflers. He felt the little girl in front of him shiver as if she was afraid they were robbers. He was a little puzzled.

In the Hoblyns' cottage Jacka was waiting with an anxious scowl. Rosina was sitting on the edge of her chair, her face still white, though she said her leg was easier. In a breath she said she'd told them not to fetch him tonight, that she'd turned her leg on one of the cobbles and it had all gone tight, that she'd thought to send up for Charlie till she recollected Charlie was ill, that Parthesia had gone off unbeknown to her, that it was leaving off the bandages that had done it and she was sure by morning . . .

Dwight put his fingers round her knee, feeling for the displacement he had found before, recognizing it again, but not certain how he had set it right. An experimental pressure had done it, some knack which, had he been able to repeat it in other cases, he would have soon perfected. But it was months now. His success had surprised him almost as much as it had anyone else. He asked her to bend her knee, but at present she could not. The joint or cartilage was right out of place. It might need fomentations and some days of manipulation. But he was leaving tonight. This was the last chance. He pressed hard with his fingers and felt her wince.

'Did you say Charlie was ill?' he asked, talking to distract her attention. 'What is the matter with him?'

'Oh, sur, you d'know that. 'Twas on account of you telling him to stay abed that he's not helping wi' the run tonight. He told me that only this morning.'

Suddenly Dwight's hands got in the right place. It was as if some memory clicked into place in his mind before anything clicked in the knee. Confidence and satisfaction. He moved his fingers, pressed. The girl cried out but, as once before, more from shock than from pain. The displacement was gone.

Dwight released her and straightened up. 'You have the bandage?' he said to Mrs Hoblyn.

'Yes, sur.' She fled, squeezing past Jacka, who was standing in the doorway now.

'You can stand up,' Dwight said.

Rosina flexed her knee carefully. Colour came and went in her face, and for a moment she looked as if she was going to cry.

''Tis all right again, maid?' asked Jacka apprehensively from the doorway.

She stood up. 'Oh, sur, I'm *that* grateful. I was so afeared that 'twas gone for good. I – I can't thank ee enough! 'Tis like a miracle.'

With lessons to be learned. 'I was overconfident,' Dwight said. 'I think you should wear a bandage always. Or for a year to begin, till the tendons knit together.'

Mrs Hoblyn came scurrying back. Dwight bound the knee, telling Mrs Hoblyn to watch carefully. It would not do for this to happen again. He could not come one hundred and fifty miles even for Rosina. Time was getting on. It must be well after ten-thirty. Time to go. They could drive all night if necessary, or stop after putting a comfortable distance between themselves and Killewarren. Dr Dwight Enys and Miss Caroline Penvenen, travelling as friends.

Jacka had brought out a bottle of rum, slopped some into a cup, and was pressing it on him. Dwight did not want it, but he knew this expressed the height of Jacka's approval, so he sipped a little while they watched Rosina walking gingerly about the room. Dwight occupied his last moment or two telling Mrs Hoblyn what she must do and what she must not do if it ever happened again. Mrs Hoblyn didn't make things any better by saying with shining eyes: 'Why, sur; we should just make 'er sit quiet like till you came!'

Sometimes a remark is like an insect's sting which at first is scarcely felt but grows uncomfortable as time passes. What Rosina had said about Charlie Kempthorne had at first been barely noticed by Dwight, and his success with the displacement had swamped it. Anxious now to be off, he was at the outer door pursued by their gratitude before the poison began to work.

As Jacka followed him out of the house, Dwight said: 'What is this about Charlie being ill? Did he tell you he was ill? Did he say I told him he must not get up?'

'Ais. Leastways, he told them as wanted him t'elp with the run.'

'I don't understand. What happened?'

Jacka peered at him. ''Twasn't Charlie's proper turn t'elp with the tub-carrying. They takes it turn an' turn about, ye know. 'Twas Trencrom's notion, to spread the risk an' to spread the reward. Men'll take a chance once in two months what they'll not take every month. But yesterday eve, Joe Trelask breaks 'is leg at the mill. Falls down the ladder, they d'say—'

'Yes. I know that. Go on.'

'So Charlie Kempthorne were next on the list, an' they sent round last night t'tell him to be ready. Then he says he's some slight. 'Tis the fever, he says, an' surgeon's told him he mustn't stir abroad on account of his lungs.' Jacka

Hoblyn's frown was such as to penetrate the darkness. 'Mean to say 'twas all make-believe?'

'So far as my part in it goes.'

'Well, the scaly little cheat! What's he about to tell such a stramming great story, 'tis hard to guess his reasons . . .'

'When is the wedding to be?'

'Tomorrow two weeks.'

'No doubt it was on account of that, Jacka. He was anxious to avoid the risk, perhaps anxious about his health too. It is a thing any man would do.'

Jacka grunted and ran a thumbnail up and down between his front teeth. 'Not any man by a long sight, surgeon. Not you, I'll wager; not me. He's no right or title to lie about'n. I'll tax him with it first thing in the morning.'

'Let it be,' said Dwight quietly. 'As you say, it is not our concern. Good night, Jacka.'

'Good night, sur. And thank ee.'

Dwight led his horse up the steep hill, Jacka watching him go. Charlie Kempthorne's cottage was at the top of the hill, just out of sight of the Hoblyns. Dwight stopped in front of it, stared up at the window. There was a light in the upper room. Twenty minutes to eleven. He could be at Killewarren comfortably in twenty minutes – if he started now. But he must start at once. Caroline would already be putting on her cloak, perhaps was now sitting waiting in her bedroom ready to snuff out the candle and steal downstairs. Bone would be at the gates with his valise.

But this monstrous suspicion grown in his mind was something which overrode his obligations to himself and to her. If he had not fancied the ride to Bath with the thought of Rosina lame again and unvisited, how much less could he face it with this problem unresolved. Five minutes would not make him late. In five minutes he could be sure.

Chapter Ten

Ray Penvenen's habits were sufficiently set to make his movements predictable at most hours of the day or night; but tonight, his last night here, he was perversely late going to bed. Old-maidish mannerisms had grown on him, and final preparations for going took the form of innumerable scribbled notes to be left with this servant and with that to remind them of their duties. Caroline stood it until half-past ten and then said:

'You are working overlate tonight, Uncle. There's all tomorrow morning to spend before we leave, and it would be the greatest pity if you found no way of spending it. Are you coming to bed?'

He looked first at the clock and then at her over his glasses. 'I have a little more to do, Caroline. An estate in the country is not like a London house, it cannot be locked up and left unoccupied. It must continue to be – looked to or it will run into chaos.'

'And are not Garth and the other men you employ capable of doing this? I should have thought so – or you would not employ them.'

'Oh, they know what to do within their limitations. But they lack initiative and, since we shall be away a month, it is necessary to supply it. For instance . . .' He went on to explain some of the decisions which might need to be made. Since she had asked, he supposed her to be interested in the answer; but once or twice he caught her eyes straying, and they were straying in the direction of the clock. 'Why do you inquire?' he ended quite suddenly, breaking off in the middle.

Her eyes came quickly back. 'Why? Shouldn't I be interested? It's not unladylike, I suppose? But I am also interested in your health. I don't think you have been looking so well of late, and it would be a woeful pity to wear yourself out with the effort of making ready to take a holiday.'

He looked at her suspiciously, but his suspicion was only of sarcasm not of deeper motive. When he saw no hint of mockery in her eyes, he patted her hand and said: 'There, there, I shall not be above half an hour more. Go to bed if you are tired, my dear. I am grateful to you for your solicitude.'

She turned away to hide her frustration, and for the next ten minutes pottered about the room on one pretext or another. But still he remained seated, making no move to go. At length she came back to the desk and said:

'Well, if you will not leave I must, for my eyes will not stay open. You'll come now?'

'Almost finished. Good night, Caroline.'

He put up his forehead to be kissed, and she brushed her lips perfunctorily over it, forgetting in her anxiety that this was her leave-taking of him, certainly for many months, perhaps for ever.

Out on the landing above the hall she remembered, but now it was too late. Her shadow kept her company along the corridor to her bedroom, preceding her like a welcoming innkeeper. In the bedroom she lit a candle and stared at her cloak, her hat, her scarf, her gloves, all waiting. Her bags were downstairs and in the coach, as also was Horace.

She pulled the bell twice to show that she wanted her maid Eleanor.

When the girl came, she said: 'My uncle is late tonight. We shall have to delay a little while. Tell Baker, will you . . . Are the other servants abed?'

'All but Thomas, miss. 'E be waiting for the master, to put out the lights and bar the doors, miss. He be grumbling, Baker say, at being kept abroad so late.'

Caroline bit her lip. 'Tell Baker to make no move until he has gone. It would be a great disaster if Thomas saw the horses being harnessed.'

'Very good, miss . . . Will that be all?'

'No. Make a move as if you were going to bed. If you can, slip out of the house unnoticed and sit in the coach. Thomas otherwise may wonder why you are hanging about. Also I'm afraid Horace will get terrified in the dark. And he yaps loud when frightened. Stay there until I come.'

'Very good, miss. I'll go fetch my bonnet and cloak.'

'But careful! Don't let anyone see you.'

When Eleanor had left, Caroline paced up and down the bedroom a half-dozen times, still biting her lip. Then she abruptly took up her outdoor things, glanced round to see that nothing was left which should not have been left, propped the letter for her uncle more prominently on her dressing-table, and snuffed out the candle and left the room.

Her shadow was sulking in its corner. As she moved along the passage, it jumped quickly to follow at her heels. The light was still under the door of the big drawing-room. She hesitated and then slipped into the maid's cupboard on the other side of the landing. Just room for her among the brushes and the dusters, but she was afraid to move lest something should topple over.

So she stayed another ten minutes, stiff and cramped, the door sufficiently ajar to see the lighted angle of drawing-room door. It must be close on eleven by now.

Mr Penvenen came out. He was carrying a candle, and a leather case under his arm. The room beyond was now in darkness. He closed the door after him and walked to the candlelamp in the corner and put it out. Then he came straight across to the cupboard where Caroline was standing.

Hypnotized, like a child caught in a terrible dream, she watched him walk towards her. Then the door slammed shut in her face and she heard his slippers creaking away . . .

In total darkness she let out a slow breath, began to count, determined not to move too soon. At five hundred she lifted the latch and looked out. The landing was in darkness.

Knowing she might yet bump into Thomas on his rounds, she crept along the corridor to the stairs and stole down them. They had never creaked so much before. Once down, she made for the servants' quarters, which directly adjoined the stables. There was a light in the kitchen and the door was ajar. Baker, her coachman, sat before a low fire in his shirt sleeves and stockinged feet, sharpening a piece of wood. He looked sleepy and ready for bed. If it was assumed, he was acting well.

He got up sharply when she came in. She put a finger to her lips, breathless in spite of herself. These last minutes were minutes of unexpected tension.

'Thomas?'

'Gone up, miss, three minutes since. I doubt 'e'll be down again.'

'Wait another five, then get the horses.'

'Yes, miss.'

'I'll go straight out to the coach. Eleanor is already there. We'll wait for you to come.'

'Very good, miss.'

As she turned to go out of the kitchen she looked up at the clock. It was five minutes after eleven. Dwight would be waiting.

Lottie Kempthorne wakened almost as soon as the cold night air fanned her face. She did not move but saw her father quite close to her at the window, peering out.

She heard his lowered voice. ''Tis just a fever and I thought to send for ee, surgeon, but then I thought to wait till cocklight afore I give ee the trouble. Maybe tomorrow if you was passing this way—'

A voice outside said: 'I'll see you tonight.'

'I b'lieve it has been brought to an intermission, an' by tomorrow—'

'Let me in. I want to speak to you.'

When grumbling to himself her father shut the window and began to pull on his breeches, Lottie still did not stir. She had learned that she must take no heed of her father's comings and goings, and a question now would be likely to earn her a growl and a cuff. So she lay comfortable enough on the thin hard bed, listening to May's quiet breathing beside her.

Father went down, taking the candle and she heard him unbar the door below. (Most people in Sawle never locked their doors day or night, but Charlie was an exception.) She heard him talking to the man who came in, and presently sat up, scratching herself in the darkness. She wondered what Dr Enys could possibly be wanting calling so very late and speaking in such a strange voice. Dr Enys had been so kind to her and usually he was very gentle. Perhaps something terrible had happened.

Her curiosity would let her rest no longer, and she slid out of bed and crept shivering to the trap door which led down to the room below. She lifted it a couple of inches and peered down.

Her father was being examined; he was in a chair, hedging and protesting while Dr Enys stood over him, his face white and hard. The first words that came up to her were:

'You have no fever, man, as you well know. Nor have you had any. Why did you tell people that story?'

'Maybe 'tis not fever to you, surgeon; but three hours gone I was sweaten like a weed. An' what with Lottie just free of the pox . . . And see now! Feel my 'and. If that edn clammy . . .'

But the face of Dr Enys, kind Dr Enys, did not change. 'This is an excuse, isn't it, Kempthorne, this sham illness – thought up to avoid any part in the tub-carrying tonight? Why did you want to have no part in it?'

Lottie's father, whom Lottie loved, licked his lips and began to button his shirt. 'I was all of a shrim. First it comed on me back like cold water, like ice. Then—'

'For two years or more there's been an informer about, carrying tales for gold. You know that, don't you, Charlie?'

'Course I know. Everyone d'know. Have you caught him?'

'I rather think I have.'

Lottie shifted her cramped feet and lifted the hatch another few inches. Father had got up.

'What, me? Dear life, surgeon; that's a purty notion to get in your head! And not a nice one, I must say! Proper insulting. And all on account of a fever that took me sudden. Why, just afore you came my teeth was rattling—'

'Where did you get these things?' Dr Enys asked, pointing angrily about the room, and Lottie was afraid he might see her. 'How did you pay for them? Curtains, rugs, window glass; all paid for out of sail-making? Or out of selling your friends?'

Her father was smiling, but she who knew him knew it was not a friendly smile. 'Out of sail-making, surgeon. That's true as my life. An' no one can show different. Now ye can *go*, surgeon, and leave me be, and take your nasty evil suspicion likewise! Coming here in the dark of the night, casting such sneavy untruths—'

'It is you who'll have to go, Charlie; and go quickly if you care for your life. You've informed on your friends tonight, haven't you? What time is the run to take place? Is there still time to warn them?'

'And what shall I say 'bout you, surgeon? That you've coveted Rosina ever since ye laid eyes and hands on her, eh? That ye suspicion me to try and stop the wedding, eh? I know. *I* know all the things ye've done to her, all the fingerin' and fumblin' there's been – on the quiet like, when her mother warn't there. She's told me, Rosina has. Ye should be grateful that somebody'll still marry her—'

Dr Enys made a swift movement, and her father broke off as if he expected violence; but the surgeon had turned towards a side table where she and May had been playing that evening. She craned her neck to see what he had picked up, and saw with astonishment that it was a picture book of hers called *The History of Primrose Prettyface*.

'Where did you get this, Charlie?'

'I buyed it.'

'Where did you buy it?'

'In to Redruth.'

'You lie. This book first belonged to Hubert Vercoe, the Customs Officer's boy. I saw it first in his house.' The doctor was flipping through the pages.

'Nay, that edn clever at all, surgeon. It proves naught. There's many such books on sale in Redruth. Why—'

'I doubt if there's one. But here is the identification, here on the first page. Hubert Vercoe coloured the wings of this angel red. He told me so himself and I saw it in his hands.' Dr Enys shut the book and slipped it in his pocket.

In the silence that followed Lottie could hear May turn over in bed and whimper, as if aware that her company and her warmth had gone. Below the two men watched each other like dogs Lottie had seen, bristling and tight-muscled.

'What are ee going to do?'

'You shall know when I've done it.'

The doctor picked up his riding crop and made a move towards the door, but her father was quicker and was there before him. Even Dr Enys couldn't believe that that smile was friendly now. 'Stay, surgeon. What are ee going to do?'

'Get out of my way!'

Neither of them moved.

Dr Enys said: 'What time is the run?'

'Midnight. Ye're late, surgeon. Too late by a long chalk. Go home and go to bed. That's the proper place for ee.'

'What made you do it, Charlie? What made you a traitor to your own folk?'

'Nobody's my folk, surgeon! Who did ought for me? My first wife was drownded before folk's eyes. None of the women made move to save 'er. Not one! They left her drown. And me? Who put forth a hand t'elp me when I was low? Not one. Everyone looks only for theirselves in this life.'

'Not to betray. Not to sell other men for money. Judas was no worse.'

Lottie saw Father's hand close round the wooden stake he used for barring the door. It was behind his back, but she saw it.

'There's naught I care for your fancy names, surgeon. I looks to myself just the same as you. An' ye'll get no admission more'n that. When me and Rosina's wed, we'll clear out of this place—'

'If you did this to gain Rosina, you're likely to lose her by it—'

'I done what I done, surgeon. You cured me of the consumptives, but ye don't order me life. Oh, *no . . .*'

Lottie cried out as her father jumped at the other man with the wooden bar raised. Dr Enys must have seen it coming, for he jerked his head back and the stick cracked on his shoulder. The pain creased across his face and he fell against the table behind him. Transfigured, unrecognizable, her father leaped after him, swinging the stake again; but the doctor's fall saved him. Crash went the table, Dr Enys rolled into the corner, sat up while her father was picking a way towards him among the legs of the table. The surgeon clutched a stool, raised it, and the stick jarred against it, hurting her father's hand for he almost dropped it. The doctor pulled himself up, caught the stick; they grappled, reeled against the wall.

Lottie swung the trap, let it fall back, went down a few steps into the room, tears trickling unheeded down her pockmarked cheeks. She called to them but they did not hear, these two men who meant more to her than all the rest of life; they were fighting to kill, to maim, you could see it in their eyes. She wanted the courage to come between them, to stop them, to put life back where it had been an hour ago. A terrible nightmare, worse than any of her fever, worse than personal pain.

Father had his hands on the other man's throat, but seemed to lack the strength to do what he wished. She saw his bloodshot eyes, murder still in them but fright also. Crash to the floor again, he under.

Behind her own crying Lottie heard a thin echo. May was awake now. May often cried if she woke in the night, without reason, without good cause. Lottie took two more steps down, nearly tripped over the ragged edge of her night shift, her mother's once.

Father had kicked himself free, was crawling again towards the stick; but the surgeon caught his ankle, pulled him flat. Her father kicked with his free foot, caught the surgeon's face, just grasped the stick. Dr Enys freed him, started forward, leaped at his back; down again. A familiar sound; something Lottie had known all her life; her father coughing. It seemed to affect the doctor at the same time. He released his grip, straightened, a look of concern, something not to do with tonight, out of other nights, other days. Her father was down, stayed down, climbed slowly to his knees, then did not move. For a few seconds both children had stopped crying and the only sound was the familiar rustling cough. Dr Enys pulled himself shakily to his feet. Blood on his face, his neckcloth torn.

Her father looked round. Then he leaped up, clutched a knife lying on the side under the crockery. As he took it up, Dr Enys saw his danger, moved after him. The knife up, but the doctor struck at the same time. The knife clattered. The doctor seemed to measure his distance and hit twice more. Father coughed again just once; he might not have been hurt, but he crumpled up, went on his knees, rolled over, and was really still.

Lottie had her hands to her ears now, helplessly, as if words and sounds would hurt more than sight, the tears beginning to trickle again. Her mouth grimaced to speak, but she could not. She stood and wept bitterly for a lost illusion. A great desolation was in her, a sense of being forsaken as no one had ever been forsaken before.

Chapter Eleven

No official word had reached Demelza, but she knew. As soon as dark fell she drew the curtains across the windows and lit all the candles to give the house an extra feeling of home and security. He might not come until early morning, but she had no thought of bed. Tonight was doubly important. She felt she would know as soon as their eyes met whether he had good news or bad.

She delayed supper until nine before sitting down alone at the table and pecking at the cold leg of mutton and the apple jam tartlets. After, she went into the kitchen, anxious not even to hear the telltale clop of horses' hooves, the jangle of harness, the occasional gruff voice. Jane Gimlett was there alone, John Gimlett being out looking for a lamb which had strayed; and to give colour to her own presence, she began to re-iron the ruffs on Ross's shirts. All of them were well worn, well darned, should long since have been cast aside.

Jane Gimlett chattered for a time; but presently, finding her mistress silent, her own talk dropped away. Upstairs Jeremy slept soundly.

Feathers, the kitten, came and rubbed its head against Demelza's skirts. Then, finding itself unrebuffed, it wriggled under the hem of her skirt and put its forepaws round her ankle. After another minute or so it somehow got its back legs tangled up and began to wriggle and kick.

Demelza bent and disentangled it and put it on the table beside her. It arched its back and opened its infant mouth in a silent snarl and then stepped sideways as if blown by the wind and almost fell off the table. She picked it up again and put it in its basket beside the ancient Tabitha Bethia, who was asleep and let out a single mew of protest.

She turned the chicken, which was cooking on a spit in case Ross should be hungry on his return, and thrust forward the potato saucepan on its iron trivet so that it stood over the hot ashes. The tide was right about midnight, and she thought he would be here by then or soon after. She took the piece of bacon out of the smoke chamber over the flue of the fire to see if it was sufficiently cured. Then she returned to the table.

On this came Gimlett, bucket in hand, out of breath, stumbling over the mat as he pushed open the door.

'John!' said his wife. 'What's amiss? Did ee find him?'

'There's a soldier!' said Gimlett, clattering the bucket down. 'By the stile at the turn of the Long Field! I nigh bumped into un! I thought 'twas one of the tub-runners.'

Demelza put her iron down. It was as if a colder iron had moved in her. 'Are you *sure*, John? How are you sure?'

'I catched a glimpse of his tunic, mistress. And he was carren a musket too! I says to him, "Fine night, my son," and he says "Aye." Just the word "Aye." 'Twas no Cornishman, I knew; and then I catched sight of his musket!'

'Did you see anything of the traders?'

'Yes, mistress, about an hour gone. I seen two moving down to the cove.'

Oh, God, to think, to think, this might be Ross's liberty, even his life. It was what she had feared often before, but then it had not involved Ross except as an accessory. This time of all times, when he was coming home. The room closed on her like a prison. 'John, do you think – do you think you can get out of the house unseen, make your way down to the cove? Go out of the back again, quickly, quick, by way of the cliff. And Jane, how many candles have we? Enough to lighten all the windows d'you suppose?'

'A score, I b'lieve, ma'am. We was to have bought more last week—'

'John, waste no time. Do what you can even if it means—'

Demelza stopped. Gimlett said: 'The sky's clearing. The stars is bright as frost, but I can—'

He had looked at Demelza, and he too stopped. She was staring past him at the door. Captain McNeil was standing there, in uniform this time; and another figure could be seen in the background.

'Good evening to ye, Mrs Poldark. I'm sorry to break in on your privacy. Your man saw one of my troopers, so I shall have to ask you all to keep within doors for the next hour or two.'

Demelza picked up one of Ross's shirts; with trembling but controlled fingers she folded it carefully.

'Captain McNeil . . . This is a surprise. I'm – at a loss . . .'

'I will explain it to ye, ma'am, if you will give me a moment in privacy. Is Captain Poldark at home?'

'. . . No. He's away . . .'

A look passed across McNeil's face. 'I see. Then a word with you, if I might have it.'

'Certainly . . .'

'One moment. How many sairvants have you in the house, ma'am ?'

'Two. These two only.'

'Then I'll ask them to stay here in the care of my trooper. Wilkins!'

'Aye, sir.'

With uncertain steps, her heart choking, she led the way into the parlour.

'Please sit down, Captain McNeil. 'Twas quite unthoughtful of you to appear sudden at my kitchen door like – like a pedlar with a tray of rings, when I thought you miles away, in London or – or in Edinburgh. You should have written.'

'I ask your pardon, ma'am. I had no intention of disturbing anyone in this house, but your man blundered into one of our pickets. I—'

'Pickets? It has a very military ring. Do you suppose that there is an enemy about?'

He screwed in his great moustache. 'An enemy of a sort. We have news that smugglers have the intention to use your cove tonight. Vercoe, the Customs Officer, has repeatedly appealed for a reinforcement of his men. Tonight I and my troopers are providing it. That's why I asked to see Captain Poldark.'

She had gone to a cupboard and taken out a decanter. He was still on his feet, and in his uniform he looked enormous and cumbersome beside her slightness.

'You'll take a glass of wine?' she said.

'Thank ye, no. Not while on duty.'

'But why Captain Poldark? What have we to do with it?'

'Nothing, I trust – I hope. But it is your land, ma'am. I think you can hardly be so innocent as you look. Where is Captain Poldark?'

She shook her head. 'From home. I told you. He is in St Ives.'

'When will he retairn?'

'Tomorrow – I b'lieve. Please sit down, Captain McNeil. When you are standing, the room is too small for you.'

He half smiled as he obeyed her, took out his watch, replaced it. 'Believe me, it grieves me, ma'am, to be in this position relative to yourself.'

'So 'twas what some said, that when you were staying with the Trevaunances you were really acting as a spy.'

He said sharply: 'No, *most* untrue! I came as a convalescent. Whilst down here I did nothing but pay a courtesy visit on the Customs authorities, since I had been concairned with them three years before. I ask you to believe, Mrs Poldark, that it is not in my nature to do what is – dishonourable!'

'Then why – now?'

'This is different, quite different. I came as a soldier, ma'am. This Trade, this organised Trade, must be stamped out. I can only obey the orr-ders I am given!'

She was surprised that the note of contempt in her voice should have pricked him so.

'Yet you wish to lock me in my own house . . .'

'For the rest of tonight. I cannot leave you or your servants free to run down and warn the smugglers.'

'So you cannot trust me, Captain McNeil?'

'In this I cannot.'

She looked at him through her lashes. 'You ask me to believe in your honour but will not believe in mine.'

'With your husband out of the house and perhaps implicated?' He got up and stood a moment with his hands on the back of the chair. 'Captain Poldark has been a soldier himself. It will grieve me if he is involved – I trust for his sake that he is not. I do not lightly make war on friends. But once before I warned him of the danger of flying in the face of the law. If he has done so now, he must take the consequences. Believe me, ma'am, for the favour of your good will I would pay a very high price. Indeed, almost any pairsonal price that you ask. But not one which involves a – a neglect of duty.'

A gruff voice could be heard in the kitchen. It was on her lips to tell McNeil the truth, to explain the cruel mischance of Ross's involvement, this once alone, and to throw herself and Ross on his understanding and good will. But she stopped in time. Her meetings with McNeil had been few, but already she was coming to have an understanding of his character. In justifying his actions to her, he had revealed both his quality and his limitations. Good-natured, shrewd, susceptible to women, he yet pursued his duty with a single-mindedness which was above weakness. Mercy was as little likely to move him as money or sex.

'What do you wish me to do?'

'Stay in here, ma'am. I can ill spare Wilkins, but he must stay with you since it was his blunder that gave you warning. It should not be many hours.'

'And when you have taken your traders and locked them up – then we shall be free to go to bed and – and forget you?'

He flushed and bowed. 'That is so. And if anyone is taken connected with this house, it will be to my deep regret as well as yours. I trust this is the last time I'll be involved in such a mission. From now on we shall have better work to do.'

'What do you mean?'

'Fighting people of a different race, ma'am. And of a different way of belief. France declared war on England yesterday. Had they done so a few weeks ago, we should have been spared this unhappy meeting.'

*

Dwight got out of the cottage and shut the door and leaned against it. Dark here, but it was the darkness of the frosty night, not that inner dark which had nearly swamped him. Bruised and shaky and in pain, but now no fear he would faint. Air revived him; as he stood there trying to think, it was a tonic – a cold breath penetrating through sweaty clothes, chilling but enlivening.

Walk to your horse, unloop the reins, struggle, pull yourself into the saddle. Already after eleven. Caroline waiting by now. Bone there, might have explained. (But he could not explain what he did not know.) In ten minutes could be there – fifteen anyhow. In half an hour away.

But that was a mere hypothesis which could not be put to the test. There was still more than half an hour to midnight. Even for Caroline . . .

He pulled on the reins and turned his horse. Unused to carrying up this steep and stony path, the horse stumbled, struck sparks from the loose rock. Good to get away from that cottage into the cold dark. Two children crying, staring at him, who'd been their friend; terrified hostile eyes, while Charlie lay in his own hearth. As he left he heard them move; as soon as the door closed they would come padding down, staring at their father; Lottie would damp a rag, try to revive him, in the end no doubt would succeed. But what was his future? What was their future?

At the top of the hill he spurred his horse away from Killewarren, away – for the moment – from Bath and elopement and his love and his new life. Left shoulder heavily throbbing, though no bones broken; blood from the scratches on his neck drying down the front of his shirt.

Had there been more time he might have gone back for Jacka Hoblyn. *He* would have been quick enough in such an emergency; they might have put out in a boat to warn

the cutter. But time would have run out before anything
was begun. Even now perhaps too late.

In Grambler two lights, but the same objection: by the
time anyone was roused. The full responsibility was on his
own shoulders.

The officer he had seen in Truro; the two horsemen
who had drawn silently off the track tonight to let him and
Parthesia go by. This was no ordinary ambush; he had read
as much in Charlie's eyes; the grand betrayal; perhaps
Charlie had decided that after his marriage he would give
up the dangerous game. Imprisonment or transportation
for a dozen men, worse if there was resistance; imprisonment and ruin for Ross.

The night was dark enough to make quick movement
dangerous; when he reached the ruins of Wheal Maiden,
he slid off his horse, tethered it inside the broken wall.
Then he went down the valley, haste and caution warring.

All the way he saw no one. A couple of lights over at the
mine. The ground was dry underfoot and hard with frost;
impossible to tell how many others might have passed this
way before him. A light in the parlour window of Nampara.
By now, no doubt, Demelza knew to expect Ross back
tonight.

On the way down plans had been forming. The Nampara household could help. When every second
counted . . .

Perhaps the silence of the valley made him suspicious,
or the obvious light so late. He went to the front door and
lifted a hand to rap, then lowered it and moved round the
great lilac bush across the flower bed to the lighted window.
Curtains were drawn, but there was a chink. He peered in.
On the table a grey busby.

A stiff and curious tableau. The big soldier by the door

in his red coat and gold-braided trousers, stolid, glassily staring; John and Jane Gimlett, on chair edge, strained, uncomfortable; and Demelza by the fire. Tonight, rather than the beauty in her face, you saw the strong bones underlying it. Normally they were imperceptible; it was as if she had ceased to be man or woman and become something common to both. The knuckles of her hands were white.

Dwight thought he heard a movement behind him, sharply straightened up, but it was only some stirring of the light breeze.

So what he had to do must be done himself. Round the house; a light burning in the kitchen window. He picked a way across the cobbled yard between the stone sheds. The curtains of this window not drawn; the room empty. He tried the latch and the door opened. Warmth and kitchen smells. An iron upended on the table and a cat asleep in a basket before a dying fire. A kitten, lying almost in the cinders, mewed and stretched at sight of him. The solitary candle near its end.

He saw what he wanted just inside the door, a small lantern used for carrying out of doors. As he took it down, Garrick began to bark. In haste, fumble with the shutter which had jammed. He could not leave and do it outside, for then he had no means of lighting the candle. As he pulled at the catch, he thought he heard a movement in the parlour. He stepped quickly behind the door, but there were no footsteps. Garrick stopped barking, and as silence fell the catch moved and the shutter came open. Move to the stub of candle and light the lantern from it. On a trivet on the fire a pan with some potatoes had boiled dry. The kitten was lying on its back near his boot waiting for a friendly hand to bite. He closed the shutter, slid out of the house. The latch of the door clicked.

Greater haste now across the yard, with Garrick barking again, over the stile at the back. Cloak covering the lantern, run towards the Long Field. This field occupied all that was cultivable of the headland which separated Hendrawna Beach from Nampara Cove. It reached up as far as where the outcroppings of rock and the gorse and bracken began. Over its newly ploughed surface he stumbled, climbing till he could see the sea on both sides. Only a thin surf whispered on the beach tonight; its irregular hem demarcated the sand. The inlet of Nampara could just be seen from here, a rift in the mounting cliffs towards Sawle.

He had gone a few yards more when he saw a man standing beside a boulder, silhouetted against the low stars. Dwight's lantern could not have been entirely hidden, and only that the man was staring out to sea saved him. Back inch by inch, slowly pivoting until the boulder was between them. Exertion or tension had made him sweat again, but now it was welcome, warming his body to the night. Crouching low he skirted the sentry, going round the north side of Damsel Point until he was near the edge of the cliff. There he lowered his lantern behind a low stone wall and peered down into the darkness of the cove.

At first he saw nothing; and then, dawning on his eyes at no definite moment, he knew the ship was there. Something unnatural in the sea, low and black, unlike a rock even if a rock could be there. Straining, he could suddenly detect even the single mast and – for a second only – a glimmer of light aboard.

No light ashore. The cove, the centre of the cove, where sand and shingle met the stream, was empty. In the darker corners there might be men and beasts waiting; but so far as one could tell, nothing breathed or stirred under the frosty sky.

He lugged out his watch and peered at it like a blind man, then knelt beside the lantern to see. Ten minutes after twelve. The run had not yet begun.

In despairing haste he swung round, staring at the land about him. The other side of the wall was as good a place as any.

He wrenched out his pocket knife, opened it, and went back a few yards to the nearest gorse bush. Gorse is a nightmare of prickles but is brittle to the boot or the sharp twist. Part with knife, part with hands he tore a big piece off, dropped it over the wall. Then the next one. He could afford no time to build a stock. The thing must be fed while it was burning.

So he hacked a dozen bushes, dry stuff and highly inflammable. Together a fair pile to begin. Abandoning secrecy, he uncovered the lantern and climbed over the wall. Taking out the single candle, carefully shielding it from the air, he held it under the lowest part of the pile.

For a grievous space he thought the light would blow out; then a flame ran suddenly like quicksilver among the gorse, and in a moment the pile was blazing and crackling.

Chapter Twelve

Ross had borne the trip home with impatience. The eagerness and anticipation of the outward voyage was all gone, and once he was in sight of Cornwall he wanted to land at once instead of tacking about just over the horizon for twelve hours.

Not that there was anything useful to do when he reached Nampara, nor any good news to impart. The pricked bubble of his hopes had left nothing in its place; all he wanted was to get home, to turn his back on mining for ever, and to forget what he had thrown away.

For the first time in his life he began to feel old. Often these last years he had known himself a failure, but always within him there had been a fundamental conviction that this was a temporary phase, a 'down' which in the nature of events must be followed by an 'up'. At least a part of this conviction had derived from a knowledge of his own youth and vigour. His meeting with Mark Daniel had shaken that belief.

His realisation again of the façade of mining expectations he had erected on the chance words of this man, uttered four years ago, shook his confidence in himself and in his own judgment. He bitterly blamed himself for his rash overconfidence, for an enthusiasm which in the light of experience looked wanton and silly. He had thrown away a profitable investment in a mine of his own starting and had poured everything he had, and persuaded Francis to do likewise, into a played-out mine which had failed his father a quarter of a century ago. Not only had he gambled with money, he had gambled with security and the security and happiness of his wife and child.

Mark's appearance had upset him. There had been a close tie between them in the old days; they had played together as boys, fished and wrestled as youths. This ageing man, grey-haired and puckering his eyes at the map ... Was he, Ross, as untouched by time as he imagined? Was he deluding himself into believing that youth was still on his side? How many other misconceptions had his sanguine brain given room to?

He was not in his most companionable mood, and after a few attempts Farrell and the rest of the crew gave up the effort of engaging him in conversation. After nightfall the cutter edged her way slowly inshore until by eleven-thirty she came to anchor not a cable's length from the mouth of Nampara Cove. The flat-bottomed longboat was lowered, and Farrell readily agreed with Ross's suggestion that he should go ashore with the first cargo. But Farrell would make no move to have any cargo shifted until the signal came from the shore.

It came at ten minutes to twelve, a single dark-lantern at the sea's edge, shining only seawards, and exposed for half a minute. Farrell gave his orders, and the barrels were lowered into the longboat.

A mixed bag, as Ross had realized when he looked at the cargo on the way home, but an immensely valuable one. No wonder Trencrom did not need to make runs more than a few times a year. Tea and tobacco and five-gallon casks of brandy and Geneva; and a good quantity of rich materials; gold and silver brocade, silk gloves, ribbons, and girdles.

The spirits made up the larger amount of the cargo and these were loaded first. It was for the most part white brandy, with a tub of colouring mixture supplied. Its strength was 120° above proof; and in his own time Mr Trencrom would dilute his import before selling it, making three tubs to sell for every one that came ashore. He paid four shillings a gallon in France, and the price in England duty paid was twenty-eight shillings. Even sold at half that price, the degree of profit escaped Ross, since there were some four hundred tubs of brandy alone aboard tonight; but he thought he would have less compunction than ever in levying his toll for the use of his land.

The boat was so filled that the gunwale was only an inch or two above the water, and Ross settled in the bows as the six oarsmen began quietly to row ashore.

For a little while there was no sound but the liquid dip of oars and the lap and bobble of water as it ran against the boat. The arms of the cove closed round them and shut out the great sounding emptiness of the sea. Instead, close at hand was the whisper of the surf, for once innocuous and sibilant. Inshore the stars were not as bright as they had been at sea: a faint haze had crept across them too tenuous for cloud. Presently the boat lifted and fell and grated on sand, and two of the men jumped out and held fast to prevent the run back. Out of the darkness around them four figures instantly came, two to help pull the boat more firmly ashore, two to wade into the surf to begin the unloading.

Ross stepped upon the wet sand. A new wave licked his boots as he walked inshore. He recognized Ted Carkeek and Ned Bottrell, and after a moment Paul Daniel loomed out of the darkness.

'All right, sur? Did ee find Brother?'

'Yes, I found him . . .'

'Was 'e well? Did 'e give a message?'

'There's a message for you and for Beth and for his father. Tomorrow morning I'll come round and see you.'

'And did 'e help? Where was the good country?'

'I'll talk of it tomorrow, Paul.'

Behind them there was scarcely any talk at all, just a rapid businesslike unloading the first barrels. Often it was different from this; often they had to fight the surf and float in the tubs as best they could. Ross moved on, and Will Nanfan came towards him leading a mule. Knowing he would have some of the same questions to answer again, Ross prepared to make an excuse and pass quickly by. But the excuse was never made. Behind him came a sharp exclamation from one of the men. Ross saw someone staring, and at once a reflection of light showed on the beach. A bonfire was leaping and smoking on Damsel Point.

Events moved more quickly than the mind accepted them. Muttered curses from the men around him, a clear shout from a voice not belonging, and then a shrilling whistle. Suddenly in the flickering light extra figures were climbing down the sides of the cove; then lantern lights, not shaded.

A surprise – gaugers – the long-expected – but this night of all nights . . . Ross swung round, saw confusion about the longboat. He ran back.

'Quick! Relaunch! Get out there and tip the tubs . . .'
He flung his weight against the side of the boat; two or

three others joined him. The boat slithered and grated. Two figures in it began heaving out the tubs together. Figures racing, strangers in flat caps, and some in tall. Nanfan had gone plunging away with his mule. A wave came and swirled around their knees; the boat floated but was being washed farther up the beach. 'Hold her! Steady! Give way!'

One of the men had gone down in the sea, his feet from under him, but two others joined. They held their ground, and as the wave slid back the longboat went with it. A musket exploded somewhere. One man jumped on the boat, then another. Ross followed until almost waist-deep. Oars were out, anyhow, but just enough to keep her straight. A man stood in the bows, held out his hand to Ross. Ross made a move to jump, then changed his mind. To be aboard again, isolated, perhaps tacking up and down for a week; he'd take his chance.

He turned, saw the place alive with men – the way up the track blocked with mules – confusion and men fighting, laying about them with sticks. As he ploughed his way out of the water a tall man in a busby: 'Halt, there! In the King's name!' Ross veered sharply. '*Halt* or I fire!' Turned again and ducked. The musket exploded in his ear as he knocked the man flat in the water.

Nothing he could do. Another shot, and then another. He ran left towards the cave where he kept his boat. An easy climb from there. Someone lurched at him out of the shadow – this time evasion came too late. He went down, the other on top. 'Got you, now! Lie still, you bastard, or I'll— *One over here, Bell!*' Bearded. Vercoe. Ross doubled and sharply stiffened. Vercoe toppled, still clutching. They rolled, Vercoe under. Running steps. Twice he hit the

Customs Officer, wriggled free, rolled over as the footsteps came up. Vercoe shouted: 'Not me, you fool! Over there – he's just gone!'

Ross at the cliff face turned as the newcomer caught him – the hard wooden stick of the gauger. They grappled. The stick clattered. A lucky swing with all his weight. The gauger fell in Vercoe's path.

As he climbed, Ross heard them following. In the cove a small war. Lights dancing. Untended, the gorse fire had waned. Climbing with all the knowledge of childhood, he pulled away. But a musket ball smacked into the rock beside him. Someone on the cliff taking careful aim. He reached the top, breaths gulping, crawled around the gorse, made diagonally for the first wall of his own land. He sucked the blood off his knuckles and spat. The two gaugers reached the top; lovely target if one had a gun. So the trooper must have thought, for the two men suddenly checked and Vercoe's voice bellowed an order across the cliff. It gave time for Ross to leap over the wall and begin to run doubled along the other side.

Demelza's sharp ears had caught the first distant crack of a musket, and she could stand it no longer. She started to her feet and was halfway to the door before the soldier was able to move.

''Ere, no, ma'am! None o' that! You heard what the Captain said.'

'I have a little boy upstairs! He will be frightened. I must bring him down!'

'No, ma'am. Cap'n McNeil said ye was to stay here in this room.'

'Please let me pass!' she said furiously.

'Now calm you down, ma'am. I has my orders and—'

'I'll not calm down! You don't make war on babies, do you? Get out of my way!'

He hesitated, glanced at the Gimletts. 'Is there a baby?'

'Course there is!' John Gimlett snapped.

The trooper turned to the drawn-faced young woman before him: 'I don't hear nothing. Which room is 'e in?'

'The one at the head of the stairs!'

He rubbed his finger along his chin and slowly drew back. 'I'll watch for ye, then. Have a care there's no trickery, ma'am.'

He followed her out into the hall and stood almost in the doorway where he could see into the room and also up the stairs. Demelza flew up the stairs and into their bedroom. Unaware of the dangers that pressed upon his parents, Jeremy slept peacefully.

This room had dormer windows looking both north and south. Demelza ran to the first of these, peered out. At first the night looked quiet and still, but then she detected the flicker of the bonfire on Damsel Point. She opened the casement window. From here the roof sloped sharply to the recently added guttering. But at the end, over the kitchen, it joined to the thatched end of the linhay where the carts were kept.

She wriggled her body through the small window and out on to the roof. Then she crawled along it like a cat to the end and slid off it into the thatch. She followed this to the lowest part, where there was a five-foot drop, and jumped.

She landed on all fours, tearing her skirt and bruising wrist and knee. Then she was on her feet and running towards the Long Field.

Breathless, she had just reached the stile when a figure

climbed it. She had no difficulty in recognizing the set of
his shoulders, the long lean head. They stared at each
other in the dark.

'Demelza!'

'*Ross!* I thought you was killed ... Thank *God* you're
safe! I thought—'

'Not safe,' he said. 'Followed. Which way is best into the
house?'

'Neither. There's a soldier there. I said you was in St
Ives. Are you hurt?'

'Nothing.' While they spoke, they were walking rapidly
the way she had come, he behind her in case of a shot. 'I
think I was – recognized. Not sure. Is the – upper valley
guarded?'

'Don't know. I've been crazed with worry. You could go
towards Mellin.'

'They'll send that way—' At the entrance to their yard
he stopped, listening. The yard was quiet except for a
scratching at a stable door where Garrick was waiting to
welcome him. 'They're coming – down the field now. Are
you safe here? They offer you no hurt?'

'No, none, of course. But you—'

'Go in then. I'll hide in the library – in the cache. Safe
enough there.'

'You can't get ...'

'Yes – round the side. I have the key.'

'But *is* it safe? ...'

'Must risk it.'

In a moment he had disappeared from her side. She
heard the running footsteps. She hastily slipped back into
the house – stumbled through the dark kitchen and into
the hall. The soldier swung his musket on her, surprised
and then angry.

'Where've ye been? How did ye get down?'

She took a deep breath. 'By the back stairs.'

He said: 'What back stairs? Ye never told me! Why did ye—'

'Well, I'm back! Is that not enough!'

The soldier too heard the running feet on the cobbles and again lifted his musket. Vercoe and his assistant Bell burst in on them.

'Put your musket down, man!' Vercoe said in a quarter-deck voice. He was blazing with anger. 'One of your kind has took pot shots at us already!' He turned to Demelza. 'Where is Captain Poldark, ma'am?'

'In St Ives, I believe.'

'Then you believe wrong! I was wrestling with him on the beach not ten minutes gone. Has he come in here, trooper?'

'Nay. No one's come in here but you.'

'We last seen him making this way. He'll be somewhere about the house, never doubt!'

'You've no right to come breaking in here!' Demelza protested, finding relief in anger. 'What right have you to trespass on our property? My husband will hear of this! Why, if—'

'He surely will! And soon, I trust—'

'How do you know 'twas him? Is it daylight outside? Did you speak him by name? Of course not! I tell you he's from home and—'

'Look ee, ma'am,' said Vercoe, controlling his anger. ''Twas Captain Poldark I seen on the beach or his brother an' twin. I'll beg your pardon if I've the need to, but I don't suppose it likely ... An' what's that blood on your gown?'

'Blood?' she said, looking at the smear. Her stomach

twisted. So Ross was hurt. 'It came from my wrist. I grazed it against the wall just now. See—'

Vercoe made an impatient gesture. 'You'll give us permission to search the house?'

'If I did not give it, you would take it.'

'Well, mebbe. The law must be served. Will you please go in the parlour with the servants.'

'No I surely will not! You may force yourself into the house, but you may not order me about. I shall come with you!'

Before Vercoe could argue about it, there was the sound of more footsteps in the kitchen and another trooper appeared. With him, half dragged and half led, was Dwight Enys, a bloodstained rag about his head. The soldier had caught him in the process of feeding the bonfire, and had knocked him out.

In the cove the pitched battle in the dark had died down. Seven of the smugglers had been captured, of whom two were wounded and one killed. A soldier and an excise man had been wounded. But owing to the premature alarm, the others had escaped. What was worse, the cutter had been able to weigh anchor and haul off from the lee of the land before the government cutter, standing rapidly in from the north-east, had been able to head her off. Shots had been exchanged, but the *One and All*, built in Mevagissey especially for the Trade, had run clean away from the government ship.

The smuggler killed was Ted Carkeek. He left a widow of twenty-one and two young children. The soldier wounded was Captain McNeil. Someone had shot him in the shoulder. An inch or so lower, and he would have companioned Ted.

He was almost the last to reach Nampara House, where by orders his men had forgathered with their prisoners. He came into the parlour holding a rough pad to his shoulder. The parlour was already part hospital, with Dwight, paper-coloured from loss of blood, trying to help those who were worse off than himself. As McNeil surveyed the scene and exchanged a word with his corporal, Vercoe and Bell and Demelza came down the stairs.

'Well?'

Vercoe shook his head. 'No, sur. Captain Poldark's not here, though I'll swear he was on the beach!'

'I've still three men posted: they may bring him in. You've tried the cellars?'

'Yes, they're empty.'

'No contraband?'

'None.'

McNeil met the angry flash of Demelza's eyes. 'Ross is in St Ives,' she said. 'I've told these men. And I told you.'

'I should be happy to believe you.'

'You're wounded,' she said. 'Your coat – all that blood . . . I'll get Dr Enys.'

'When my work is done.' He turned to Vercoe. 'We must comb the cottages round. You've examined the outhouses of this place, the stables, the library?'

'The stables. Not the library. 'Twas locked. I left that till you came.'

'We'll go now, then.'

Demelza felt as if this time her face must betray everything.

'The library?' she said, when they turned to her. 'I –

have the key somewhere ... But your wound, Captain McNeil.'

'Will keep a little while. It is not the first time I have been blooded.'

They went through into Joshua's old bedroom, Vercoe and McNeil, and Bell carrying a lantern. With fumbling fingers Demelza unlocked the door to the library and went in. The long shabby room showed up, never used for its named purpose, full of mining samples and boxes of lumber and two desks and an iron safe. As soon as the lantern followed her in, she knew he had come as he said he would. The metal trunks which normally stood above the trap door had been moved.

She stood against the door, not able to trust her legs. while the men went round the room. Vercoe carried a musket belonging to one of the troopers. He looked like a hunter after game. And the game was gone to earth.

First they examined the things in the room itself, opening the desks and the boxes, looking for contraband. After a moment or two she followed them halfway, watching them from the centre of the room. Then quite close to her she saw a spot of blood. It was tiny and already drying. She moved a little and put her foot on it, rubbed it into the boards.

But she might have known it was no use. Something in Vercoe's words or the way he spoke them had forewarned her that this was to be no ordinary search. They began to examine the floor.

So the informer had done his work.

They had come to the metal trunks, and Vercoe had seen the joins in the floor boards. He knelt by them and motioned Bell to bring forward the lantern. Demelza said: 'I want you—'

Malcolm McNeil straightened up and looked at the girl who had come up behind him. He said: 'I think you would do well to leave us.'

She shook her head, not trusting her voice any more. He gazed at her a second longer, and then made a gesture for the two gaugers to continue.

Vercoe had found a spade and was forcing it into the narrow nick of the floor boards. With a squeal of strained wood they began to come up, for they were being lifted from the wrong side. After a minute he got his hand under the lifted boards, and Bell, putting the lantern down, knelt to help him. The trap door came up and the cache was open. McNeil took a step forward.

From where Demelza stood she could not see in. The room was humming and drumming about her ears. Rectangles of wall and roof began to dissolve into the uncertain geometries of faintness and nausea. All three men were around the hole, like jackals about a fallen beast, like hounds at the kill. For a few seconds they were involved in the general unreason of failing eyesight, of distortion and instability. Then she put out a hand and with a great effort steadied herself against a chair.

She did not know who would speak first, whether it would be Ross or one of his captors; but in fact it was McNeil, and all he said was: 'Well . . .' and made a gesture to Vercoe. Vercoe grunted.

Then no one spoke again and no one stirred. At last she forced her limbs to move. She looked down.

The cache was empty.

Chapter Thirteen

At three o'clock the following afternoon, having been granted his freedom on recognizances of £20, Dwight rode in at the gates of Killewarren. If there had been need for subterfuge before, the time for it was over.

For a while he could get no answer either to his rings or his knocks; but eventually the door was opened by the footman Thomas who had often shown him in before. He raised his eyebrows at sight of Dwight's bandaged head and bruised face.

'I've called to see Miss Caroline Penvenen.'

'She's gone, sir. This forenoon with her uncle.'

'Gone?'

'They've left for London. House be closed, sir, except for the servants. I don't know when they be coming back. A month may be.'

Dwight was unable to think what to say. 'What time did they go?'

'Just after ten. They was both anxious to be off, so they decided to dine on the way.'

'Was any message left, do you know? I had expected one.'

The man stared at him doubtfully. 'Not as I know. But I'll ask the housekeeper if you'll step inside.'

'I'll wait here.'

The man was gone several minutes and then brought

back a sealed letter. 'Miss Penvenen gived this to the housekeeper, just as she was leaving. No address. Just Dr Enys. I suppose she knew you'd call, sir.'

Dwight turned away from the house and, ignoring the man's talk, stood by his horse fumbling with the seal.

The letter was dated: '9 A.M. Sunday, the third of February, 1793.'

Dear Dwight,

I am leaving with my uncle for London within the hour, a move which cannot surprise you after the fiasco of last night. Need I tell you of it? Your servant will already have given his account.

I waited. Oh yes, I waited like a dutiful Bride, you will have been gratified to know, for nearly two hours, while my coachman and my maid yawned their heads off – and no doubt snickered behind their hands and your servant made so many excuses that I wondered at his invention.

But at the beginning he had told me all it was really necessary to know.

It is for the best this way, Dwight. Certainly far better that it should have happened now than later. I have known of your unhappiness for more than a month. Ever since we agreed to elope I have seen the struggle going on, the fight between your infatuation for me and your real love, which is your work in Sawle and Grambler. Well, your real love has won, and won so triumphantly – on the very day when I might most have expected to occupy your mind – that I am quite put to Rout.

Now you need not worry about it any more: you need give up nothing but me, and that you have already done. Perhaps it is for the best in more ways than one. We know so small a part of each other, I of you and you of me. No doubt we should have learned more in Bath, and then it would have been a little late.

So this is goodbye, Dwight. Do not fear I shall come to Cornwall to disturb you again. Not by two hundred miles. Thank you for the lessons you have taught me. They at least will not be forgotten by

Your sincere friend,
Caroline Penvenen

At five o'clock that afternoon, just before the first dusk, six men waited on Charlie Kempthorne in his cottage at the head of Sawle Combe. Their faces were as grim as their mission merited; but they found no one to welcome them. Charlie Kempthorne had gone, taking with him his easy smile and his cough, and a bag of silver he had saved and hidden under the floor. He had also taken his wedding clothes, which he had been making himself, and his Bible and such of his more recent purchases, like the cups and saucers and the mirror, as he could carry.

All he left was Lottie and May crouching terrified in a corner of the room upstairs. When they could be persuaded to speak, they said their father had given them a silver piece each and had gone at daylight, warning them not to stir out of doors for fear of their lives. They did not know where he had gone. Frustrated and angry, some of the men wanted to burn the cottage and beat the children; but moderate views prevailed, and word was sent to St Ann's to the aunt of the little girls to come and claim them quickly.

Charlie also left behind his wife-to-be. Dwight's interference had broken two romances. Rosina, at first incredulous, presently found in her memory small factual proofs. She had never really loved Charlie, but after a while she had responded gratefully to his admiration and attentions. It needed an emotional somersault now to realise and to condemn; for a while it was more than she was capable of and she went about in a daze, knowing hurt but not hate, answering the questions put to her flatly and without interest. Only occasionally a spark of anger showed when someone's question seemed to suggest that her own innocence could not be as complete as it seemed.

The six men who had called on Charlie did not give up their efforts at the sight of an empty cottage. They believed he would not move very fast or be able to travel without leaving a trail. News travels far in country districts, and the informer is the most hated of men. They thought they might catch up with him yet.

At seven o'clock that evening Ross came out of the cache where he had been hiding without food or water for eighteen hours – and in air that no one unused to the bad air of mines would have been able to tolerate for a quarter of the time. He had forced himself to wait until full dark, knowing that other men could be as patient as he. When he climbed up into the library, his eyes – so long accustomed to darkness – were able to pick out the window, the articles of furniture, and the door into the garden. He tried this, expecting it to be locked; but it was not and he stepped into the fresh air. There were lights in the house, but before he would approach it he made a cautious detour of the outbuildings and the surrounding garden and stream. Then he approached the house and looked in at each of the lighted windows. All the troopers had gone.

So at last he went in to Demelza, who for eighteen hours had been wondering what had become of him and had been imagining that the blood from his knuckles had been escaping from some untended artery.

The cache, having been dug to Mr Trencrom's specifications, had a false side moving on a central swivel, with a secondary and larger cache beyond. It was a not uncommon device among the more intelligent of the smuggling fraternity of Cornwall, but it was one that seldom failed to deceive.

The men who had done this job, being all miners except for one farmer and one carpenter, had completed the work with exceptional thoroughness and skill. They had made the second cache large enough to conceal a considerable amount of contraband, but Ross had not supposed when he watched it done that it would ever be used to conceal himself.

BOOK THREE

BOOK FIVE

Chapter One

Dwight's intervention, if it had not done everything that was intended, had saved Mr Trencrom's cargo. The *One and All* put back to the Scillies for two weeks and later landed her goods in three separate lots at different points along the coast. It had also saved Ross, for Mr Trencrom looked after his friends. Those who had been caught on the spot he could do nothing to help, but those who were luckier received his able support. Ross was informed that when the case of Black Saturday came up at the Quarter Sessions at the end of the month, a farmer and his son from Gwithian would be produced who would swear that Captain Poldark had spent the night of the second of February at their farm.

A week or so after the fight a surgeon called Wright came to stay with Dr Enys and helped him on some of his cases. A few days afterwards Dr Enys left for London.

Later Dwight was sorry that he had been so precipitate, that he had not waited until after the sessions, but at the time he felt he could delay no longer. He had bribed Caroline's London address out of Thomas and had written twice giving her on each occasion – lest one letter should go astray – his full account of the adventures of the night and his reasons for acting as he did. Knowing her to be fundamentally reasonable, he had expected that her letter of farewell – written in understandable heat and haste –

would sooner or later be retracted and that they could eventually make new plans. He had hung on day after day and had said each night, I'll wait until tomorrow, and then at last had dropped everything and gone.

So in the event, with a journey of five days each way and the sessions compelling his return, he was left with only one day in London to make his apologies and bring about a reconciliation.

It was enough had Caroline been half willing. They were staying with Mr Penvenen's sister Sarah, and Dwight called twice and twice was refused admittance. Then in the evening, reasoning that her uncle was likely to be behind the refusal, he called a third time, knowing her in, and tipped a footman to take up a private note to her. He waited impatiently until the footman returned with a reply which ran:

Dear Dwight,

Yes, I received your letters. I am glad that the choice you made was of salve to Ross Poldark and the other smugglers. But the choice – your choice – was made before ever you knew this man was an informer. So it cannot affect mine. Do you not see that? I am very, very sorry. It is better for us both that it should be so.

Caroline

Early the following morning he made a final effort to see her, but it was useless and so he came home.

While the Quarter Sessions were pending, the coastal district of Sawle and St Ann's had more urgent and imminent things to concern it than the new war with France. The bench of magistrates, it was known, had been chosen to represent impartiality, but many considered it had been chosen for its partiality for the letter of the law. Its chairman was the Revd Dr Halse, who had always been known for his severity on the bench, and it was not long before the free traders caught were summarily tried and convicted. Four of them received twelve months' imprisonment and two, Ned Bottrell and a man from St Ann's, were sentenced to transportation for ten years. These were savage sentences for Cornwall, where smugglers even when they were convicted usually got off light, and feeling was high by the time Dwight Enys came before the bench.

The case of Dr Enys was a peculiar one. It had not been clearly established how far he was implicated, and the witnesses who were called went no further towards making the position clear. Dwight himself refused to offer any explanation for his movements, and Dr Halse's exasperation became obvious. No man, no educated man, could suddenly appear on the cliff edge and start building a bonfire without certain conclusions being drawn. This much and a lot more Dr Halse said in a long homily which followed his consultation with the other ten members of the bench. It was, he said, a peculiar disgrace that a well-known physician of the neighbourhood should allow himself to become so involved in this reprehensible traffic. A heavy responsibility rested upon all men of reputation to help to stamp out the illegal conduct of their less enlightened neighbours, not to encourage it, not to participate in it, as, failing any other explanation, it must be assumed Dr Enys had been doing. The opinion of the bench was that Dr Enys should be fined £50 or serve three months' imprisonment.

Dwight accepted the censure and the fine unmoved;

and when the hearing was over, he refused to accept either sympathy or offers of help from those who had heard the case. All through this month, for a young man normally so kindly and tolerant, he had shown unexpected brusqueness and rancour towards friends and sympathizers. His popularity in Sawle and district had shot up to new heights – except in the house of Vercoe – and there were many who wondered why he would not be befriended. He showed impatience at any friendly move and a blank face to all advice and condolence.

Even Ross and Demelza he had seemed to avoid; and when he and Ross rode home together from the sessions, it was almost the first time they had had a private conversation.

For a while they discussed the outcome of the day. Ross thought that neither Bottrell nor the St Ann's man would serve their sentences. Already the Navy was crying out for men, and the two prisoners, both with experience of the sea, would probably be given the choice of fates. 'Not that one is much better than the other, but there's a matter of self-respect involved. I should suppose Bottrell at least will choose the Navy.'

'I was glad you were not charged, Ross. I thought they might have tried to pin something on you seeing that it was your land and knowing how hard they worked to get you convicted at the Assizes.'

'So they very well would have but for Trencrom. He provided me with witnesses to show that I was far away at the time of the run.'

'A man came to me just as I was leaving the court, said he was from Mr Trencrom and that Mr Trencrom would insist on paying my fine.'

'What did you say?'

'I refused, of course! I did not go to that trouble for Trencrom's sake.'

'No, you did it for mine. Have I told you what I feel about that?'

'You need not bother.'

'I am under an enduring debt.'

'Oh, nonsense.'

They went on for a few minutes. The day was windy but not cold. Seagulls were wheeling and screaming overhead and a gleam of sun gave sudden brilliance to their wings. Ross was the last person to push inquiries where they were unwelcome, but he was aware that something was very much amiss with this young man.

'I saw your friend Wright the other day. I suppose you still intend to leave the district now that this fuss is over?'

'I've no settled plans at all.'

'Then – your marriage to Caroline?'

'Is off. It was an adolescent folly. Fortunately we discovered it in time.'

Ross stared at his friend. 'As an outcrop of this smuggling affray?'

'No, of course not.'

'Demelza insists that it must be. She says you told her you were leaving late on the Saturday night. How was it affected by your arrest?'

'Not to my detriment, I see now. We should never have made anything of it, Ross. We were – incompatible, in the grip of a foolish passion. It couldn't have lasted and would have led to misery on both sides.'

'What has it led to now?'

'A temporary unhappiness that later we shall be grateful for. If you but realized it, I am in your debt, not you in mine.'

Dwight spoke firmly enough, but Ross saw that it was costing him a good deal. He would have liked more than anything to say something to help, but privately he was of the same opinion as Dwight. The relationship had been foredoomed. Far better bitter disappointment now than the humiliation and misery of a lifelong *mésalliance*.

After a time Ross, having searched his brain for a new subject, said:

'McNeil the dragoon officer looks none so well from his wound. Is it true he's staying with the Bodrugans?'

'Yes. They'd known him since his first visit and invited him. I still attend him.'

'You? That surprises me.'

Dwight smiled slightly. 'I know. Both sides of the law. But I took out the ball and dressed his wound at your house on the Saturday night, and he seemed grateful that I did not bleed him. Anyway he requested I should see him again, and I've done so.'

'You'll have had some good talk on the ethics of smuggling.'

'We do not discuss it. But I don't think he bears any ill will – except to the man who shot him. He's by no means fit to travel yet and should not have been in court today; he bitterly begrudges every day which prevents him from joining his regiment and fighting the French.'

'I think if he's patient, the opportunities for glory will not all go in the first months.'

'No, possibly not. It's hard to foresee how long it will last.'

'Well, when a nation with less than fifty thousand troops, mostly in foreign parts, engages to fight one with an army of half a million, all at home and striking from central lines . . .'

'We have allies.'

'Prussia and Austria? They blew hot and cold last year when their opportunities were greater. Holland? I think the Dutch will need more than a few of our gunboats and a regiment of Foot Guards to give them the will to fight.'

Dwight said: 'I have thought these last weeks I should wish to do something myself. It's difficult to know what, but the notion attracts me now – and it would I think help to relieve the – the sense of futility.'

'Well, take your time. Think all round it, for once you're in the pan it's hard to jump out.'

Just before they separated Dwight said: 'And your visit to – to Mark Daniel, was it all to no purpose?'

'It was to some purpose, for it showed me what an over-sanguine fool I've been.'

'He had no advice that was of use?'

'None at all.'

'How long shall you go on?'

'Until the coal is done.'

Dwight was silent until he drew rein to turn off.

'How was Daniel, Ross?'

'The thing had left its mark, as you'd suppose.'

'Yes . . . as I would suppose.'

Ross rode down the valley. Another matter of importance to himself came out of the events of Black Saturday. Nampara Cove was now useless to Mr Trencrom. The gaugers could not watch it every night, but the notoriety of the raid and all that had gone with it put the cove out of bounds for a long time to come. There could be no question now of the Poldarks taking the risk, for Mr Trencrom would not take the risk. That was going to make a great difference to Ross's income, just the vital difference he had not counted on. He had gambled again, and again lost. . . .

He had asked Demelza not to come to the Quarter Sessions; and since he was not in danger himself, she had agreed. Now he had it all to tell, and supper was late as a consequence. Afterwards they talked of the mine. The venturers of Wheal Radiant were interested in the head-gear; and this morning before the sessions began he had seen a representative of another mine for the sale of the surplus stores.

Demelza said suddenly: 'Ross, I have never mentioned it; but one day at the beginning of the year I went into St Ann's to buy a few things we needed – you remember, I asked for Darkie – and while I was there I met Mr Renfrew the chandler . . .'

He had picked up the *Sherborne Mercury* to glance through its pages; now to give himself time to think he carefully folded it and took it across to the shelf by the window where the old copies were stacked.

'And Mr Renfrew said it was a poor thing you'd sold the last of your shares in Wheal Leisure. I've never sought to ask you about it because – well, if you did not want to tell me, you did not. Perhaps you thought to save me worry. Or perhaps Mr Renfrew is mistaken and he was speaking of the first shares you had sold.'

Ross came back to the fire and stood beside it. 'No, it is true. I sold them in early January. I made £675 for them, which showed a handsome profit on my investment. Of course we have not the income . . .'

'Has all that had to go into Wheal Grace?'

Because she made it easy for him to lie to her, he could less than ever do so. 'No. Only £75 of it. The rest I used in discharging a debt of honour . . .'

After a moment's silence Demelza said: 'Oh, well, I thought he would know, being in the mine himself. Ross, do you think that the beer we brewed last will be right to drink yet? The other is gone, and John I know favours a little with his supper.'

'Tell him to try it. It should be fair enough. Demelza, I have wanted to explain about this for a long time but have not known quite the best way to do it. I was waiting in fact for a good opportunity, waiting for a time when it would no longer matter what I had done with the money. Instead the explanation comes on me when it matters more than ever.'

She looked thoughtfully at him. 'It is your money, Ross. You must do with it as you please.'

'Not entirely. My obligations are various. But one, in this particular, seemed above the others.'

Something in his expression gave her a hint of what was coming. She put down the thing she was sewing.

So he told her what he had done.

'Sometimes,' he ended, 'one feels an obligation in one's mind. Regardless of whether it is so truly or not, it *seems* a matter of conscience and so becomes one. I had induced Francis to sink his money in the mine. Now he's dead and Elizabeth and Geoffrey Charles are penniless and alone. However indifferent a protection I am to you and Jeremy, I am alive and active – constantly doing what I can; I offer some sort of shelter from – from the wind. Elizabeth has none such. With this money they can do a great deal, tide over these first difficult years.'

'Yes. I see that.'

'Before Christmas, of course, I was in no shape to help anyone at all. But my unknown friend gave me the breathing space. And he gave me the idea that I might copy him.

It was rash, but I needed – for my soul's sake – to be free of the burden of the sense of obligation. Of course I was then relying on the money from Trencrom continuing for the next few years.'

Demelza did not speak. She broke the cotton and stared at it with narrowed eyes.

'With Trencrom's money,' he said, 'we could spare this interest and capital. Without it we're in difficulties again – or shall be in time. Fortunately there's nine months of the year still to go. But I repent my generosity, and unhappily so must you also.'

She began to thread her needle again.

'Do you blame me?' he asked.

'Of course not. Not for myself, I don't. I am not so sure for Jeremy. But then 'tis done, and no good will come now of talking of it.' She hesitated, pushing her dark hair away from her forehead as if it was some unwelcome thought. 'Do you think Elizabeth is in so much need?'

'I think she *was*. Why?'

'Well, I have heard that George Warleggan is being very obliging to her.'

'I've no doubt he would be if she would let him. But she will not. Who spoke to you of it?'

'Sir Hugh Bodrugan.'

'Has he been here again?'

'Yes, he came to call one afternoon last week. He was passing, he said.'

'You didn't tell me.'

'I forgot. He wanted for us to go to the Meet at his house last week. I said we had another engagement because I knew you would not go.'

He bent to light his pipe, but the mouthpiece would not

draw so he knocked out the tobacco and began to fill it afresh. He was surely the last person now to complain either at someone's fancy for his wife or at her failure to tell him of a passing visit. But perhaps the irritation he felt rose not from Sir Hugh's visit but from what he had said.

'One of George Warleggan's ambitions, long before Francis died, was to drive a wedge between them and me, and the easiest way to attempt it was by befriending them. Once he succeeded, and both Francis and I suffered as a result . . . In trying to help Elizabeth now, he is only continuing the same tactics. Although that wasn't my aim in arranging for her to get this money, it does have the effect of strengthening her hand against him.'

'Yes,' said Demelza, and went on with her sewing.

On the twelfth of March, which was a Tuesday, Captain Henshawe came to see Ross in the library, where Ross was working. There was a peculiar expression on his face, and he carried a small sack which he put down on the floor while he took off his hat and wiped his forehead.

'You're hot?' said Ross. 'You'll soon cool off here. There's a draught that's been mislaid from January blowing under the door. What's that, the last of our coal?'

Henshawe said: 'Young Ellery's just come up and brought this bag with him. I thought you might like to see what was in it, sur.'

He emptied the bag on the floor. There were about a dozen pieces of quartzose rock, not noticeably different from a thousand others that had been mined and crushed in the last twelve months. Henshawe's eyes travelled curiously over Ross's face as Ross looked at them.

'Pick 'em up,' said Henshawe.

Ross did so, weighed one or two in his hand, put them on his desk, tried a couple more. Very heavy.

'What is it – lead?'

'Tin.'

'What sort of proportion?'

'Goodly. There's a thin streak or two of copper, as you can see, and some siliceous minerals. It's in that main shaft we've been sinking below the sixty fathoms. Plumb light-blue killas. They come on it today.'

'You've been down?'

'Yes. They've been driving through granite and hard black killas, as you know; but they passed out of that yesterday, following the eastward split of the old copper lode, as we decided. There's been tin mixed with it for twenty fathoms, but never in much quantity, and the copper even poorer. Indeed, as you know, 'twas only just alive. This is the first time there's been any rich indications.'

'Is there any size to the thing?'

'This is from a reg'lar bunch of ore, as you can tell by the weight. The lode is narrower than 'twas, and generally comby; but this bunch is six feet or more across, and we don't know how deep.'

Ross tilted his chair back and stared at his desk. 'I was in the process of closing the books of the mine. Saturday is the end of it. The infidels from Wheal Radiant are coming nearer to my price for the headgear. I have kept them waiting two days as a business tactic, but I shall send over tomorrow and accept.'

'And this?'

Ross turned over a piece of the rock with his foot. 'As we have spent eighteen months and all our money seeking copper, you can hardly expect me to become excited over the discovery of a small parcel of tin.'

'From the look of it below, I should say it was worth a second thought.'

'Do you want me to come down?'

'Yes. I'd like for you to.'

'Who found it?'

'Ellery and Green.'

'And they think they've discovered El Dorado?'

'They're keen enough, as you'd imagine. After so much wasted effort . . .'

'In their eyes it appears much bigger than it really is, eh?'

Henshawe said cautiously: 'I'd like for you to see it before we say more about that.'

Ross got up and shut his ledgers. They went out and began to walk across the valley. Low grey cloud was blowing across the sun, and the thin smear of smoke from the mine chimney merged and blew away with it. Farther west, rifts in the shifting canopy showed distant sky, blue and pale-green and misty indigo. It was a quiet day and should have been mild, but some northern air had infected it and the wind was chill. The trees in the valley were still as black as mid-winter.

There had been silence all the way. As they neared the mine, Ross looked up at the slow, measured swing of the balance bob. Trevithick had said the engine would last fifty years, and no doubt he was right – given the opportunity. Ross could tell that Henshawe was quietly very interested in this discovery; but there had been so many bitter disappointments that in self-defence he would not allow himself to perceive any novelty in this one. And unless they had actually struck a bed of tin which needed the absolute minimum of further outlay, with a quick return for what was raised, there was no chance at all of keeping the mine in operation. In any case, tin was basically less profitable than copper, the ore being so much more expensive to extract at surface. There had been tin mines in this area before – Grambler had begun as one in the seventeenth century – and there were still a few alluvial workings, two- or three-man concerns eking out an existence; but he had never seriously thought of finding or mining the mineral in any big way. And the tin industry was still in a depressed condition; no one would be willing to finance an exhausted copper mine on the strength of a few samples of rock.

They went down, and Ross inspected the find. Work had stopped in other parts of the mine – only the great engine still patiently sucked water out of the sump – and men were more or less taking it in turns to pick at the rock, weighing this lump and that in their work-seamed hands, bending over it and talking and nodding and comparing experiences of the past. Most of them were stripped to the waist, for the heat had much increased in the last twenty fathoms. Ross took the pick himself and worked away for a few minutes, while Ellery stood beside him pointing out the breadth and inclination of the lode.

Ross didn't say much; every one of the workers knew the state of things in the mine, but every one no doubt hoped this would just make the difference. He did not disillusion them, for that would come soon enough.

On the way up again he said to Henshawe: 'I agree. It is not unimpressive.'

'You said all along you had the feeling to go deeper.'

'Yes, but not for tin, man, not for tin. Anyway it may still be the merest pocket.'

As they reached the top and the now apparently bright day greeted them, he added: 'I'm glad Ellery found it. He and his partner are good men. We can get what little they have time to bring up stamped and dressed, and it will make a difference to their last earnings.'

'They'll take it some hard to be deprived of the chance to work a few weeks more. They would have given up more easier if there had been no such find. What we need's a breathing space to see what this means.'

'I agree, but where's it to come from? Who's to pay? I tell you frankly I haven't twenty pounds in the world.'

Henshawe said: 'I'd never much faith in you seeking the lodes at a greater depth. It's not been my experience in this district – they die on you. But this has a keenly look to me. And it's queer; copper under tin you expect – but not tin under copper.'

'Well, there's four days still to go. They'd be advised to work hard until Saturday.'

Ross did not tell Demelza of the discovery. There was no virtue in raising false hopes. But the whisper spread behind his back, and in no time she had heard of it and wanted to know what it meant.

'It means nothing,' Ross said. 'At best it would be a minor lottery prize. A few months ago we could have worked it as a side product; no one objects to an additional mineral, and the receipts from it would have kept us struggling a while longer. But there is nothing more to it than that. It will be a blow to many families when the mine closes, and I suppose it is not unnatural that they should be hoping for the impossible.'

'So was I,' said Demelza, and after that nothing more was said.

Nothing more until Thursday evening, when Captain Henshawe called. He found them both at home, so the conversation took place before Demelza.

'I've just been down again, sur. They've opened of her up a tidy bit since Tuesday. More and more it look to me like a lode of value and not just a freak bunch. The stuff that's come up, as you know, is as rich as you'd want. It go more and more against the grain to let her fill with water at the present stage.'

Ross frowned his discomfort. 'It goes against the grain to let her fill with water at any stage. Let someone only provide the coal to keep the pump working . . .'

'That's what I been thinking,' said Henshawe apologetically.

'What d'you mean?'

'I been thinking that if I'm eagerer than you I'm also the more able to back my judgment. Leisure is doing a fine job for me and I've made savings. Not all that big, but I could see us through a month or more. I could put down a hundred pound if need be. It seems only right, and I'd be willing to do that.'

Ross stared at him. 'You would?'

'Yes, I would.'

Ross had known Henshawe for twelve years, since he was made mine captain at Grambler. He was an honest man and a clever one. His education, he sometimes said, had cost his father a penny a week for eight months. He had raised himself – at one time before the depression came – to a position of consulting manager to five mines solely on the strength of his own ability and acumen. His friendship with Ross had grown closer ever since the opening of Wheal Grace. But Ross had no fear that Henshawe was making this offer as a gesture of friendship or on a charitable impulse of the moment. Unlike certain other people who might be brought to mind, Henshawe had never disguised the fact that he felt his first duty to be to his own wife and family. He would perhaps have given five pounds to save a friend from prison; but nothing would have induced him to risk a further hundred pounds of hard-gleaned capital in a mining venture which had already absorbed so much unless . . .

Ross met Demelza's eyes across the room. He knew what she was thinking.

'Are you wholly satisfied, then, that this thing is worth pursuing? After all the other failures you feel so sure of this . . .'

'Not sure, sur. But I thought to proceed slowly. In another week we shall know far more. If 'tis disappointing we can still close and I shall have lost twenty or twenty-five pound. If it go on as I think it will go on, I'll back it for a month longer. But we must move tomorrow. I thought with your permission I'd send over to Trevaunance or Basset's Cove for coal to carry on. 'Twill only just reach us in time.'

'Send over by all means,' said Ross, but neither his face nor his voice was easy to read. He was carefully combating a feeling within him which he was afraid to recognize as hope.

On the same day towards the evening George Warleggan went to see his father and mother at Cardew and told them that Elizabeth Poldark had promised to be his wife.

Chapter Two

In all prospering human affairs there is a streak of hazard, a blending of good fortune with good judgment which gives the lucky man a sense of having earned his deserts and gives the deserving, if he is modest, an awareness of his luck.

That George Warleggan was able to break such startling news to his family came in part from events over which he had no control and in part from that sharp sense of timing which had stood him in good stead before as a man of affairs.

They met at Cusgarne on the Thursday afternoon, and Thursday was the last and most trying day of four which had been trying for Elizabeth.

First there had been the unpleasant scene with George Tabb, who had been a faithful servant of the Poldarks all his life. As the last manservant, he had felt himself able to claim certain privileges even before Francis died; and since then he had become subtly less easy to handle. On Monday a trial of strength, and Elizabeth came out of it bitterly aware that she had let things slide too long. Now she must either accept his defiance or discharge her two remaining servants and take new ones who would not possibly get through the same amount of work.

The choice was temporarily but uneasily shelved. Then Mr Nathaniel Pearce arrived fresh from his gout, with new problems to face, the results of negotiations to report, and new decisions to be made for which only Elizabeth could be responsible. A tithe of £1 6s 8d per year on the seines of certain of the fishing boats in Sawle was payable to the Poldarks, and in the case of most boats this was long overdue. For the last four years catches had been poor. Should the fishermen be pressed for the money? Whose was the greater need now? A long-standing complaint from Garth, Mr Penvenen's agent, on the condition of the bridge over the stream behind Grambler village where the two estates ran together. Repair was Poldark responsibility, but now Mr Penvenen, newly returned from London, offered to pay one quarter of the cost of a new bridge if Mrs Poldark would meet the rest. Would she meet the rest? What about the pastureland to the west of the house? Ross advised her to have it ploughed; for now that war had come, corn growing would be likely to pay handsome dividends. But already it was late to do anything this year, and it would mean engaging and paying farm hands. Finally there was the making of a complicated dispute with some tinners who were claiming their age-old right under the Stannary Law to enter enclosed ground and prospect for tin.

She slept badly that night, and so in the morning in the very first light was the less strong to meet the news that it brought. A man from Cusgarne to say her mother had had an apoplexy and would she come at once. Elizabeth was in Kenwyn by eleven and found her mother paralysed in one arm and hardly able to speak. Over a silent meal with her father she faced up to the inescapable. There was now no choice for her. Already there was one bedridden woman at Trenwith, tended on unsatisfactorily by the village girl Elizabeth had been able to engage. The Chynoweths would bring a little money but trouble and difficulties out of proportion. Elizabeth looked into the future and saw it as one in which sickness and age and responsibility were her only companions.

Into this picture came George Warleggan, saying he had only just heard of her mother's illness and that he had come straight up from the bank, apologizing that he should be a little untidy, solicitous for Mr and Mrs Chynoweth, and more than solicitous for Mrs Poldark.

She told him all there was to tell, and without emotion told him what she proposed to do. While they were talking, her father shuffled out of the room, a man who for thirty years had accepted his directives from his wife and now without her was helmless, drifting as the first wind took him.

They talked on for a time. George seemed reluctant to go. He was watching Elizabeth with his attentive eyes. At length he said:

'Do you know what I wish?'

'No.'

'I wish, my dear Elizabeth, that you would allow me to make all the arrangements necessary, and that you would permit me to engage a separate establishment for your mother at Trenwith, so that no further burden would fall on you.'

'I couldn't let you do that.'

'Why not? You're so *frail*, Elizabeth. I fear for you. One does not expect the lily to stand the storms of winter. It needs protection. *You* need protection. I can only offer it you in this way.'

She glanced at him through her lashes, her face pale and withdrawn but not unfriendly.

'You're truly kind. But I'm stronger than I look. Now – just now – and perhaps for a few years, I shall have to be. I regret it – you don't know how much I regret it – but it has to be. One must take what life sends.'

'But one must not take what I send, eh? Is that it?'

She smiled at him. 'I have already taken so much.'

'Oh,' he made a gesture, 'a little for my godson, and that very reluctantly; certain concessions in the matter of Francis's debts. But nothing for yourself. And now nothing for your mother. I should like to do it for your mother's sake.'

Always in the past he had found this the surest avenue to Elizabeth's sympathies, and it was so now.

'Oh, you know how very deeply I have appreciated what you've done for her in the past, George. Your kindness makes me ashamed to refuse you anything. But what you suggest—'

He said: 'If there was one thing you did not refuse me, it would solve everything.'

'What is that?' she asked, looking at him; and instantly knew.

'Yourself,' he said.

She turned a little away from him, with a sudden sensation of finding herself on the edge of a precipice. It was a precipice she had quietly known of for a long time but disregarded because she felt her balance so sure. There was no danger – except perhaps in allowing him to think there might be. Now suddenly the equilibrium was changed.

'Before you say anything,' he went on, 'let me add something to that one word. Although I've never spoken of it, you will be aware, I dare suppose, that I have loved you for ten years, ever since we first met. In that time I have served you only as I could, by paying back half Francis's card debts with my cousin Sanson, by waiving the interest on his ordinary debts to our bank, by allowing no thought of retaliation to be considered when he – persistently insulted me. All this I did willingly and would have done twice as much if the opportunity'd been present – as you also know. Since Francis's death I have served you in any way you would allow me, and will continue to without thought of anything *I* may gain by it.'

'Yes,' she said. 'I'm more than grateful – more than grateful.'

'But now I ask you to marry me. As I said, I love you. I don't think you love me. But I think you like and respect me; and I think – indeed I'm sure that in time such liking would become something more than liking, something closer than a common interest.' He hunched his shoulders and stared at her. She had not moved any farther away, and he could see her face. He thought there was a slight flush under her pale composure. He flattered himself that, considering all that hung on the outcome, he was putting his case well. 'I can't bring you breeding, my dear. But I can bring you a certain kind of gentility which is the more punctilious because it is only one generation deep. And so far as material considerations go—'

'Please,' she said.

'Oh, I know you would not marry me for my money or my possessions. If you did that, you wouldn't be the person I know you to be. But at the risk of offending you I want to tell you what I can offer.'

She tightened her lips, a little more tense, as if ready for another protest. The window through which she looked was full of trees and hedges, overgrown, overbranched, blowing in the wind.

He said: 'When I marry, my father has promised that he and my mother will vacate Cardew. That means I shall be able to take my wife to a house four times as big as Trenwith, everything in it almost new, twenty servants, in a park of five hundred acres. You've seen it. You know. If you marry me, Trenwith could be repaired and refurnished, kept as a second home where your father and mother could live with adequate servants, and where we could visit them as often as you chose. I already have my own carriage, you could have one also if you wanted it, or two or six if it pleased you. I could take you to London and Bath and introduce you into society there. Local society is already a thought provincial for me. I have undertaken to educate Geoffrey Charles. But as my son he would be differently placed from what he is now. I am heir to all Warleggan interests. So would he be. We're still young, Elizabeth, you and I. There's very little we could not achieve if we put our minds to it. For ten years you've lived in a cage. Give me permission to turn the key.'

'And the devil taketh him up into an exceeding high mountain and showeth him all the kingdoms of the world and the glory of them; and saith unto him: "All these things will I give thee . . ."' It had been one of the lessons read last Sunday in Sawle Church, where Elizabeth sat alone with Geoffrey Charles in the family pew.

She picked up her bag from the table, fumbled in it without knowing what she wanted. She hadn't spoken and now he was waiting. The light was already poor in the room, as poor in its way as the worn furniture; but some reflection from the mirror above the sofa lit up his heavy, intent, constrained face. She knew that every moment he waited his hopes of a favourable answer would rise. To her own astonishment, she realized that a favourable answer was no longer impossible for her. It was as if life were mesmerizing her into acceptance of a situation which at one time, and not so long ago, would never have been allowed to come into being. There was still enough critical detachment in her to notice the occasional gaucheries of his proposal; yet reason told her there was not one single statement he had made which was exaggerated or untrue. He *could* offer her all that. He, George Warleggan, very close to her now, known so long that easy familiarity led to an underrating of his achievements and his charm; but in fact formidable, wealthy, powerful in the county for good or ill, still young, not bad-looking, a person already become a personage, one of the few who counted and who would count still more as time went by; he was offering her all this as the price of marriage: her son lacking for nothing, *all* her problems solved. All except one, a new one, the problem of George.

'Elizabeth,' he said. 'Can I suppose that—'

She stopped him with a gesture, instantly, suddenly flushing into a rare colour and brilliance of expression. 'No, please, I don't want you to think . . .'

And there in her refusal she halted. Upstairs was her mother, crippled and fretful, and her father, indecisive and endlessly complaining. She had ridden over in the rain and tonight or tomorrow she must ride back to Trenwith, which would greet her unlighted and unheated and with all its problems still to solve. And years of loneliness and sick-nursing lay ahead. And on the other side was light and warmth and companionship and *care*.

'Oh, George—' she said, and put up her hands to her flushed face. 'I don't know what to say.'

Instantly he was beside her, one arm gently round her shoulders, aware of a startling triumph that he'd not dared to expect, but aware of how nearly it still trembled in the balance.

'Say nothing more now, my dear,' he urged. 'Nothing at all, please.'

'I am so depressed. Please don't ask for an answer now.'

'I ask you for nothing. Only give me permission to give.'

'But if you give—'

'Don't say any more, Elizabeth.'

'But I must. It's the – loneliness . . . What I'd not imagined – the lack of a person, a partner. But to pretend now, or to let you think . . .'

'I think nothing for the present. But I hope. Loneliness is not one-sided, Elizabeth. A man can feel it too, especially when he has loved anyone as long and as hopelessly as I have you.'

So they stayed for a time. And while she held her head down as if in defeat, he held his high in victory and looked over her bright hair at the wild, untended garden and the rain. He watched the water trickling in grey loops down the glass.

Though intention had not been in it, he suddenly found the prospect before him dazzlingly good – first because it gave him this woman whom he had loved and wanted for so long, second because by the same stroke it dealt what he knew would be the deadliest of blows at his bitterest enemy. It was not given to many men, he felt, to achieve so much by a single coup.

Chapter Three

The tin lode did not peter out. In a week they found that ore-bearing rock existed in a great mass at this point. No one knew how far it yet extended, but Ross began to feel himself infected with some of the general excitement. In another week they were raising the ore in quantity; and even allowing for the difficulties of dressing, there was the prospect of a return.

To keep down expenditure, all work on the copper lodes – such as they were – was suspended, and for the same reason other trying decisions had to be made. They were working an underhand stope, and already there was a worked-out open space above them. Very soon it would be dangerous to go on without timbermen and props for support. Already it was uneconomic, for no lode is constant in size and quality; and instead of eating at it in this unscientific way, they should have been making a series of right-angled shafts and levels to cut the lode at different depths and to create reserves of explored ground. That was the methodical way; but lack of capital forced them to live from hand to mouth.

No rumour of the momentous decision taken at Cusgarne reached the outside world. On a visit to Truro, Ross met Richard Tonkin, whom he had not seen for a year, and told him of the discovery of tin. Tonkin drew on his own experience to be encouraging, and, having at one time been manager of United Mines, his experience was considerable. He himself was no longer in mining, having six months before bought a small boatbuilding business in East Looe in partnership with Harry Blewett – another sufferer in the Carnmore Copper failure and one to whom Ross had lent money at the time of the crash. They were making a good living out of their venture.

Ross parted from him slightly encouraged by his comments. If one could just keep *going*, even with the most modest return, it would justify all manner of things within himself, it would maintain the men working on the mine, it would help everyone connected with the venture to a new self-respect . . .

The following week-end, Verity, Francis's sister, visited Elizabeth. She had not been to Trenwith since her brother died; but this was a long dated invitation, and the ice had to be broken sometime. Elizabeth too forced herself not to go back on the arrangement, though with so much milling in her heart and head . . . Verity brought her stepson James Blamey who had arrived unexpectedly for a few days' leave. Young, noisy, warmhearted, attractively fond of his stepmother in a boyish, roughly gentle way, James helped to keep the spectres at arm's length.

They were much concerned when they learned of Mrs Chynoweth's illness and offered to leave at once, but Elizabeth would not hear of it. Her mother was well looked after – now. A nurse had been engaged and two new servants, and one could only wait and hope that in a few weeks she would be well enough to be moved. Verity wondered at the word 'now', which seemed rather often to creep into Elizabeth's conversation.

James was open-mouthed at Elizabeth's beauty – as young men so often were – and enjoyed himself cantering about the countryside on a borrowed nag. He joined Verity on several of her visits to old friends and went with her to Nampara for Sunday dinner and tea. Demelza was waiting for them, and she and Verity hugged each other while Ross shook James Blamey's hand. Then James had to kiss Demelza, so that it was some moments before she had the breath to ask the question Ross had forced himself not to ask.

'But – isn't Elizabeth with you?'

'No. She was to have been, but a severe headache came on. She's much worried, you know, over her mother. She sent her love as well as her apologies.'

They went in, and talked and laughed perhaps more easily than they might have done in Elizabeth's presence. While they were talking of Ross's mission to see Mark Daniel, Verity's eyes strayed out of the window and confirmed their earlier impression that the engine chimney was still smoking.

She said: 'But I see you have not yet given up.'

Ross explained.

'We exist on a shoe-string and everything's against us. But the quality of the ore this week is remarkable – fortunately, for every expense of development must be paid for out of what we raise and a single fault in the lode will see our end.'

'D'you know,' said James Blamey in his big voice, 'I have never been down a mine yet, though it is unnatural in me to be so neglectful. How deep is your bilge, Captain? Do you climb all the way or do you have one of these newfangled buckets?'

'Perhaps after dinner James would like to go down, Ross,' Demelza suggested.

'By all means.'

'Ha! so I should,' said James, 'though I've a fancy I shall get dizzy climbing the wrong way from usual. When you're in the foremast shrouds, 'tis most comforting to see the deck below you, even if 'tis only the size of a visiting card. In a mine I should expect to fly up to the surface if I lost my grip!'

Just before dinner Dwight came. A week ago Demelza had tackled him about the break-up of his plan to marry Caroline and so now felt a greater than ever responsibility for his welfare.

Nevertheless he was no damper on the party, being specially interested in James Blamey and medical conditions in the Navy. James laughed at his questions. When you were afloat, you didn't dare to be ill. If you were, you got dosed with a purge or an emetic according to where the pain was. Last voyage on his ship there'd been thirty deaths from scurvy alone. James had left the *Thunderer* and had joined the frigate *Hunter* in a squadron under Admiral Gell. They were at present in Plymouth Sound but under sailing orders for next week, destination yet unknown but probably the Mediterranean. James's concern, like Captain McNeil's, was lest the war should be over before he could have any part in it.

After dinner Dwight left and Ross took James off to the mine, so the two women were left alone.

At first they talked of Jeremy, and then quite suddenly Verity broke off the conversation to say:

'Tell me, my dear, have you noticed anything strange about Elizabeth?'

'In what way strange?' asked Demelza, her senses instantly alert. 'I've scarcely seen her.'

'Well, it's hard to define. But I think she has recovered quickly from her bereavement, has she not? Oh, I know it's six months, and no one would expect her to grieve for ever; it is not quite that – but she seems different in some way, a little on edge, as if innerly excited. Once or twice in conversation she has checked herself, as if afraid of saying too much.'

'To you? This week-end?'

'Yes. I believe I am not imagining it. I know her quite well as we lived so long together. One gets the impression that she thinks her circumstances are going to change.'

They may already have changed, thought Demelza, remembering the six hundred pounds. 'You should ask Ross,' she said.

Verity looked at Demelza. 'That sounds a trifle bitter, my dear. Are you sure you have reason to be?'

Demelza looked up quickly, then smiled. 'Did it? It was not at all meant to be. I know Ross loved Elizabeth once; so when he goes to see her I'd not be human if I did not wonder what they say to each other. Would I? Ross does not tell me what they say, and 'tis not in my pride to ask, so I never learn.' She got up, looking down at Verity, now stooped and kissed her forehead. 'I should not have said that much if you hadn't asked me, but you did, and so I answered. Verity, would you care for a cup of tea? It is early, but all this talking has made me thirsty.'

'I'd like one. But just let me say – and I do not say this for your comfort – if Ross were—'

'No,' said Demelza. 'I don't think you should need to say that, whether for my comfort or no. Having a husband, it seems to me, is a small matter like going to church. Either you trust in something or you do not. If you do not, then there's no benefit in going to church at all, is there? But if you do believe in him, then you've no excuse to be asking for proofs all the time.'

'That's a very admirable outlook—'

'Oh, yes, and I am not always very admirable. Seldom, indeed. But it is true, isn't it; and that's more important than the feelings you feel sometimes. Verity, tell me about yourself for a change. You are happy, quite happy? I dearly love James. I should like Jeremy to grow up like James. He's like a west wind, gusty and clean and no breath of malice. I think he has quite fallen in love with you.'

Verity caught her smile and swiftly answered it.

'I love James like my own son. Yes, I'm happy, Demelza, or would be without the fear for Andrew's safety. So far there has been no trouble for the packets, and he says he takes a more westerly course to avoid possible attack. But he must come through the narrower waters between the Scillies and Ushant, and there is never any knowing now. You know what that feeling is.'

When they were in bed that night Demelza told Ross that Verity was going to have a baby.

'What?' Ross leaned up an one elbow. 'That is a surprise! Brave news! Are you sure?'

'She told me so herself. As yet it is a secret. Andrew doesn't know and she wishes to keep it to herself for the time. Isn't it good? I'm that pleased for them both.'

'So am I. When is it to be?'

'About October.'

'She will be thirty-five this year. I hope all will go well.'

'Oh, it is no age, Ross, though I believe she is a little anxious in that respect herself. It will be strange for Andrew with his daughter nearly twenty; but I know he'll be delighted and I urged her to tell him so soon as possible.'

'I have never noticed you overready with your own news. Indeed, it was my greatest complaint on both occasions.'

'Let's not go into that now,' said Demelza.

Later, in the darkness, her thought moved on to that other subject which had been nagging at her all afternoon. Why had Elizabeth given Verity the impression that her circumstances were soon going to change? In what way could her circumstances now change more than they already had done from the receipt of the six hundred pounds? It didn't make sense; and the more she went over the ordinary explanations, the less satisfied she was by them. At length Ross, who had been asleep, said:

'My dear, are you eaten by ants that you must toss and turn all night long?'

'I'm sorry. It is something that will not let me sleep. I will be quieter now.'

'Are you upset or feeling ill?'

'No, no, in rudest health. Just can't settle. I shall be better now.'

Easy enough to predict. No sooner did her limbs compose themselves in momentary ease than the urge began to move them elsewhere. Even an inch. Even a half inch.

Were Ross and Elizabeth planning to run away together? Was *that* the change of circumstances Elizabeth foresaw? That would not bring any greater prosperity to her, but perhaps she did not refer to financial circumstances at all. Demelza would have taken this more seriously if Ross had not been lying beside her now, his breathing becoming deeper again as he went off to sleep. It was not at all improbable, she felt, that they would like to do that; but, knowing Ross so well, she was certain he would not do it this way. He was far too honest a person to do anything underhand. If he was going to leave her and go with Elizabeth, he would force himself to tell her.

Very well, but perhaps he would tell her when the time came. Perhaps Elizabeth had said: 'Keep it from her as long as you can – for her sake.' In the dark of the night Demelza could hear her say it. Yet even that did not tally with Ross's manner or moods. Yesterday he had been cheerful, more highspirited than she remembered him since Julia died. That was because of the mine, not Elizabeth. Demelza would have staked her head that it was a mine-cheerfulness and not a woman-cheerfulness.

Then did George Warleggan come into Elizabeth's picture somewhere? Demelza suddenly went rigid. Something Sir Hugh Bodrugan had said, more than she had told Ross. A hint, no more. Did he know more?

Had Demelza been certain at this stage that the mystery she was trying to solve concerned only Elizabeth and George, she would have gone no further with it. But she was still by no means sure.

So tomorrow . . .

In visiting Sir Hugh Bodrugan she knew she was on thin ice. Ross strongly disapproved of her giving any encouragement to his attentions. In the second place Sir Hugh, though playful enough most times, was becoming less easy to keep at arm's length. The rumour was that he was deep in an affair with a woman called Margaret Vosper. If it were so, it did not abate his interest in Demelza. Perhaps having one easy conquest had made him less patient with young women who were too long on the hook.

To avert these twin dangers, or to reduce them, she waited until the Wednesday when she knew Ross would be most of the day down the mine, and she went in the morning when Sir Hugh's gallantry was likely to be at its lowest ebb.

In the event she was a little unfortunate, for Sir Hugh was out and was not expected back until dinnertime. Constance Bodrugan was also off with her dogs, so Demelza found herself drinking chocolate with the one member of the household able to entertain her and the one she least wanted to see.

She had not expected to meet Malcolm McNeil again, and she half expected him to show some resentment; but he greeted her like an old friend. His arm was still in a sling and he had put on weight from the enforced idleness. She always dressed her best to come to Werry House, and McNeil's eyes, she thought, were bolder than usual in his assessment of her. No doubt the degenerate influence of the Bodrugan household was having its effect.

When she was trying to think of the best excuse to leave, he suggested that as it was a fine morning they should stroll across the park and try to find Sir Hugh. It should not be difficult, since he was rounding up his young deer and his gamekeepers would be with him.

They set off down the steps and along the path between the unkempt lawns. He found her long stride unusual in a woman.

'And how is Captain Poldark?'

'Brave, thank you. That busy with his mine.'

'I had hoped I should receive an invitation to visit you before I left.'

'. . . Last time you came without an invitation.'

'That was in the course of duty. This would be in the pursuit of pleasure.'

'Then come any time, please. I know Ross would be glad to see you.'

'And you?'

'And I, of course . . . When do you expect to go?'

'Not for some weeks. That's if I continue to take notice of your doctor-smuggler friend.'

'He is a very good man to take notice of.'

'I still find it har-rd to understand his association with the smugglers.'

'Have you asked him about it?'

'Frequently.'

'If he has refused to explain, Captain McNeil, I don't think I should begin.'

They walked on in silence, passing a herd of about thirty deer who without exception raised their heads and watched suspiciously until the danger retreated.

'Captain Poldark was somewhere in the house that night, wasn't he?'

'How should you expect me to answer that?'

'You don't need to. I could tell that you expected him to be in that secret cellar when we opened it. I knew ye had seen him that night.'

After a moment she said: 'Is that Sir Hugh in the trees over there?'

'No, he's on a chestnut horse. I thought it probable that if I posted a watch on your house long enough we should discover where he was hiding.'

'And did you – post such a watch?'

'No.'

'Why not?'

'Because I had too great a regard for you, ma'am.'

Demelza glanced quickly at him, expecting a conventional insincerity but not quite finding it.

McNeil went on: 'Or that is the half of the truth, to be honest. Had I conceived it my duty to do so, I would have.

But I am a soldier not a spy and was already sickened of the affair. The men who were caught were caught and that was an end on it.' He screwed up his moustache. 'And now. Well, now it is all forgotten so far as I am concairned. I hold nothing against Captain Poldark except that he married so charming a wife.'

Demelza said: 'I don't hold even that against him – so far as it is true.'

'It is true.' McNeil stopped and she had to stop also. He smiled down at her. 'So I trust you hold nothing against me for my part in the affair?'

She gave him her very best smile in return. 'Far from it. I hold naught against you for what you did do, and thank you much for what you did not do.'

He bowed slightly. 'Would ye take my arm, ma'am? The good one, I mean. I think that is Sir Hugh in the distance now, and it would be more seemly to approach him in the proper manner.'

In the end Demelza got the information she wanted, though not without tactical manoeuvre. She said she had come to see Sir Hugh about a new seed drill he had talked of on his last call. It was a poor story, but he was indulgent enough to break off his own work to show her the drill in operation. Fortunately it was to Sir Hugh's purpose as well as to Demelza's that they should get rid of McNeil, so in the end they managed it.

Sir Hugh said: 'Now you see the seed fed into the hoppers falls into the seed boxes fixed on the bottoms of the hoppers just as in Tull's old drill; but here's where the improvement is claimed— Why d'you come in the morning, m'dear, when you interrupt my work, damme, when there's three evenings a week free, eh? Wednesday's not a good evening, for I'm often bespoke; but Thursdays, Saturdays, and Mondays I'd entertain you in a fashion proper for a young woman of your trim. Come Saturday; Connie's often away, and—'

'I should have thought 'twould have been a poor time to see a seed drill, after dark.'

'Oh, pooh, yes; but if you stop the night, I'll show you the drill Sunday morning. 'Twould be an excuse to stay from church.'

'And what do you suppose my husband would say?'

'What? Well, what would he say? Is he a spoilsport? Then come when he's from home and will not know the difference. I have an idea—'

'You were going to tell me, Sir Hugh, where the improvement in this seed drill was claimed.'

Sir Hugh grunted impatiently and told her. After a while she said: 'Do you remember when you called to see me last that you mentioned George Warleggan and Elizabeth Poldark, saying that George was paying her attentions? Do you know if it is true? What made you say that to me?'

Sir Hugh paused with his hand over hers on the handle of the seed drill. His thick eyebrows crouched like furry caterpillars.

'Nay, rumour, that was all.'

'And what was the rumour?'

'What I told you. Now look ee—'

'What was the rumour exactly, Sir Hugh?'

'That he was paying her serious attentions. No more and no less. Indeed I was surprised you'd not heard it. Gossip is always a pleasant topic over tea, especially bawdy gossip. I'll tell you some when you come on Saturday.'

'About Elizabeth and George?'

'Nay, I know nothing more of them and misremember where I heard that. But stay, there was one other thing. I was in to Truro on Monday ordering some new cravats, and my tailor told me in confidence he'd just received an order for a wedding suit from George. 'Twas all secret at present, he said. So what George's relations are with your cousin-in-law, I'd not pretend to say. Either he's going to be legal about it or he's keeping her for the side door. I hope for your sake it is the first, for it would be a grand thing for the Poldarks to get George Warleggan in the family. I wish Connie would marry again and marry some-one like that. We need the money. I'm always nagging her to, and she's always nagging me to, but I say I ain't a marrying man; and then without fail she says I'm a bedding man and what's the difference except for a service and a gold ring, and I say, ah, but the gold ring is just what I can't face, for you can't turn your wife out to grass like a prize mare. Now, m'dear, when you come on Saturday—'

'I'm sorry, Sir Hugh, but I can't manage Saturday. You see—'

'Saturday sennight then. This army feller is accompany-ing Connie—'

'I'm sorry, Sir Hugh.'

He bent his eyebrows at her again. 'You're a damned unaccommodating minx, ma'am, if you'll excuse the fam-iliarity. If I didn't like you so well, I'd like you not at all.'

Demelza still had her hand in captivity. 'I'm glad you like me so well, Sir Hugh, for I like you well too and I should be grieved to think I displeased you. But you've told me you look on women as prize mares which can be turned out to grass just whenever you think. Then can you not forgive a woman for wanting to gallop off as she pleases with no hand to bridle her and no man to order her where or how she shall go? Isn't it good to have the exception as well as the rule? Must all women be just what you say so's to win your approval?'

He stared at the V of her collar, not bothering to follow her argument but liking the paling colour and gentle swell of her skin there.

'I'll tell you what, miss,' he said. 'It will be my birthday in a few weeks' time, and Connie and I are thinking of giving a party and a dance. Just a few friends – forty or fifty maybe. We get asked out here and asked out there, and I say to Connie it would be a good thing to push it through while the war's on. We'll do it in very good style, though; not like that fellow Trevaunance who's too mean to spit. A band and what not. Now if I sat down and wrote a formal invitation to your stiff-necked husband, d'you think the two of you would come? Would that be right enough for you, eh?'

Demelza stared into his beady eyes, trying to read what ulterior purposes might be there.

'Thank you, Sir Hugh. You're being that kind to me now. Much kinder than I deserve.'

'You can't judge what you deserve, ma'am. Leave that to me, and one of these days I b'lieve you will get it.'

She reached home without the necessity of having to tell Ross where she had been. She had discovered what she had gone to discover, but was unrelieved for knowing it. She knew at once that she could not break the news to Ross, she found she could not even hint at it. What his response would be, how he would act, she had no idea. All she knew was that she did not want to be the one to tell him or to be present when he was told.

Chapter Four

Weeks passed, and the primroses flowered and the first bluebells. Dwight's physician friend went home and Dwight made inquiries about joining the Navy as a surgeon. But he took no further action because the war was coming to an end. The optimists had been right and France was breaking up. Defeated by the Austrians, who had at last moved, General Dumouriez followed Lafayette into the enemy's camp. Two thirds of the provinces were in revolt against Paris. The invasion of Holland had failed, and the British had taken Pondicherry and Tobago. For the second year running, Paris lay open to any army with the enterprise to take it. Obviously this time someone would, even if it had to be the grand old Duke of York.

Among the results of a general rise in spirits was a fall in the price of copper and tin. But the fall was not enough to make the difference. Success or failure at Wheal Grace still depended on their ability to eke out their finances during the change-over, to preserve a delicate balance between earnings and outgoings. Henshawe's hundred pounds was already gone, but they were existing on credit provided for them by Pascoe's bank against the next coinage. Trains of mules carried the black tin into Truro, where the bank issued its tin cheques on the quality and value of the white tin which would be extracted; and on the credit of these cheques the mine was able to continue.

Most of the economies they could make were eaten up above-ground, where a rearrangement and extension of the dressing floors had to be undertaken. Not only did it mean more dressers and spallers, it often meant new ones, for a good copper worker often did not understand how to treat tin. Much of the ore was sent out to the tin stamps of Sawle Combe.

On the second of May, Charlie Kempthorne's body was found floating in the sea off Basset's Cove. Dwight went to identify him.

The man had been in the water several days. There were no signs of violence, but the sea had not been kind to him. Dwight stared for a while at the remains of this person he had cured of miner's phthisis, one of his few real medical successes.

Traitor, informer, bridegroom for Rosina, sail-maker, father, decaying eyeless flotsam, no ready-made deceitful smile now, only the black gape of corruption. Familiarity with death had not lessened Dwight's essential distaste. The more he saw of it, the less he understood it. The instant disappearance of personality, light from a candle, leaving nothing of value or interest except to the surgeon with his scalpel able to probe now at will. And it was not in his temperament to want to do that. *All* his preoccupation was with the living, even when the living lied and cheated and sold their friends.

Rosina Hoblyn came to see him at the Gatehouse. Dwight had avoided her since the night of his fight with Kempthorne.

'Is it true, sur,' she said, 'was it Charlie that was washed up?'

'Yes . . .'

'Had he been – done to death – killed, afore he was dropped in the water?'

'Not so far as I could tell. It's possible. But he may well have fallen in.'

'Charlie wouldn't fall in, sur. 'Twasn't in his nature.'

Dwight knew in his heart that she was right. Rosina understood her man.

'Or he may have committed suicide – have done himself to death. He cannot have been happy the way things turned out.'

'Nor me, sur.'

'You – are you very unhappy for him?'

She flushed sharply. 'Yes, sur. Or I don't rightly know. He was always that kind to me . . . 'Tis part that and part the disgrace. It don't seem right somehow, hard to believe; for it to have been the same man: him that was kind and him that played Judas. And I feel the disgrace so bad – as if I'd done it myself – like I'd known about'n all along. And I didn't, sur; I didn't; I never knowed a thing!'

'Of course not, Rosina; nobody could possibly suppose you did.'

'Sometimes folk *look*, so much as to say . . . They d'think if you're walking out with a man . . .'

'Be thankful at least that you didn't marry him. Has your knee been any trouble since that night?'

'No, sur. I'm that grateful. It seems funny, though, that if you'd never come t'help me . . .'

He would be married, living in a strange town, Ross perhaps in prison or deported; much, so much, hanging on a single thread; three, four, five, countless people's lives altered by a single wanton circumstance. Here the girl at the centre of it all. Rosina's knee. Ludicrous. After Francis's death Ross had railed at the sudden changes of fortune that made nonsense of man's striving and contriving. So it had been once again, more outrageously than ever.

When Rosina left, Dwight felt the urgent need to talk to somebody. Other people discussed their troubles with him, but there was no outlet for himself. He repressed his own troubles and they festered and grew worse.

He knew now that he must get away. It was necessary to restore his self-respect. For no reward he must give up the things he had been reluctant to give up for Caroline. That was not the whole of it: the issue was not as simple as he sometimes tried to believe; but he knew he could not stay here with the memory of his failures.

There were only two people he could talk to, because they alone knew the truth – or part of it. But the opportunity had to be sought, the breaking of the ice. He decided to go at once, without more thought, before the old hesitations and the old embarrassments came. What mattered was the unburdening of his mind. Since his friend Wright went home, the long hours alone had become more than he could bear.

It was a rough, blustering evening for early May, with lowering cloud. The sea was as wild as winter, and between the white lines of breakers was a vivid oily green. In the distance the horizon was hidden in a pale grey mist, and he wisely waited a time in the porch. Sure enough the rain came, blinding in the stronger wind that brought it. It lasted some minutes and then as abruptly ceased, leaving everything guttering and dripping, and the sun flung a single sabre of green across the sea.

As he topped the hill, he could see both people he wanted. Demelza was brushing the water from her steps with the energy of one whose time is limited; and Garrick, nose on forepaws on the wet grass, was obviously waiting for some inner prompting or perhaps a fluttering jackdaw to set him galloping across the valley. Ross was just leaving one of the sheds of the mine.

Their tracks would not converge until near the house, and Dwight saw that Ross would be there well before him. He did not hurry. From this high ground he could survey the whole valley. Presently Demelza saw Ross coming and waved. Garrick, although through all his years at Nampara he had remained obstinately Demelza's dog, got slowly up and went to meet his master.

At that moment Dwight felt a slight tremor in the ground and a consciousness of noise which he could not specify and could not locate. It might have been an explosion far out to sea, but somehow he knew it was not. By the time the sensation was a few seconds old, he had decided it was some trick of his ears or an extra gust of wind.

Ross had paused to whack Garrick on the flanks; this was what Garrick really liked: pats were no use and he clearly despised anyone who attempted them. Demelza came down to speak to Ross and they were discussing something in the garden. Here Dwight went into the first ring of hawthorn trees, whose tops were bent at sharp angles by the prevailing wind. Between these and the apple trees was a clear gap; and as he came out into this, he saw a man running towards the house from the mine. He looked then at the mine and saw that, in addition to the ordinary coal smoke from the chimney, there had gathered about the engine house a sort of haze which gave the impression of being neither smoke nor steam. As he watched, the balance bob of the engine slowed and came to a stop.

Dwight also stopped. Other figures were emerging from the engine house. The man running had not yet reached Ross, but Demelza had seen him. They were going to meet him. Dwight began to run towards the mine.

Casual accidents in Cornish mines were common enough – a man would fall and break a leg, blasting work was unreliable and hazardous – but major accidents were rare. In the five years of his being mining surgeon there had been none in these parts. Ross was running back now with the man and with Demelza a little behind him.

But Dwight would be there ahead of them. The first person he met was Peter Curnow, who, grey-faced and dirty, had just come out of the engine house.

'What is it, man, what is it?'

'A stull's run, sur, and filled all the bottom with deads! Jack Carter's just give the alarm. He d'say there's four, five trapped. The others is coming up now!'

'Some hurt?'

'Aye, half of 'em or more.'

'Look, will you do something for me? Run straight to the Gatehouse and fetch my bag and instruments. Tell Bone. He'll know what to bring.'

'Aye, sur. I'll do that!' He went off racing.

The stuff about the engine house was dust. The wind was clearing it now, but down below it would be still thick. Three or four more men had come out, but they waved Dwight away – nothing serious, scratches or bruises – and many had stayed below, some to tend the injured, others already beginning to dig.

As they spoke, Ross arrived. Dwight could see from his expression what he felt. Every day the great cavity above them created by the hasty mining of the tin had grown larger. It had not looked too bad a risk. There had been some hasty shoring up which might well have sufficed. Other mines had taken and were taking similar risks. Often such gunnies existed for twenty years without collapsing. But the luck had been against them and the work had caved in. With it had fallen thousands of tons of rock, burying the lode deep and the men as well.

Two men were killed by the fall and three seriously injured. All the work at the bottom of the mine had collapsed, carrying with it ladders, pumping gear, platforms; and nothing was to be seen in the flickering dusty light but a great pile of shattered rock, at which a dozen subhuman figures were frantically digging. The death toll would have been five, but the three who were recovered alive had heard the collapse begin and had run up part way and flattened themselves against the wall of rock as the stuff crashed down. The most seriously injured were Ellery and Joe Nanfan, who were buried four hours before they were rescued. Dwight went down for a time; but he soon realized that he could do more good aboveground, and he went up with the first seriously injured man to be recovered. The changing-shed had been turned into a sort of hospital, with six men lying in it. Someone in the first panic had sent for Surgeon Choake, and he temporarily overlooked his dislike of his young rival. One man had his arm broken, and Choake had the arm off above the elbow almost before a sickened Demelza could turn her head away. Knife in hand, he looked round for the next victim and knitted his brows in disappointment when there seemed no more carving to be done. When Dwight came up, he was binding a head injury, and the two men exchanged a few cold words before concentrating on their common task.

Midnight was past before the last two survivors were brought up, and it was soon plain to Dwight that Joe Nanfan was near death. A beam had fallen on him; his right hip was crushed and a great bruise was spreading across the abdomen, which had suffered internal injury. He was wet with sweat and his breath came in agonized gasps. Dwight did what he could, administered laudanum, and bound up the abdomen to give it support.

Ellery was unconscious, with a deep wound in the temple. There was some prospect of a trepanning operation to remove bone pressing on the brain, and Choake said it was worth attempting anyway because he needed the practice; but eventually it was decided to see how the man went on unmolested.

Ross did not come up all night, and Demelza was not unaware of the dangers of a further fall. While others took it in turns to dig, he remained below. At four Demelza wanted to go down herself, but Dwight would not let her. Instead he sent Gimlett with a message asking Ross to come up. Ross sent word back that he would come when there was no more to do.

Light began to grow soon after four, but the black dawn sky was as torn and ragged as a beggar's coat. The sun rose in another flurry of rain and a rainbow arched its back across the head of the valley. The second vigil, Demelza thought, that she had spent in this engine house. But this time even the engine had stopped. In the cold morning light she shivered and stretched – tried not to yawn, aware of fatigue and ashamed of it. Sitting on the steps above her Daniel Curnow was quite motionless, as if a part of the engine he had stopped. Six others. The wife and sons of one of those buried; two sisters and a father of the other. Hoping for the impossible – or if the worst, then for a body to bear away.

At five o'clock Jim Ellery, having been wrapped in warm blankets and kept perfectly quiet, began to come round without any operation. By seven he was taking a little light broth, and at nine he was able to walk home.

At nine Ross came up, having been below thirteen hours. He had no energy and no speech left. They had been unable to recover the two others, and the water was slowly rising.

Contrary to Dwight's every conviction, Joe Nanfan lived the night and three days later appeared to be on the mend. Fascinated, Dwight compared him privately with one of those insects that you crush underfoot and which still contrive to move away as if nothing has happened.

On the seventh of May, Wheal Grace officially closed. There was nothing much else that could be done. It would take six weeks' work to remove enough of the debris to reach the lode again. Twenty fathoms of pumping gear had been destroyed. Two hundred pounds would not set it working.

Ross was not sure that he even wanted to see it working again. It had cost the lives of three men. It had been an ill-wished venture from the start.

On the ninth of May he received a letter from Elizabeth.

Chapter Five

He had been in Truro all day, once again making arrangements with the venturers of Wheal Radiant for the disposal
of the headgear of the mine. Half his life, it seemed to him,
he was active in starting business ventures which he spent
the other half winding up. Well, this was the end of them.
From now on he farmed his land and, if he was allowed,
lived on in debt-ridden poverty for the rest of his days. Now
he had no mine, and no interest in a mine, and that was
the way it would stay.

He was taking this failure very hard but not saying much
about it. Looking back, he thought sometimes he had over-
dramatized his disappointments as a younger man. As one
grew older one saw that no good came of kicking at the
table like a hurt child. You took the bad luck and swallowed
it and shook off the injury and pretended to yourself as
well as to other people that it didn't matter.

That was a lesson hard to learn. It was particularly hard
for Ross.

In the afternoon he met Richard Tonkin again and told
him the news, receiving his sympathy with a better grace
than most people's because they had once been fellow
sufferers together. They had a meal in the Seven Stars, and
it was nine before Ross arrived home.

There had been a faint suggestion of summer heat
about the day, and Demelza looked very fresh and cool in

the garden in a white ruched bodice and a cream poplin
skirt with a little green apron. He got off his horse and she
walked with him back to the house.

'You've supped, Ross? I thought you must have. I waited
until a quarter after eight. Did that heavy shower catch you
this morning?'

'No, I had none on the way.'

'Dry both in and out, truly surprising. These bull-horns
are something terrible; I suppose it must be all the caudly
weather. They eat my flowers and slime my stones; and
if I *step* on them, it makes me feel sick. I have a lady's
instincts where a snail is concerned. Funny, for I can wrap
a bad wound or clean a baby or pick up a mouse without
distaste.'

'You should train Garrick to eat 'em. Or perhaps if
we're more reduced, we shall do it ourselves. I haven't seen
that before. Is it new?' He touched her bodice.

'New?' she smiled.

'Well, I have not seen it, I'm sure.'

'I made it out of two of your old shirts which were far
gone for patching. There is good material if you pick out
where the wear does not come.'

'When I asked you to marry me, I did not suppose you
would be driven to making your blouses out of the tails of
my shirts.'

'Not tails: sides. And the lace I got from an old shawl.
But I have been in much worse straits.'

Gimlett was not about, so she walked with Ross round to
the stables.

She said: 'I'll unsaddle Darkie. If you go in, I'll follow so
soon as he's comfortable. There's two letters for you.'

'Two? Who from?' Something in the lightness of her

tone. 'No, Gimlett will be in soon, won't he? Have you read them?'

'The one that is addressed to us both. It's from Sir Hugh, inviting us to a party at his house next Saturday. He mentioned it when last I saw him. It's his birthday – I did not dare ask which – and he seems to be planning something to outdo Sir John Trevaunance.'

Ross thought that he had solved the slight peculiarity of her tone, and so forgot to ask about the other letter.

'I hope you'll not be disappointed if we answer no.'

She said: 'I would have thought it reasonable enough to go, as so many of our neighbours are likely to be there. But it don't matter if you'd prefer not.'

He went in, glad that she'd so readily given up the idea and rather surprised that she had. Perhaps she was growing as tired of the man as he was.

He did not notice that she had not followed him into the house. He went through into the parlour and picked the two letters up off the spinet. The long twilight was ending and the light was very shadowy, so he took the letters to the window. Recently he had seen more of Elizabeth's writing, on documents and things, than at any other time, and he at once recognized it on the outside of the second one. He broke the seal.

My Dear Ross [Elizabeth had written],

I do not know how to write this letter; I do not know where to begin it or where to end it or how to tell you what I have to tell. I know it will upset you, and I, who gave you so much Pain once before, would rather do almost anything than hurt you again, and in the same way. Yet it seems that I must.

Oh, Ross, my life has been a very frustrative one; it has been an empty one and very cold. Never more so than in these lonely months since Francis died. Perhaps I am the wrong sort of person to be left alone. I seem to need the strength and protection that a man can give.

I have promised to marry George Warleggan.

It will be just ten days from now. We are to be married by Licence at St Mary's Church. At my insistence it will be very private, only our parents and the necessary witnesses. We will live mainly at Cardew, so that from now forward you will see little of me. I feel that is what you will wish.

Ross, I cannot give you Reasons for marrying George, for Reasons suggest I need justification, and I cannot begin my second marriage by being disloyal even in thought. If Affection has existed between us all these years, between you and me, I pray that you should use it now to reach an understanding of my position. For to understand all may be to forgive all. Or if not that, to excuse in part.

Your sincere and affectionate friend,

Elizabeth

While he read, it had gone dark. Or was the darkness in his heart and in this mind? He listened to the drumming of his own blood. After the first moments of utter incredulity, his brave, civilized thoughts of this morning were gone, completely swallowed up. You could not fight the imponderables of life, he had thought. But was this such? Was this something to be accepted with resignation and a sigh?

That was as far as recognizable thought went. Beyond

was all feeling, all feeling. The thing struck at him two ways together, at his love and at his hate. Either by itself he could have mastered. Together they were overpowering.

He swung round and out of the room.

'Demelza!'

There was no answer.

He picked up his cloak and went through the kitchen, out to the stables.

'Demelza!'

No answer. Darkie was still saddled.

Jane Gimlett came hurriedly out of the stillroom.

'Can I help ee, sur? John'll be back any minute now.'

'No. Tell your mistress—'

'I'm here, Ross,' said Demelza, coming out from the shadow of the stables.

Jane Gimlett looked from one to the other. She could see little, but there was that in their voices which made her go quickly indoors again.

He said: 'Demelza, I'm going to Trenwith.'

She had been hiding from him, not because she was afraid of him but because she could not bear to see him receive this news. 'Do not go tonight, Ross.'

'I must. I have to see Elizabeth.'

'It will be better in the morning.'

'You – know something?'

'Is it about George?'

'How did you guess?'

'Something I heard.'

'You never told me.'

'How *could* I . . .?'

'This . . . thing . . .' He found he was still holding the letter. He crumpled it into a ball. 'This thing must be stopped.'

'How can you stop it? You can't!'

'You think not. We'll see.'

'Ross, I don't want for you to go tonight!'

'Perhaps you don't want me to stop it at all.'

'I don't want you to – in the only ways you can,' she said distressfully.

New anger grew in him, one wave overtoppling the last. 'Please get out of my way.'

For a moment she did not move, watching him, striving to see. 'Always – always I had thought . . . I had never thought it would be like this . . .' There was anger within her too, responding to his, striving to form itself. But as yet she would not let it. 'Don't you see, Ross, that you cannot go. For if you do . . . Meaning what you do . . .'

Although she barred his way, her white figure seemed already withdrawn, a little unreal. He tried to force himself to make some move, some affectionate gesture towards her. But for the first time he failed. The spectre of Elizabeth was immovably between them, more real, more tangible to his hurt than Demelza.

She saw that she could not stop him. He could not stop himself. This was something fundamental. She stepped out of his way. He mounted his horse and clattered out of the cobbled yard.

Trenwith House was in darkness, except for two lights on the first floor. From his close acquaintance with the house he knew that one was on the landing and one in Aunt Agatha's room. Elizabeth's room looked out on the inner courtyard, as did Geoffrey Charles's. The Tabbs slept over the kitchens. He slid off his horse and pulled at the bell beside the front door. Nothing now lingered of the dying day but a bluish tinge in the far west. Stars glimmered brightly, and as he looked a meteor flickered across the sky. The ride had cooled him but not altered his purpose. His resolutions were finer pointed, less unreasoning and impulsive. The ring being unanswered, he pulled the bell again. After another minute or so he rapped at the door with his crop. Then he stepped back and stared up impatiently at the house. The Tabbs were most probably quite out of earshot. If they were asleep, he might ring till morning. And it would be easier to rouse Charles from Sawle churchyard than Aunt Agatha from her room. There was only Elizabeth and Geoffrey Charles.

He went back to the door and rapped very loudly on it. Was this a diplomatic retirement on Elizabeth's part? He had not asked what time the letter had been delivered, but perhaps Elizabeth had been expecting a visit from him all afternoon. She could hardly imagine that he would make no move at all. Perhaps as darkness fell she had bolted all the doors and gone up to bed, determined she should not see him tonight. ·

Well that was where she might yet be mistaken. He tried the door and found it locked. He stepped away again. The front of the house was impregnable, but he did not suppose it would all be.

He walked round to the east side, and an owl flitted away before his crunching footsteps. Here was the herb garden, much overgrown but doubly aromatic in the late evening. 'Larded with sweet flowers which bewept to the grave did go.' Words running through his head. Something was stirring in the bushes now besides himself, a rat or a stray mongrel, mute as he was mute, no business here.

Near the house a sycamore tree grew, some of its lesser

branches brushing the window which had once been Verity's. Needed lopping. But it had not been lopped. He tested the lowest branch, then swung himself into the tree. At this stage he unhooked his cloak and dropped it over a bush below him. 'There's fennel for you and columbines – there's rue ... I would give you some violets but they withered all when my father died ...' He went on and up, a shadow moving it seemed with no great care, till he was level with the window.

A small-paned leaded casement. From below he had thought it an inch open, but this was not so. Only a single tiny pane in the upper part of the window was open, too far from the catch. The one suitable thing he had was the key to the padlock on his own library door. He took this out and rapped against one of the panes until it broke. Then, almost before the glass had stopped falling, he had thrust in his gloved hand and lifted the catch. A minute later he was in the room.

He had made some noise but distinctly less than at the front door.

He came out in the east passage. At the end, towards the front of the house, a faint glimmer shivered on the panelled wall. It was the candle on the front landing, just round the corner from the great hall. He went towards it, and was nearly there when a door opened and Elizabeth came out.

She gave a scream half stifled, stepped back against the wall. They stared at each other. She looked as if she were going to faint.

'Ross! ...'

'I came to pay my respects.'

'*Ross*, I thought ...'

'That I was a burglar. So I am as to means of entry.'

She continued to stare at him with great eyes in a white face. She was wearing a green velvet frock, an old one and in better light shiny, but it suited her. Everything suited her. That was the trouble. 'I heard a noise. How did you get in?'

'I came to thank you for your letter.'

'I thought it was Geoffrey Charles. I thought it was strange.'

'Is there somewhere we can talk?'

She knew him well enough not to be taken in by his even voice. There was no escape for her now, from this interview.

'Yes . . . I'll get a candle . . .'

She turned back into the room she had left. Irrationally suspecting she might be going to call someone, he followed her in and closed the door.

'This will do.'

It was her bedroom, and she lifted her hand from the candlestick. 'I don't think . . .'

'There's no one else to consider. I want to talk to you, Elizabeth, and now.'

A nice room. The brown draped curtains hung with cord, the gilt dressing-mirror, the rocking horse, the blue slippers, the white lace nightgown over a chair. He had never been in there before.

He could see the blood coming back to her face, to her lips. And some of the confidence.

'I so *much* hated sending you that letter, Ross. The *last* thing I wanted – as I said . . . But you can't come here like this, now. In the morning . . .'

'The morning's too late. I want to know tonight.'

'To know what? What I've already told you in my letter? Is there anything more to say?'

'Well, yes.' He moved away from the door, pulled off his gloves and dropped them in a chair, came closer to her. She took a step away. 'I had a certain impression of how things stood. Tell me, Elizabeth, where I have gone wrong . . . George Warleggan I have long thought of as my greatest enemy. You I have long thought of as my greatest friend. In which particular am I farthest adrift?'

She flushed. 'It isn't like that at all, Ross. But it has been a grievous position for me. Of course I'm happy and proud to think of *you* as my greatest friend—'

'Well, it was more than that, wasn't it? How long is it, not more than twelve months, since we met one evening at the Trevaunances? What did you tell me over the dinner table then? That when you turned me down and married Francis you made a mistake which you discovered a few months after and have regretted ever since. It was a – an astonishment and humiliation to you, you said, that you should have made such a mistake. I remember the words.'

She stretched out a hand to the back of a chair. 'Your coming like this, Ross . . . The shock has made me feel faint . . .'

But he was not to be put off. 'That mistake you confessed to, Elizabeth, was one Francis suffered for all his life. And you suffered for it, and I. What sort of a mistake are you making this time?'

'No,' she said. 'What I told you that night – I'll not go back on it – though I should never have spoken if I'd thought anything was going to happen to Francis. Please, Ross, understand. I felt that some day I had to tell you, to let you know that if you were unhappy in those early days, it was not long before I was too. I thought it would please you to know that the mistake had been mine and not yours!

310

It was too late, years too late to put things right; but I wanted you to *know*. As soon as I'd spoken I realized it was wrong to have spoken. And when Francis died ... then more than ever.'

'It explains nothing. Where does George Warleggan come into this?'

'Not at all at that time, of course. Only now – much later. He's been so *kind*, Ross, so good—'

'Do you marry a man out of gratitude?'

'Not alone out of gratitude. But you're far wrong to think of him as your greatest enemy. I think – I *believe* – that I can bring you together, that truly you can and will be friends. He has no bitterness—'

'Are you marrying him for his money?'

She said nothing for a minute, her eyes narrowed in an effort to be calm. So far they had faced each other like adversaries, she content or able only to parry each thrust that he made, and with no time or thought for manœuvre. So far only the situation made the encounter worse than her imagining. She had known how bad it would be; and remembering her expectation of it, she took a grip of herself. She was injuring him, not he her; therefore she must bear his insults, try to lead him to reasonableness and perhaps later friendship again. To evade the issue wasn't possible. To give him detailed reasons for her decision to marry George was a waste of time. Each one she put up he would demolish in a moment.

'Please, Ross.' She smiled at him but avoided the searching look in his eyes. 'Will you come tomorrow and we can talk more calmly and more properly than here? Believe me when I say I am not marrying George for his money. I have not been very clever with my life. But I've tried to be loyal to the people I care for. What may seem disloyalty to you, isn't really that at all. What would you suggest for me, Ross? Thirty years of widowhood and loneliness? I might well live thirty years. Is that what you ask for the mistakes I've already made? Can you offer me anything else to hope for?'

He was silent, studying the curves of her brow and cheek and mouth.

'I'll go if you can answer me one thing. Do you love George?'

The clock struck eleven, accenting the other stillnesses. Far in the distance, communicated to an inner ear, was the sound of the sea.

'Yes,' she said.

That settled it. He took her by the shoulders, quietly but firmly, so that her eyes flicked up quickly to his in surprise and alarm.

'This is a very similar imposture to the one just after you married Francis. You told me you loved him then, and you didn't mean a word of it. I was simpler then and believed you. I don't believe you tonight.'

She tried to free herself. 'Don't, Ross. You're hurting me.'

'You ask me if I'd condemn you to thirty years of widowhood. The answer's no. But with your looks you could have the pick of six men. I do not like this betrothal to George Warleggan. I ask you to wait awhile and try again.'

'Let me go! I'm my own mistress and shall please myself! I'm – sorry that you feel like this. But I can't help it.'

'You never *have* been able to help anything, have you? It has all been beyond your control. All your life you've drifted helplessly down a stream of good intentions. You can't help this either.' He kissed her. She turned her face away but could not get it far enough round to avoid him.

When he lifted his head, her eyes were lit with anger. He'd never seen her like it before, and he found pleasure in it.

'This is – *contemptible*! I shouldn't have believed it of you! To force yourself . . . To insult me when – when I have no one—'

'I don't like this marriage to George, Elizabeth. I don't like it! I should be glad of your assurance that you'll not go through with it.'

'I'd be surprised if you believed me if I gave it you! You called me a liar! Well, at least I do not go back on my promises! I love George to distraction and shall marry him next week—'

He caught her again, and this time began to kiss her with intense passion to which anger had given an extra relish, before anger was lost. Her hair began to fall in plaited tangles. She got her hand up to his mouth, but he brushed it away. Then she smacked his face, so he pinioned her arm.

She suddenly found herself for a brief second nearly free. 'You treat me – like a slut—'

'It's time you were so treated—'

'Let me *go*, Ross! You're *hateful*, horrible! If George—'

'Shall you marry him?'

'*Don't!* I'll scream! Oh, God, *Ross* . . . Please . . .'

'Whatever you say, I don't think I can believe you now. Isn't that so?'

'Tomorrow—'

'There's no tomorrow,' he said. 'It doesn't come. Life is

an illusion. Didn't you know? Let us make the most of the shadows.'

'Ross, you can't intend . . . Stop! Stop, I tell you.'

But he took no further notice of the words she spoke. He lifted her in his arms and carried her to the bed.

Chapter Six

Demelza stayed awake till four and then woke again at six to hear him come into the house. He did not come upstairs, and that confirmed what she already knew. For she had known it from the moment he left.

Jeremy woke soon after and began to play and crow in his cot. Jeremy didn't talk much yet, but his two favourite remarks were 'Aberdare' and 'No anemone,' which he employed in a system of his own to meet the varied circumstances of life. He had become a happier child recently as well as more robust, not so liable to fly off the handle if things didn't come his way, but as full as ever of intense nervous energy. It was one of Demelza's pleasures to wake early and lie in a drowsy contentment listening to the murmurs and chuckles of Jeremy in his cot.

Not so today. She got up at half past six, which was about the usual time, and went to the north window out of which she had climbed not many months ago. The sun had risen two hours since, and the rhetorics of dawn were long past. The morning was cloudy but very still, the sea a shadowy slate blue and deeply calm, having fallen away in the night. Sometimes there seemed to be no movement at all, it was a stretched silk cloth, but every now and then an apparent ripple would form under the surface and at rarer intervals one of the ripples would topple over, betraying its size by the crackling roar with which it broke the stillness of the day. Gimlett was already up and about, tirelessly and persistently busy in the farmyard. Demelza often wondered at his quietness in the morning, for he never woke them with the clatter of pails or other untoward noise.

This morning there was in her a pain so deep that it derived from some part of her she had not known of before. She had never known such despair. *Everything* was in ruin and in ashes. Whatever consolation her brain turned to crumbled at the first touch. *Nothing* would ever be the same again, for she had lost faith.

Not long ago, talking to Verity, she had said that trusting one's husband . . . If one did . . .

Well, now the faith was gone. Of course it was not so clean-cut as that really. She had lived with Ross too long not to know his faults, his weaknesses; if you thought of your husband as godlike and perfect, you were a fool and asking for disillusionment. But it was the principle of trust that mattered. All his life Ross had been in love or partly in love with Elizabeth. The discontent had been more active since Francis died; but all the same Demelza had known him in and out of love with herself, more in than out, and had felt that that intense sense of loyalties which was one of the faults and one of the virtues of his nature would preserve him to herself in the last resort.

It was more than that, of course. The loss was more than that. However sane and civilized she might be, however she might reason it out, Ross had always been one step more than a husband to her. From the moment when, a little over nine years ago, he had taken her into his kitchen as a starving miner's brat, he had represented a kind of nobility, not of birth but of character, a person whose standards of behaviour were always, and always would be, slightly better, surer than her own. Often she argued with him, lightly, flippantly, disagreeing with his views and his judgments; but underneath and on fundamental matters she gave him best.

So whether one expected complete fidelity from one's husband or not, there was so much else lost besides. Demelza's pride had been in him more than in herself. She had believed herself better than other women because a man like Ross had married her. In his visit to Elizabeth last night he had not only let himself down, he had let her down. It was a joint betrayal, something which destroyed the whole basis of her life.

Jeremy was waiting to be picked up, no longer content within the confines of his cot, becoming fretful. She ignored him and went to the other window while she brushed her hair. Somewhere within herself there was still a tiny thread of protest that perhaps this thing had not been; yet consciously she knew the truth. She had known it before he did, known what his purpose was before he rode away. And now? Why had he returned? Had he come to fetch his things and was he going to live at Trenwith with Elizabeth? Was the marriage between Elizabeth and George finally abandoned? Demelza was not a good hater, but she felt she could kill Elizabeth. Elizabeth had done her best to ill-wish the first years of their marriage. She had failed; but indirectly and innocently she was responsible for the death of Julia. *That* had been the first breach between Demelza and Ross. An estrangement, though barely perceptible, had grown from that day out of Ross's grief, and Elizabeth had made the most of it. Now, since Francis's death, she had had a free hand. One wondered if she had ever seriously meant to marry George, or if it had not been a gauntlet thrown down to provoke the reaction that she had in fact provoked.

Jeremy began to cry, and Demelza at last picked him up, changed him, and dressed him. Then she carried him downstairs. Jane Gimlett was in the kitchen.

'The master's 'aving his breakfast. I put on the cold gammon. I thought you was sleeping, and he says not to disturb you.'

'Is there tea?'

'Yes'm. Not made ten minutes. Shall I cut ee some bread and butter?'

'No . . . Can you keep Jeremy for a few minutes . . .?'

She went into the parlour. Ross had changed his clothes and shaved, had almost finished his tasteless breakfast. He looked up and they looked at each other. In that moment she knew finally, and he knew that she knew.

'I thought you might be asleep,' he said. 'I thought I'd begin without you.'

She did not speak, but after a moment she came forward and sat at the table some distance from him. She poured herself out a cup of tea, added milk and sugar. The light from the window fell on her pale eyelids, the dark gloss of her hair.

'It won't be the last time, will it?' she said.

He didn't speak, but looked down at his plate and pushed it away.

She was suddenly visited with an overwhelming gust of anger. It came upon her and took her utterly by surprise. She had been afraid of crying, but now there was not a tear in her.

'Is – their wedding to go on?'

'I don't know . . .' His scar was very noticeable this morning. Often it was as if that chance sword-thrust in Pennsylvania remained with him and had become a

318

symbol of the nonconformity of his nature, the unabiding renegade.

She found her lips were trembling with anger.

'When are you seeing her – seeing her again?'

'I don't know.'

She swallowed, tried to control her voice.

'What time did you get back?'

'I think it was about five.'

There was silence between them then. She would not ask anything more, and he could not explain the unexplainable.

Trying hard to make talk, to be matter-of-fact, as if this was like any other breakfast there had ever been, he said: 'I called at Mistress Trelask's yesterday about the ribbons for Jeremy. She says she will have cheaper ones in a month or two.'

Demelza did not speak.

'I was with Harris Pascoe a good part of the morning and so did not have the opportunity to buy the other things you mentioned.'

She stirred the tea, took a sip, felt the hot liquid go down, stared out of the window with unseeing eyes. He picked up a fork, made twin marks on the tablecloth with it.

'I supped with Richard Tonkin. He has bought a boat-building business in partnership with Harry Blewett in East Looe. It had prospered since the outbreak of war.'

'Oh.'

'They have more orders, he says, than they know what to do with. Small craft . . . At least it is satisfactory to hear of someone doing well.'

'Is it?'

Ross looked at his wife. 'You do not see that satisfaction?'

'No, I do not.'

'I'm sorry.'

'So am I.'

'You're spilling your tea, Demelza.'

'Yes,' she said and deliberately dropped her cup on the floor. The most frightening blazing anger was alive in her now. It was not only Elizabeth that she could have killed but Ross. She could have thrown every piece of crockery at him, and knives and forks too. Indeed she could have attacked him knife in hand. Fundamentally there was nothing meek or mild about her. She was a fighter, and it showed now. She struggled with herself and gasped and met his grey gaze. Then she swung with her arm, knocking off teapot and milk jug and sugar basin and two plates, sweeping them all to the floor.

She went out.

Ross did not stir an inch until Jane Gimlett came running in.

'My dear life! What happened, sur? The teapot's scat all to jowds! And your rug . . .' She bent to clear the mess.

'I caught my coat,' said Ross. 'It jerked the tablecloth. Pity.'

'Dear life, it is so! Where's the mistress?'

'She went out. She does not want breakfast this morning.'

All the week a great thunderbolt hung over the house. All her life Demelza's principle, though she did not know it as such, had been never to let the sun go down on her wrath. But she could very well have been buried with *this* wrath, because it came from a wound that knew no cure.

It was not that she could not forgive. She did not know that he cared about her forgiveness, or in any case that that was of importance. You can forgive someone for cutting down a tree, for smashing a precious vase, for burning a picture; it makes no difference to the thing destroyed.

They met only at meals, and then often contrived an avoidance by beginning early or coming late. When they had to meet they spoke little, and of things about the house or farm. Ross had a bed made up in Joshua's old bedroom, where Demelza had slept the first night she came. To him it seemed impossible after what had happened that he should force his presence on her upstairs; to her it seemed that one contact with Elizabeth had rendered his wife disgusting to him.

That so far he had made no effort to see Elizabeth again was rather a surprise, though of course he could have walked over every day for all she knew. At least he was continuing to eat and sleep in his own home. She would have died rather than ask him what he intended to do.

After that one outburst she was calm, though the anger had not left her. It had become a recognizable companion, colder, more deliberate, and she could not order it away. She didn't want to. Sometimes afterwards she thought it was only her anger during that week that kept her alive. It was her opium, to which she turned when ordinary thought became intolerable. She knew he was busy all week over the sale of the mine gear. It was fetching about a quarter of what it cost. It would upset him when it began to go; but perhaps by then he would no longer be here. On the Thursday a letter came for him which he did not show her; but the following day he said:

'I shall have to be away tomorrow night. I am going to

Looe and cannot be there and back in the day. Harry Blewett has written and wants to see me.'

'Oh.' So this was the excuse he must make. It lowered the relationship even further that he felt he had to lie about it. Why not say, I am going to Elizabeth?

'If you like to, you can read what he says.' Guessing perhaps, he pushed the letter across the table to her.

'No.' She pushed it back unread.

After a moment or two he said: 'I do not know what his motive is. Richard Tonkin must have told him I have no money to invest in his shipbuilding. I wish he would pay me back some he already owes me.'

She nearly said: 'Then you could give it to Elizabeth.' But at the last she had just too steady a sense of proportion to be petty.

On the Friday afternoon a man rode over from Werry House with a verbal message. Sir Hugh had received no answer to his invitation. Were Captain and Mrs Poldark able to accept? Demelza almost laughed. Sir Hugh and his party. Who felt like partying? Not she. And Ross would be away partying on his own. Partying with Elizabeth. Perhaps she should suggest that Ross should take Elizabeth and then she, Demelza, could pair off with George Warleggan.

She was not sure whether Ross intended to visit Looe at all, but she knew he would spend the last part of his week-end at Trenwith House, in Elizabeth's arms. He would not want to be bothered with attending a reception and dance. Elizabeth's reception was all he cared about. Demelza wondered if Ross used the same endearments to Elizabeth as he sometimes had to her. No doubt she would be charmed with her new lover. She'd got what she wanted at last, at long last. In her own bed she was welcoming him. Slender as a lily in his arms. Patrician and well bred and distinguished in a way Demelza could never be. For a woman who traced her ancestry eight hundred years there were perhaps refinements of love of which a miner's daughter knew nothing. It was impossible after such a union that Ross should ever come back to common clay. Impossible. Impossible. He could go his own path while she drooped and languished at home, and drudged and cared for his child and tramped through the muck of the farm.

He could, could he? A light like a flame fell upon Demelza and illuminated all the dark places of her heart. Captain Poldark could not attend Sir Hugh Bodrugan's party. But Mrs Poldark could. An unrestricted Mrs Poldark. A Mrs Poldark bent on avenging herself upon her husband and salving her own hurt, on bolstering up her own pride in the only way she could at this time. Let Ross take the consequences, for the situation was of his creating.

She gave the appropriate message to the footman who was waiting, and saw him go off up the valley on his horse. The light was still playing in her mind and she knew it would not go out. She began to prepare for her visit on Saturday.

Chapter Seven

Werry House had been built at the time of Edward IV, when all the Bodrugan interests were at their peak. Later, when Richard's lust for power had ruined the Yorkist cause, the main Gorran Bodrugans had come crashing down; but the Werry Bodrugans had managed to find some favour at Henry's court and had preserved their inheritance. Now the stock was petering out of its own accord. Neither Sir Hugh nor his stepmother cared anything for appearances. They kept servants to wait on their needs but preferred to live in disorder. They liked to slop about the house in muddy boots and throw them anywhere when discarded, and Sir Hugh had been known to say that the sight of a tidy room or a polished floor put him in mind of his old grandfather, whom he was trying to forget.

But there had been some effort to better the place for the time of the party. The lawns were cut, some of the walls and ceilings brushed, and most of the menagerie of strange animals had been cleared out and herded into two rooms. If one were not too particular or took more notice of the company than of the chair one sat in, the whole thing passed muster pretty well.

Much the biggest room in the house was the hall, and this had a stone-flagged floor, a great fireplace, a raised dais at one end, and a high hammer-beam roof. The lower half of the walls, below the windows, was covered with moth-eaten tapestry, and above were numerous candelabra usually not lighted. It was in this room that the ball was to take place.

It was fortunate for Demelza that her decision to go, and to go in such a mood, was taken with so little time to prepare, otherwise she might have wondered a good deal what to wear. Problems of transport she had been quick-witted enough to solve before she dismissed the footman yesterday. Knowing that Ross would take Darkie, she had sent a message to Sir Hugh asking him to send over a groom and a horse; and this he did about five. So she arrived at Werry House in stylish manner, followed by a liveried man on another horse carrying her bag.

The drive of Werry House led out upon a coaching road, so most of the guests who came from central and southern parts of the county had arrived in their carriages. Six was evidently the fashionable time, for Demelza had to wait her turn before she could ride up to the front door, and she was the object of numerous raised quizzing glasses. She bore the scrutiny coldly, sitting straight-backed in her dark riding habit and tricorn hat.

Hugh and his stepmother were just inside the door, having been lured into the hall from an interesting discussion with John Treneglos on farcy in horses. Demelza came just on the heels of Mr and Mrs Nicholas Warleggan and heard Mr Warleggan's apology. George had very urgent business and presented his compliments and regrets. Following her were a couple whom she vaguely recognized as Lord and Lady Devoran. Lord Devoran was a friend of Ross's.

Sir Hugh came up to her and said: 'Ha! ma'am, so you've ventured to trust yourself to me care and left your husband by the fireside. Good. Good.'

'Yes, Sir Hugh. I thought 'twas not the weather for firesides.'

'Nor is it, m'dear. I'm with you there. But it is a very respectable gathering this week-end, damme. Or most of it gives that impression at a distance. You'll be quite safe with us, ma'am, I assure you.'

'That's what I was afeared of,' said Demelza.

He chuckled dryly and looked at her with his beady black eyes. ''Tis comforting to hear you talk so even if you don't mean it. Respectability bores me to madness, and I fancy there'll be moments this week-end when I shall be glad to slip away. Did I not promise you bawdy talk? Yes, I did, and you shall have it. We'll nip into a corner somewhere and—'

'Hughie!' called his stepmother. 'Miss Robartes is here with Dr Halse. Go and see 'em down! God damn it, I can't be everywhere!'

As Demelza was shown to her room along the floor-creaking corridor upstairs, she reflected that she would have to be very far gone in drink before she could throw herself at Hugh Bodrugan's head. He had tried to make love to her in Bodmin, and even now her flesh crept at the thought.

That no doubt was always the trouble with wronged wives. The will to retaliate was there but not the object to make it possible.

The bedroom she had been shown into was big and low with heavy beams and panelled walls. When she was alone she at once went to the window and threw it open before beginning to unpack her dress. The window looked out on the side of the house, across two sloping lawns towards a belt of beech trees. The trees were just in their first entrancing green, dappling in the sunlight like watered silk. Bisecting the lawns was a broad low-walled path sentinelled with statuary, much of it now showing the effects of wind and weather.

Coming along the path towards the house was Malcolm McNeil of the Scots Greys.

Sir Hugh's preferences seldom leaned towards the conventional; and since this was to be a dance, his view was that the thing should be got under way as soon as possible and kept up as long as possible so that no one should complain they hadn't had their money's worth. Also he wanted his money's worth out of the orchestra. Still further, he was no great hand himself at these stately minuets and gavottes, so that if he could get them disposed of before supper they could concentrate on the country dances after and everyone could get hot and sweaty and enjoy themselves.

She deliberately kept her room for a time. A maid brought chocolate up for her and she sat in her lawn morning-gown sipping quietly and enjoying the view. She had no plans and no thoughts. Her mind did not go to Ross and Elizabeth, nor did it to Sir Hugh or Captain McNeil. She was like the captain of a ship just before an action, drained of emotion and free from apprehensiveness, detached from what had gone and what might come.

About seven she began to dress, sponging her body and putting on clean and flimsier underclothes. There was very little one could wear under this dress which Ross had bought her for the Celebration Ball of '89 and which she had not worn since. She had changed very little in figure since then, but found it a little tighter in the bodice and a little less tight in the waist. She put on her only pair of silk stockings – a present from Verity the Christmas of '91 – liking the feel of the silk against her skin.

She decided to do her hair, or try to do it, the way the Warleggans' maid had dressed it four years ago, piling it up and up, only allowing wisps to fall in front of her ears and that bit of a fringe to curl on its own. No maid had come to help, and she was grateful. Nor any patches on this dressing table, but she had brought her own powder and rouge – present from Verity the Christmas of '92 – and she used these very sparingly, and lengthened her eyebrows about an inch each.

All that done, she at last began to struggle into her frock. It was curious the warmth there was in fine silver brocade. Unimaginable contortions were needed to fasten it, but at last it was done. She stared at herself in the mirror and considered that she might have passed herself in the street without recognition. But not without a second glance. Did not this appearance proclaim her pretensions far too obviously? Did decent women look like this? She decided after sober consideration that they did.

Out in the dusty, shadowy corridor the first strains of music came to her ears. So she was not too early. The thing had begun. Dancing – or at least music – before eight o'clock with the sun still in the sky and the birds twittering. More suitable in high May to have dancing on the lawns. She bitterly regretted not having included a bottle of port in her luggage. Facing the company in cold blood.

In this house the stairs did not come down directly into the big hall but into a smaller hall at the rear of the house, so she was saved the ordeal of descending in full view. As she came down, John Trenelgos was at the foot of the stairs and immediately caught sight of her. Neighbour Trenelgos, eldest son of the master of Mingoose House and himself already almost master of it; a clumsily built, sandy-haired, freckled man of thirty-five or -six.

'Why, there, if it isn't Mistress Demelza! Tally ho! Where've you been hiding yourself, eh?'

His trumpeting tones drew everyone's attention, and Demelza thought, I must be careful. She had no particular affection for John Treneglos and less still for Ruth, his wife, who always tried to take her down a peg; but she well knew John's feelings for her. It would not do to repeat the performance of four years ago at the Assembly Rooms when, in this very frock and hair style, she had had four or five men nearly fighting for her – and herself meaning *then* no more than to be polite and accommodating.

He came up a few steps and held out his arms. 'You'll allow me to escort you into the ballroom, eh? And the first dance, eh? Same as once before! History repeats itself. 'Twould give me pleasure to spike your husband's guns for once. Where is he?'

She gave him her hand. 'He was called away. Where is your wife?'

'In pup as usual. And 'tis near her time or she would have come whether or no, you know her. This is all very well met. Damn it, I believe it was arranged by Providence!'

'Damn it, I believe it was not,' said Demelza.

He laughed heartily, and they went into the ballroom.

Her impression of the first hours of the dance was hazy and confused. Above all at the first she needed a stimulant to give her poise and possession and to steady her nerves, but it seemed hours before anyone offered her one. Then it was some dry-tasting wine and not enjoyable to drink. But in the end it had the right effect.

Six in the orchestra, three violins, a tabor, a pipe, and a

French horn. The conductor, who was also one of the violinists, was the roundest man she had ever seen, everything about him rotund, from his gold-rimmed spectacles to his gold-fobbed belly. His coattails were never still; they beat time metronome-fashion and were only subdued when he sat on them during the negligible intervals.

All of fifty people in the room, which had been decorated with lilac and daffodils. Sir John Trevaunance had come but not Unwin. Mr Ray Penvenen was there, although he did not dance and looked very pale and austere among it all. Robert Bodrugan, Sir Hugh's only nephew and heir presumptive, had come, and she had two dances with him during the early part of the evening. All the Teague family, and three of the Boscoignes, and Richard Treneglos, John's second brother, and Joan Pascoe, the banker's daughter – but not Dwight Enys; and William Hick, and Mrs and Mrs Barbary, and Peter St Aubyn Tresize, and the Hon. Mrs Maria Agar, and Lady Whitworth and her son, who was now a parson, and Lieutenant and Mrs Carruthers, and dozens more.

One person very noticeable in the company was a tall handsome woman in black, with so many bangles and trinkets that she clinked every time she moved, and it wasn't until she was to be seen hanging on Sir Hugh Bodrugan's arm that Demelza placed her as the notorious Margaret Vosper with whom Sir Hugh had been consorting for twelve months. During the evening they came towards her and Sir Hugh said:

'D'you know my friend Mrs Vosper, ma'am? Mrs Ross Poldark. You two should have something in common; both pretty women and only need to crook a finger at a man, eh? Or have you already an acquaintance?'

Margaret laughed in a loud husky contralto: 'I don't

know this one well, but I've had dealings one way or another with all the male Poldarks. Maybe we've more in common than you think, Hughie.'

Sir Hugh cackled and Demelza's soul went black within her. She didn't doubt the woman's insinuations; it all fitted in with Ross's perfidy.

'You have the advantage of me, ma'am,' she said, 'but I expect that would be before I was born.'

Sir Hugh's laughter became louder. 'I hope you're enjoying the dance, mistress. I confess I've not seen you sitting out much.'

''Tis a very beautiful dance, Sir Hugh, and I'd no idea there was so many handsome men in all Cornwall. 'Tis fortunate that you need not fear the competition.'

Sir Hugh took out his snuffbox and tapped it, hiding his expression from Margaret.

'This fancy talk's giving me the vapours,' Margaret said yawning. 'I've buried two husbands and been straw widow to a number of others – naming no names – and I never see the point of beating about the bush. If you feel a taking for someone, go up and ask 'em yes or no and have done with it.'

''Twould be very businesslike,' Demelza said.

'Businesslike and honest,' said Margaret. 'A man knows where he is and so does a woman—'

'She knows where she's likely to be,' put in Sir Hugh with a rumble.

'Do you not think,' said Demelza recklessly, 'that there is a case to be made out for a thought more daintiness in love? I should better prefer to take my time in making up my mind. Even if it seem like beating about the bush to you, I should rather do that than get scratched and worn on every bush I see.'

Fortunately, John Treneglos came up just then and claimed Demelza, and Margaret drew Sir Hugh away and soon gained his attention again.

But it was Demelza whom Sir Hugh led in to supper.

She had not seen anything of Malcolm McNeil in the early part of the evening. He had not been in the room at all to begin; but when he caught sight of her, he at once hurried across, pushing his way between Peter Tresize and Lieutenant Carruthers, who were talking to her.

'Why, Mrs Poldark, I'd no idea! A glorious surprise on a man's last night! When may I have the favour of a dance? Are you engaged for supper?'

'Yes, I'm that sorry.'

'And the dances before?'

'I'm five deep already.'

'Then after supper? The first?'

'Very well. The first.'

'Why,' said Tresize, 'that's unfair, ma'am! It was the one I'd just asked you for.'

'I'd been saving it for Captain McNeil. I'm that sorry, Mr Tresize. Perhaps the second?'

'The second then.'

'I want the third,' said Lieutenant Carruthers. 'I've heard the third is to be an *écossaise*. They are rare good sport and—'

'I think if 'tis that dance, I should dance it with a Scotsman. That is, if he would condescend to ask me.'

'Great plaisure, ma'am,' said McNeil, pulling at his moustache in agitation. 'And many more if I may have 'em.'

Demelza thought of Margaret's philosophy. 'What you care to ask for, sir, so long as you ask now.'

'The first, the third, the fifth, the seventh, and all thereafter, if there be an after.'

'I believe strongly in a thereafter,' Demelza said.

'I see it as naught but gluttony,' said Tresize. 'And you should not encourage gluttony, ma'am; it gives rise to other appetites.'

'Captain McNeil tells me he is leaving on the morrow. Or so I b'lieve. Perhaps he may be permitted special indulgences on that score.'

'You're immensely kind, Mrs Poldark!'

Later, when Sir Hugh took her in to supper, she was aware that all the events of four years ago were being repeated, except that she was keeping a better control on them. The knowledge was headier than the thin French wine.

But to go on drinking in careful moderation, not enough to get drunk but enough to maintain her present condition, was vitally necessary not only for reasons of poise and confidence. In her spirit, in the very deep parts of her spirit, the desolation which had been there nearly a week was no different at all. *Nothing* she could do tonight could change it. Margaret could rub it freshly raw, but even that didn't vitally matter. She had already lost all there was to lose. To use her own simile, she was like a Christian who had lost God, a believer turned atheist, knowing relief and unexampled liberty, trying to rejoice over the outworn beliefs she had thrown away, conscious of the immense winds of freedom and utterly determined to make the most of them; but at heart lost, irretrievably lost.

Chapter Eight

Supper was immense, and after supper, to shake the food down, the country dances. Full of good things and fumed with wine, even the most dignified members of the gathering unbent. Demelza was surprised at the way the upper classes let themselves go. Inherently she had felt that Lord This and the Hon. Mrs That were by virtue of their titles only fitted for performing the minuet and the gavotte. That was not their view at all. Wigs bobbing and skirts swaying, they pranced about with the relish of Borneo natives. Some of the stouter women, following the low-cut fashions of the day, came very near to endangering their modesty; and if Demelza had been observing the thing from a distance, she would have been hot with anxiety for them. But instead she was in the fray herself, anxious from time to time that no clumsy shoe should step on her beautiful gown or clasping hand pull it from her shoulders.

She would not have denied that there was a sense in which she enjoyed it. She loved dancing; and now that Malcolm McNeil was her close attendant, she could encourage a man without hypocrisy – or without too much hypocrisy.

In a breathless fan-waving interlude between a galop and a Sir Roger de Coverley she said:

'You are truly leaving tomorrow, Captain McNeil?'

'Och, yes, I am truly leaving tomorrow. I should have

been gone on Thursday but for an accident of post which I then abused but now believe the work of kindly heaven. As a special favour for tonight, would you consider calling me Malcolm?' McNeil had received such encouragement that he was taking the play out of Demelza's hands.

'Perhaps I'm mistaken,' she said, 'but was that not the name of one of the kings of Scotland?'

'More than one. You're very well informed on Scottish history – Demelza.'

'I read sometimes. I'm sure that surprises you. You think I do naught but milk cows and feed pigs and tend babies and bake bread.'

'No, no, I assure you.'

'Well, thank you for the assurance. Do you know, I b'lieve only two men have ever called me Demelza before: my husband and my cousin-in-law.'

'What of your father?'

'Oh, he did not, so far as I can recollect. When he liked me he called me "daughter", and when he disliked me he called me a name which being now a lady I have long since forgotten.'

McNeil laughed his big laugh and nearly stopped the band.

'Oh, you may laugh, Malcolm, but it is true! And now tell me something of yourself. How many ladies have called you Malcolm before?'

'What?' He stared at her, stared into her direct dark eyes, seeking the bubble of laugher but not finding it although he still suspected its existence. 'A few, I confess; but *few* considering the temptations of a soldier's life. I'm hard to please, as I fancy you are. I was brought up to like the best only, and it is a constricting circumstance as you'll agree. Nevertheless it has its rewards, for when the occasion arises—'

'What occasion?'

He laughed. 'To call a woman by her Christian name is the first endearment. It is like – like touching hands without gloves, like lifting her down from a stile, like receiving a smile that has more in it than friendship. I admire your name, Demelza. Where did you get it and what does it mean?'

'I got it where you got yours, I suppose, Malcolm – from my mother. I do not know where she came by it. An old gipsy who came to the door once told me that in the true Cornish tongue it meant "Thy sweetness". But he was an ignorant old man and I do not suppose he was right.'

'"Thy sweetness". Very apt. Though I think I should be more happy still if it were "my sweetness".'

'If I'd known so much was meant by this using of Christian names – that is, as you tell me – I should have trembled to let you be so free with mine.'

'But why so? Did you not say when we first met this evening that whatever I cared to ask for . . .'

She smiled into his eyes. 'I don't think there was an "ever" in it.'

'There is certainly an "ever" in my wishes.'

Neither spoke for a moment. Then, before she could frame the right reply, someone came towards them and said, 'I think this is our dance, ma'am,' and she was led away.

But McNeil, having advanced thus far, was not to be denied. He was in the cavalry and knew all the moves from now on. When it came time for their next, he suggested they should go upon the terrace for a breath of air. There were several other couples out there. The long twilight had at last faded and night had fallen blackly, without moon or stars. They paced up and down, her neck and shoulders showing palely in the dark. They talked for a few minutes, and then she shivered.

'You're cold, darling?' At once he put his arm round her shoulders. 'Forgive me, I'll get you a wrap.'

'I have none,' she said, very gently disengaging herself. 'I did not bring one, for I have never possessed one. But I am not cold; it was just – some feeling.'

'Describe it to me.'

'Oh, that I could not. There's an old Cornish word, shrims, which is nearest. But the feeling is gone, so we'd best forget it.' She had never had quite this *sort* of attention before, not even from Ross. It won her, though she tried to stay detached.

'What good fortune kept me here two days longer!' he said. 'I well see that you would not have gone unattended tonight; indeed the other men will snarl over you at the least excuse; but I fancy, I hope, that the others would not have suited you so well.'

'They would not have suited me so well,' she said. 'Are you quite recovered now from your wound? It is late to ask, but—'

'Quite recovered. Look.' He stretched his arm. 'It's as good as new. And the wound was worth the having. Just because of meeting you.'

They came to the end of the terrace and stopped. She moved to turn, but he did not. She thought, this is the first choice. He's bending his head to kiss me. Well, I've asked for it. I've often wondered what it was like, those moustaches . . . now I know . . . Is this me, looking up at a strange man's hair, with his hands and lips on me? This is the moment to turn back; Judas, this is a long kiss, I like it and dislike it both at the same time. Oh, no, this isn't really me; I'm home by the fire with Jeremy asleep upstairs, and Ross . . . Ross is in Elizabeth's arms . . .

When at last he released her, she leaned back against the balustrade and glanced round rather belatedly to see if anyone was watching. But the night surrounded them. She took a breath, which was overdue, put a hand uncertainly to her hair. He was a big man, perhaps not as tall as Ross but heavier, stouter. And he was no beginner.

'Ever since I first met you,' he said, 'ever since that first time years ago, I've wanted to do that. Och, it is a very great thrill to me.'

'Och,' she said, 'I'm glad you enjoyed it.'

'Madam minx. But it is always the way with humankind, Demelza; the realization of an ambition leads on to greater ambition and greater ambition, until—'

'Until there is none left. What then, Malcolm?'

'What then? Why, then one achieves fulfilment of the most desirable kind. Were ye suggesting futility? It hasn't been my experience. And I am sairtainly convinced it would not be so in this case.'

'And for me?'

'I'd not be a disappointment. Do ye think it likely?'

Their heads were still close, within six inches of each other. The conversation had got completely out of hand, had run suddenly amok. Momentarily she did not know how to control it.

'I think we should go in. I think, I b'lieve, it is very warm out here and would be cooler in the ballroom.'

'Will you not give me a word of encouragement before we go?'

'It seems to me that there have been many words of

encouragement. Or I don't know how else you would call them—'

'Encouragement yes,' said McNeil confidently. 'But will you not fulfil the promise of your looks, my darling? Perhaps later. Later tonight. Which is your room? Demelza . . .'

Well, what was she waiting for? Was this not why she had come to the ball? Was this not the only way of getting back at Ross? Had she not a few hours ago been bitterly reflecting that no eligible man existed? Sir Hugh, in such a connection, filled her with repugnance. So did John Treneglos. But here was McNeil, off tomorrow, personable, quite attractive to her, eager and loving. What more could she ask? Unless the whole of her rebellion, the whole of her protest, was the empty breath of so many angry words, words spoken within herself and never seriously meant. A windbag, pretending to be daring. Bolstering herself up on glasses of wine so that she might reach the ultimate peak of wickedness by allowing someone to kiss her. How many casual carnal kisses had Ross given, not only to Elizabeth but to that bold coarse creature stalking about indoors? Margaret Vosper. Margaret Cartland, Margaret Poldark. Demelza Poldark. Demelza McNeil.

She lowered her head and said in a low voice: 'I am not well acquainted with this house.'

'I am. I have lived here many weeks.' His lips touched her ear, his hand on her arm. 'Thank you, my sweet, thank you . . .'

When she got to her room much later that night, the conductor's coattails were still swinging. A few of the energetic younger couples were making the most of the emptying floor, but the majority of the guests had departed or were beginning the process of retiring for the night. Constance Lady Bodrugan had long since left them to it and was feeding her animals. Sir Hugh was drinking a last rum toddy with Lord Devoran, and Robert Bodrugan was making heavy going of a flirtation with Miss Tresize.

Demelza shut the door behind her and went across to the window and parted the curtains to look out. The heavy evening clouds had lifted and it was less dark. The silhouette of the trees bloomed against the lighter night sky. Light flooded out from the ground-floor window underneath her, reflecting back upon the ivy-covered walls. What she thought was a gargoyle on the turret of the porch suddenly came to life and flitted silently past her window: a barn owl looking for prey.

She let the curtain fall and turned to warm her ice-cold hands at the single thick candle which burned like a beady yellow eye on the table. She was now in process – in rapid process – of becoming what her father would have described as a whore-bird. She only wished she knew how whore-birds generally behaved. Did one wait in one's gown, presenting the exact picture which had enticed the man in the first place, but with all the hazards of a spoiled and crumpled frock? Did one undress first and put on one's morning coat, which was not one quarter so attractive but which had the merits of accommodation? Or did one get into bed in one's night shift – or even without it – and pull the sheet up to one's chin?

She wished now she had allowed herself to become a little drunker. If one felt dizzy and silly, it was all so much easier – one simply let him make the running and probably giggled one's way into infidelity. She had never felt less like giggling in her life. Of far more use to her now than wine was the mental picture she had of Elizabeth, with her pale fey face and golden hair flowing, lying in Ross's arms. The picture was extraordinarily vivid, as if it were painted and hanging on the wall of the room.

She wished her hands were not so cold. It was the only outward sign of nerves. She wished all was not to happen so much in cold blood. He should have carried her off while they were on the terrace – got it over, like having a tooth out. No, that was unfair to him. It would all be better when he came. He was attractive, handsome, ardent. She should be flattered by his attentions, *was* indeed. She must think *hard* about *him*. It helped. It helped a great deal.

She decided that the morning coat was the thing and began hasty contortions to remove the frock. Eventually it slithered down in a beautiful shimmering heap, and she stepped out of it, long-limbed and black-stockinged and white. Well, if he came in now! She grabbed the morning coat and struggled into it. As she tied the cord, there was a just perceptible knock on the door.

Only just in time! She picked up the gown and laid it hastily on a chair, then tiptoed to the door. In a moment Malcolm McNeil was inside.

Dressing-gowns evidently were the correct thing. He looked bigger than ever in his, more down to earth, more *real*. Absolutely frighteningly real. And rather fat.

'My sweet, I was afraid I might have picked the wrong door and flushed some antique dowager. How adorable you look! How old are you, eighteen? If I did not know to the contrary, I should not suppose it to be more.'

'I'm forty-seven,' she said, playing for time with her own brand of humour, opposing it to her temporary sense of shock. ''Tis the light in here which is so becoming, Malcolm.

I should not suppose you a day over twelve. Though, in truth, the candle has had a thief in it and has guttered half away. Did anyone see you come?'

'No one. The maids have gone to bed, and the guests that are left are yawning their heads off. But for us, my darling, the night is young—'

'What time do you leave tomorrow?'

'I catch the noon coach from Truro as it passes the gates—'

'And shall I then not see you again?'

'You shall if you wish! Only write me at Winchester . . .'

He put his arms round her, still talking, and kissed her several times with great energy, allowing one hand to slip inside her coat and rest on her shoulder. I'm supposed to be *enjoying* this, she thought. What's the matter? Has it come too sudden, or doesn't he attract me so much as I believed? Am I liking being kissed like this? Not now. Not this way. But it will pass. I will try to forget everything. I wish I was drunk. Dear Malcolm; how he wants me. Soon I'll want him. Just surrender yourself up. It's naught but shyness that makes me all curled up and cold. Or am I really, truthfully, a prude and shocked at myself? . . .

'Malcolm,' she said, when she could get her mouth free.

'Yes, my angel,' he said, and gave her no time to reply.

For the moment at least she was able to keep his endearments within bounds, and while doing so she stormed at herself. Ross is unfaithful! Ross is unfaithful! He is gone from me as a lover for ever. Elizabeth has won him. He has even been with that *terrible* woman downstairs. What an insult, a *humiliation*! Ross has gone, I tell you. There is no more of him, nothing but desolation, and this: the furtive appointment in the bedroom; Malcolm is kind, upright, sincere, so much *more* than I might have expected,

even if a little fat. I *wanted* him to make love to me; I almost
asked him! Now am I not satisfied? Keep to your bargain.
In a few minutes you will be enjoying it. It is just the
beginning that seems so strange, so foreign, as if one had
never been made love to before. Foreign, that was the
word. Being seduced by a foreigner.

His endearments were becoming progressive.

'Malcolm,' she said breathlessly, part breaking away
from him. 'Are you kind?'

'Kind? You will find me so,' he said, following her slowly
backwards. He had exhausted his finesse downstairs.

'Then, Malcolm, I want you to listen to me. Please. Just
for a moment or two. I – I want you to be kind and
understanding. I want you to understand why I led you to
suppose . . . You see it is because of Ross. I thought because
of what he has done that I wished to do the same. And of
all the men I could have preferred to have chosen . . . *you*
were here . . . And it was not until this moment – a few
moments ago – that I have begun to wonder—'

'Och, yes, darling,' he said. 'I quite see what you wonder.
It is not an uncommon feeling at the last . . .'

'No,' she said. 'Hear me out, please. It is of great
moment. I—'

'Of course. Of course. No one is denying it. Have I told
you how beautiful you are? I've rarely seen a woman so
beautiful as you tonight . . .' She could retreat no farther.
She had her back against the wall.

Up to that moment there had been a strong element of
doubt in her feelings. The terrible sick hurt within her
goaded her on in spite of these very peculiar feelings which
were attacking her now, which swept over her, wave after
wave. Hurt pride and all the other things were working
hard on Malcolm's behalf. But she knew then that she *must*

have a breathing space, still a little time to relate one emotion with another, so that there should still be an ultimate freedom of choice, a rejection or an acceptance within her heart. Had he been a subtler man and given her time, she could have done this. But he did not give her time, and so the new feelings grew stronger than the old and his compliments slid past unheeded.

He stood smiling over her, a hand on either side of the wall, not touching her but about to. And suddenly, abruptly, knowing him and liking him, she breathlessly began to try to explain. Perhaps it was a lost cause but she went on, telling him of Ross's misconduct, of her own decision to come tonight, of his personal charm which had led her to the point where she was willing to do this thing; and then of her sudden humiliating recognition but a few moments ago that she could not go on. It was something quite fundamental, within herself, primal and entirely unrecognized until now, an adherence to one man however he might neglect her.

She did not use those words but she did her best, groping around to explain feelings as yet only half acknowledged. She had never felt so debased in her life, she said, not because of what had been proposed but because of the way she was behaving now. Only her absolute *certainty* that she could do nothing else gave her the courage to seem such a cheat and a prude. She didn't suppose he would like what she was saying; but they were not strangers; in a manner of speaking they were old friends, and she threw herself upon his friendship now, begging him to appreciate her position . . .

She said these things at considerable length and hoped and prayed that he understood; and then she looked into his eyes and realized with a sense of shock that he wasn't listening.

'I quite appreciate your feelings, my angel. It does you cr-redit to be so scrupulous. But think of me a moment, who's been looking to this rendezvous as to a mortal's taste of heaven. I well know your tender heart. It would not, I know, deny me the privileges it has promised. Ye have two duties now, my angel; not one alone to your faithless husband. The first is to me . . .'

He took her and began to kiss her again. She struggled, turning her head away, but not with great vehemence, hoping that her obvious reluctance would make an impression. It did not. He got hold of her morning gown and began to pull it off. She bit him.

He stepped back a moment, and she slid along the wall out of his reach. The look in his eyes changed. He glanced at the teeth marks in his wrist. The blood was beginning to come.

He said: 'Well, that is a pretty way of showing affection. I confess it surprises me in a lady. But perhaps it is the way you like it.'

'Oh, Malcolm, please, don't you understand . . .?'

He came after her and captured her in a corner of the room. They struggled desperately for a minute or two. Then she broke away again, leaving a sleeve of her gown in his hands. They faced each other across the room. Her breath was coming in great gulps.

He took a deep breath himself. His intention had been so predetermined when he came into the room that no words of hers would have been sufficient to turn him from it. Nor would a solitary act of resistance. But this last struggle had shown him how much in earnest she was. And for all her slenderness she was as strong and lithe as a young animal. Of course he could still have his way if he chose. It was simple enough: you hit her just once on her obstinate little chin. But he was not that sort of a man.

He slowly rolled the sleeve of the gown into a ball and mopped his hand. Then he dropped the material to the floor.

'I like to think of myself as civilized,' he said; 'so I give you best, Mrs Poldark. I hope your husband appreciates such fidelity. In the peculiar saircumstances I do not. I like a woman who makes up her mind and has the courage and grace to stick to it. I thought you were such a one. My mistake . . .' He walked slowly to the door and gave her a last glance. 'When admiration turns to contempt, it is time to go.'

He went out. At the last moment she almost spoke to him again, making a final effort to bring him to understand something of her feeling, so that, even though he might condemn, he would not despise. But as he moved she just did not dare to open her mouth.

And when he had gone, when the door had closed and she was alone again, she walked trembling to the bed and sat on it. All the tension of defence was moving out of her. She couldn't quite believe in her own vehemence. Every muscle in her body ached. Her arms and shoulders were bruised. Her teeth ached.

She didn't cry, but she put up her hands to her face. 'Oh, God, I want to *die*,' she said. '*Please*, God, let me die . . .'

Chapter Nine

About half an hour later, as the big clock in the hall was striking three, when the band had finally worked itself out and peace was settling on the house, when those still up began to move more quietly for fear of disturbing those already retired, a short stocky man came slowly up the stairs and turned towards the east wing. It was Sir Hugh Bodrugan himself, and the exaggerated stealth of his movements showed not only that he was on illicit business but also that the spirits he had drunk had had the effect of making him abnormally sober.

Wine had been spilled down his red hunting coat, and the lace of one cuff had been torn in a skirmish, but that was all the obvious damage, and he was sure the ball had been a great success and that everyone had enjoyed themselves. Now to put the cap on the evening he was bent on enjoying himself in another way. He'd cunningly given Margaret the slip, and she no doubt was still pacing about in the library waiting for him. Presently she would get tired of waiting and would swear roundly and go to bed. That was as it should be. He was going to bed, he hoped, but not with her.

There were few guests in the east wing, and that naturally made his purposes easier, although the confounded floor creaked and moaned all the way. His choice of bedroom for the lady had not been undesigning, in case she should give him any encouragement. It was therefore with surprise and indignation that as he neared the door in question he saw another figure move towards it out of the shadows and peer at the handle as if to make certain of his bearings. As this figure stretched out a hand to open the door, Sir Hugh said:

'Hi, there! What the blazes . . .'

The other man straightened up sharply. It was John Treneglos. He said: 'Hullo! What?' and blinked. 'Oh, it's you, my friend! Is this my bedroom, did you say? I remember 'twas on the right-hand side as you turned up the stairs. This wandering great house of yours, it's worse than my own. Look ee—'

'You're not so foxed as that, sir,' said Bodrugan sternly. 'Oh, dear no, sir. One may make a mistake by a room or two, sir, but not by half a house. That's your way, straight down the corridor; and I should be obliged if you'd take it.'

'Ah,' said Treneglos. 'Is that so? Yes, I see where I went wrong now.' He made a move and then stopped. 'Yes, I suppose 'twas all the jigging in the dance that put my bearings out. Thank ee.'

He waited. They both waited. Sir Hugh said: 'Well, good night to you.'

'Now, Hughie,' said Treneglos. 'Don't be a damned spoilsport. I never thought to think you a damned spoilsport.'

'You may think what you please, sir. That's your way to bed. This is Demelza Poldark's room, and well you know it!'

John Treneglos grunted. 'I'll confess if you want me to, though it's a thought unmannerly to need me to be so explicit.' He put his hand firmly on the other's shoulder.

'You know how it is on these occasions. Damme, you of all people shouldn't stand in a feller's way. You've done enough tile-walking in your time. The little bud was oncoming tonight. As good as invited me, y'know. Can't turn a good thing down. What with Ruth out of the way. Golden opportunity. I suggest you turn a blind eye and toddle off to bed.'

'Blind eye!' said Sir Hugh explosively. 'I was going in there myself!'

Treneglos stared at his host in startled fashion. 'What? What? You're joking! Damn it! Don't tell me she invited you too!'

Sir Hugh scowled. 'Not *invited* in so many words. But a nod's as good as a wink, man—'

'Ah, you put too much store by these nods, my dear. No doubt she wished to be polite, as any woman would to a handsome old war horse like you, but—'

'Well maybe she'll go on being polite . . . And war horse be beggared!' said Sir Hugh, as the second half of the sentence registered. 'I'm inclined to suppose I'm just as good a man as you. What did she say to you – tell me that, eh? What did she say to you, sir?'

'I misremember the exact words, but 'twas plain enough in the meaning. And half of it was the look. She has a very suggestible look when she sets herself out to it—'

'Pshaw!' said Bodrugan. 'You've less claim to an invitation than I have. You thought to try your luck, that's all. Confess it, man! She's always been a tantalizing slut, and there must be an end of all things. How did you know which was her bedroom?'

'What? Oh, I squeezed that wall-eyed maid you have, and she gave off the information. Now look, Hugh, it is plain enough I was here first, if only by a short head, so I have a certain priority in the matter, even if we discount the exact manner of the invitation. After all, you have your own doxy here in the very house, which is more than Ruth would ever put up with. Don't be greedy. What do you say to giving me best? Then perhaps another time – '

'Rubbish!' The injustice of the situation welled up in Bodrugan. 'Who helped her in Bodmin two years gone and nothing for it but a few kisses? Who showed her how to use that new seed drill everyone's talking about? Who's sent her presents and called upon her regular? And who invited her here, sir? Whose house is this? Ecod, if 'twas in your house, I fancy you'd put in a substantial claim . . .'

'Hush,' said Treneglos. 'If you argue in that tone, the whole house will be out in the corridor . . . I grant that 'tis your house and welcome to it; but you're the host, Hughie, and it is your place to give way to a guest. Any book of behaviour will tell you that. The convenience of the guest should come first – always first. Damn it, you haven't a leg to stand on! Manners aren't what they were but—'

'I stand where I stand,' said Sir Hugh angrily. 'And if you go in that room, I go with you!'

John sighed, and wiped the back of his sleeve across his forehead. 'I don't fancy we'll win her that way . . .' He was struck with a thought. 'It may be she meant the invitation to apply to us both and that 'tis just ill fortune we have come together. But if we go *in* together, that will finish it. What do you say to tossing a coin? Winner goes in right away. Loser chances his arm in an hour or so. Ecod, it seems the only reasonable argument . . .'

Sir Hugh grunted. 'You're worse thoughted than I ever supposed, John. But no one shall say I wasn't a sportsman. If it is the only way to settle the matter peaceable, I'll accept it.' With some difficulty he fished a coin out of his fob pocket. 'Now if you'll toss, I'll call . . .'

'Naw. Hold hard a moment. Let's see the coin . . . Ah, just as I suspicioned: two heads. All's fair in love, but let's be fairer than that.' With equal difficulty John Treneglos fumbled another coin into his fingers and showed it to his rival. 'This one was born natural and has a top and tail. Now call, will you, while I spin.'

'Heads,' grunted Sir Hugh furiously, and at once bent and then went on his knees to see the result.

'Tails!' said John in triumph. 'Tails it is, by the beard of Moses. You've lost, Hugh, and the filly's mine!'

'It struck the edge of the carpet! Just as it fell I saw it. I demand we should toss again! Why, damn me—'

'Nay, fair's fair. You'd not go back on your word, I take it?'

On hands and knees they eyed each other, and Sir Hugh perceived that if he quarrelled with the fall of the coin he would have a fight on his hands. And Treneglos was the second-best amateur wrestler in thirty miles. Grumbling, grunting, sweating, he got to his feet. He bitterly regretted having agreed to any such hazard now. He knew, in his bones he knew, that things had been propitious for him tonight; and now this clumsy, bungling fool had come along to spoil it all.

With seething resentment he watched the younger man tiptoe to the door of Demelza's room, gently turn the handle, and slide inside. Unable to bear the sight of it, he turned sharply away and stumped off to the end of the corridor. But there he stopped. It would be a mistake to abandon his position too early. It did not after all turn entirely on the fall of a coin. There was the lady to consider.

He flattered himself that she had a soft spot for him, and John Treneglos was the sort of bumptious ass who, given an inch, would assume a yard. He might well come out again at any minute with a cracked head. She was a quick-tempered girl and if his advances were unwelcome . . . Sir Hugh decided to linger in the shadows at the end of the passage and wait a minute or two. To while away the time he took a pinch of snuff and dusted the loose powder away with the torn end of his cuff.

The sneeze that had been in gestation was stillborn with delight, for the very thing he had hoped came to pass. John Treneglos came sharply out of the bedroom with a dazed expression on his face and stared right and left. He spotted Sir Hugh and beckoned him. Preening himself, strutting, Sir Hugh came.

'Is this the room, Hughie? I've made no mistake?'

'Nay, of course not. She wants me—'

'Well, there's no one in it. See for yourself.'

'What!' Sir Hugh pushed past him. A candle guttered in the draught between door and window. The bed was not disturbed. A chair was overturned, but no articles of clothing were to be seen about the room. Sir Hugh went straight to the great wardrobe and flung it open. The cupboard was bare. He pulled the curtains farther back from the bed. Then he went on his knees and looked under it. John Treneglos brought the candle over. United in adversity, they ransacked the room. All they found was a number of hairpins, some powder spilled before the dressing-table, and the sleeve of a lawn dressing-gown.

'She's maybe gone visiting herself,' said Treneglos. 'Ecod, I well call to mind a serving maid we had at Mingoose: you'd never be sure where she was to be found next. Once I remember—'

'I conceit it's different from that,' said Sir Hugh, scowling. 'Shut that pesty window, John; all the harmful night air's blowing in . . . There's McNeil, now. He was making a mighty fuss of her after supper . . . But he sleeps some way distant; and even if she went to him, she would surely leave some of her draperies behind.'

Treneglos had had his head out. 'I suppose she wouldn't be madcap enough to climb down this ivy, eh? What would be her purpose? Has it all been done to hoax us, d'you suspicion? I think she couldn't have done it, could she? Or would our noise have scared her? If you flush a hen pheasant, it flies farthest.'

Bodrugan put his head out tentatively and then quickly withdrew it. 'Bah, no, you're dreaming, man. Why should she go that way and risk her neck? 'Tis all very confusing and provoking too. I've never known a woman like her for promising much and performing little. I could put her over my knee.' He thought of that pleasurably for a moment, and then the long-delayed snuff-sneeze occurred. 'Shut the damned window, I say. We shall both have a distemper in the morning.'

The window was shut, and the two men returned disconsolately to the corridor. Sir Hugh was reflectively crumpling the gown sleeve in his fingers.

'It is a mortal pity,' said Treneglos. 'With Ruth away and all . . .'

They tramped down the passage together, no longer on tiptoe or careful of creaking boards; the house might wake now for all they cared. In the distance at the head of the stairs a coat of mail armour glimmered in the light from below.

'When's her time?' said Sir Hugh, trying to take an interest.

'Whose?'

'Ruth's.'

'Oh ... it was to have been last Wednesday, but she's always late in coming to the boil.'

'How many will this be?'

'Four. If she keeps up her rate of fire, we shall soon have our share of livestock. And you'd never have thought it to look at her before she was wed.'

They stopped at the great black banisters and looked down into the littered hall. A footman yawned in his hooded leather chair. Treneglos seemed to expect his host to walk with him into the west wing, but Sir Hugh stopped.

'You run along, dear boy. It will be daylight soon and the cocks crowing. The band'll be waiting for their settlement. I promised they should have it prompt. It was the only condition on which they'd agree to come.'

'Don't forget your Margaret in the library.'

'No,' said Sir Hugh. He brightened a little at the thought and his brow cleared. 'No, there is that. I'll call in there on the way.'

Chapter Ten

Ross stayed three nights at Looe. Propositions were put to him, and he needed time to think them out.

Blewett, to Ross's infinite surprise, was in a position to repay him the £250 loaned when the copper-smelting company smashed. The small boatbuilding business had been a moderate investment when they bought it; but with war came boom conditions, and in six months they had doubled their capital. So £250 was there for Ross's taking. He had been invited to Looe because Blewett, well aware that Ross's loan had saved him from bankruptcy and prison, was keen to repay the unwritten debt as well as the actual one and was prepared to offer Ross a share in their business. In order to judge fairly, he must see the yard.

Ross saw the yard. It was plain that money was being made there. His £250 would double itself in a year. As a business proposition it was first-rate.

But the yard was remote from where he lived. He could either find permanent lodging in Looe or he could allow the work to go on in his absence and look on the thing simply as an investment. Or he could take the £250.

And if he took the £250? Was he to put it aside for the emergencies of next Christmas? Or was he to pour it down the bottomless drain where £1,500 of his had already gone?

Buried under twenty fathoms of rock and broken props was a lode of tin. He knew that. That much was not a speculation any more. Captain Henshawe had sacrificed a hard-earned £100 to prove it. But it had been an unlucky venture from the start.

During the last weeks Ross had bitterly blamed himself for taking the risks which killed the two men. He knew that whatever the inducement he would never take those risks again. But if he let it be known that he was thinking of restarting work on the mine, all the men who had worked on it would flock back, eager to go down. Not one of them would bother to inquire the number of timbermen he was likely to employ. For them it was the luck of the game.

Although much had been agreed for the disposal of the headgear, scarcely anything had yet been moved. Two hundred and fifty pounds would by no means be an excessive sum to get the mine restarted. It might indeed be insufficient. He wondered what Henshawe would say. He knew what Henshawe would say.

He took the £250.

As he set out on the last stage of the journey home, his mind returned to the familiar devils, those which had occupied so large a part of his waking thoughts during the last week. He had not seen Elizabeth since his visit to her that night. He could not evaluate his own feelings yet and did not know hers. The only ones he was sure of were Demelza's, and as he neared home he knew that some personal decisions had to be made and faced quickly if his own attitude was not to go by default. But how could he explain or justify what he did not understand himself?

Ever since he left Elizabeth in the early hours of the morning he had been tormented with new problems. What he had done had brought Elizabeth very much down into the arena. That might have simplified everything. In fact, he found it had not. All his old values had been overthrown and he found himself groping for new ones. As yet they were not to be discovered.

This might have been a useful corrective had he supposed himself to be finding a solution when he broke into Trenwith House six nights ago, but in fact the thing had blown up like a squall in his brain; there had been no time for calculated motives or reasoned intentions. Reason came after and reason was still out of its depth.

When he got home, Demelza was out. She had been out all day, Jane Gimlett said in a peculiar voice. Ross had his supper alone, and then when the sun set he asked which way she had gone, and Jane said across Hendrawna Beach. He went to see if there was any sign of her.

It was a good two miles to the Dark Cliffs on the other side. The tide was high, and in the orange afterglow the sea had become an unusual willow-pattern blue, so full, so overflowing, that it looked as if the land would never contain it. Halfway across he saw her coming. She was walking slowly, stopping now and then to examine some offering of the tide or stir a pile of seaweed with her foot. She was in an old dimity frock, and her hair was beginning to curl as if it had been wet. He remembered there had been a heavy shower not long since.

He had to wait some time before she came up with him. At length they were within speaking distance, and she smiled in a brilliant brittle fashion.

'Why, Ross, how kind of you to come and meet me! Have you had a pleasant week-end? Did it come up to expectations? Mine did not. I went to the Bodrugans; but 'twas nothing in my line so I left early. Have you had supper? Yes, I suppose you have. Jane will have seen to that. Jane's a rare good seer-to-things. I have been a long walk, miles beyond the Dark Cliffs. There's other sandy coves beyond there, but none with any deep water so I suppose they're no use to Mr Trencrom. Now—'

'They're no use to Mr Trencrom,' he said. 'You're wet.' He touched her arm, and noticed how she shrank away at his touch. 'That shower. You'll be taking a chill in the evening air.'

'How thoughtful of you to think of it! But 'twas only a surface wetting. I have been wetter than that today. One of the little beaches was so pretty that I swam in the sea. There was no one to observe but the choughs. And how is Elizabeth? Is she still to wed George or have you fixed another arrangement? I do not suppose she meant seriously to marry him, do you?'

'I haven't seen Elizabeth this week-end,' he said quietly enough but the muscles tight in his cheek.

'Was there some hitch at the last moment? I thought 'twas all arranged.'

'I was at Looe,' he said, 'with Tonkin and Blewett. I don't lie to you, Demelza. When I go to Elizabeth, I will tell you of it.'

'Oh, but does that not constrain you unfairly, Ross? Might it not be thought even a little pompous? To have to tell one's wife every time one intends to visit one's mistress . . . Is it not making a burden of one's enjoyments—'

'No doubt you feel entitled to these pleasantries. No doubt you are. Tell me when you have done, and then we can talk.'

'No, Ross, you tell me when you have done. Isn't that the way it should be?'

They faced each other. At that moment she hated him deeply – as she had done all week-end – so *much* more deeply because she knew she was bound to him by apparently unbreakable chains, which he it seemed could cast aside at will; because she had discovered it at great personal humiliation to herself – greater than she had ever imagined possible.

Ever since her escape from Werry House with its valise-burdened five-mile trek across broken country in the dark; the desperate haste to be home before daylight to be spared the final humiliation; the bruised knees and scratched hands of her climb made worse at every gate and hedge – ever since then the knife had been in her, turning hourly, the *awful* degradation of her struggle with McNeil, the *utter* disgrace of her flight. Had she yielded to McNeil, she would not have felt one quarter as bad, not one tenth as bad.

Ross's adventures might have wounded her desperately, but the result of her own was not so much a wound as a goad.

Knowing nothing of this, he was taken aback by the hostility in her eyes. Especially because it had not been present – or not so noticeably present – after his return from Elizabeth.

He said: 'You still think I've been at Trenwith this weekend. I haven't. I never had an intention of going.'

'You must do what you think best, Ross,' she said. 'Go and live with her if you want to.'

They began to walk again. A shag flew across the surface of the brimming sea so close that it might have been skating on it.

Ross said: 'It is quite possible that Elizabeth's marriage to George will still take place.'

'Well, I'm sure you did your best to stop it.'

'No doubt I did.'

She said: 'Does she love George, then?'

'No.'

She perceived suddenly that not she alone was in torment.

'Did any good come of your visit to Looe?'

'Blewett has paid back what he owes.'

'What shall you do with it?'

'It is enough to restart the mine.'

She laughed. That startled him too, for it was not a winning laugh. He had never heard or seen her like this before.

'I can think of no better way to use the money. It is not enough by itself to discharge our liabilities.'

She would not answer.

'Oh, I know this mining is some taint in the blood, inherited, a fever. I shall make the excuse that I am doing it for Henshawe's sake, but it is not true. I do it for my own sake. If I did not do that, I should go to the war; and at the moment I have no special wish for that again.'

After a while they reached the stile which marked the end of the sand and the beginning of grass and meadow. She went over first. No one would have thought her dependent on anyone. Their words tonight had immeasurably widened the gulf between them. The fact that she had been wrong in supposing him at Trenwith did not seem to carry the weight it should. Acts had been succeeded by principles. Hostility by omission had become hostility by commission. They were both desolate people, needing friendship and sympathy and finding none.

As they reached the garden Demelza said: 'When do you want for me to leave, Ross?'

'Have I said that I wanted you to?'

'No . . . But I thought 'twould be better for you – for us both. I can find work easy.'

'And Jeremy?'

'Jane can see for Jeremy, for the time being anyhow.'

'Do you want to leave?'

'I – think so. I want to do what's right.'

There was silence for a minute or two. He tapped some mud from his boot, his face half turned from her.

'God *knows* what's right, Demelza! And I don't believe there's anything to be gained by trying to do the right thing or the wrong thing in a situation such as this. We can only follow our own feelings so far as they lead and judge from day to day. I don't want you to leave if you're willing to stay.'

They had reached the door. She put her hand against the jamb, suddenly very tired. It was a long time since she had eaten.

'I'd like you to stay,' he said. 'That's if you feel you can.'

'Very well. It's as you wish. But what I said about you going to live with Elizabeth – please do that if you want. George can't marry her if you're there.'

He didn't speak.

'When will you know?' she asked.

'What?'

'About George and Elizabeth's marriage.'

'I can't tell . . . We'll hear.'

'She didn't promise to let you know?'

'She didn't.'

It was going dusk. The afterglow had ended. Demelza stared out over her garden. A bat flitted before the fading face of the sky. A hundred times before she had taken a last look here before going in. But never like this. She had never thought it would be like this. The garden was nothing to her any more. Let it run to waste and let the giant weeds grow. It would match the desolation in her soul.

An hour before this George had come in haste to see Elizabeth.

He said: 'When I had your letter, I came straight away, Elizabeth. I knew if I didn't see you tonight I should not sleep. What's the meaning of it? I can make neither head nor tail of your reasons. Explain what it is that is troubling you.'

He spoke more sharply than he had ever done before to her, but she was far too caught up with her own feelings to notice it.

'All this week, George, I have been thinking, worrying. It seemed – somehow it came home to me that I was plunging into this marriage without due respect for Francis's memory. It isn't yet twelve months. Dear George, please try to appreciate my feelings. I've no one to advise me. I— To be married in secret – oh, I know it was my own request – but in such haste does not look seemly. All this week I have been turning it over in my mind, and at last I plucked up courage to write to you—'

'Three days before the wedding—'

'It is only a *postponement!* Perhaps two months – or even six weeks – and I should feel better about it. I don't somehow feel I can go into it with relish so soon. People will say that I have married you for your money and—'

'People will talk if you sit all day by your own fireside. They concern me no more than the gnats on a summer pond. What is your real reason for asking a delay?'

Elizabeth's troubled eyes widened. She looked very

lovely in her white dress against the dark wainscot of the room. 'I have given my reasons. Aren't they sufficient?'

He smiled. 'No, they are not.'

She made a little gesture of helplessness. 'I have no others, George, but they're sincere. Will you not humour me?'

'All the guests are invited.'

'Guests? But we agreed there were to be none! This was to be an entirely private wedding.'

'And so it is. A few of my closest friends would be hurt if they didn't come to the house afterward. I have had to notify them. I am proud, so proud of my bride. I would have asked five hundred if it had been left to me.'

'How many are there? What numbers have you asked?'

'Oh . . . about twenty-five.'

From the way he spoke she knew it was more. She bit her lip.

'I feel so ashamed to be asking for a postponement; but . . .'

'But what?'

'I have promised to marry you, George, and I'll try not to go back on that promise. But it would – somehow, I feel it would not be fair to you – to either of us – to marry in such haste.'

He watched her with his careful, possessive eyes. She was more nervous than he had ever seen her, fine-strung; her eyes did not meet his but went anywhere about the room.

'Is it something to do with Ross?'

She instantly flushed. The colour came almost before he had stopped speaking. 'It is nothing to do with *anyone* but myself! That day you asked me – at Cusgarne – I was so beset with worry, not able to see which way to turn. I said I would marry you—'

'You regret it?'

Her head went up. 'Not in the very least. But time then seemed unimportant—'

'So it is.'

'Not altogether. I was forgetting Francis. It's only right to allow a decent interval to pass.'

'Many marry after three months – some less. You know that, my dear. No one would think anything of it at all. Ross has been here, hasn't he?'

'He came, of course.'

'You quarrelled?'

'. . . In a way.'

'He naturally does not like the idea of our marriage.'

'No.'

'And he is at the bottom of this change of heart on your part.'

She hesitated. George had so exactly stated the truth that she didn't know how to answer.

'Please. I don't want to discuss Ross. What we decide, you and I, is quite our own concern. I've asked as a great favour, George, that you would postpone the wedding. When I wrote you, I did not know it would inconvenience you so much, because of the guests. But I still request it. Believe me, I don't ask lightly or capriciously. It is a – a feeling I have.' She touched her breast. 'Please don't be angry with me. I – can't stand that . . .'

George's fingers moved round the knob on the end of his stick. He was disappointed, angry, suspicious, and jealous. But fortunately he did not suspect the truth. He was jealous of Ross's influence and bitterly resentful of it, that was all. Thanks to Ross, thanks to something he had said or done, the prize that he, George, had coveted for so many years had slipped a little out of his grasp. No money could buy it, no power obtain it. At present he had no control over it at all. He must go carefully, walk gingerly, lest it slip away altogether.

He said: 'I want to be indulgent to your wishes both before and after marriage, my dear. It's a *bitter* disappointment to me. When I read your letter, I could hardly believe it true. I have the licence, the ring, the ... But whatever you wish in the way of a postponement I will do – if you'll promise one thing.'

'What is that?'

'That you fix another date tonight.'

She hesitated again. Her impulse to postpone had been overwhelming. Whatever else, she was not a liar and a wanton. To go from one man's bed to another in the course of a few days – however disgracefully she had been taken advantage of ... Still less could she go from Ross's caresses to George's. Perhaps that was at the root of her feelings. Well, now the postponement was achieved. George had given way.

But there was a sting in the tail. To gain her end she must bind herself for the future – to an exact day, not a vague time such as she had promised herself.

'A month from today,' he said. 'That's surely a sufficient concession.'

'Oh, no ...' She stopped. Did she want and need to marry him or did she not? If she did, she owed him some consideration. But in the meantime, what would Ross do? 'I had thought of August,' she ended lamely. 'That would then be almost the twelve months.'

He shook his head decisively. She knew that shake. It meant business. 'I may have to go away in August. Besides, that would upset other arrangements relating to Cardew – and to your own mother. Whom do you fear?'

'Fear? Why, no one!'

'Whose opinion do you fear, then? Ross's?'

'No, no, of course not. It is entirely what I feel myself—'

He took her hand and tried to look into her face again. 'Come, my dear Elizabeth, let's not shy at bogies. And let us compromise in this arrangement so that we may both have something out of it. You disappoint me grievously by wishing to postpone our wedding at all. Give me the consolation of being able to fix it for this day month. I know you are not a changeable-minded woman, and I know you will stick to your word. Let me take something home with me tonight . . .'

Elizabeth freed her hand, but not ungraciously, and walked to the table, stood turning the leaves of a book with beating heart. If Demelza had been in tribulation this last week, hers had not been much less. She had not seen Ross since the night he had called. In some moods she felt she never wanted to see him again. But those moods were by no means constant.

Not a changeable-minded woman! Was that what George thought her? All, all that had happened was a result of it. If she had not changed her mind, she would have been married to Ross these ten years and neither George nor Demelza would have been anything in their lives. But what had Ross to offer her now? A sudden wicked climbing in at windows, an incursion on her privacy, a violent taking of what was not rightly his. Demelza lived and would live. They had no money to run away. Ross had not proposed it. He had not even been near her since. That was the crowning insult.

'I know you will stick to your word,' George had said. 'I

do not go back on my promises,' she had said to Ross that night. Were these things true? Yes, but the whole *purpose* of this postponement was that she should have time to think, to consider, and perhaps leave others with time to consider too. What was the good of time if she was bound at the end of it?

He had come up behind her. So far he had kept his attentions within the strictest confines. A half dozen times he had kissed her cheek; sometimes he held her hand. No more. She was not so foolish as to think him cold because of it. He disciplined himself to meet her varying moods. Only a man of his calibre could do it and she respected him for it. Now he lightly rested his fingers on her shoulder – in such a way as to make it quite clear that she was free to escape. She made no move to escape.

'Can I rely on you, Elizabeth?' he said. 'A month from today?'

'Very well,' she said. 'A month from today.'

At that he put his lips on her neck. She thought: other lips have been there. God, I am in a cage! Lost for ever! Why did Ross have to come? How I *hate* him for coming! And despise him. There'll *never* be any friendship between us again! Only *enmity*. I shall be George's heart and soul, his faithful wife and faithful friend! *Anything* I can do against Ross. *Why* did he have to come? God, I am in a cage. Lost for ever.

BOOK FOUR

Chapter One

Elizabeth and George were married on the twentieth June. Contrary to her wishes, a big reception was held at Cardew at which more than a hundred guests were present. This had been George's intention all along. The bride and groom went away for their honeymoon and did not return to the county until late August. Then they took up residence at Cardew. Elizabeth found that Nicholas Warleggan and his wife had not yet moved out, which according to George they had promised to do, but which, also according to George, they were still preparing to do.

Cusgarne was sold and Elizabeth's father and mother moved to Trenwith, where two elderly gentlefolk and a number of servants were engaged to look after them. George wanted to have Aunt Agatha turned out so that Ross would be forced to look after her; but Elizabeth would have none of that and Aunt Agatha stayed.

Sale of the headgear of Wheal Grace mine was countermanded, and work rebegan on the fourth June. By July the debris was cleared and the lode was being worked agin. Among the first miners to go down were Ellery and young Nanfan. The money ran out, but Ross borrowed another £50 from Blewett and then another £50, and that saw them through.

Life at Nampara moved on with the change of the seasons. The hay was gathered and ricked. The wheat and the barley turned from green to yellow, and deepened and grew ripe. This year they had sown close down to the back of the house, and the stalks whispered together all day long. Even when the sea roared you could still hear the other sibilant voice close at hand.

The Allied armies had still not taken Paris, and now it looked as if the opportunity had passed for yet another year. Perhaps it had passed for longer than that, for the latent energies of the revolution were at last beginning to work. General Custine had been thrown to the guillotine for the crime of being unsuccessful, and an unknown Burgundian, Lazarre Carnot, had been appointed to organize victory. His first decree was a *levée en masse*, calling all Frenchmen to the colours and marshalling the services of France down to the last woman and child. It was a new conception of war, or an old conception revived, reversing the civilizing influence of a thousand years.

There had been no proper reconciliation between Ross and Demelza. Sometimes she wished she had left. Sometimes she thought of it even now. Yet she couldn't be sure of what he was feeling. Elizabeth was married to George. The thing had gone through in spite of his intervention. Therefore unless he was prepared to take Elizabeth from Cardew by force he had nothing to hope for from her. Therefore he would stay at Nampara married to Demelza. If she was prepared to be content with second best, then she could be of service to him.

But was she content with second best? Sometimes she thought yes, often emphatically no. Still the goad of her refusal of Malcolm McNeil worked in her. She, Demelza Poldark, had proved herself to be chaste and virtuous, that was what almost killed her. She had given up praying to die, but only just. The next time she met Sir Hugh

Bodrugan he had questioned her peevishly on what had happened, and she had lied to him, telling him she never intended to stay the night and had slipped away soon after the end seeing him surrounded by friends and not wishing to intrude. She prayed that she would never meet McNeil again. That would be the crowning horror.

Ross still slept downstairs. He had never made any attempt to resume a normal relationship with her, and this was a second alienating influence – even though she would have refused him if he had made the approach. She supposed him to find her distasteful after the rare and delicate joy of Elizabeth's arms.

So two acids worked, both corroding to her self-respect, both in turn standing in the way of her customary impulses which always were to forgive and forget.

Often he was inscrutable to her, in a way he had never been since their marriage, though some days he was friendly and companionable enough within the limits of ordinary living. When news of Elizabeth's marriage reached them, he did nothing and said nothing unusual; only his face expressed strain for a time, but he changed the subject and did not mention it again.

The mine was his escape from his own thoughts. He buried himself mentally as well as actually, working longer hours than any of the men, and his face grew paler instead of browner with the summer's advance. The uncomfortable hours were in the evening, but usually Demelza contrived to be busy while the long days lasted.

As the nights drew in, the mine began to show a small profit. He worked it over twice with Henshawe to be sure there was no mistake. Henshawe proposed that they should frame the cost book which recorded it. They could none of them expect money back yet, but at this rate they would

creep slowly away from the red line. With four months still
to go before the next reckoning of Ross's personal account,
he estimated that if he could see a hundred pounds clear,
or a hundred and twenty, by the end of the year he might
somehow, somewhere, scrape together enough to satisfy
his creditors for another few months. His unknown well-
wisher, being a well-wisher, could hardly foreclose on him
for the sake of seventy or eighty pounds.

In September it became known that Mr and Mrs George
Warleggan were staying at Trenwith House. This news
served to incense Ross more than the news of the wedding,
for which he had been in some measure prepared. For two
days he contrived to spend all his time out of the house,
and at mealtimes it was more than he could do to behave
as if life were moving in a normal way. News soon followed
that extensive repairs were being undertaken at Trenwith.
One could not help but wonder at George's generosity in
doing so much for Elizabeth's parents. If he was doing it
for them. Both Ross and Demelza wondered, but neither
spoke of it to the other. Speculation on such a subject was
better not voiced.

Demelza received a letter from Verity.

My dear Cousin,

Thank you for your warm and Affectionate letter,
and for all your Warnings and advice, which, coming
from one who used to seek mine, reads a little
strange. Howsoever, I fully admit that in respect of
Babies your experience has been greater than mine,
and I defer to everything you say.

We had a great Scare last week when news spread
through the Town that five French Privateers had
been sighted, one of them but three miles off the

Castlehead. Everyone was in a Consternation, and
the *Iris*, Captain Soames, the Barbadoes Packet,
which had just sailed, had a near escape of being
taken. However, he put back in time, and an Officer
was sent hot to Penzance to deliver a message by
swift Cutter to Admiral Bell, who was cruising off
Scilly. There is no doubt that he would have
intercepted the Privateers, but a thick sea-mist came
down a few hours later to Blanket our sight and
theirs. Much *Qui Vive* all night lest the Privateers
should take advantage of the Fog; but they did not
and when morning came the Horizon was clear. But
it has given us all, I believe, a salutary shock.

I hope Ross is prospering. I need hardly be told
the effect Elizabeth's marriage to George Warleggan
will have had on him, and now that they are coming
to live beside you it will be an added Offence. Pray
be patient with Ross at this time. I have not seen
Elizabeth since the day of the wedding, but have had
one letter from her. We went, of course, to the
wedding, Andrew and I; for Elizabeth's sake we
could not well refuse; she had Few enough of her
own people about her. From the start I do not think
I liked greatly the thought of this Union. I have no
feud such as Ross has to support me, and I have
nothing against the Warleggans because they are
new rich. Most of our aristocratic families were
founded by successful traders at one time or
another. But George has never quite carried his
money *Rightly*. None of them do, and when you see
them in Aggregate, it is specially noticeable.

The wedding was a very brilliant Affair; St Mary's
Church decked with lilies regardless of cost, a

splendid Crimson Awning outside, and crimson carpet all the way up the aisle to walk on. The Revd Dr Halse performed the ceremony, and he used just the same voice that he uses on the Bench for malefactors. You will want to know what Elizabeth wore. Well, it was a gown of heavy cream satin, with a crepe train decorated with small bouquets of white and purple lilac and a wide sash with a thick silver fringe. She told me afterwards when I admired it that it took twenty-six yards of material. Old Jonathan must have had a long stocking somewhere. But you will know without me to tell you that she looked very beautiful in it – like a queen – yet nervous, ill at ease, inclined to flush up and go pale at the least thing. George of course was unruffled by anything, even when his great friend Paul Boscoigne dropt the ring; he was very smart in a rich gold-laced coat and a scarlet waistcoat with broad gold lace.

Andrew is due home on Wednesday. Only one packet, the *Trefusis,* has had trouble as yet – what can a single ship do if she finds herself attacked by five? I ask myself that sometimes, in the night.

Is it true, do you know, that Elizabeth is with child? She makes no mention of it in her letter, but Mrs Daubuz tells me that her mother had been saying so. It will be strange to have a family of Warleggans founded in the home of the Poldarks.

My dearest love to you both, and a special hug for Jeremy.

Your loving cousin,
Verity

Demelza did not show this letter to Ross. She had her own reflections on parts of it, but she thought it better he should not share them. As it happened he came home that day more than ever pre-occupied, though earlier than usual. It was Lobb's day, but he did not even ask if there were any letters. Demelza began to feel she could not stand his silences much longer. They dined in silence and Jane cleared in silence. Demelza stuck on, determined not to be frozen out, and more and more certain that a conflict must come. At length, her heart swelling, she said suddenly:

'Ross, if this is to go on you will have to eat alone! For days now you have scarce spoken and today has been the worst of all! I know why you are like this and cannot help you to a solution. Perhaps there is no solution any more. But there can be one for us. If I stay, if you want me to stay, then let us behave like human beings. But if you want for me to go, then say so, for go I shall if this be the way you expect us to live!'

Ross looked up, and the surprise in his face was a surprise to her. 'Has it been as bad as that?' He laughed. She did not remember when he had laughed before. 'I'm sorry. I hadn't realized. I should explain—'

'Is that necessary?'

'Very necessary, considering I have not been thinking about Elizabeth and George this evening at all.'

She stared at him. 'Is there some other bad thing then?'

'No, good rather. I was hesitating yet whether to say anything of it because so often before . . . I hadn't realized my face naturally set into such morose lines that—'

'What good thing?'

'But of course you're right – I have been in a mood all this week, and for that I . . . My feeling about Elizabeth's marriage need not be gone into now. That's something I've had to think out – fight out in my own way. But George's coming to stay at Trenwith and showing signs of remaining, that's a – a crowning indecency. Trenwith is part of the Poldark family! It is our *home*, if you understand! I cannot accustom myself at all to the idea of its belonging to George. I really can't, Demelza. It's – unnatural, a monstrous perversion of the right – or so it seems to me. That has been my trouble all this week. But today . . .'

'Today?'

'It is the mine. I thought it wiser not to tell you as yet. I have been almost afraid. The lode has split today. One half of it, the best half, is twice the size of the old lode. It appears to be over twelve feet thick. The first assays are very rich too. Henshawe says he has never seen richer ground.'

Demelza felt confused, as if she had braced herself to fight something that wasn't there. 'But – why not tell me? Why sit there . . .'

'I'm *sorry*. I was so preoccupied, calculating . . . Why not tell you? Because we've grasped at so many false hopes. I can't help having them, but I thought of saving you.'

'That I b'lieve is something you need not save me from. But will it mean so much? The mine is already paying its way, you said.'

He stared back at her and his face was no longer set in the old lines. She perceived that she had mistaken the tensions behind it.

'Let's wait,' he said. 'Let's hatch the chickens first.'

They waited. Ross kept his head down and would not allow his thoughts to progress beyond the day's work. Only

Henshawe, with his more detached mind – having so much less at stake – would allow himself a jubilant tone. After another week Ross told Demelza that she need not worry about a debt settlement at Christmas. One month's work at this rate would pay all the interest. Two months would see part of the debt gone. They could already see two months ahead.

Demelza said: 'Do you mean – in any case?'

'In any case. The assay is as rich as the ground. It can't help but pay! There's little skill now in this part. We just have to get it up and dress it and sell it.'

'I can't hardly believe that.'

'No more can I.'

The flaw for them both was that success had been too long in coming. This venture had raised so many hopes before and then dashed them. It no longer seemed *entitled* to become a valuable property. Had mineral been found eleven months ago, it could have saved them dramatically from immediate bankruptcy. Thirteen months ago it would have saved Francis's life. Now, when hope deferred had made the heart sick, when everyone had grown past the stage of expecting anything any more, when bankruptcy was not quite so immediate a danger – though still existent – when a bare living from it was as much as anyone felt entitled to expect, now suddenly it began to give off riches.

Riches. That was the queer thing. Not just an income, not just a business return, but riches. This was quite different from Wheal Leisure, where cost books were still balanced and profits still calculated. The profits were here in lump sums. The money was here in lump sums. The gamble had come off. Ross felt he had to handle the coin sometimes. It was all very well to accept tin cheques and the rest, but gold and silver in bags was what he needed.

He also needed Demelza to help him savour it, for success after long tribulation can only be fully enjoyed if it is shared. They tried conscientiously to share it; but in that they failed. The division between them was too deep.

In late October, Dwight received a letter from Dr Matthew Sylvane of Penryn. It ran:

> Sir,
>
> One of my patients, Mr Ray Penvenen, of Killewarren, near Chasewater, has for some weeks been suffering from a wasting condition which has not responded to accepted medical treatment. After due consideration I have thought it desirable to have a Second Opinion, and Mr Penvenen has mentioned your name as a physician with some former knowledge of his physical condition.
>
> Should you be willing to be called in Consultation, I suggest that you meet me at his house on Friday the Eighteenth at or about Five o'clock, when we can discuss the Symptoms privately before proceeding to examine the Patient.
>
> Perhaps you will favour me with a Reply by the hand of my groom who has instructions to wait.
>
> I am, sir, your obedient servant,
>
> M. Sylvane

Dwight wanted to send word that Mr Penvenen could turn yellow and rot before he would enter his house again; but after a struggle he replied accepting the invitation. He had never met Matthew Sylvane, but knew of him as a man with small private means, like Choake, who practised among the gentry. At ten minutes to five Dwight rode in at the gates of Killewarren. Such a pang at the mere entrance, the gateposts. The droop of the pine trees, the long thatched house, even the servant who came to the door . . .

Dr Sylvane was in the big upstairs parlour over the stables. He was a narrow adenoidal man of forty-five or so who seemed to do nothing without the help of his nose. Dwight would have preferred to see Mr Penvenen first, but Sylvane was having none of that nonsense. The young fellow must enter the sickroom armed with the theories and observations of an experienced apothecary. Mr P. had gone down in the first place about ten weeks ago with what was clearly a spasm of the common gall duct, creating a low fever and slowing the circulation of the blood, dissolving the tissues and affecting the elasticity of the fibres. From that a wasting and possibly tumorous condition had sprung. The primary symptoms had given way to treatment: a little bleeding and a suitable draught: salt of wormwood and ammoniac, ginger powder, sugar candy, oil of cloves; jellies and broths to eat, beef teas, minced veal. No fish. Fish in this close weather smelled very quickly; Dr Sylvane was against giving it to sick people, who smelt already.

But Mr P. had never lost his appetite. When the fever was brought off, he began to eat like a horse – still did. And white wine. Down it went, bottle after bottle, quite astonishing. There was slight pulmonary congestion of an edematous nature, and plenitude of urine; not surprising really. Bleedings, blisters, potions, he'd tried 'em all; but the patient remained very inert and was losing strength. A second opinion was really unnecessary, but sometimes a confirmatory diagnosis gave the patient confidence . . .

Scarcely listening, his mind on earlier visits, Dwight

followed his colleague along the passage to Mr Penvenen's bedroom. It was all horribly reminiscent. But his memories left him when he saw Ray Penvenen in bed, crouching like an injured weasel, grey-faced and dry. He had never been handsome but now . . . The skin was in folds on his face and hands.

As Dwight came up to the bed, Penvenen said in his precise voice: 'I do not believe we parted very good friends, Dr Enys. I am the more obliged to you therefore for coming.'

Dwight bowed slightly but didn't speak. The man should have his attention but nothing more.

'I insisted on its being you, in spite of your youth, because I believe you have the courage not to be influenced by what other people say. Dr Sylvane has done his best, but his best does not appear to be good enough—'

'Well, Mr Penvenen, what I have done—'

'It is the first time for a great many years, Dr Enys, that I have been really sick. I have a feeling that unless something is quickly done it will be the last.'

'I trust not.' With a stiff face Dwight bent to examine him.

Certain symptoms at once. 'There's no fever now, Dr Sylvane.' 'No, as I told you, it has responded to treatment.' 'It did so nine weeks ago, Dr Enys. I have never had none since.' That acetose smell on the breath. He was almost too weak to turn himself. 'You drink a great deal, Mr Penvenen?' 'To excess. Nothing strong; a light canary.' 'Water?' 'Yes, even water sometimes.' 'And eat?' 'And eat. Enough for four, yet I have become as thin as a shotten herring. Hitherto I have thought the gluttony of my neighbours a trifle disgusting.'

After a thorough examination Dwight allowed the curtain of the bed to fall and walked to the window. No Caroline today in her black riding habit and her flame-coloured hair. No little yapping pug. No Unwin Trevaunance with his great lion head. Only a sick man, sick to death.

'I have also considered,' said Dr Sylvane, following him nasally, 'the possibility of a cestoid worm in the alimentary canal. This ravening hunger. But I have examined the stools and have been unable to find any evidence—'

'And the urine?'

'Unusually sweet to the taste. But with all that unfermented wine . . . Then again I have considered a tuberculous infection of an atmospheric-cosmic-telluric nature induced by the moist heavy weather in a county teeming with metals and minerals. There's a natural malignancy to the mineral effluvia, and folk here are hectic and consumptive at the best of times. Do you know, sir, it is fortunate there are few large towns in this county. Do you know, sir, that three thousand men living within an acre of ordinary ground make an atmosphere of their own steams seventy-one feet high. How much more dangerous then, in a county—'

'It is surely the sugar sickness,' said Dwight.

'Ah?' Sylvane breathed out through his nose, a thin reedy sound. 'Ah.'

'A man – I've forgotten his name – Willis was it – years ago. And more recently . . . And all these other symptoms, the hunger, the wasting, the sour breath—'

'Polydypsia,' said Sylvane warily. 'I had thought of it. It could be considered; but there are contradictory indications. The fever—'

'There has been no fever for nine weeks, he says. I believe it to be a mistake to consider it as a symptom now.'

'There is a gouty condition. And the pulmonary congestion—'

'Very typical and very dangerous.'

'I have not found it so.'

Dr Sylvane squinted suspiciously along his nose at Dwight, but Dwight was not giving way. 'I believe there is no other diagnosis.'

'Mr P. is fifty-seven. So sudden an onset in a man of his age . . .'

'It does occur. Anyway, that is my belief.'

'You cannot intend to tell him your views. It will be a serious shock. I'll not be answerable for the consequences.'

'I'll not be answerable if he goes on as he is.'

'How else can he go on? You do not suppose he will recover if that is his complaint!'

They talked for a few minutes in low tones, then Dwight turned back to the bed. Ray Penvenen watched his approach with red-rimmed eyes.

'Well, Dr Enys, is it to be the knife?'

'No, sir, no knife. I think possibly we can do something for you. And you can help yourself.'

'How?'

'By giving up most of the things you eat and drink. The wine especially.'

'But that is the only thing which relieves me! How shall I quench my thirst?'

'By cold water and some dilute milk. And you must eat very much less. I would urge the strictest possible diet. It will not be an easy treatment, for I know how hungry you will be.'

'You don't know how hungry I'll be for you've never felt as I feel! It's very well to prescribe these things. D'you mean I am to starve?'

'Not starve, though it may well seem like it. I'd also suggest warm baths and a greater amount of air in your room.'

Dr Sylvane was heard to mutter something under his breath, but when Mr Penvenen glanced up at him he was sniffing the perforated end of his gold-headed cane.

'You don't agree with this treatment, Dr Sylvane?'

Sylvane shrugged. 'We have talked over it at length, and I regret to differ from a colleague – I positively cannot accept responsibility for a lowering treatment on one in such a weakened condition as yourself.'

'I am in an extremely weakened condition,' said Mr Penvenen, 'in consequence of twelve weeks' illness and ten weeks of your treatment of me. That suggests I am in need of a change of treatment. Can you cure me, young man?'

'No, sir.'

Mr Penvenen blinked and passed a tongue over his lips. After a moment he said: 'Well, that's honest anyway.' He motioned to his servant, who was standing by the bed, to pour him another glass of wine from the decanter. Then with a continuing gesture he stopped him. 'On second thoughts no, Jonas. The doctor advises me to take water.'

Chapter Two

Dwight had no patience with the view that because raw meat turned putrid when exposed to the air human beings necessarily did the same. And he was as much a crank in matters of food and drink. Fasting and fresh air had done good in several cases of bilious fever and the tertian ague, and he had tried a similar treatment on Charlie Kempthorne with his consumption of the lungs. Miraculously it had worked on him. Not on many others, but one success was something in a disease notoriously fatal. Then he had experimented with gout, to the annoyance of his few substantial patients.

Now Mr Penvenen. As a physic he prescribed Theban opium after each meal. It was all a shot in the dark and likely to kill or cure.

Mr Penvenen began to come round.

On his fifth visit he found his patient sitting up in a chair muffled in rugs and cloaks before a window open more than half an inch to the mild afternoon. After the usual examination Mr Penvenen said dryly:

'You said you could not cure me, Dr Enys, but you seem well on the way to having me out and about again. I'm very much in your debt.'

'It is partly your own doing.' Dwight had never unbent in his attitude. 'Without your will to deny yourself . . .'

'The effort has been considerable. How much longer am I to deprive myself of the ordinary pleasures of life?'

'If by ordinary pleasures you mean ordinary food and drink, I should say for many months yet. Perhaps for the rest of your life.'

'And how long is that likely to be?'

'I can't tell you. Provided you take care of yourself, there is no reason why it should be short.'

Silence fell between them. Dwight took out his pulse watch, but Penvenen said:

'I trust you now feel able to overlook the unfortunate circumstances which attended my niece Caroline's last visit. No one regretted the situation more than I, or the measures it was necessary for me to take. Now that it is all past, I should like to assume that I may call on you when necessary; and perhaps sometime you will favour me with a social visit when we may dine together – assuming of course that your own diet will not be as strict as mine.'

It was a gesture of friendship, or as near as Ray Penvenen could get to making one. Dwight didn't answer. Penvenen went on:

'Perhaps I should tell you before you answer that Caroline will shortly be announcing her engagement to Lord Coniston, the eldest son of the Earl of Windermere. I hope the information will not now distress you.'

'I congratulate her,' said Dwight.

'Thank you. She was clearly predestined for such a match, and I should have been failing in my duty as her guardian if I had not prevented an unsuitable attachment from developing. I hope you understand it was no reflection on your personal capacities or that it showed a lack of esteem for them on my part.'

'Yes, I understand.' Dwight put his watch away. He did not know his patient's heartbeats and he didn't care. He went across the room and stood by the fire. 'When is the wedding to take place?'

'My sister does not say. I don't believe the date has been fixed yet. Caroline hasn't been well and that—'

'Not well?'

'One of the customary summer indispositions. She's quite recovered. But the wedding is not likely to be until after Christmas.'

'Will you give my wishes to Miss Penvenen. I'm sure it will be an entirely – suitable match.'

Dwight didn't deceive himself, but he evidently deceived Mr Penvenen.

'I'm glad you feel as you do about it. That is the attitude of a generous man. I was sure I could rely on your good sense and understanding.'

Dwight felt like asserting that no one could rely on either. 'Continue with the physic,' he said. 'A little more exercise when you feel like it; but no overexertion. I'll be in again on Wednesday morning.'

He was going to leave then, but the older man said tentatively: 'I – hope I shall be well enough to travel up to London after Christmas. There is business I should attend to as well as the more social purposes.'

'We must see how you progress,' Dwight said.

He did not suppose that his patient's improvement would be maintained at its present rate. If his diagnosis was correct, there was nothing whatever he could do which would affect the underlying disease. However, there was no point in telling Penvenen so, and one never knew with the human constitution. Obviously the prospect of seeing his niece married into the nobility would be the strongest possible stimulus.

*

Verity had her child on All Hallows E'en, a boy of seven
pounds, and both were well. He was called Andrew after
his father, and Ross and Demelza went for the christening.
Because there was a Coinage due that week, Ross rode
there and back in the day; but Demelza stayed four days.
She felt better then than she had done since May, and
Verity's happiness was reflected in her. She was taken
aboard Andrew Blamey's ship and went a trip up the river
and to a reception in the town. She said nothing at all of
her own trouble to Verity. For the first time this was
something she could not discuss even with her. In any case
she could not say anything without telling of things which
she hoped nobody but herself and Ross and Elizabeth
would ever know. With George and Elizabeth now so close,
it seemed more than ever important to be absolutely silent
about the events of the ninth of May.

The day after he returned home Ross received a note
from George.

> Dear Poldark,
>   As you are a trustee of Francis's estate, certain
> formalities cannot be gone through without your
> signature. Since June nothing whatever has been
> done, and it therefore seems necessary that we should
> meet. If you will come to Trenwith on Friday or
> Saturday morning next I shall be there to receive you.
>   Yours etc.,
>   G. Warleggan

Ross replied:

> Dear Warleggan,
>   As you are not a trustee of Francis's estate, I do
> not consider that the business concerns you. If you

wish to see me on any other matter, I shall be at
Nampara on Friday or Saturday morning next.

Yours etc.,
R. V. Poldark

George replied:

Dear Poldark,

It may have come to your notice that Elizabeth
and I were married in June. In attending to Francis's
estate I am only trying to take the burden off her
shoulders. She has not been well this month, and it
would be more convenient for her to meet you here.
Perhaps you will let me know a time suitable to
yourself.

Yours etc.,
G. Warleggan

Ross wrote that he would call on Saturday at noon.

As soon as he came inside the gates he saw the difference. In less than three months money had worked miracles. The undergrowth of ten years had been cleared, the
hedges clipped, the unnecessary trees cut down, specimen
trees newly planted; the pond had become a lake and
bobbled with fish, flower borders were laid out and a few
late flowers were still in bloom. Fat cattle grazed on the
other side of the lake. Fresh gravel had been laid on the
paths before the house.

When he went in, he saw that the great window of the
hall had been repaired and long crimson satin curtains
fitted. New rugs were laid, new hangings on the walls. Many
of the old cracked portraits had been put away, and in the
big parlour where he was shown by a liveried footman – no

hasty, aproned Mrs Tabb – all had been changed. Even Elizabeth's spinning wheel and harp had disappeared.

No one was in the room, and he was allowed to wait ten minutes tapping impatiently at his boot before George came in followed by a tall, thin man with narrow shoulders and eyes too close together. George was in a fine buff-coloured suit with darker buff nankeen trousers. Then another, older man entered. Jonathan Chynoweth, Elizabeth's father.

They bade good day to each other distantly. George said: 'This is Mr Tankard, my attorney. You know Mr Chynoweth, of course. We need not take much of your time. Several papers have to be signed. Then you can go.'

'Where is Elizabeth?'

'Resting. We can complete the business without her.'

'I don't think so. She is the co-trustee of Francis's estate. I shall do nothing without her presence.'

'We anticipated that,' said George pleasantly. 'She has signed a power of attorney, so that I can act for her in these matters. Show the document to Mr Poldark, Tankard.'

Ross fingered the parchment, vaguely suspecting a sharp practice but unversed in law. He turned to Mr Chynoweth.

'It is true, my dear boy. There is nothing underhand about it, I assure you. I think you can acquit me of being party to any – hm – dubious expedient.'

'If you wish to know the truth,' said George, 'though it will not pleasure you, Elizabeth especially asked that I should do this on her behalf so that she shouldn't have to meet you. Her health is not perfect at the moment, but she is fully capable of transacting any business she wishes to transact. She wants to have nothing to do with you, so I'm helping her to avoid a meeting which would be distasteful.'

Ross returned the document to Tankard, who put it crackling back into his brief-case. 'Is it true that she is with child?'

Tankard's head came up. George said: 'It is true. What is it to you?'

Ross shrugged. 'Let us get on with the business.'

There were various papers to discuss and sign. He had no intention of being amenable to their plans, but in fact there was little to query. Mr Chynoweth did not speak again but watched it all, fingering his thin little beard. George was honest enough in his day-to-day transactions. But when it was all done, Tankard said:

'Er, Mr Poldark, these shares, this half share in Wheal Grace – held on behalf of Mrs Warleggan's son – which was disposed of at the beginning of the year for a sum of six hundred pounds. Can you tell us how it came about? The transaction seems to have been irregular, and we are not satisfied that it was legal.'

'It was legal.'

'Well, sir, we have applied to Mr Harris Pascoe for details of the arrangement, but he tells us he is not at liberty to divulge them. We shall be glad of your explanation.'

'No explanation is necessary. Mrs Poldark – Mrs Warleggan received six hundred pounds on behalf of her son for a half share in a worthless mine.'

'Supposedly worthless,' said George. 'Who was so foolish as to pay her that sum?'

Ross put down his pen, dusted sand over the paper, shook it. 'I was.'

There was a moment's silence.

'Ah,' said George. 'I wondered if there was not some such explanation.'

'I understand,' said Tankard, 'that the mine is now into rich country – that it will be very shortly paying a high dividend.'

'It already is paying a high dividend.'

'Ah,' said George again. 'And no doubt at the beginning of the year—'

'I take exception,' Ross said, 'to your suspicions. I take exception to your lack of common intelligence. Good life, d'you suppose that if we had found rich ground in January, we should have waited until November to exploit it?'

'Why did you buy the other half of a worthless mine, then?' demanded Tankard.

Ross gave him a look. 'Listen, man, I am not here to be cross-examined by out-at-elbow attorneys! Go back to your law books and speak when you're spoken to.'

Mr Chynoweth drew his spatulate first finger along the polished surface of the table. 'Come, come, I think we're getting a little heated, eh? No need for that, quite uncalled-for I assure you.' He stared at the tip of his finger. There was no dust. 'I don't doubt you had other and good reasons, dear boy. If you care—'

'In January,' said Ross, 'your daughter was in straits for money. I felt responsible for having persuaded Francis to sink his last six hundred pounds in a mine. I wished to give her the money back but knew she wouldn't accept it as a gift. So I devised a means whereby I could do so unknown to her. I thought the mine was a failure. I thought it as late as July.'

'A dubious story,' said George. 'No one—'

'What you think doesn't matter. But don't expect me to listen to your speculations.'

'Wait,' said George, as Ross seemed about to leave. 'I think we must give the devil his due. Eh, father-in-law?

On certain conditions I am prepared to accept the explanation. It was a device – as you say – a thought cumbersome, no doubt, but one which would probably appeal to an unbusinesslike mind. Well meant. Eh, father-in-law? But cumbersome. The legality of the arrangement need not be questioned, for its moral aim was good. Indeed one views it as a gesture – a rather overdramatic gesture such as one would have anticipated – but let us accept it and wait for the following gesture which plainly will succeed it.'

Everybody waited as bidden. Mr Chynoweth had not followed George's meaning and blinked in perplexity.

'What following gesture?'

'Why to return the half share of the mine, now that it is successful, into the custody of Geoffrey Charles's trustees.'

Ross took up his gloves. They were still patched. 'Why d'you suppose I should do that?'

'Well, you acted to save Elizabeth in a difficult situation. Now that gesture is no longer appropriate because what you took from her has become worth more than what you gave for it. The situation's quite changed.'

'So have her circumstances.'

'Naturally. With her marriage to me. But in this you were acting for Geoffrey Charles. Francis's son has no claim on my generosity. All he has is a half share in your mine.'

'He *had* such a share. He sold it to me.'

'In fact what happened was that as Geoffrey Charles's trustee you sold this property to yourself.'

'Yes. Thinking it worthless.'

'We have only your word for that. And it's no longer true.'

'Fortunately for me, no.'

'It's obvious therefore that if you truly meant this transaction to be a gesture of friendship and affection in

Geoffrey Charles's favour, it must in order to stand as such now be reversed. Otherwise it becomes a sharp practice.'

Ross continued to tap with his gloves. 'What is obvious to you, George, and what is obvious to me are two very different things. As cotrustee with Elizabeth of Geoffrey Charles's affairs, it was my duty to do the best I could for him and for such property as Francis left him. In January of this year I sold his half share in Wheal Grace for £600. That was *more* – far more – than the best I could do. Had the stock come on the open market, he would not have had fifty pounds for it. No; nor ten neither! You wouldn't have given me ten for my half share. The mine was finished. I thought so with the rest. By hook and by crook we kept her working through the summer. After an accident she closed, but we reopened her. And now we have struck tin. Tin where we were looking for copper. But tin in such abundance that it stretches out whichever way we go. Well, so now I deem the profit legitimately mine. I don't consider it belongs to Elizabeth or Geoffrey Charles or to Mr Chynoweth or to you. And if ever you had hopes of jockeying me into thinking otherwise, you'd best give 'em up for they will not benefit you.'

Tankard coughed and blew on his fingers and looked at George. George said:

'Since you've put your case so plainly, we can hardly do less. We shall contest the legality of the sale.'

'On what grounds?'

'You will get that information in due course.'

'I shall be waiting to receive it.'

'In any case, you will not come out of the litigation with a savoury character. A man who cheats his ward.'

'Up to now,' said Ross, 'I have offered you no violence. I don't want to spoil your vulgar new furnishings.'

'You would not,' said George. 'I have three servants within call.'

'Never stir without them,' said Ross.

George flushed. 'Go back to your scullery maid,' he said.

Chapter Three

Unlike Julia, Jeremy seldom prospered in his mother's absence, and Demelza returned to find him with a stomach upset. Dwight said Jeremy had a mild colic, and mixed a sedative draught. When he had done and they went downstairs, Demelza said:

'You will stay to dinner? Ross has gone to Trenwith but will be back soon.'

'To Trenwith?'

'Yes. He is a whatever-they-call-it for Francis's estate and must visit them on some business matter.'

'Oh . . . I see. Thank you, I'll stay, for I wanted to see you both sometime this week. I wanted you to be the first two to know my plans. I have put in for a post as surgeon in the Navy.'

'Oh.' Demelza stared at him, troubled. 'Is it final? Have you quite decided?'

'Yes, it will be for the best. I have a friend at the Admiralty, Sir Ralph Slessor, who has promised his influence. There's no trouble, of course, in getting a ship; but one wishes a good ship.'

'This is the second time you've threatened to leave us, and this time . . . Are you certain sure you are acting for the best?'

'Well, I cannot settle here. I've tried but it is useless. This – war is unsettling for one thing. I'm in a backwater.

It is the wrong place for a young man. There's so much experience to be gained elsewhere.'

'Does it mean you must leave us altogether for a term of years, like going to prison; or shall you be able to come out when you are tired of it?'

'It will be for a term, but I've yet to hear how long. They're equipping the old ships as fast as they can press men to serve in them, but it is slow work. They say hardly more than forty thousand have been added since the war began.'

She went to the window and narrowed her eyes at the slanting sun. Sun fell and made luminous patches on her hair.

'And Caroline? Have you heard nothing from her?'

'After Christmas she's marrying Lord Coniston, whoever he may be. Her uncle told me last week.'

She knew now the final causes of his flight, for in a sense a flight it was.

'I'm that sorry especially for the way it happened. It grieves me that much when I think—'

'Well it grieves me no longer. I am thankful for the escape ... Oh, I loved Caroline – still do.' He turned his eyes away from her. 'But we were not for each other.'

'Here is Ross now. 'Tis peculiar that I can tell Darkie's hooves from that of other horses ... Dwight, did you not go to see Caroline and explain? Did you not see her in London? I am unhappy to feel that this came about, whether for good or bad, because of what you did to save Ross.'

'No, I think she sensed it long before that, and in that respect I am to blame—'

It was not often that Demelza cried out, but she did so

when Ross, leaving his mare to find her own way to the stables, came stooping into the parlour.

He had lost his coat entirely except for one cuff which hung round this wrist. His shirt was split up the back, and he had used his neckerchief to tie up his head. There was blood oozing through the improvised bandage.

'You have an aptitude,' he said to Dwight, 'for being in the right place at the right times.' Then he sat in a chair and so put himself on a level to be examined.

'You fell?' said Demelza. 'Have you broken any bones? How did it— No, but you did not fall! Ross, who did this? You've been fighting at Trenwith! Oh, your head is so cut! Dwight, I'll get water . . .'

She flew into the kitchen, and in a moment Jane Gimlett was flying too – for unguents and towels. When Demelza got back, Ross had already begun his explanation.

' – nor was the least thought of it in my mind. But it's no good! Every time I see him – and seeing him in Francis's old home; it has been almost as much my home as this; and his airs . . . Then when he said that, I could stand it no longer and suddenly the respectable little scene broke up. My, but it did me a world of good! And his parlour—'

'Good!' said Demelza.

'And his parlour is in ruin. We batted to and fro across the room for three or four minutes, with that squint-eyed attorney crouching in a corner and Mr Chynoweth under the table. George is getting soft, I'll swear it; it is this city life or his wedding or something; I have never beaten him so easy before. But then three of his flunkeys came bursting in— Ach! what are you doing, man?'

'Putting some stitches in your head. You don't want to be scarred this side as well.'

'And then three of his men came in and set on me. It was weighted the other way then, but two of them were puny fellows and had no real stomach for the thing. I threw one of them through the window. Then at the last they got me and threw me out after him. So I whistled for Darkie and she came trotting round. Even then I rode over their new flower beds. This eyetooth is loose; should it come out?'

'No, leave it. The gum is bruised, but the tooth is unbroken.'

'And where was Elizabeth during this?' Demelza asked quietly.

'I didn't see her. She was unwell or unwilling. You'd not believe the difference they have made to the place, with Turkey rugs and brocade curtains and new pieces of furniture. Already it's ceasing to be the home of the Poldarks and becoming the home of the new-rich Warleggans. I was impressed.'

'But what was it started it?' said Demelza. 'How did you come to blows when 'twas to have been just a business meeting and a signing of papers?'

Ross lifted his good eyebrow. 'He made an offensive remark.'

'What did he say?'

'Nothing I should wish to repeat to you.'

'Was it *about* me?' she asked, scenting as much from the expression of his face and thinking instantly of the Bodrugan party.

'It was about nobody I have any connection with.'

'Why then did you take offence over it?'

'Because I chose to.'

They stared at each other, and presently he laughed at her expression. It was as if the fight had done him the good that he claimed. She found herself warming to his attitude of mind.

When dinner was over and Dwight had gone, Ross told her what had passed at the meeting earlier. She was indignant and incredulous.

'I don't know if Elizabeth is party to such a manœuvre,' he said, 'but I must see Pascoe this week to know if the sale was watertight.'

'Not this week,' she said, looking at his head.

'Well, as soon as possible. George is marked too – that's some consolation. Until I see Pascoe, I shall not know what there is to be met.'

'I'm glad at least that you do not intend to return the share to Geoffrey Charles.'

'Well, I do not believe Elizabeth will have neglected Geoffrey Charles in any marriage settlement she has been able to arrange. He is the last person. If I see him short of money when he comes of age, I shall give him a share then. But not until then. I'm not having George with a finger in *this* pie!'

'I hope this new quarrel will not make things worse betwixt you and George.'

'I wouldn't wish it to improve them.'

'We live too close now for feuds, Ross. You may meet any time, accidental, about other business. Or he may attempt reprisal. Remember Jud. It will not do for you to be out at night alone.'

'Violent solutions seem to be the only ones that come natural to me at present. I'm very sorry, Demelza. It is an uncivilized attitude. But at least I can have no room for complaint if someone fires back.'

She did not reply, and he grimaced as he changed his position.

'You know the big parlour,' he said. 'They have a set of new chairs in there of fine polished – well, mahogany I suppose it would be, with delicate carved backs and satin-covered seats. I am not one with an expert eye for furniture, but they seemed to me as good a sort of work as any I've seen.'

'Oh, yes,' said Demelza.

'A great many things had been done to the room – some good, some bad. They have blue damask curtains with a broad gold fringe, and the new Turkey carpet is very thick, inweft with human figures. There were some considerable number of china ornaments on the mantelshelf – very rare no doubt – but these I did not care for. And they have a great candelabrum of cut-glass suspended from the ceiling. And before the door, to shut off the draught, a Chinese screen.'

'You seem to have taken in a very fair number of changes.'

'I was kept waiting ten minutes, which naturally put me in a good mood to begin. One does not realize until one has seen it the variety of things money can buy these days.' He looked around, a man seeing his own house afresh. 'We're poverty-stricken here, aren't we?'

'Yes, I believe so.'

'Well, it need not be quite so much so any longer. What do you say to coming in with me, when I go to see Harris Pascoe, and we could buy a few new things for the house.'

He watched her as he spoke, but as always when the conversation took a personal turn she seemed to draw in from the natural response.

'It is just as you say, Ross. I'll come with you if you want me to.'

'Yes. I want you to.'

'The interest on our debts is due next month.'

'The south lode is twenty-five feet wide and still increasing. Our profit last month was £580. For a month only. If this goes on, we shall have no debts at all.'

Demelza got up, began collecting together the building bricks that Jeremy had left in a corner. 'I still can't hardly believe it.'

'Nor I. I shake myself twice daily. Don't do that, not just now. I saw the look in your eyes when I come in with a bloody head. I believe you still care for me.'

It was the first challenge, the first direct approach.

'Of course I still care for you, Ross. What a thing to say . . .'

'Then listen to me, please. Tell me what you think we should buy. Women know better than men what are the first essentials. We need so much that I should not know where to begin.'

She came over to him. 'Suppose I made out a list and you take it in.'

'That was not what I suggested.'

'Well, there is so much to see to in the mornings. And Jeremy . . .'

'That was not what you promised.'

'Well, there's only Darkie.'

'We've shared her before. We can buy a horse for you to return on if you dislike the proximity.'

She smiled, trying to release her hand. 'There are many things we need more badly than a horse. Let me fetch pen and ink.'

'And you'll come with me to get them?'

'Yes, Ross, I said I would. If you want me to.'

A fortnight passed before Ross's head was clear of its plaster, and then they went in together. He went first to see Harris Pascoe, before any purchases or extravagances were begun. Pascoe said:

'Th-they haven't a leg to stand on. The investment was legally transferred. I do not believe a civil court would waste time even on hearing their case; but if they did, there could be only one verdict, in your favour.'

'It may be George was making an idle threat. I thought that, but I came to you for reassurance.'

'You have it. I am sorry this quarrel has broken out afresh, though. With Warleggan your close neighbour on both sides ... I don't b-believe feuds of this sort ever profited anyone.'

'What do you mean, a neighbour on both sides?'

'I was speaking figuratively. Mr Coke has sold his holding in Wheal Leisure to the Warleggans.'

'It is what I expected, but I don't welcome it all the same. Wheal Leisure is on Treneglos property, but the workings enter my land underground.'

'I should not be astonished if the Warleggans soon gain a controlling part.'

'Well, George may organize his days as he thinks best. I shall seek no brush with him so long as he seeks none with me.'

Ross got up. Demelza was waiting for him in the room outside. He had often promised himself the pleasure of taking her out to spend money as she pleased, but the promise had gone sour with keeping.

'Oh,' he said, turning from the window; 'very soon I shall be able to clear off my debt to the man who saved my skin last Christmas. It's an agreeable thought. You should give me his name now, so that when I do pay him I shall be able to thank him in a suitable fashion.'

Mr Pascoe stroked his pen along the line of his cheek. 'The matter is one of confidence, as you know.'

'Which you are now entitled to break. D'you realize what he did? – but of course you do—'

'Yes, I do—'

'Without his timely help I should be in a debtor's prison with probably little hope of release. The mine would have closed. My wife and son would be paupers. It's no longer a question of confidence, Harris. It's one of common gratitude.'

'Oh, yes, I agree. B-but it does not absolve me—'

'I contend that it does. I owe him virtually everything and would wish to tell him so. What is his name?'

Pascoe wavered. 'I will write and ask his permission.'

'Nonsense. It was not *you*, then?'

'It was not I. I said so at the time. I only wish my position would have allowed me—'

'Does he live in Truro?'

'No. In fact . . .'

'In fact what?'

'Well . . . In fact it was not a man at all.'

'What?' Ross stared, thunderstruck. 'What do you mean? That it was a woman? A child?'

'A woman.'

'Who? Your daughter?'

'No. Dear me, I feel that I have already—'

'There cannot be many heiresses of my acquaintance. In fact I can think of none! I know no one, not one single woman with fourteen hundred pounds to put down for me. The thing's *impossible*! You're joking, Harris! Tell me you're joking.'

The banker looked upset. 'I feel I have already been

guilty of a breach of confidence. Only the fact that you will soon be able to pay the capital back ... It was Caroline Penvenen.'

'Caro ...' Ross swallowed and stared. After a moment he said: 'Oh, but I don't believe that!'

'It's the truth.'

'Caroline Penvenen? But I hardly know her! I spoke to her two or three times, no more. We said ... How could she know? I don't go about confessing my financial situation to every slip of a girl. It's – monstrous! How did she approach you?'

'She came into this office one morning, said she was looking for an investment and that she considered the best investment she could make was loaning fourteen hundred pounds to you. She knew all about the bill, about the Warleggans possessing it, about the straits you were in. I felt it my duty – forgive me, but I felt it my duty to warn her what a risk she ran of never seeing her money again. She paid no attention to it. If I would not arrange it for her, she said, she would go elsewhere. Having done what I could to p-put her off, I was of course only too gratified to do what she insisted.'

'I positively can't believe it.'

'I don't know what she will feel at my having told you.'

Ross rubbed the new-healed scar on his head. As it healed it itched. 'Well, I have never been so upset with astonishment. *Never!* I can guess, I suppose, how she came by the information. But that she should choose to act on it ... No wonder I could not think who had helped me. God's life! What a strange creature! I – can't begin to understand. I must tell my wife. She too will be taken aback.'

'I'd appreciate it if you allowed the information to go

no f-further,' said Pasooe. 'It is the first time I have ever broken an undertaking of that nature. I'm sorry that you forced it out of me.'

'I am not,' said Ross.

They bought several new items of furniture: a fine dressing-table for Demelza's room, for which they paid £5 10s 0d, another clock to replace the one they had sold two years ago, a new table – new secondhand – with a splendid polish on it and latest-fashion pedestal legs, two Turkey rugs at £4 each, fine calamanco cloth for bedroom curtains, and a rich cream silk paduasoy for the curtains for the parlour. Some cloths Ross bought because Demelza liked the feel of them – a piece of crimson velour and another of green satin – without an actual purpose in view for them, unless it was the purpose of tempting Demelza into a new attitude of mind. They bought six new-shape wineglasses, which cost them 28s, and a dozen pewter tankards – cheap enough, these, at 4d each – and new crockery and new cutlery – very expensive – and a cane-bottomed rocking chair.

Demelza bought two pairs of Dantzig shoes and some fine wool for a coat for Jeremy and a toy horse and a rattle. Ross bought neckcloths for himself and two for John Gimlett, and Demelza some striped muslin for Jane.

And in their minds the whole time, at the back of all their purchases, was the news they had learned about Caroline Penvenen.

By the time they had finished, the afternoon was well on, and it meant a long ride in the dark. So they went home as slowly as they came in, closer together physically than they had been for many months. In the old days when she was a child she had sometimes ridden on the pommel of his saddle, but that had been out of the question today. He found it pleasurable to feel her hand on his belt, and the occasional rub of her shoulder against his back; one could talk easily too, without raising one's voice or having it carried away by the wind.

He had not devised this shopping expedition with any motive other than the most obvious one; but on the way home he wondered if it had achieved a double end. Once or twice this afternoon he had noted a richness in her tone which he had not consciously missed until it came back.

Halfway home Demelza said: 'Ross, the more I think of Caroline the more I feel we have gravely misjudged her.'

'I know it. We're more in her debt than anyone has a right to be. I don't feel it should be left where it is.'

'No more do I.'

They were silent for a time. Demelza said: 'The more you think of it, the worse it gets. Caroline Penvenen saved us from the bankruptcy prison. Dwight saved us from another prison. There's no doubt he still loves her. There's no doubt that but for what he did that night they would now be married and living in Bath.'

'I cannot understand her doing it for us – unless it was with Dwight's connivance. He must have told her of our trouble and have pressed her to help, I suppose. But he seemed as surprised as we were when we told him of our good fortune – I don't believe him to be that good an actor. I'd like to go and see her, to ask her about it.'

'I think she is very impulsive, temperamental,' Demelza said slowly. 'She would jilt one man, or help another, because she has a sudden feeling that way. She has perhaps a strong liking for you—'

'For me? But we only met two or three times.'

'It would be enough. Oh, I don't mean to take away from her. But the good things and the bad things go together in her, and often I'm sure most for good, as Dwight found.'

They jogged on a little farther. It was a mild evening but damp, and every now and then a flurry of rain would beat against their faces.

Demelza said: 'I think you are right, Ross; you should go and see her.'

'She's in London. I have her address from Pascoe and intended to write.'

'I think you should go, not write.'

He tightened his grip of the reins as a badger sputtered across their path. When Darkie had settled again, he said: 'I don't see we can do anything to bring Dwight and Caroline together again. She is engaged now to marry someone else – and in any case the very shortcomings which have helped us are precisely the reasons why she would not make a suitable wife for Dwight . . .'

'I'm not saying anything about bringing her and Dwight together. Dwight is going to sea, and she cannot jilt yet another man. But I do not think a letter from you would do, Ross. It – isn't enough. I think you should go'n see her in person – and tell her what we feel and how we should like to thank her. Maybe she doesn't know how much she's helped us, maybe fourteen hundred pounds don't count much to her; but it don't leave us any less in her debt.'

He couldn't question that. 'I'll go before Christmas. It will take a fortnight, but I can leave Henshawe in charge of the mine. I'll take the first year's interest with me and tell her I shall hope to repay the whole by Easter.' Already his mind was springing ahead to details of the journey. It was over ten years since he had been to London, and then it had been only to pass through.

'One thing,' Demelza said. 'I think you should do one thing about Dwight and Caroline, even if it is nothing to do with bringing them together. I think Caroline must have had some better reason for jilting him than just because he didn't turn up that night. She may be impulsive, but that's not the way a woman would be impulsive. Leastwise, she might well go off in an anger, but she wouldn't stay in an anger after he had come to explain.'

'And you think I should ask her?'

'Yes, Ross, I do.'

'All right, I'll tell her that my wife thinks it unfeminine to have acted as she did.'

'Tell her,' said Demelza, 'that we find we have a new debt and should dearly like to pay it any way we can.'

As they came to their own land, the lights of Wheal Grace glimmered over the valley. Mines, Ross thought, could wear expressions just like human beings. Or was it that men read their own thoughts into objects of slate and stone? Three months ago such movement as had existed seemed to be the motions of an animal already doomed and feeling the languor of death. Now everything moved with an invigorated air. Five lights burned where one had burned before. The steady rhythm of the engine was unchanged, but some new purpose had crept into it. Fifty new hands had been engaged this month, twenty for underground and thirty for the rapidly extending surface sheds. Some of the work of dressing was still farmed out, for the amount of mineral-bearing ore brought to the surface was still increasing faster than the dressing capacity grew. Young Ellery and his five partners were in the richest part of the lode, and Ellery had confessed to Ross that often he couldn't sleep at night for thinking of his work and wanting to get back to it. When men were on tribute, the percentage they received on what they raised was adjusted month by month and was reduced in proportion to the richness of the ground they worked; but Ross and Henshawe had been very generous in their bargains, and many of the miners were making big profits.

Once Demelza might have sighed for the disfigurements of a hillside and the south end of their pretty valley. The stream which ran beside the house was yellow with mud, and the bal girls worked almost on the fringes of her garden. But now she would have turned her flowerbeds into ditches to dig out the tin.

When they got home, Gimlett was waiting for them, tireless, friendly, anxious to please. He took Darkie and his presents, it seemed, with equal gratitude. Presently he disappeared into the rear of the house. Demelza ran upstairs to see for Jeremy. He was asleep, looking more angelic, more frail than ever. Despite his vastly improved health, he clung to that look. He had a round, graceful head, dark hair, a slender neck, a wide, mobile mouth, a Poldark mouth. There was a look of distinction about him even so early – and an air of restlessness. Only in sleep was his energy dormant.

Hearing a movement, Demelza looked up and saw that Ross had followed her. He so seldom came in here now. He smiled without looking at her, nodded down.

'He has survived without you.'

'So it seems.'

'I wonder Jane has had no children of her own. We must get more help in the house now. Do you think Jinny would come back?'

'We could perhaps find someone younger. I only need another young girl.'

'Two would be better. You will have to grow used to giving orders instead of doing things yourself.'

She did not reply, and he thought perhaps his words had sounded like criticism. 'Soon, if the prosperity lasts, I want the library rebuilt. It has never been anything but a barn of a room. We need an extra room downstairs; and if that were in a proper state, it would transform the house.'

'At least we might fill in the cache.'

He smiled. 'I think it should be left as a warning.'

Jeremy turned over and breathed uneasily in his sleep.

'We should move,' he said, 'or we'll wake him.'

'Oh, no, that is past. He takes no notice of anything now.'

'Perhaps he's easier for my not being in the room.'

She looked up, half veiling her look with a swift glance away. 'I do not suppose that.'

'Some say children are jealous of their fathers. Jeremy has had little to be jealous of, of late.'

Demelza said: 'I think perhaps that's a subject we should sleep sounder for not discussing.'

There was silence for a few seconds. A shade experimentally, he put his hand on her shoulder. She did not move.

'I intended to have bought him some building bricks,' he said. 'I knew there was something else.'

'You'll be able to get them in London now.'

'Do you think you might come with me? Why not try? Jeremy is well enough with Jane.'

'Me? . . . Oh, no. No, thank you, Ross. Not this time. Though next time gladly. I think you should meet Caroline alone.'

'Why?'

'It is a feeling I have.'

'You could stay at the inn while I went to see her.'

'No. This time I'd rather not.'

He had moved a little closer to her. 'Demelza.'

'Yes.'

'There have been a lot of unhappy things between us these last months. Not said – but felt. I should be glad to think they are all forgotten.'

'Of course, Ross. I feel nothing now.'

He put his face against her hair. 'It is not nothing that I want you to feel.'

'I'm sorry . . .'

They stayed thus for a moment more. Although unable to feel any tautness within her, he knew it was there. He had not removed it, he had not defeated it. He knew he could take her if he wanted, and her resistance would only be token; yet the token was there, and while it existed the reconciliation would be ashes.

He kissed her abruptly on the hair, released her, went across to the north window, and pulled aside the curtain to look out. Her eyes followed him.

He said: 'Perhaps you're right; we don't ever regain what we lightly lose.'

'I don't think 'twas lightly lost on either side.'

'But lost.'

'Well . . .'

It was so dark outside he could hardly see the sea.

'And lost to no good purpose,' he said, half speaking to himself.

'That I don't know.'

'Oh, there was a purpose, a good purpose served, if you come to think of it; though perhaps you would not agree. I don't know . . . I have not wanted to talk of it.'

She stood by the cot watching him.

'Perhaps sometime it will have to be talked of,' he said, 'if we are ever to straighten this out between us. Yet I have a prejudice, a feeling that it is a bad thing . . .'

'What is a bad thing, Ross?'

He turned from the window, let the curtain fall from his long fingers, said wryly: 'I think there is an etiquette even in adultery, and I cannot bring myself to discuss one woman with another, even when the second happens to be my wife.'

'You don't suppose I should want to hear it?'

'Yet it might not displease you.'

'I can't see how it would be likely to please me.'

'Then you are less perceptive than I suppose.'

''Tis very likely.'

There was another pause. Ross came slowly back from the window and after a moment's hesitation bent and kissed her on the lips.

'Yes, it is very likely,' he said, and went out.

She did not move for a time. Jeremy's breathing was a little more hurried now, as if he were dreaming. She turned him over expertly, firmly; as if knowing the touch of the familiar hand, he settled more comfortably after it.

She straightened up and went to the window herself. There were movements of warmth in her heart where she had not expected to have feeling again.

Chapter Four

The next day Dwight received news of his appointment. He was to be surgeon of the frigate HMS *Travail*, fitting out at Plymouth, and was to join her on December 20.

Ross said nothing of his intention to go and see Caroline, but he told Dwight of his discovery about the money. Dwight's face flushed up. He had known nothing of it, he said, and hid his other feelings behind a mask of apology for having spoken so freely of his friend's business affairs. Ross told him he had never been so much obliged to anyone for talking freely of his business affairs.

He left for London on the following day, dining at St Austell and spending the night at Liskeard. They crossed the ferry at Plymouth and lay the next night at Ashburton. Friday they dined at Exeter and slept at Bridgewater, and Saturday saw them eating at Bath and sleeping in Marlborough. The last day was a full one, for they were up early making a stage before breakfast. They dined at Maidenhead and reached London just before ten at night. The ground was snow-covered as they neared the city.

It was snowing the following day when Ross set out to find Caroline. Her address was No. 5 Hatton Garden, which he knew to be a superior residential district; but he had to ask many times on the way. The streets were more crowded than he remembered them, and people seemed to have no manners, pushing and thrusting each other aside to get along more quickly or to gain some temporary advantage. Twice he saw people knocked into the gutter. And there were enough in the gutter to begin: blind beggars, tattered ex-soldiers short of an arm or a leg, children with sore eyes, bent crones holding out acquisitive claws. Snow had made things worse, for there were a half-dozen pitched battles in progress between apprentices of one sort and another, and often the women joined in. In the middle of one fight a carriage came along, and suddenly everyone turned on it so that the coachman was nearly pelted off his seat. Whoever was inside knew better than to open a window to protest.

Ross bought a daily paper, but it was filled more with quacks' advertisements than news of the war. Anyway, since the execution of Marie Antoinette, people had become inured to the bloodstained horrors of Paris. The French had gone mad, that was plain. And England was at war. That was the main thing. What fighting there had been had been disappointing and inconclusive, almost as if the combatants hadn't yet got their hearts in it. But even that was a relief to overburdened feelings. More would follow. England was at war. Eventually the insanity would be purged. It was only a matter of time now.

A liveried manservant opened the door of the house when he rang, stared petulantly at Ross's clothes, which he had not had time or patience to renew since his change of fortunes. 'Miss Penvenen?' said the manservant, after being stared down. He would inquire. A considerable wait. He came back. Miss Penvenen was in and would see Mr Poldark. Ross was shown into a fine, rather empty, rather cold room overlooking the street. The manservant's heels clicked on the polished inlaid floor.

His eyes newly alive to decorations and furniture, he took note of the elegant walnut writing bureau with the claw feet; the inset oval-shaped cupboards displaying fine china on either side of the great marble mantelpiece. The panelling of the room was of carved pine, and there were few pictures but many miniatures and silhouettes. A fire burned in the grate but did not seem to warm the larger spaces of the room. Downstairs somewhere children were laughing.

The door opened amd Caroline came in.

'Why, Captain Poldark, I could not believe it was you! But the name was so unusual. London is honoured. I have seen no flags out for your visit.'

'They don't put flags out when I come to a place,' Ross said, bending over her hand. 'They put them out when I go.'

He was quite shocked by the change in her. She had gone so much thinner and lost much of her beauty. She was a person whose looks would always be volatile, but just now they were at a low ebb. She wore a dress of a fashion Ross had never seen before, with the waist under the armpits and falling straight to the floor. It had short puff sleeves and a gold cord and tassel.

'You should have told me of your visit. How long shall you be staying?'

'Two or three days. I couldn't have forewarned you, for I didn't know of it myself until a few days ago.'

'Urgent business? You'll have sherry and biscuits? It's nearly time. The apothecary tells me I must have sherry every two hours, and I don't find it an unpleasurable remedy.'

He watched her sit and then took a seat himself at the

417

other side of the fireplace while she talked on rather aimlessly and at some length. She was ill at ease in his presence.

'You've been ill, Miss Penvenen?'

'I am a little out of sorts, and the heat of a London summer took my energy. How is your wife?'

'Very well, thank you. We are all very well. And the mine has come into paying country, so that I am making money for the first time in my life. And all thanks to you.'

She looked quite convincingly surprised; then to give herself an escape from his heavy-lidded look, she turned and pulled the bell tassel beside her.

'I drew it out of Pascoe last week,' he said. 'Afterwards he was a thought repentant of his confidences, but I gave him your full absolution.'

'Indeed.'

'Yes, indeed. So it would be a pity to waste time denying the indictment. You are convicted, Miss Penvenen, of wilfully saving three people from the worst disaster that bankruptcy can bring. You had no possible excuse for doing it, no ties of friendship or relationship, and it is a very grave charge.'

'And what's the sentence?'

'To receive my gratitude for a selfless, kind, and Christian act that I shall never be able to understand and shall never forget.'

The colour came to her face, perhaps more at his tone than what he had said. She laughed and turned towards the door, glad before it opened of the interruption. When the sherry was on a table between them and the servant had left again, she said:

'You make altogether too much of it, Captain Poldark.'

'Ross,' he said. 'Christian names for a Christian act.'

'Captain Ross, then. You make far too much of it. I have always been used to indulging my whims, and that was such a one. Sherry?'

'Thank you. I disagree as to making much of it. You should have been in my shoes.'

'But I was not. And don't forget, spinsters are unpredictable at the best of times. I might well have endowed a sailor's home instead, or indeed turned against you as easily—'

'I don't believe you.'

'In any case, the money is nothing to me. A few hundred pounds—'

'Dwight tells me your personal fortune is not large.'

At that she was silent a moment, took up a biscuit, and chewed it slowly. 'You have answers all ways. I see there is nothing for it but to accept the halo you offer me.' She put up her hand to her hair. 'I imagine it would look comic on a redhead, and in any case I shall surely tip it off at the first fence. But if it pleases you, Captain Ross, then don't let me interfere with any arrangements you wish to make. The canonisation could be arranged for tomorrow at eleven.'

Ross sipped his sherry. 'My journey took me five days. I have been thinking a good deal about you on the way – Caroline.'

'I pray not for the whole five days. I do remember my ears burning once, but I thought it was the fever back.'

'I came to tell you – one thing I came to tell you is that I shall be able to repay the whole of the money very soon. I have with me a draft on Pascoe's bank for £280, which is your interest for the year. But the capital should also be forthcoming within a few months.'

'There you are, you see! You elevate me merely for a

shrewd stroke of business. I don't believe my uncles earned me anything near twenty per cent when the money was in their charge.'

'You talk of being a spinster, but I believe you're not to remain so very much longer. I heard of your engagement just before I left – to a Lord Coniston, is it?'

'Does that affect the safety of my investment?'

'No. It only points my interest in your future.'

She rose and poured him another glass of sherry. Her arm was freckled along its outer curve.

'You were not about to make me an offer yourself, Captain Ross?'

He smiled. 'I'm not a Muslim. And have seldom regretted it before . . .'

She curtsied slightly before she sat down. 'Thank you for being so gracious about it. But your compliments come a trifle early. I'm not promised to Walter.'

'Not? You mean you are not promised to Lord Coniston?'

'You look astonished. Does it matter – I mean, to you?'

'Well, yes . . .'

'He has offered himself once or twice, the last time as recently as last month. He's personable enough, but I don't think I shall marry him.'

Ross stared at his wine. Her reply had taken him completely by surprise. All he had planned to say to her – and all he had planned not to say to her – had been built on this belief. He felt as if his attitude of mind suddenly needed rethinking, and he had only a moment or so in which to do it.

'Your uncle in Cornwall told someone I know that you had definitely promised to marry this man.'

'My Aunt Sarah – whom I live with here – is always

premature. He's eligible and he had asked me; that was enough for her. But why does it upset you?'

'If it's not an impertinence, may I ask why you don't intend to accept?'

She smiled. 'Oh, the usual capriciousness of my sex.'

'And you do not love him.'

'As you say. I do not love him.'

'In fact it's probable that you are still in love with Dwight Enys.'

She took another biscuit. 'Could the impertinence be in that question and not in the other?'

'You know he has joined the Navy?'

She looked up quickly. 'What, Dwight? No, I did not.' For the first time he had got under her guard.

'He's joining his ship at Plymouth this week. There has been no settling him in Cornwall since you left.'

'How very unwise of him! I should have thought he would have behaved with the utmost common sense.'

'One does not always behave very sensibly when one loves a person as he loves you.'

'Did you really come to thank me for the money or to act as his ambassador?'

'He knows nothing of this. But he told Demelza last week that it was because of you he was leaving us.'

'And what am I supposed to do, go into a decline because of that? Would it suit you if I gracefully fretted away?'

'It would suit me if you told me why you left Cornwall when he failed to meet you that night. Oh, not that. I can understand that very well. Why you didn't later accept his very reasonable explanation.'

She got up and went to the window. 'What business is it of yours?'

'It has suddenly become my business. I've long had a sincere affection for Dwight. I'm now under the deepest obligation to you. I want to know.'

'It doesn't give you the least excuse to interfere.'

He came up beside her. 'I want to know, Caroline.'

Two young girls were just coming out of the house in the charge of an older woman, a governess. One girl glanced up at the window and saw Caroline and waved. She raised a hand in return.

'How is your cousin-in-law, Elizabeth Poldark?'

'She's married again. She married George Warleggan.'

'Oh . . . That does surprise me. Are they living at Trenwith?'

'Yes. On my doorstep.'

'That will not be welcome to you.'

'It is not welcome to me.'

'And your mine? It's really paying?'

'We can't compute yet what the returns will be.'

'My uncle has been ill. Do you know if he's better?'

'At the moment, yes.'

She turned, her fingers still holding the curtain. He noticed the little amber specks in her eyes. 'Yes, I loved Dwight, if that's any joy to you. It's no joy to me, for I know we could not have been happy. I came to London with my uncle that day because I was vastly angry, piqued, disappointed – all the feelings you'd suppose. I did not know then that Dwight had been doing what he did for you – to help you. I knew that he had gone into Sawle, answering a medical call at the last moment from someone who needed him more than I did. The fact that *afterwards* he had involved himself in some scuffle with the preventive men and got himself knocked about and arrested did not really make the important difference which you seem to imagine.

His going to see the Hoblyn girl was a – a symptom, a *symbol*. That is what you don't understand and what he surely must. At least I tried to tell him in my letter. Captain Poldark – Ross, as you say I must call you – did you see anything of Dwight during those last weeks when we had arranged to elope and live in Bath?'

'I suppose I did. I don't remember.'

'Well, he behaved as if he were preparing to do something *shameful* and underhand. Oh, yes, he was in love with me in his way, and that made him set a bright front on it; but underneath he was miserable! He thought he hid it from me, but it was plain to see. He was leaving his charge, his people, his cures, leaving them disgracefully, deserting them at dead of night and going to live in a fashionable and wealthy city. He may have had reasons for feeling that way – I don't say if it is the right attitude or the wrong attitude – but there could have been no happiness in it for me. You think me a fickle and capricious woman; but in fact I'm not quite so featherbrained as you suppose. At least I could see that we should have a miserable future if he spent the rest of his life blaming himself for the desertion and trying not to blame me! It is true; don't shake your head, it is true!'

'Yes, I see it; I'm not denying that. I didn't know. I didn't know it all. And you explained all this to Dwight in a letter?'

'As much as I was able.'

Ross took a turn about the room, and for a while neither of them spoke.

He said: 'The desertion as you call it was especially difficult for Dwight because of his affair with another woman years ago, a patient—'

'Yes. Keren Daniel. I know about her.'

'I am not defending him, but I suppose that gave him a bad background for any later move which might look a trifle sordid to himself. There would not be wanting people who would say he had married you for your money.'

'Oh, people! If you spend your life thinking what people will say, you will not stir from your own fireside.'

'I entirely agree. And in principle I'm sure Dwight would. But he's a deeply sensitive and punctilious person. I see his point; and I see yours now . . . But if you both loved each other, surely there was some other way out of the mess.'

'For me to live with him in three rooms at the Gatehouse, with my uncle kicking up a rumpus a few miles away and everyone in the district knowing of it?'

'No . . . But would it not have been better to see him, when he had travelled all that way to speak to you?'

She looked at Ross with a little deprecating expression. 'I'm not made of iron, though no doubt you think that also.'

'No,' said Ross. 'I don't think so. I find you more and more a woman after my own heart.'

With a swift-flushing colour she said: 'I believe I shall have a proposal from you yet.'

'You may shortly have a proposal from me of a different nature. Do you still love Dwight?'

'Extravagantly!'

'No.' He put his hand on her arm. 'Tell me, Caroline.'

She shook her head. 'I find this a very embarrassing interview.'

'Dwight will be in Plymouth all this week and part of next. If you travelled with me when I return on Thursday . . .'

She stared at him blankly, angrily. 'You must be mad!'

'Am I? It depends what you feel for him.'

'It depends not at all on that—'

'Then on what? You could be in Plymouth Sunday. Don't you suppose it worth a final meeting? You've never talked over it sensibly together, in the presence of a third party, have you?'

'It's seldom possible to be sensible on such occasions.'

'I doubt that. Anyway, it's your last chance of seeing him.'

'I don't think you should appeal to my sentiment.'

'Well, you cannot ignore the facts.'

'That's just what *you* are doing. The facts have not changed since we separated. There's no better way out now than then.'

'But they *have* changed. You are not making him leave his friends in Sawle. He's doing it of his own free will. I didn't understand before why he thought that so necessary. I do now. If you meet him now, he will be free of all those associations.'

'And tied to the Navy.'

'Yes. There's no comfortable escape to Bath. The facts have changed both for the better and for the worse. They should be worth reconsidering.'

For a moment she seemed to waver. Then she shook her head emphatically. 'Impossible . . .'

'Only one person can make it impossible and that is yourself.'

'Yes . . . you're right! You're wholly right, Ross. I have spoken as if all the weakness, all the shortcomings, were on his side. Do you think I've not had time enough since to look into my own? What happened, the way it happened, showed me up to myself. Do you know what it's like when your anger and bitterness are so great that you can only hurt yourself – and go on hurting yourself for ever and ever, it seems, so that there's no escape? That hasn't changed. The possibility of its happening again hasn't changed.'

'Why not?'

'Well, it may have lessened, but it doesn't disappear. How can it? If I had brought a different understanding to his feelings, I should be a different person. I am not a different person. I'm only myself. Not only did I expect too much of him, but he expected too much of me. I know less of married life than you, but I should have thought it the worst way to begin. The break went both ways – and *very* deep. I haven't such a plenitude of courage to hurt myself again, and him too.'

There was silence for a time. She said: 'Nor would what you think come out of a single meeting. I have done too much of it already – arriving to turn his life upside down and then leave again. Let him go – in peace.'

Ross took out his purse and unfolded a piece of paper. 'Here is my draft. Your banker will send a receipt.'

She took the paper. He did not like his defeat at all; not one bit.

He said: 'There's one other thing I should tell you. Your uncle is not altogether better. Dwight tells me the disease is held in check, but it's not probable that he will improve much from his present condition. When Dwight is safe at sea, I think you should come down.'

'Very well.'

The life had temporarily gone out of her, in a way he had not known before; the emotion had tired her. She asked him to meet her uncle and aunt that evening, but he refused, making the excuse of pressure of business. As he was leaving he said:

'If you should change your mind before Thursday, you'll find me at the Mitre in Hedge Lane. It is just off Leicester Fields.'

'Very well,' she said again. 'But I cannot.' And he went out into the crowded street.

Chapter Five

While Ross was away Demelza had an unpleasant experience. She received an invitation to tea from Mrs Frensham, Sir John's sister, who was visiting him again; and, it being a fine day and Darkie in Truro, she decided to walk. The shortest way took you along the cliff, dipping into Sawle and across the shingle, then up the other side skirting Trenwith land by way of the cliffs until you came to Trevaunance Cove.

On this journey Garrick decided to accompany her. It was funny about Garrick. You could walk to the end of the combe of an evening and he wouldn't lift an eyebrow from his after-rabbit sleep; but if you were *going* anywhere, he knew instantly and it was the hardest thing in the world to get started without him.

He followed perseveringly close beside her all the way, grumbling only now and then in his throat. By now he was ten but bore his years like his great size lightly. His black astrakhan coat looked more than ever as if the moths had been at it, he had lost several necessary teeth in several unnecessary fights, and he could not see much out of one eye; but these were the ravages of battle not of time. Demelza sometimes suspected that he was developing a middle-aged outlook. He had learned to distinguish between a rabbit, which had to be galloped after before it escaped, and a tossed bone, which lay where it fell until one came up with it. And he no longer disappeared for days on wild rampages of his own. Jeremy loved him dearly and pulled him about into improbable postures.

When he strayed from her today, she did not call him, knowing that after a snuffle down some promising hole he would be back soon enough and there was nothing he could hurt on this scrubland. When she heard the shot, her mind had been far away and it took a few seconds for her to relate it to the savage yelping which followed. Then she saw Garrick down, rolling on the ground, and she ran across the heather towards him, alarm and anger hardly fledged. In his anguish as she knelt down he bit her wrist, but she forced his jaws open and tried to see where he had been hit. A part of one ear had been shot away; a piece hung loose; blood was dripping over his eyes and terrifying him. But there seemed nothing else.

There was a crackle of dry wood behind her and a voice said: 'That your dog, Mrs?'

She looked up. A strange man, rough-dressed, carrying an old fowling piece under one arm. Another man of the same sort was coming over the heather.

'Did you fire that gun?'

'Aye, Mrs. Looks as if I only nicked 'im . . .'

She got to her feet, blazing. 'Nicked him! You might have killed him! Judas God, you should be put in prison! What right've you to be firing your piece without looking if there's people about! Here, Garrick! Here, boy!' Garrick had jumped away from her and was running round, shaking his head then rolling over trying to stop the pain.

The man wiped a hand across his nose. 'Just obeying orders, Mrs. You'd no right to be on private land.'

'Private land! This is public land! Orders! Whose orders? What are you talking about?'

The second man had come up. He was another big fellow, older than the first, and there was a family resemblance.

'All right, Tom, I'll 'andle this. This is private land you're on, Mrs, and all dogs straying are shot. You ask whose orders. This is Trenwith land right to the sea—'

'Never!—'

'Oh, yes 'tis. And there's another thing. There's been too much sheep worrying of late—'

'Garrick doesn't do that sort of thing! You did ought to know it's young dogs—'

''E's cutting a fine caper now,' said Tom, snickering. 'Fair old dance he's doing, edn'e.'

'So would you, you great fool! I'll report you to Mr Warleggan! I'm Mrs Poldark, Mrs Warleggan's cousin, and I'll see she hears of this!'

Tom went on snickering. 'Oh, aye, we've heard tell of you, Mrs. A bit like your dog, ain't you: bit of a mixed breed, eh?'

If there was a characteristic for which Garrick was noted, it was his obstinacy rather than his intelligence; but at this moment he chose to show his insight into the situation by going for Tom's leg. Tom shouted and jumped away and swung his musket and missed. The other man stepped back and Demelza called to Garrick and in the confusion they were slow in seeing the horseman who was coming towards them across the heather. Trouble was saved by Demelza capturing Garrick, and then the older man said:

'Here's Mr Warleggan now. He'll see for you his self, Mrs . . . Damnation take that great mongrel—'

They waited, all breathing sharply, for the arrival of the man who was to settle the dispute. To hide the pain in her wrist, Demelza bent trying to help the dog.

George came slowly. The ground was dangerous for riding, and he had no intention of being thrown. When he recognized Demelza, he took off his hat.

'Mrs Poldark in person. Were you about to call on me?'

'Far from it!' said Demelza, wishing her face would cool. 'I have an invitation to tea at Trevaunance House and was walking there when these two impudent louts first shot my dog and then insulted me! Look at my skirt! And they've sorely wounded my dog! I don't know what they think they're at! Judas and my gloves too! 'Tis nothing less than disgraceful—'

'There's some mistake,' George said. 'They took you for a trespasser, which of course you are. But they exceeded their instructions—'

'I am not a trespasser! This has been open land ever since I came here—'

'Francis was overindulgent. Poachers and gipsies stray wherever they choose—'

'Do I look like a poacher? If I came within twenty feet of your window, I should not expect to be treated with such rudeness! Do you mean you *support* these men?'

'The Harrys were obeying orders. But perhaps they have been overzealous . . .'

'Overzealous! . . .' Demelza suddenly perceived that George was not going to help her. 'If that's how you feel, then there's no more to say.'

'I think your dog will recover. It will teach him not to stray.'

Trembling with anger, Demelza bent to pick up her other glove. 'We shall be poor neighbours, George.'

'Your husband has already shown himself to be that.'

She moved to go on her way, but young Tom Harry put out a hand like a plate. 'Not that road, Mrs.'

Demelza looked up at George. For a moment she could not believe that he would not allow her to go on after all this was said. Then she realized that even his permission now would be an insult. In any case she was in no fit state to go visiting. She whistled to Garrick and he came lolloping back, still shaking his head and keeping well clear of the men.

'Have a care, George,' she could not refrain from saying; 'I might send Ross to visit you.'

It was strange how Ross was always George's weak link. She saw that there was a mark on his face, under his chin, which had not been there before.

'If he comes on my property again, he'll be dealt with.'

'It will take more than two clodhopping bullies to do it!'

''Ere, you keep your insults to yourself, Mrs,' said Tom Harry. 'Else we'll send you 'ome with a clip out o' *your* ear.'

'Hold your tongue, Harry!' said George sharply.

She turned and left them; to retire with dignity is a hard and bitter thing, especially with three men staring after you and no doubt talking behind their hands. When she got home, she wrote an apology to Mrs Frensham and in the evening sent it with John Gimlett, telling him to go by way of the villages.

Dwight Enys was lodged at the Rising Sun, in one of the narrow streets off the Barbican. He had arrived in Plymouth to find the *Travail* much farther from being fully commissioned than he had expected. Captain Harrington was still in Portsmouth; the crew was barely a quarter of its full complement; and the first officer – a black-browed, long-jawed Welshman called Williams – said they were pitifully short of stores. *Travail* was a frigate of 860 tons burden, 46 guns, nine- and twelve-pounders, and her full complement was 314. When Dwight went below into what were to be his quarters, he found all Williams's gloomy views confirmed. His own tiny cabin next to the common wardroom was adequate enough, but the ship's medicine chest was bare of supplies and the stench below decks was already hard to be borne. It was his instinct to set about cleaning things up right away; but a feeling that it would be untactful to initiate any move without the permission of the captain sent him mute ashore.

He decided for the time being to stay ashore, although he made a daily visit to the ship, and for the next week spent much time wandering about the seaport, himself idle and restless and depressed. He kept thinking of Caroline and of his own failures and the constant futility which had dogged his efforts to make a recognizable and satisfactory pattern of his life. He knew that this act of his in going to sea would be regarded by most of his profession as a monumentally silly one. The pay was poor, the life arduous, his standing when he came out, nil. It might be patriotic to serve one's country; there were easier ways. What he had seen so far of the crew was the pick, the volunteers, from whom would be selected the petty officers, the top men. The remaining three quarters would either be pressed men or debtors, rogues and ne'er-do-wells, the sweepings of jail and port. It would be on such material, lice-ridden, diseased, that he would work for the next two years. For weeks on end it would be a monotonous round of purges and vomits, of rough-and-ready treatment with the minimum of medicinal scope. If there was an action, it would become a sudden blood-bath of brutal and hasty surgery in nightmare conditions deep in the heart of the ship by the light of a swinging lantern. Was this what he sought from life, this confined and disciplined escape? At least it was what he had chosen. He was not prepared yet to regret it.

On the Sunday, Dwight received a letter from Ross saying he was staying at the Fountain Inn overnight, having business in the town; would Dwight take dinner with him?

Dwight was surprised and pleased. He had had more than enough of his own company and had thought himself without a friend in the place. About six he walked over, and Ross was waiting for him in the front parlour of the inn.

When they had greeted each other, Dwight said: 'This is pleasant and unexpected of you. When did you arrive in the town?'

'This morning. I slept at Ashburton. When do you sail?'

'Heaven knows. Not before Christmas it now seems certain. How did you know where to find me?'

'Sent a boatman out to the *Travail*.' Ross eyed his friend speculatively. 'A handsome uniform, that. At least it must be some satisfaction to look the part. I've ordered dinner in a private room tonight; I thought it would be more comfortable. And what is your impression of the Navy up to now?'

'That everything is done in a very haphazard way,' said Dwight, following the other upstairs. 'It is plain that this lack of method must be an illusion, for they always produce the results; but at present I can't see how. *Travail* was to be one of a squadron of three for patrol work in the Channel; but the other two left last week. I suppose when Harrington does arrive, he will have fresh instructions from the Admiralty . . . You're staying in very regal style, Ross. It must be a rare pleasure to have money in your pocket again.'

They had come into the private room where a servant

was tending the crackling fire and a table was set for dinner for two. The curtains were drawn, and the warmth and comfort of the room contrasted with Dwight's bare lodgings.

Dwight said suddenly: 'Did you say you slept at Ashburton?'

'Yes. I've been farther afield and am on my way home. Sit down and I'll tell you of it.'

Dwight warmed his hands at the fire and accepted the glass he was offered. Ross went on talking, his long strong fingers running along the edge of the mantelshelf, curiously purposive, Dwight thought, though the conversation was idle enough.

'You said you had been farther afield,' Dwight prompted as the servant curtsied and went out.

'Yes. To London. I saw Caroline.'

Dwight did not move. When he was sure of his voice, he said: 'You went to see her about the loan, I suppose.'

'Yes, in the main. I went to thank her. Of course we had a considerable conversation on general matters also.'

'Indeed.'

'I found she was not engaged to marry anyone.'

'But her uncle said—'

'No. I asked her about that. The report was premature. She had not come to any definite decision.'

Dwight frowned miserably at the fire. 'It's hard to understand that—'

'We discussed you. I hope you didn't mind.'

'Naturally not,' he said in a voice that showed he did.

'What she said convinced me that it was worth while your meeting again. In fact, I tried to persuade her to come back with me, officially to visit her uncle, and to stop in Plymouth one night on the way.'

'Which she refused to do.'

'Which she refused to do. How well you understand each other! I visited her on Monday and used all my persuasion in vain. But on Tuesday I went to see her again. Possibly the effect of twenty-four hours' reflection – and the somewhat overbearing tone I used – had the effect of persuading her different. The fact that her uncle—'

Dwight got up. 'What do you mean?'

'The fact that her uncle was ill did, I think, make the project savour of respectability.'

Dwight said: 'Ross, what do you mean?'

Ross said: 'I mean she is here, Dwight. The servant has gone for her.'

'Good God, I— She has come to see me? But I—' Dwight had gone pale.

'She has come, but very reluctantly. Very reluctantly, and with, I think, quite a new and sober attitude of mind. Let me emphasize that there's no settled idea of reconciliation in her mind, yet the fact that she *has* come makes reconciliation at least a possibility. The next move is with you, Dwight. And if I may offer advice—'

Ross broke off. Someone had tapped at the door.

Ross said: 'I have been explaining to Dwight that you are on your way to visit your uncle, are spending one night in Plymouth, and are here now at my invitation. I strongly feel you should both meet once more as friends. It may be the last chance you'll have of meeting for years – or the last ever. Sit down, will you? Here, Caroline . . . You there, Dwight.'

He had the authority to impose his will on them as perhaps no one else could have done. Neither spoke. After a single glance they didn't for some time look at each other.

Caroline sat down by the fire and smoothed out the skirt of her travelling dress like a bird spreading its wings to the warmth. The tensions of the moment had given her back her colour.

Ross said: 'Believe me, I'm not by choice a tomfool meddler in other people's lives, especially in affairs which touch you both so close as this. The *last* thing ... But sometimes, however mistaken, one conceives it one's duty to meddle, and this is such a time. So far as I know you have never talked over your differences quiet-minded and without haste or anger or recrimination. I think you owe that much to each other – and in a degree to your friends. It took time to bring Caroline to my view. She positively felt that such a move on her part would be misinterpreted, and I undertook to explain to you – as I have done, Dwight – that this meeting is to be taken only for what it is, a gesture of common good will before you leave England. Of course, I believe it to be the only neighbourly way to behave.'

Dwight looked up and met a glance that wasn't in keeping with all this politeness. But in fact he was not inclined to disagree. His throat was dry.

'Nothing – would give me greater pleasure than to dine with Caroline – to talk with her again.'

Caroline looked at the table. 'You're staying, Ross? The meal is only set for two.'

'It was meant for two. I shall dine elsewhere. But I'll be back. You'll both wait here for me?'

It was an insidious request, ruling out as it did any angry breakup. After a second Dwight nodded and Caroline gave a little acquiescent shrug.

Dwight said: 'You have not been well, Caroline?'

'I am in good health, thank you.'

'I thought . . .'

'My complexion has always been poor. I am going off rapidly.'

'No, no; your uncle said you'd been ill.'

'Oh, I'm recovered. But I have found the prospect of this interview trying.'

It was plain that having been brought almost forcibly to make this first big move Caroline, being Caroline, would be defensive and prickly to begin. Dwight had started off on the wrong foot. She looked cool enough, a little disdainful, far more collected than Dwight, but Ross knew she was not. It was time Dwight discovered that. If he did not, he was lost and all would be wasted.

She had come in too soon, before he could say any of the things to Dwight that he had hoped to say. Ross wondered now whether to try to help still more or go, leaving them to struggle alone. He poured out a glass of sherry for Caroline and moved to take it to her. But Dwight quickly intercepted him. Ross watched him hand it to her and her quick, cool upward glance which betrayed nothing at all. But something in Dwight's look encouraged Ross. In ten months Dwight had suffered a lot. It had matured him in a new way.

Ross said: 'Before I go, I suggest that we take a glass of wine together. Nothing formal. No more than a friendly gesture. That's if you both still regard me as a friend.'

They drank. Caroline said: 'I do not know how Ross behaves to his own wife, but if he treats her one half so cavalierly as he has me this week, I shall call her very downtrodden.'

'You compliment me too highly,' Ross said. 'And your-self too little.'

Their eyes met. They had came to an understanding of each other, these two, among the conflicts of the last few days.

Ross said: 'But since you mention my wife, I'll mention her too, for she would have views on the situation tonight, though different in some particulars from ours. She would argue that if a man and a woman care for each other, then the obstacles which keep them apart *must* be substantial – otherwise they are pretentious and unworthy or are contrived by one or the other with insufficient reason and should be disregarded. She puts emotion above intellect, and the result is what you'd expect.'

No one challenged him.

'I do not wholly agree with her; there's something to be said for both sides. But I think her side is worth the consideration along with any other. She would say that a man was a fool and a woman was a fool . . . that they were cowards too. She'd say life holds only two or three things worth the having, and if you possess them the rest don't matter, and if you do not possess them the rest are useless.' He went to the door. 'If you look round you, I suppose you would have to confess that her view works out in the majority of cases. It is sentimental; but by and large we're creatures of sentiment and cannot escape. Nor is it always wise to want to. You see people every day who take a chance and damn the consequences. Many of them suffer for it, but I do not think they come off worst. The people who come off worst are the people who draw back at the last moment and spend the rest of their lives regretting it. No, don't get up, Dwight, I'll see myself out.'

Chapter Six

Christmas Day was on a Wednesday, and the Tuesday came without any word at Nampara from Ross. Not that Demelza expected a letter, since letters travelled no faster than people; but she had hoped he would be back before this. She had not spent a Christmas alone at Nampara before, and this of all years would be most uncomfortable to bear.

Being in constant expectation of his coming was being on the constant *qui vive*, so she spent much of the day indoors, the first part of it casking some beer which they had brewed. Almost every footfall caused her to turn her head; but in the end she was out when he came, having gone to see Prudie Paynter, who was laid up with her leg and bitterly complaining of Jud's neglect and misbehaviour. When she came back, he was already in the parlour and she walked in unsuspecting.

She gave a squeak as he turned. 'Why, Ross, I didn't know. I was up at Prudie's. How did you come?'

He smiled as he kissed her – it was just a formal salute between them. 'On four legs and then two. Should I have brought the carol singers?'

'You're an hour or so early: they don't belong to be here before dark. When did you leave London?'

'Last Tuesday. In snow. They manage things more seasonably up there. I stopped at Plymouth and saw Dwight and left there yesterday afternoon.'

Conversation was broken by the arrival of Jeremy – but
he helped to ease the constraint which now was sought by
neither of them. Ross had brought him presents, and some
he gave him now and some he saved until tomorrow. Over
Jeremy's head, punctuated with squeals and shouts, he told
her some details of the journey; but twenty minutes passed
before he was able to say what he should have said at the
start.

'Have you three extra bedrooms you could get ready for
tonight?'

'*Three?* ... Why, who is coming? What have you
arranged?'

'I have brought Caroline back with me. Caroline and
her maid.'

Demelza opened her eyes. 'Where is she? Do you mean
at her uncle's?'

'She is with him now. But I invited her here to
supper, and I want you to put her and her maid up over
Christmas.'

'Over Christmas? Gladly. I'd lay special carpets for her
if I had them. But it's *awful* short notice, Ross! And I don't
quite understand . . .'

'We stayed a night in Plymouth and then came on. The
story of her engagement was overhasty. There was no truth
in it. When I heard that, I felt most of our old misgivings
should be set aside and I tried my hand as matchmaker. Of
course I hadn't your skill, and at first she would have none
of it. But on my second visit she decided to nibble at the
bait. We saw Dwight in Plymouth.'

'Yes?'

'I believe they have made it up. He travelled back with
us and, if we can fix him in, will stay here too.'

'They have? Oh, Ross, I'm *very* glad! More than glad.

The longer I have thought of it ... But how did you contrive it? Can he get out of the Navy?'

'How did I contrive it? I thought, what would Demelza do, and I did it. That was all. It was really not very difficult once the first resistance was overcome.'

'And Dwight?'

'He's at the Gatehouse. There's been delay in commissioning his ship. The captain arrived only yesterday morning. He gave Dwight three more days ashore. That means he must leave here after dinner tomorrow and be in Plymouth Thursday evening. What's that on your wrist?'

She had put up her hand and fine white bandage showed.

'It's nothing; a scratch. Ross, I'm delighted for what you did. Above all, 'twas *common sense*. There is so little of it in this world! What time are they coming? I must fly. If you'd—'

As she went past him, he took her arm and lifted the lace back from her sleeve again.

'It's nearly healed. What can I give them for supper?'

'Don't worry, I bought a goose in Truro and some ribs of beef and a fillet of veal. I have never known you tie up a scratch in your life. Who put this bandage on?'

'Jane. To tell the truth, it wasn't exactly a cut.'

'Then what was it?'

'Garrick bit me by accident, like. I must tell Jane at once—'

'Garrick *bit* you? Nonsense. What are you trying to hide?'

'It is the truth. Last week something happened to excite him. I'll tell you of it later. Just an unpleasantness. What time are they coming? Do you think it will work out right this time, Ross?'

'Right.' Ross still held her arm and was now untying the bandage. Seeing no way out, she suffered it without complaint, not entirely unflattered by his refusal to be put off. 'Yes, I think it will work out this time. It is a great pity they have no longer. At the best it can only be a reconciliation before he leaves.'

He took off the last bandage and the lint. The bite was healing cleanly, but the marks left no doubt as to what it had been. Ross looked up.

'Where's Garrick?'

'I left him asleep in the kitchen. You're not going to . . .'

'I don't know. How long is it since this happened?'

'Yesterday sennight.'

Ross was silent a moment. The dreaded rabies was ruled out. 'Has he been quiet since? Even if he is, I don't think we can run risks, for Jeremy's sake.'

'No. No, it's not that at all.' In defence of her beloved Garrick she found herself forced to tell him what had happened, though she toned it all down until it sounded like the merest accident for which no one was in the least to blame.

When the bandage was tied again, she said: 'Ross, which bedrooms shall they have? We have only two nice rooms, and I dearly wish they were not so shabby. And I cannot well get out of my own in so short a time, with Jeremy already settled there. I do not suppose Dwight will heed where he sleeps. But Caroline . . .'

He went across and put on two fresh pieces of wood. 'You had best prepare her my room.'

'Yes,' she said after a moment. 'There are new curtains in there. And Dwight we can give the room over, though it is in poor shape.'

'You can set up my bed in the little room behind if you like.'

'Whatever you say.' Demelza fingered the bandage and glanced at him. When she pushed back her hair, the candles made of her movements a mystical confused replica on the ceiling. 'Jane and I could carry my new dressing-table down. It would be nice for Caroline. And I'll fetch out the lace bedspread—'

'I'm sure she will appreciate anything you do. But I'm also sure that her pleasure will not turn on the newness of the furnishings. Demelza, it's not yet six-thirty. I thought to go out for an hour. You'll have a free hand then, and I shall be back well before our visitors arrive.'

'Will you go far?'

He smiled at her. 'I want just to drop over and see George.'

'I was *afraid* of that!' she said. 'Ross, you must *not*! You'll come back with your head all bloody – if you come back at all! Ross, I tell you, no!'

'Don't fret this time. I shall go in peace.'

'So you may, as you have before. But have you ever left in peace? It is very well for you to go to talk to him, but you know you will get thrown off his lands the very least! Something worse happens every time you meet! You cannot mean to create more ill will just because of a silly mistake on the part of his gamekeepers! George as good as apologized for them when he came up.'

He did not answer, but she felt no awareness of victory.

She said: 'We have Dwight and Caroline coming. I do not wish to be bandaging your broken head, or – or talking to them, trying to be nice to them, and all the time waiting for your return. It's a season of good will. Let us be content for today and tomorrow.'

The new wood was hissing as flames discovered the moisture within it. Occasionally it sputtered a protest. Ross pushed one piece farther on with his boot.

'George seldom seeks violence – I introduce the violence, not he. As for his servants – they are nothing. I shall talk to him and come away. I'm *very* sorry, my dear. I very much want to please you tonight. I hope still to do so. But this is something . . . It is not wholly because of your brush with him. I have been thinking about him a good deal on the journey.'

George and Elizabeth supped at seven. It was early but a convenient hour for them both.

Immediately after Christmas they were to settle in town until after the baby was born. The one thing that irked George about his new country house was that no turnpike road existed. You could get a coach through the last five miles, so long as the mud was not too deep, but it was a crazy lurching journey which shook you up more than travelling on horseback.

Elizabeth had kept well since her marriage, except for one or two diplomatic indispositions. In a looped-up polonaise gown of yellow brocade she looked as lovely tonight as she had ever done in her life, the extra fullness in her cheeks softening the fine-drawn classic oval of jaw and chin – that ultimate beauty of bone which would never fade. At Trenwith they always supped alone. George had let it be known early that he wanted his evening meal in the company of his wife, so the Chynoweths ate in their sitting-room upstairs. The winter parlour had been transformed: much of the panelling ripped out and the walls hung with expensive flock paper; a new dining table with such a polish on it that the slightest thing left a mark; twenty extra candles; a liveried footman to wait on therm At the opposite end of the table George sat, full-bodied, self-possessed, well groomed. In the summer they would dine in the hall. George had plans for the hall.

Elizabeth had found life with her second husband a mass of contradictions. He lived, she found, more genteelly than the people of her own kind. Although he was putting on weight, he ate considerably less than Francis had done or her father did. Accustomed to a society in which men considered the courtesies observed if they didn't slide under the table before the ladies left, she found his sobriety attractive. He drank but never got the worse for drink. He never spat or blew his nose in her presence. His courtesy towards her was unchanged whether they were in company or alone.

But of course it was impossible to treat him as she had treated Francis. He was not one quarter so malleable, so mercurial, so easy to understand. She missed Francis's dry humour and easy sophistication. Somehow she never seemed able to meet George on equal terms. While she was absolute mistress of the small things, she found him absolute master of the large. She did not love him; she was not even sure that he loved her; but she felt herself to be a treasured possession, cared for and considered in every way. Often it was delightful to be so treated. It was what she had longed for during her widowhood. Occasionally she found it oppressive.

He kept all his other feelings under as good a control as his feelings for his wife. It seemed as if in climbing the ladder of society he had been so afraid of betraying the wrong emotions that he had grown afraid of showing any at all. He was morbidly sensitive about his humble beginnings, though even that he was clever enough to keep from her for some months. Then one day she made a remark that could be taken two ways, and she saw the instant resentment before he could hide it. After that she walked carefully, watching her own words when necessary so that no hint of condescension could be gathered from them.

Tonight in the first part of dinner they talked about the news which had just come through to Falmouth of the fall of Toulon. Its surrender to the British last August, together with thirty battleships and great quantities of naval stores, had looked like the end of the war. Lord Hood in grateful astonishment had taken possession and had sent an urgent appeal for forty thousand troops to consolidate this magnificent opportunity. The government had sent two thousand British soldiers, some Piedmontese, and a few Spaniards. Now in December the Republic, freed of its other preoccupations, had sent a large force and reduced the town, led by a new young general of whose name the Falmouth news-sheet had three different spellings in the length of a column but of whose ability no one seemed in doubt.

George had always been for war as against Revolution. The Warleggans were founding their dynasty within the framework of a settled and ordered society. Anything which might undermine that society was to be resisted and condemned. War was far the lesser of the evils.

'. . . small forces,' he was saying, 'which we reduce to complete incompetence by distributing to the corners of the globe. Our campaign in Flanders is bogged in mud. The Vendeans have asked for our help in vain. This would bring about Pitt's downfall if there were anyone to replace him. But Dundas, Grenville, Richmond, none of them have the parliamentary command . . .'

Elizabeth saw the door open just behind the manservant and Ross come in. So certain was she that it must be another servant with the wine that for a second she disbelieved her eyes. Then George saw her face and turned.

He instantly pushed back his chair.

Ross said quietly: 'I have not come to make a disturbance this time – unless you force it.'

George did not move his chair any farther.

'And *you*,' said Ross, as the manservant, catching some glance from his master, moved towards the bell pull.

'How did you get in?' George said.

'I want a word with you, George.'

The servant said: 'Shall I . . .'

'No,' said George, watching Ross like a snake.

'That's wise. There's no need to wreck your dining-room: I have committed enough violence in this house . . .'

Nobody spoke. Ross's eyes flickered across to Elizabeth. She met this gaze with bitter hostility. It was the first time they had seen each other since the night in May. He looked at her a moment longer, in surprise, a little in assessment. 'I am sorry to upset you, Elizabeth.'

'You don't upset me,' she said.

'I'm glad of that.'

'You may be glad or sorry. I'm not interested.'

George, gratified, said: 'Pray forgive me for exposing you to this intrusion, Elizabeth.'

'It need never happen again,' Ross said. 'I have no ambitions here ... But I'm tired of our relationship, George. Whenever we meet, we snarl like dogs – and every now and then it comes to the point of a scuffle, but inconclusive even then. It seems now we're to be neighbours, close neighbours perhaps, for years to come. A disagreeable prospect for me, but not one that I can alter.

There are really only two ways out of it, and I have come to suggest that we should choose the better one.'

'Is there a better one?'

'Well, I think so. I'd suggest that we agree to avoid heedless provocation and live as peaceable as we can. What is your view?'

George looked down at his fingers. 'I should have thought your visit tonight a very heedless piece of provocation.'

'No, for I came to put the alternatives before you. I am lawabiding now, George, and prosperous. Think of that. Prosperous. That must gall you. But never mind. It surely must be in the interests of both of us that we should make the civilized choice.'

'And what other do you suggest exists?'

Ross listened to the sound of footsteps in the hall. 'I'm a little unsure as to details, because my wife would not supply them, but I believe an insult was paid her while I was away.'

'No insult was paid her that she did not invite.'

'I understand you're claiming the cliff path as your property between Sawle and Trevaunance.'

'It is my property.'

'I'm not sufficiently interested to dispute it, though there may be others who will.'

'I have already made sure of the legal position.'

'I thought you would have. But the possession of property doesn't entitle you to be affrontful to people innocently using a footpath which has been public for years.'

'Your dog was straying. In what way was your wife harmed?'

'She has left me in no position to argue about it. But I suggest that you take care she's not molested again.'

'The remedy is in her hands not mine.'

'That is where we differ, and differ beyond the point of peaceful enmity. As I say, I have no wish to come here again—'

'You will not, I'll see to that.' George took out his watch. 'You may have three minutes more.'

Ross said: 'I am trying *very* hard to put the choice intelligibly before you, and you asked me as to the other alternative. Well, that is it . . . Age has mellowed us both; but you must know of my ability to incite miners, for you once tried to get me convicted for doing so. It would not be difficult to bring three hundred, and you know what they are like. I don't wish to threaten or to dramatize a simple promise; but they would trample across your lawns and pull up your trees, and in a night it would look as if a hurricane had blown. And any bloodshed caused by trying to keep them out would certainly lead to more bloodshed. The law will not protect you; for it knows no way of offering protection except with a company of infantry, and soldiers now are scarcer than battleships.'

George turned as the door opened and Tom Harry put his head in.

'Begging your pardon, sir. The cook— Ah . . .'

He had seen Ross. Ross did not move. Harry sidled in and another man stood in the doorway.

Ross said: 'That's an alternative you'll have time to think over. The present alternative is before you.'

George hunched his shoulders. 'You've finished what you came to say?'

'Yes.'

Tom Harry said: 'Now, see 'ere—'

'Wait,' said George. 'Let him go.'

There was a pause. Harry's hands dropped to his sides.

Ross said: 'It is Christmas tomorrow and believe me, I

have come in no carping spirit. We cannot be friends, but it's tedious to spend all one's life with one's hackles up. I certainly don't want to; and I hope you don't want to. In coming to live in my district, you have vastly annoyed me; but you have also offered up certain hostages for your own good behaviour.'

He glanced at Elizabeth. Seeing her had upset him in a new way. 'Explain to George, will you, that I'm in earnest.'

She said: 'I know nothing of any insult to Demelza. But I've complete faith in my husband's capacity to order his life as he thinks best.'

Ross stared at her. 'Then see to it that he appreciates the choice.'

He went out, pushing past Tom Harry, who only shifted an inch or so. The man in the doorway retreated more quickly, and Ross walked across the hall, half expecting some attack from behind. He glanced round that great hall which had been a part of his life ever since he was a child. Here he had come with his father and mother when he was just old enough to walk. He had played here in a corner with Verity and Francis while words from the sober elders grouped round the fire had floated across to his half-attending ears: Chatham's illness and the Wilkes controversy and the repeal of the Stamp Act. Here, returning from America, he had found Elizabeth celebrating her engagement to Francis. Here he had come for the christening of Elizabeth's child, for his uncle's funeral ... Something belonging intimately to his family had existed in this room.

But not any longer. The familiar wood and glass and stone were not enough.

Warleggan ground. George's influence was all-pervasive.

The bitterness of Elizabeth's tones and looks had only

surprised Ross in their degree. He had expected her enmity. But he did not suppose all of it derived from the ninth of May. He was not proud of his adventure then, nor ever a man given to passing off his own behaviour with an easy excuse; but after the initial resistance that night there had been no particular indication that she hated him. Her attitude towards him during a number of years, and particularly the last two, was more than anything else responsible for what had happened, and she must have known it. Her behaviour that night had shown that she knew it.

But there had been other – and later – sins on his part. Over and over again during those first weeks following he had known he should go and see her and thrash the whole thing out in the light of day. It was unthinkable to leave the situation as he had left it, but that was precisely what he had done. He had behaved abominably first in going, then in not going; but he did not know what to say, and the impossibility of explaining himself had stopped him. If the history of the last ten years had been the tragedy of a woman unable to make up her mind, the last six months was the history of a man in a similar case. For a long time he had been quite unsure of his own feelings; then they had crystallized; and from that moment a private meeting with Elizabeth was impossible.

Now it was too late.

Chapter Seven

He was back in time to soothe Demelza's fears, and just before eight Dwight and Caroline came.

Caroline had been sobered by her visit to her uncle's. In spite of what they had agreed, she had been determined to tell him at once of her meeting with Dwight; but sight of her uncle had shown her how ill he was, and she was silent.

Demelza was nervous and excited too; and as dinner wore on, her attitude helped Caroline to an easier frame of mind.

Demelza said: 'But how long shall you have to be away, Dwight? Have you not heard yet? It is a matter of some importance to us all.'

'The naval surgeon is neither fish, flesh, nor fowl – but I'm told my appointment can be considered to be for two years or for the duration of the war, whichever is the shorter.'

'And if the war go on after that?'

Dwight hesitated. Caroline said: 'He will stay. I feel it in my bones he will not reconcile it with his conscience to retire.'

Dwight smiled. 'For once you overrate my conscience. Since Caroline came, my patriotism has been running out fast.'

Demelza said: 'But you will not have to wait until then, until you are out of it—'

'No. I think she will marry me – I believe she will – on my first shore leave. That may be in three months or six, no one knows . . .'

'And until then?' Ross said to Caroline. 'What shall you do in the meantime?'

'Stay with Uncle Ray for a time. Then perhaps go back to London.'

'I'd prefer you to stay here,' Dwight said. 'The air is good and London hasn't suited your health.'

'Oh, yes, do you know,' Caroline said to Demelza, 'he spent the first morning of our reconciliation sounding my chest. Faith, I found it more embarrassing than any conjugal endearment.'

Dwight went very red. 'Nonsense, Caroline, you make it sound much worse than it was! I was less than half an hour, and your maid was present—'

'Oh, yes, my maid was present, which made it even more overfacing. What allurement can a woman hope to have for a man who has already examined her tonsils and her teeth and has counted her ribs in the harsh light of day?'

Dwight took a gulp of wine. 'Well, if you want to know that, let me tell you! You have every possible allurement for me. I love you and am fascinated by everything you do, and no amount of medical attention, either on you or on myself, will ever cure me of *that*!'

It was a change to hear Caroline getting more than she asked for, and to save them both Ross said:

'When Dwight has gone, so long as you stay with your uncle, I hope you'll come and sup with us once or twice a week. It will help the time to pass.'

'After Dwight has gone, I shall wake up sometimes and wonder if all this week has been a dream. I think I shall have to come here for reassurance. I hope my uncle improves so that I can tell him the truth.'

'If you are in any difficulty, come straight here,' Ross said. 'We will put you up for as long as necessary.'

Caroline looked at Demelza before replying. 'Your husband's committing you very deep.'

Demelza said: 'Well, no deeper than I'd want to go or be willing to go tomorrow.'

It was Caroline who eventually smiled and glanced away. 'I have told Ross. It was just a whim. Anyway, perhaps this war will be over next week and then I shall not need your kindness. In Plymouth the landlord's wife was whispering news of some sacrilegious feast the French have been celebrating in Notre Dame. It all sounds very decadent, and I trust their armed forces will be corrupted by it – especially the Navy.'

'Next year will see a change when I am at sea,' said Dwight. 'The lice at least will notice the difference.'

At half past nine the carol singers came from Sawle Church, and Demelza thought of the many other Christmasses ... Six years ago at Trenwith, the Trenegloses had come unexpectedly with George Warleggan, and Elizabeth had sung and she had sung, and she had tasted port wine for the first time and had loved the flavour of it and what it did to you in spite of feeling sick with Julia four months forward. And then two years later, when she was alone here and the same carol singers as tonight – though a much depleted stock – and she had asked them in and had sympathized with them over their ailments, nervous only for her new status and anxious to behave well, not thinking or dreaming that in two weeks more Julia would be dead and she a drawn and wasted invalid. And the wrecks that had come in on the great January gale, and Ross, like herself only worse, spiritually worse, bitter and lost, going down to the shore and the teeming, struggling miners.

The choir was at full strength tonight and in good form. Uncle Ben Tregeagle was in charge, ageless and gipsylike with his thin black curls, and Mary Ann Tregaskis, and Char Nanfan and Johnny Kimber and Betty Carkeek, whose husband had been killed in the tussle with the gaugers; and even Sue Baker got through the singing without going into one of her fits.

When they had gone, the four sat round the fire for another half hour drinking tea and eating homemade cake. Then Demelza excused herself and presently Ross followed.

He went up to the mine and was gone some time. When he returned, Demelza was still in the kitchen and told him that Caroline had just gone to bed. He went into the parlour and found Dwight about to leave too.

Ross said: 'We thought you might like a few minutes alone.'

'Thank you . . . And for so much else besides.'

'Little enough.'

'It isn't often that one man can retrieve another's mistakes for him. I want to tell you—'

'Don't try. Sometimes to be able to growl and bully is a signal advantage. And really it is very easy learned. Make the most of your happiness while it is here.'

'That I will do. Caroline . . .'

'The more I see of Caroline, the more I esteem her.' Ross poured brandy into a glass for himself and then put it down untouched. He wanted no more. 'Not until this week did I begin to understand her. You'll have a lifetime to do it, and that I imagine will not be too long. Always she will disguise her goodness as if ashamed of it. I congratulate you on your acumen in picking so exceptional a wife.'

Dwight shook his head. 'I only wish she were my wife. I'd give years of my life for a month ashore now. But she could not be rushed into it this time – in this way... Demelza likes her, I think?'

'Of course!'

'I asked for a particular reason. I hope it will not be so, but it may be that I shall not have a lifetime in which to appreciate Caroline. In war it's not uncommon for people to get hurt. I don't propose to sentimentalize on the possibility, but it might be that she will need all your friendship and the help you could give even if we marry, then as a young widow...'

'And do you suppose we should fail to give it?'

'No... no.'

The fire was burning low and needed more wood. Presently it would be made up for the night.

'There are many things on which I could not answer for Demelza. But in this I can.'

He went for the big logs into the storeroom after Dwight had gone. When he returned to the parlour with the logs, he found that Demelza had come in again. She was standing before the mirror, pinning up her hair.

She saw him in the glass. 'They're both settled?'

'Yes. All's well.'

'I hope Caroline won't want for anything. John left plenty of wood for her fire, but I expect she will not need it. Did you find London likeable?'

'Likeable enough for a visit. You must come with me next time.'

She lowered her arms and moved aside to let him put on the logs.

'I wonder why the weather is colder in London. It is four years since we had snow here . . . If Julia had lived, she would have been near on six.'

He took up the poker and began spreading out and flattening the remnants of the evening's fire. 'I know . . . And you . . . Barely yet in your middle twenties.'

'Do I look that much older?'

'No. Often younger. But you began living so young, have experienced . . . Sometimes I feel you're as old as I am. Already in six and a half years we've shared so much.'

'And lost so much.'

'We've lost Julia. Nothing else irreparably.'

She lifted her shoulders. It was a shrug half abandoned, for she was watching him. This they both suddenly knew was the moment when he was going to force past the casual guards of companionship.

She said: 'So you came away from Trenwith without a torn shirt.'

'Yes . . . In recent weeks, more particularly since I went to London, I have come to realize how silly this constant enmity is, that its chief poison acts on the man who feels it. Not an original discovery, nor perhaps one I shall always be able to abide by, but worth a run. I put it as a proposition to George tonight that we should try to live without rancour.'

'And what did he say?'

'Nothing promising; but I hope when he gets over his astonishment he'll see the reason in it.'

'And Elizabeth?'

'Ah . . . About her I'm not sure.' He got the two logs firmly settled and then, still crouching, looked up at his wife. His face was less guarded tonight. 'Demelza, I wanted to talk to you about her.'

'No, that I would rather not hear.'

'I think you must. Before I went away I thought not. But there's no other way.'

'Ross, I've forgotten it. *All* that time. It will do harm to bring it back now. I would much better prefer that nothing should be said of it.'

'I know but – in fact it can't be forgotten, can it? It is only – overlooked, set aside.'

She moved away from the fire to give herself breathing space, pulled a curtain straight, snuffed three candles on a side table so that the furniture at the end of the room slid its surfaces into an encroaching shadow. Absently she began to shake out a cushion.

Ross said: 'I want to tell you that Elizabeth means nothing to me any more.'

'Don't say that, Ross. I shouldn't want for you to say more than you feel—'

'But I do feel it—

'Yes, at present. But then again sometime, perhaps next month, perhaps next year . . .'

He said: 'Come here, Demelza. Sit down, will you? Listen to what I have to say.'

After a minute she came back.

He said: 'You're so desperately anxious to be fair, not to be self-deceiving, to make the best of what you have . . . But what you have is all . . . Will you try to believe that?'

'Have I call to believe that?'

'Yes. I wish I could explain about Elizabeth. But in a way I think you must understand. I loved Elizabeth before ever I met you. It's been a – a constant attachment throughout my life. D'you know how it is when a person has wanted something always and never had it? Its true value to him may be anything or nothing; that doesn't count; what does count is its *apparent* value, which is always great. What I felt for you has always been assessable, comparable, something human and part of an ordinary life. The other, my feeling for Elizabeth, was not. So what I did – what happened in May, if it could only have happened in a vacuum, without hurt to anyone, I should not have regretted at all.'

'No?' said Demelza.

'No. Because from it I came to recognize things which no doubt I should have had common sense and insight enough to have known without the experience but did not. One is that if you bring an idealized relationship down to the level of an ordinary one, it isn't always the ordinary one that suffers. For a time, after that night, things were upside down – for a time nothing came clear. When it did, when it began to, the one sure feeling that stood out was that my true and real love was not for her but for you.'

She was very still, eyelids pale, brows straight with a hint of concentration at their inner ends. He received no hint that she was wrestling with demons, her mind and emotions split: on the one hand struggling against the too easy capitulation ready, so ready, within herself; on the other looking at the love that he now offered with both hands, and finding it, perversely, not enough – not of itself enough as a single isolated factor.

'May I ask a question?'

'Of course.'

'How did you come to feel that, Ross? What persuaded you of it? I mean, the experience itself can't hardly have been unpleasant.'

'What experience?'

'Of making love to Elizabeth.'

'No . . . far from it.' He hesitated, a little put out. 'But I wasn't seeking just pleasure. I was – I suppose in fundamentals I was seeking the equal of what I'd found in you, and it was not there. For me it was not there.'

'Perhaps it would have come in time. Perhaps you did not persevere, Ross.'

He glanced at her dryly. 'Would you have had me do so?'

'Well, I do not know the details of your – adventure, but it seems to me you are hardly quite fair on Elizabeth. At least . . . I do not very much like her, but she is not a light woman. You came upon her, I suppose, in surprise. I should not be astonished if at first she tried to be faithful to her new promise. I do not know how long you stayed with her or how much you made love to her, but I should think there could be times when she might show to better advantage.'

'Are you defending Elizabeth now?'

'Well, yes . . . or no. I think I am defending *women*. Truly, Ross, are not all women treated by all men like something inferior, like chattels you take up and put down at will? I – I'm very happy tonight that you prefer me and I hope you always will. But I ink it is unfair to any woman to judge her, to condemn her, upon a chance encounter, like. I should not wish to be so judged. Though indeed I think I have been so judged, quite recently.'

'What do you mean?'

She hesitated, uncertain now of the chasm that gaped before her, then suddenly certain that – though all unplanned – this was the testing jump.

'If we have to talk of this, then there's something I must

tell you. I have often thought I should, but it did not seem important if you did not care for me any more. But now if it is true what you say, if you really mean this . . .'

'Of course I do.'

'Then I must tell you, before we go any further, that on my last visit to the Bodrugans I had an adventure – though it did not end in quite the same way as yours. I went – you will know the sort of mood I went in to that ball. It was but four days after you had gone to Elizabeth. I should dearly have liked to revenge myself on you in the only way I could. And as it came about, the opportunity was there. Malcolm McNeil was there.'

'McNeil?' said Ross. 'The—'

'Yes. We were something flirtatious during the evening. Then afterwards he came to my room.'

Ross looked at her.

She said: 'I do not want for you to blame him, for it was almost at my invitation that he came. But when he came and began to make love to me, I found him less attractive than I could tolerate. I do not know what standards I have created in you, but I know what standard you have created in me. And so at the last I would have nothing to do with him. The meeting did not end as happily as yours with Elizabeth. He was very angry.'

'My God! So I should think!'

'There, you see! You are taking the man's side, just as I took Elizabeth's—'

'I am not! If ever I meet with the profligate swine—'

'But it's not fair to rail at him. It is me you should be angry with, if anyone . . .'

Ross got up and walked slowly across the room. He stood with his hands behind his back, seeing without reading the titles of books on his bookshelf. After a while he said: 'I don't *understand*. What occurred between you and McNeil? Have you ever had any feeling for him?'

'At one time I believe I had a little, but not now.'

'A little . . .' Emotions disturbed his normal balance. 'Yet you allowed him the freedom of your room, of yourself—'

'Can you imagine how I felt at that time? You had just abandoned me for Elizabeth.'

'So you threw yourself at the first man available—'

'Not the first, Ross. At least the fourth.'

Their eyes met and clashed. There was an awful silence.

He said very bleakly: 'God in heaven, I don't admire your frankness after all this time!'

'Maybe I should not have told you, but I don't like to be dishonest. If there is to be something good and true between us again—'

'Good and true . . . How far did this – thing go between you and him?'

'Not any great way.'

'So I should think not!'

'Why should you think not, Ross? Should not the goose, if she chooses, be able to drink as deep as the gander?'

Anger was in him unencouraged. 'Well, I don't think I admire your attitude, either then or now! I take no pride in my visit to Elizabeth. But the thing was the outcome of a devotion which had lasted on my side for more than ten years. It was not some tawdry little passion worked up over the wine for a cheap satisfaction between dinner and supper!'

Her pulses began to beat suffocatingly. 'And Margaret Vosper?' she said.

'Margaret Vosper?'

'Yes. She was at the ball. Have you a ten-year devotion for her also?'

He could have struck her. 'The only dealings I ever had with Margaret Vosper were one night before I met you. I believe you would be twelve at the time. I can't swear to my faithfulness to you while you were in swaddling bands, and I don't propose to begin! Can you think of any other excuses to give a soldier licence of your body?'

'That was what I didn't do, Ross, as you would know if you had been attending instead of getting hot and angry about it. I could not. I found I had no love for him at all. I don't know if that gives you any gratification ... It gave him none.'

Ross said: 'How am I to know what gratification he received?'

'Oh,' she said, and stared at him blindly. 'Ross, what a thing to say! After you just told me ... That you should think ...' She could get no words out.

He said: 'How am I to know anything any more?'

There was dead silence for a moment or two. 'No,' she said. 'How are you to know ...'

She ran from the room.

Upstairs in an impossible trembling state, part anger, part grief. In a cupboard the valise she had taken to Werry House. Out with it and a few things. Anything almost. A change or clothes, shoes, a few coins. She began to struggle out of her dress, pulling at the hooks, ripping the lace. Then into her travelling clothes. Boots, crop, hat; it all took too long. Now and then tears fell on her hands. Now and then she took a breath as if there was no air left in the world. Jeremy stirred in his sleep. She must leave him now. Later she would send for him. She could not wake him, take him through the night.

Impossible end to the evening! Dwight and Caroline reconciled. They almost. It had begun so well. Ross could hardly have said more. Then her need of conviction. Then her mention of McNeil. McNeil. A test which had somehow recoiled on herself. She stared round, at this room which had been hers ever since they married. Never again. Not here. It was the end of all. Never again.

She got her hat on, pinned it, could not find gloves, must go without; picked up the valise. Handkerchief. She must go quickly or the sounds she was making would wake Jeremy.

Out in the passage and down the stairs. Ross. In the doorway of the parlour.

'Where are you going?'

She glared at him, eyes like lamps, opened the front door, and went out. Round the house, stumbling, into the yard, the stables. She must take Darkie, no other mount of their own. The stables full tonight. Gimlett had left a lighted lantern. She stumbled, dropped her valise, almost fell, pulled herself to where the saddles were. Her own. Darkie whinnied. She carried the saddle to the mare and threw it over her back.

She had saddled horses many times, but now her fingers were all ways. The girth kept slipping through her hands. Darkie was restless, sensing her haste and frightened by it. The other horses pushed against each other, whinnied; a bat disturbed fluttered with futile wings among the rafters. The seventh Christmas of their marriage. What had Verity said in her letter? They were all so wrong!

A footstep. Ross said: 'Where are you going?'

She did not turn, tugged desperately at the girth, which had somehow got twisted and now would not release to begin again.

'Demelza.'

'I'm going away,' she said. 'What else can I do after . . .'

'Are you going to McNeil?'

'No, of course not.'

He came a little farther into the stables. At last she got the strap free, but in tugging at it she slid the saddle over to one side.

'Then tomorrow would be more convenient for us all.'

'*No* . . .'

He said: 'Here, let me,' and came up beside her and took the girth out of her hands and began to fasten it properly. In the lantern light his face looked like stone.

She turned sharply away to hide her own face from him and went for her valise, carried it to the horse. In silence he finished saddling the mare and reached for the bridle. Then he stopped, weighed it in his hands.

He said: 'Since you went upstairs I've been trying to think how this began, this quarrel, how it came so swiftly on us, and the cause. Perhaps you think I was patronizing you by explaining myself in the way I did, by seeming to take your feelings for granted. Was that it?'

'. . . Does it matter now?'

'No, plainly not. What I feel for Elizabeth now is of small importance; other things have come up. Still it was the truth, what I told you, all of it. When I saw her tonight, that confirmed it – it was like seeing a stranger. Queer! Like a stranger, even an enemy, sitting there. George's wife. I'm sorry that I did her an injury as well as you, but there's no way of recovering the past.'

'No . . .'

He fastened the bridle and bit and then looked at her. 'Shall I tie the case to the back of the saddle?'

'Please . . .'

'Where are you going? It's very late.'

'I . . . The Paynters for tonight. Prudie will find me somewhere.'

'Will you come back for the rest of your things, or shall Gimlett bring them over?'

'I don't know. I'll send word.'

He said: 'Before you go, you should know that I don't seriously question your account of what took place between yourself and McNeil. What you told me came as a surprise – a shock, and in the first anger . . . or you could call it the first jealousy . . . But of course I don't want you to think that could be my eventual belief.'

Demelza turned blindly, took the reins, led Darkie to the door. Ross did not at once follow her but stayed in the stable picking up some things which had fallen from a shelf. She hesitated, put her hand to the stirrup to steady it, but did not mount. He came out. Darkie pulled her a couple of paces forward and vigorously shook the bridle.

'And there's one other thing I want you to know,' he added. 'That is how deeply sorry I am that I ever hurt you in the first place – in May, I mean. *You* were so undeserving of any harm. All these months . . . I know how you will have felt. I want you to know that. If you had gone off with McNeil, I should have had only myself to blame.'

She dropped the reins and put up her hands and covered her face with them in a sudden gesture of distress. She wanted to say something but could think of nothing at all.

After a minute or two he said: 'Does it upset you now to be told that I love you? D'you still prefer McNeil? Is he still in the district? I'll go and call on him tomorrow.'

'No, Ross, he is gone; and I care nothing, nothing.'

'Then why are you leaving? Are you not willing to overlook what I said?'

'I can't.'

'Why not?'

'Because it is the *truth*! That is what I had never realized till you had spoken it. Oh, I don't know why. A sort of blindness. 'Tis quite unbearable to think of . . . Impossible to live with! I don't know what I shall do.'

He came out and stood beside her. He looped the reins over a peg.

'Should we not go inside and talk it over?'

'No! I can't.'

'You cannot forgive me, then.'

'I cannot forgive myself.'

'That was a favourite Poldark complaint at one time, but I judged you too wise to catch it. Look, supposing we go as far as the kitchen. I don't see that need compromise either of us too deeply.'

He took the lantern and waited for her. She hesitated.

He said: 'You may leave in five minutes if you wish.'

She followed him into the kitchen.

He opened the side of the lantern and lit another candle from it. The fire was low but quite a glow still came from it. She resisted a sudden impulse to shiver.

He said: 'I've been giving good advice to two other people of late, but it's hard always to advise oneself. If—' He stopped and stared at the door leading to the stillroom. In the growing light they could see a black stain spreading under it. 'What is that?'

'Oh . . . the beer! . . . I casked it this morning.' She took the candle he had lighted. In the stillroom the cask was overflowing with froth, and beer and froth covered half the floor. She exclaimed and went back into the kitchen.

He said: 'Did you bung it too soon?'

'I don't know. The fermentation had ended – I thought.' She returned with a floorcloth and a pail. His impulse was to say, leave it, you'll spoil your dress; but in time he refrained.

''Twas the hops, I b'lieve,' she said. 'You remember you thought they smelled not quite right.'

He picked up the bung which had blown out and sniffed it.

'I should've waited till you came home,' said Demelza.

They cleared the mess. The place reeked of beer. He carried the bucket out twice and emptied it and after inspection replaced the bung. The fermentation was over now. Whether the stuff was drinkable must be decided at a later date.

When the job was done there seemed nothing more to do or say. The awful catastrophe of their quarrel had evaporated in a commonplace.

He handed her a towel and she dried her hands. There was beer on her cuff and on the hem of her dress. She did not look at him.

He said: 'There's not a drunkard in Cornwall smells worse than we do now.'

She took out a handkerchief and blew her nose, hiding behind it longer than she needed. Then she went to the window and opened it.

He said: 'My dear, I bought you something in London. I had intended giving it you tomorrow; but in case there is no tomorrow for us, it would be best for you to have it at once.'

She did not turn while he fumbled in his pocket, but then he came up beside her at the window and put a box in her hand. She was surprised to see that his fingers were not as sure of themselves as usual. She opened the box and saw a gold filigree brooch with a ruby in the centre.

'I could not get one just like the last. I believe this is French instead of Italian. The work is not quite so elaborate as the one we bought from the Jew.'

'It's lovely . . .'

'I bought it in Chick Lane, near Smithfield Bars. Quite by chance, walking that way the second day after seeing Caroline. And this also . . .'

She heard him fumbling again, and after a minute he put some tissue paper in her hand. She unwrapped a necklace of garnets.

'Oh, Ross, you'll break my heart.'

'No, I shall not; not this way surely. If there—'

'Yes, you will. You do not know what is going on inside me.'

'Can't we agree to forget what has passed? I assure you I should be well pleased to do so. Is not *our* fermentation over too?'

'Truly, it isn't that I—'

'Think of this brooch as the payment of a just debt long owed, and this necklace as a Christmas present. Nothing more.'

'I have nothing at all for you.'

'See, the catch fastens this way.'

She had been fingering it, and he took it from her, showed her how it worked, then moved to put it round her neck. For a second she shrank away and he stood with the necklace. Then she straightened up and allowed him to put it on her. The acceptance had more than its own significance. She fingered the stones uncertainly.

'There's no mirror here,' he said. 'Come into the next room.'

'I don't think I want a mirror just yet. Until I can see myself in some less – less disagreeable light.'

'No such ill light exists. I assure you.'

'Ross, you know that I didn't need or expect a present like this—'

'I know. But if you suppose or suspect that in buying these things I was hoping to buy myself back into your favour, then you're right. I admit it. It is true, my dear, my very dear, my very dear Demelza. My fine, my loyal, my very sweet Demelza.'

'Oh, *no!*' she said, the tears overbrimming her eyes again. 'You *cannot* say that! You cannot say that now!'

'Do you know of any way to stop me?'

'Well, you cannot *mean* it! I have never felt so bitter for myself . . . If we are to make it up, if we are to live together, I think it will be a good thing if you are unpleasant to me for a little while.'

'Remind me next week. I could make a New Year resolution of it.'

'But seriously . . .'

'Seriously, Demelza,' he said.

She touched his hand as she turned away from the window. 'I – I wonder you had money to get home. So generous. I *wish* I had something for you. It is Christmas tomorrow and—'

'It's nearly twelve,' he said. 'Let us sit up awhile and call it Christmas tonight.'

WINSTON GRAHAM

Bella Poldark

Pan

'*Now, hurrah, Poldark rides again through the action-packed pages of Winston Graham's long-awaited concluding volume of the hugely popular Poldark saga. From the very first lines we tingle with the sense that we are in good hands, transported by Graham's atmospheric prose back to 1818 and the treacherous coast of craggy Cornwall*' Daily Mail

Graham's magical stories of the Poldark family, together with the much-loved television series, have millions of fans worldwide. Now we continue the story:

Of Ross Poldark, strong, independent squire at Nampara and his beautiful, outspoken wife Demelza. Of Valentine Warleggan, the wayward, perverse son of George, whose existence rubs salt in the war wounds his father and Ross have inflicted on one another. Of Bella, the Poldarks' youngest daughter, who is encouraged as a singer by old flame, Christopher Havergal – this objective being deeply complicated by the appearance of French conductor Maurice Valéry, who has more in mind than simply exploiting Bella's talent. Of Clowance, the Poldarks' widowed daughter, who meets Philip Prideaux, a mysterious figure who emerges from the shadow of the Battle of Waterloo and wishes to marry her. And of a murderer who lurks in the villages of west Cornwall, and is long – too long – in being discovered.

Written with power, humour, irony and elegance, *Bella Poldark* makes a brilliant finale for this distinguished saga.

WINSTON GRAHAM

Memoirs of a Private Man

PAN

'I have always been more interested in other people than myself – though there has to be something of myself in every character created, or he will not come alive...'

Winston Graham's bestselling career spanned more than forty novels, among them the celebrated *Poldark* series, which won him the hearts of millions. When he eventually found the time to tell the story of his own life he produced a wonderful book, free from what he calls 'the fashionable sins' but rich in charm. Witty, eccentric and intimate by turns, *Memoirs of a Private Man* offers an insight into the world of the novelist who rose from the isolation of Cornwall to the glittering London film scene, supported throughout by his lifelong loves: of his wife Jean and of writing.

'To read his memoir is to meet a charming, decent, old-fashioned sort of character with an enormous capacity for friendship and a wonderful interest in other people... Every gentle page offers us a shining example of prolific creativity and a good life well-lived'
Val Hennessy, *Daily Mail*

'A must for Poldark fans... His essential niceness shines through in this endearingly self-effacing autobiography' Maggie Pringle, *Express*